D0252673

2/7/92 √s

DOMINIONS OF THE GADIANTONS

Our world needs heroes!
This is a book about such
people. I hope you enjoy it.

Sincerely
Bob Mannum

DOMINION$
OF THE
GADIANTON$

A NOVEL

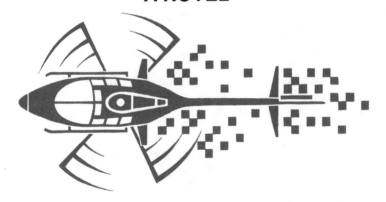

ROBERT MARCUM

BOOKCRAFT

Salt Lake City, Utah

Library of Congress Catalog Card Number: 91–75416
ISBN 0–88494–813–7

First Printing, 1991

Printed in the United States of America

To my wife and family,
patient and supportive;
my pioneer ancestors, who helped settle
the valleys of the Tetons;
and Richard Schofield,
an honest broker and former partner in
the securities business.

And it came to pass that the robbers of Gadianton
did spread over all the face of the land. . . .
And gold and silver did they lay up in store in abundance,
and did traffic in all manner of traffic.

And it is impossible for the tongue to describe,
or for man to write a perfect description of the horrible scene
of the blood and carnage which was among the people . . .
they delighted in the shedding of blood continually.

. . . [And the people] were compelled, for the safety of
their lives and their women and their children,
to take up arms against those Gadianton robbers . . .
to maintain their rights, and the privileges of their church
and of their worship, and their freedom and their liberty.

—Book of Mormon

1

July 1990.

My mind vaulted into reality as my thrashing hand banged against the oak headboard. My legs pushed against the sweat-soaked sheet that entangled me, and I tried focusing on the variegated pattern of light cast across the ceiling by the salmon-colored mini-blinds. Why the same dream, haunting, deadly, the details so clear—and so awful? What did something that must have happened so long ago have to do with me?

I liberated my body from the mint green bed sheet, shoving from my mind the annoying dream. Red numbers flashed on and off in the face of the clock radio, verifying why the room felt hotter than usual—the power had been out, temporarily interrupting the operation of the air conditioner. Midsummer power outages in Las Vegas were not uncommon.

Rubbing the small bump forming on top of my hand, I planted my feet firmly on the plush carpet. On the end table, next to the *TV Guide*, lay a worn velvet box, its contents demanding first consideration. I opened the box and removed the object. It was rounded on top and convex underneath, with a brownish green iris and dark, sunken pupil.

Step one, douse the entire shape with antiseptic liquid; step two, open the cavity of my right eye and place it inside; step three, blink and move the tissue until it falls into place. Over time I had gotten used to the slick feel of it. Over time, I had discovered, one could get used to anything.

I flipped several switches on the wall. The sound of the

stereo and television, some thirty feet across the room, replaced the deadening effect of silence. I flipped two more
switches, and muffled sounds chimed in from the den and
bathroom, the lights dispelling the last corners of darkness.
When we first moved in, the switches had been installed as a
matter of plain old self-indulgence and love for tinkering with
electronics. I appreciated a central light switch system more
since living alone.

The morning news and stock market report on FNN meant
it was eight o'clock back in New York, five o'clock in Las Vegas,
and close to time for final preparations before the opening of
the market. I was usually at the office by now, going through
a routine I had learned to love—and need.

The phone rang, once, twice, three times. I picked up the
TV remote with frustrated feeling and flipped to an old black-
and-white movie, waiting as the message machine beeped and
started to record the familiar voice. Then I picked up the receiver.

" 'Lo?" My voice sounded as if I had swallowed my pillow. I
cleared it and tried again. "Uh, hello?"

"Morning, Jeremiah. Sleeping awfully late, aren't you?"

"Morning, Kirk."

Kirk Bolt and I had been partners for four years at the Las
Vegas securities office of Banner, Stutz, and Milligan, occupy-
ing the corner suite on the twelfth floor of the Pincock Center,
overlooking the Strip. We had arrived there after forming a
partnership in a smaller firm with a limited product line. We
had made the strategic move to Banner when several multi-
million-dollar clients, both individual and commercial, had
promised us business if we could deal competitively in additional securities they needed. The move had doubled our six-
figure incomes.

Kirk had a great family and had become like a brother to
me. His family had been my family . . . our family, before Liz
passed away. Few partnerships had the remarkable record we
did, and few had created friendships like ours. Two different
people with two different ways of doing the same thing, we had
our ups and downs and disagreements, but we always came
out of the problems together. I trusted him with my life.

Kirk had taken the reins when the doctor told Liz she had
cancer. I returned to my job a year later alone and broke,
wanting to lose myself in work, wanting to forget. I had
worked—long days shorten lonely nights. Despair had turned

to acceptance. Then the bottom dropped out and put me back in hell.

Kirk had been a young thirty and had had an insatiable desire to succeed on Wall Street. Talented and hardworking, he had been the more productive half of a good partnership. He brought amounts of youth and excitement, which were necessary to offset what he called my "maturity" and "overzealous caution."

Kirk had called every morning for a few months after Banner put the screws to me. Now it was about once a week. He had been good enough to try and keep the partnership intact, even though Banner and the Securities and Exchange Commission had effectively dissolved it with the revoking of my securities license. Trust the SEC! Kirk still sent me a check for my share of commissions generated by joint client accounts. He had been good to me through everything.

We discussed the news, several client accounts, buys and sells in my personal and our joint accounts, and rumors on the Street about the possible invasion of Kuwait by Iraq. It seemed to me that our conversations were getting shorter, more about business than anything else, even a bit strained. I wasn't part of that world anymore.

After I hung up the phone, the cold thought of slitting my wrists wisped through my mind. I focused on the faces of Edward G. Robinson and a young Cary Grant to empty my mind of the morbid frustration and anger at the unseen forces that had changed my life and threatened to put me in prison, the forces which had stripped me of what little dignity I had left. Without Liz, life had gotten suddenly very hard. Work had been my way to survive; without it, I was desperate—and afraid. I slapped the pillow with my fist, venting the anger I felt toward those who had destroyed even that thread.

My head throbbed. I reached for the vial of pills; the doctor had prescribed them along with a trip to some exotic place away from my problems. I could afford the pills. I got a glass of water and swallowed two pills. A few minutes later I was asleep.

The distant sound of bells playing "Mary Had a Little Lamb" pulled me reluctantly from sleep. I hated that tune, even if I had picked out the doorbell chimes on my own. It was a joke, one of those things you did while shopping south of the border and then sprung it on your friends, a joke I had regretted ever since.

By the fourth rendition I knew they weren't going away. I pushed myself off the bed, nearly falling over. My leg was asleep from being tucked under me and gave me a painful tingle clear to my toes. I shook the leg, then stopped to rub the numbness away. It did no good; and Mary was going after her lamb again.

I turned the deadbolt and angrily flung the door open. Angry words were coming up my throat as the burglar alarm went off, sending an ear-shattering wail through my head and and into the neighborhood.

"Jerry, dear, you best shut that thing off if you don't want the police rushing in here . . . again!"

Jan's presence on the front doorstep momentarily paralyzing my mind, I hit the numbered buttons on the lighted wall plate. Wrong numbers. I hit them again. Wrong again. *Maybe a fist through the whole thing* . . . I felt Jan's body come close to mine and watched as her slim, well-manicured finger deftly hit the four, the six, the eight, and the zero, stopping the blare of the living dead in midsound.

"Liz never could get you to remember those numbers. They're so easy, Jerry. Really!"

She stepped back. The scent of body soaps and perfumes filled the hallway as I shut the door behind her.

"Don't look so shocked, dear. I promised Liz I would drop in on you, and here I am."

She turned and walked into the living room, which was still decorated with her expensive suggestions. Liz had given in to the idiocy of these furnishings to please Jan, and I had learned to live with the room by adding doors that blocked it off from the hallway.

"It has been a while, Jan. The funeral was one year, nine months, and ten days ago, as I recall."

She turned to face me, a brief moment's hesitation flashing across her *Mademoiselle* complexion, then receding into the deep blue of her eyes. She sat down on the couch, crossing her long legs, the crease of a smile returning to her lips.

Jan Delling, the former Janet Dellingham, was a small-town Idaho girl who had made it big as an international model. Her good looks and slim figure had graced the cover of so many magazines that I lost count. And the sister who had leaned on Liz whenever anything went wrong in her glamorous, cold, and confusing life wasn't there when Liz needed her most.

Jan used people and then discarded them as if they were gum wrappers. I had watched her use Liz for years. Liz allowed it even though I fumed. It had been after a whirlwind European tour, photo session after photo session, and a schedule that had dissolved her strength both physically and mentally that Jan showed up on our front doorstep three years ago. While Liz helped her regain her sanity, Jan tried to destroy our marriage, to change our home into a decorator's nightmare, and to otherwise ruin our lives. Then, like a ghost, she disappeared in the smoke of new contracts, returning only for the funeral.

"What brings you to Las Vegas, Jan? Another photo session at the Mirage, or another funeral?" The cold tone chilled the well-conditioned room.

"I'm here because you're my broker," she said acidly. I wanted to smile, but kept it hidden behind the uncaring, blank facade I had mastered over the past six months. "As long as I can be there for you," I said sarcastically.

"All right, all right. Let's stop paring. Come and sit down." She patted the sofa next to her. "I'll tell you what's happened; then you tell me if you can help me. I've messed things up a bit."

"The word is *sparring*, Jan." I smiled roughly but ignored her request that I sit down and remained standing.

She leaned forward and placed her forearms on her legs, hands tightly clasped, her eyes looking at the carpet a few feet beyond her knees. "I do need help. You're the only one I can trust."

I could see it was bad. Jan never played the humility ploy; she didn't know the meaning of humility. I slouched my two-hundred-pound frame into the chair opposite her and folded my arms across my chest.

"I'm listening," I said.

2

The cold shower bristled my skin. Jan's visit had unsettled me in more ways than I wanted to admit. Jan had been a beautiful, successful model, but now her world was falling apart . . . again. She was a scared victim caught in a world she hated on the one hand and was addicted to on the other. Younger, more ambitious models had come along and had taken her most lucrative contracts. Her career had been floundering, and she had used up what little savings she had to try and salvage it, but to no avail. Then she had received a stock tip and had desperately invested her last hundred thousand dollars, only to have the stock do a nosedive. She explained her situation to me as I was moving her luggage into the guest room; I promised her that I would look into it.

Her tears amazed me most. I had never seen Jan cry, even at Liz's funeral. But at the time of the funeral her world wasn't falling down around her, and Liz's death had seemed to be a nuisance she shrugged aside for the more pressing matters of her career. Maybe her work had been an escape too.

I sat down on the chair that I had put in the shower when Liz had grown too weak to stand for more than a few seconds. Liz didn't like the stench of dying. Her showers became the only thing she could do to try and wash the disease out of her skin and thus keep her dignity. Even when she couldn't get out of bed, she had the nurses bathe her, comb her hair, and manicure her nails.

How I missed her!

I turned off the water and dripped dry a few minutes before reaching for a towel. I toweled down my hair and slipped into underwear and a robe. Memories. Man's links to the past were often painful. The man in the mirror, drying himself with a Mickey Mouse towel, had just turned thirty-nine years old. The dark complexion, with slightly receding brown hair, slightly crooked nose and square jaw, was beginning to show the wear of months of depression and struggle against the odds—a hopeless struggle now that the opposition was winning.

My bishop had been sympathetic to me in my depression. He had felt my state of mind as only a bishop can, backing me all the way and accepting my statement of innocence without question. He had also sent people so many times I couldn't remember who and when, trying to involve me, to keep me afloat and active, but I couldn't respond. I had clients in the ward, people who had trusted me. I couldn't face them; my fall from grace had been well documented in the papers. It's a horrible thing to be innocent and feel guilty, having to face others, trying to explain. After the twentieth attempt, I couldn't do it anymore.

I still had my temple recommend, and I found some relief from going to the temple in St. George, and later the new one across the valley, trying to find answers. Then, just when I thought I had the strength to get up and go on, new incriminating evidence hit me from the blind side. I grew weary from watching for the next blow.

The Church hadn't been one of my high priorities during much of my younger life. While my friends were on missions, I was a volunteer warrior in Vietnam at the stick of a Sikorsky S-65 heavy assault helicopter trying to save lives by taking them. Luckier than most, I had only lost an eye, while witnessing death and destruction that had sent me on a personal trek to find answers. I went through everything from meditation to Catholic mass to a study of Islam but finally ended up deep in the Book of Mormon, reluctantly first, then with enthusiasm. It was there I learned about war and killing, and how the Lord and righteous men abhorred it, even as they had gone into battle. I related to Mormon and Moroni. Through their words, I found the capacity to keep my sanity intact while the world around me went nuts.

I wasn't a "foxhole penitent." What I had was a book that all LDS soldiers carried in time of war, a book that somehow gave me a thin thread of hope and a direction in which to turn that was always upward. I went to church meetings when I

7

could, and I wasn't picky about whose religion it was, or how they worshiped. I needed religion, and because of it I came home drug-free and somewhat sane but still with a lot of deep-seated hate and enough questions to keep "Dear Abby" and a good psychiatrist busy for the rest of their natural lives.

During the third plastic surgery on my face, I met Liz Dellingham of small-town America. She and Jan were opposite in appearance. Liz was five feet six and Jan was near six feet. Jan's cover-girl looks—her clear, elegant face and perfect figure—were in opposition to Liz's somewhat small-town-American look—freckled nose, green eyes, rounded features, and deep inner glow, a glow that emanated from her and affected all she touched.

Dr. Elizabeth Dellingham, thirty years old and single, had been one of the best plastic surgeons at Johns Hopkins and a devout Mormon. She had traveled to the Philippines every year to repair the faces of children who would never have had a chance without her tender, effective care. Dr. Dellingham became Dr. Daniels and moved her private practice to Las Vegas when I received an offer of work. She had been my number one cheerleader until the day she died. I was glad our vows were for more than just this life.

Liberally applying white foam to my dark stubble, I proceeded to go through a ritual I could never understand, shaving—a masochistic activity in which a person tries to slit his own throat for the benefit of appearances. And they say man is the intelligent species!

I leaned forward, placing my hands on the sink top. "What a failure you have become, Jeremiah Daniels!" I said aloud, looking into eyes that could both have passed for glass. "Murphy's Law has hit you so hard so often that the bruise is running blood. Liz would not be proud of what you have let yourself become. Get it together, quitter!"

I finished shaving and put on cotton slacks, a pale blue golf shirt, white initialized socks, and walking shoes. Then I stuck my wallet and car keys into my pocket before thumbing through the file full of legal papers for my meeting with Hank Butcher, bankruptcy attorney. Hank had appeared on the scene when I needed him most and was now trying to find out who destroyed my career and to save what few worldly possessions and dignity I had left.

After knocking quietly on Jan's door, I peeked in and found her asleep. Then I slipped out to the garage and turned on the lights. A red and white restored 1956 Chevrolet BelAir hardtop was parked in the first stall, but without air conditioning it only went out in early spring and late fall.

The second garage space was occupied by Liz's bright red restored MG convertible. The top was still down from our last ride to cooler temperatures at Mount Charleston. I hesitated a moment, then opened the door and inserted the key in the ignition. It started without hesitation. I put the top up before turning off the engine and left the key on the seat (Jan would need transportation with air conditioning).

I walked on to the third garage space where the black 1983 Cadillac Eldorado Biarritz was parked. My first real business car. I had never purchased the new models. Too much plastic. Instead, a friend of mine who was in the restoration business gave the Biarritz twenty coats of paint, chromed the engine, replaced the leather interior, and fit it with a telephone and a fancy state-of-the-art sound system. It was better than front row seats at a Sinatra concert.

Inside the trunk of the Caddy were golf clubs, shoes, and other paraphernalia. Before disaster had struck, I played most of my golf with clients at the Las Vegas Country Club, where old money resided. Today I would be Hank's guest at Spanish Trail, Las Vegas's newest addition to housing and country club development for "new" money. It was for out of towners for the most part. Hank belonged to both clubs but was sensitive to my recent fall from social grace via SEC sanctions and the talk such a fall engendered among the so-called "upper crust."

After the interior of the Eldorado was cooled sufficiently, I pulled out, looking both ways down the street of our private residential area. Fenced walls and guards at the gate protected these houses that sold for well over a half-million dollars. Liz and I owned ours free and clear before she died. However, when things went sour at Banner—well, the Century 21 sign on my front lawn wasn't there because it matched the now brown grass.

Once on the east-west expressway, I called Hank and confirmed with him our two o'clock appointment. In late July the golf course would be hot, but I liked that as long as the wind was mild and the club kept the cart's coolers stocked with ice. A person could miss the crowds and play to keep his weight down.

My mind turned to solving Jan's predicament. It hadn't

been easy for her to come to me, and there was a little guilt gnawing at the lining of my stomach. My approach to Liz's sister was hardly what my wife expected of me. *I must remember that my life isn't the only one in shambles at the moment*, I thought, *or prepare for a good tongue-lashing when I face Liz again.*

I decided to call Daniel Anthony Trevino to see if there was anything he could do to help Jan. He was a trader for Banner. As were most of my close friends, Danny and I were in Vietnam together. A paraplegic with a heart of gold and a mind like a steel trap, he could remember the details of trades he had made three years ago, along with every major rumor, fact, and figure associated with Banner's trading practices since he was hired.

His condition had left him wondering if life could ever hold any promise again. "Jerry," he said, "what woman in her right mind would ever stick herself with someone who can't even use the bathroom without help! Nah . . . that part of my life is over!"

His job had proved to be a challenge as well until we convinced him a personal secretary could take notes and do the legwork. He found a secretary, and I paid her salary until he was able to. After that he became an overnight success and a public relations gold mine for the firm. I quit paying for his secretary after the second month. He was making more than I was.

Our relationship grew from sitting next to each other in a Sikorsky for better than one hundred fifty missions and also from being nailed by the same land mine. I owed him; his body had found its way between me and the explosion, taking most of the impact and all of the shrapnel—except the piece that shattered my eye and one that tried, unsuccessfully, to lift my scalp.

I rang the 800 number set up for his personal use and waited. I looked at my Rolex. One-fifteen. The market was closed on the East Coast, and a call shouldn't interfere with the rush of market business.

"Danny, here."

"Out of business yet, Danny?"

"Hey, Jeremiah! Good to hear your voice. With recent developments I thought maybe you had flown to Venezuela!"

"Funny, Danny."

His voice got serious. "Any change in things?"

"Nope. It's looking more bleak all the time."

"You're getting a bum rap, Jerry," he said after a few seconds of silence.

"Somebody was out to get me, Danny, and succeeded. Maybe someday I'll find out who. Right now I'm just trying to stay out of prison."

Two and a half million dollars had vanished out of a Powers Limited's corporate account. Two weeks later ten percent of that amount had showed up in mine, the rest disappearing into thin air.

At first I figured it for a computer malfunction, then for a cruel joke. Then the tickets with what looked like my signature were found, and I was told not to come to work pending an official investigation. There had been demands for replacement of funds or for criminal prosecution; attorneys negotiating; desertion by the firm; and finally, my being forced out of business by the SEC when they revoked my license on the day criminal charges were filed. If I had ever entertained the idea that justice would prevail it had been dispelled by a six-month-long nightmare that nearly drove me to jumping off high buildings with nothing but concrete to stop my fall.

"What I called about, Danny, concerns Jan."

Another pause. "Your socialite prig of a sister-in-law? The one who thinks the good Lord in heaven owes her something for being beautiful? The one who tried to wreck things between you and Liz? Jerry, you are either a masochist or the most hopeless idiot I have ever known!"

Danny and Jan had met on one of Danny's frequent visits to our home in Las Vegas while in treatment. Jan looked down on him as if he had leprosy instead of a wheelchair. Having them in the same house, both trying to recuperate from emotional stress, caused war. Liz forced a truce by grounding them in their rooms until they could behave, as if they were children. When released, Danny grumbled a lot and Jan pouted. After six days they spoke to one another again, but only because Liz threatened to make them both go to church—Catholic or Mormon, she didn't care—and see the bishop or priest, their choice. Things immediately improved.

"No lectures, huh, buddy," I said. "Will you just look into a company called TriStar Oil? It's over the counter. Last traded at 1.15 on the ask. Seems she bought it at 2.50 with the promise from someone, probably one of her jet-set girlfriends' sister's husband, that the sky was the limit."

"How much has she got?"

"About fifty thousand shares." I smiled. "She spent her last penny on it."

"Are you serious! Where did this full-time social fluffball learn about moderation? Maybe on the side of a cornflakes box!" His laugh filled my car. "Listen, Jer, after what she tried to do to you, maybe you should just let her sink instead of throwing her a life preserver!"

"Give me a little slack, will you, Danny? What are you hearing on the Street?"

"I don't know much about it. Small over-the-counter stuff with Richards and Company out of Denver as market maker. It looks like typical pie-in-the-sky stuff. It has nearly 10 million shares out there and has dropped better than a point since the day before yesterday. The Vegas office of Banner has sold quite a bit of it." He paused, a habit of his when trying to emphasize a point. "Mostly your old partner, Kirk."

"Any chance of getting Jan out, tomorrow?"

He tensed; it wasn't a small request. He would have to call in a favor or two. Someone was going to have to eat the stock if it was bad, and he liked the idea of that someone being Jan.

There was a long pause, then a sigh. "Okay," he said finally, "I'll look into it. I'll do a little research before we get somebody to bury the stuff at a loss. We may get a better picture in a couple of hours. I'll get back to you.

"One other thing," he said. "The Mideast is getting hot. If you have any oil stocks, hang tight. They might drop some, but knowing how greedy the oil company monsters are, I'm sure they'll grab the opportunity to raise prices and make a killing. Shouldn't hurt their stock at all. Also, get some oil futures."

"From the sound of things, you expect a serious upset in the balance of power over there," I said.

"A strong possibility of people going back to war. Maybe another Nam, heaven forbid." I could imagine him crossing himself as he said it, a habit that had always followed "heaven forbid."

"What did you mean, her last penny?" he asked.

"What?" I asked.

"You said she invested her last penny. What did you mean?"

I told him the bare essentials.

"Mm. Serves her right," he said unconvincingly, and hung up.

Danny, the Catholic boy from the Bronx who said he stopped giving a blankety blank about life while in Vietnam, cared. But then I'd known that since he sat as co-jockey in the Sikorsky. He had the medals and broken body to prove it.

I checked my Rolex again. Ten to two. I needed to hurry so I wouldn't be late for my appointment with Hank. Hank Butcher stood six feet two and weighed in at around two hundred fifty pounds, none of it hanging over his belt. When he hit a golf ball off the tee he would drive his cart half a mile to where the ball had come to rest. The trouble was that he usually didn't hit it straight, and he cheated on his score to make up for lost balls. But at least he told you up front.

Hank had come into my life almost as a miracle. Kirk and I had been working on Hank's partners to move their accounts from another brokerage firm to Banner—under our control. They handled a lot of money for clients and had a lot of influence. It meant millions in new client funds for Kirk and me. In the attempt to get their business, I became good friends with Rod Clemens, the number two partner in the firm. McCloud, the number three, didn't care who handled the money, as long as it was safe and growing. Actually neither Clemens nor Mc-Cloud paid any attention to money matters. Hank seemed to handle it all.

In the only meeting on the subject of the accounts Hank ever gave Kirk and me, we received a cold shoulder. He had everything right where he wanted it and didn't like the idea of change. The subject was closed. Rod had shrugged his shoulders in my direction, McCloud had left for another appointment, and Hank Butcher continued to rule the firm's finances. Kirk had ranted about it for a week, but I had moved on to greener pastures while continuing to play golf with Rod. I was glad for the friendship and was sure matters would eventually change.

When the bottom had fallen out of things at Banner, Hank turned up on my front porch. He gave me the impression that Rod felt Banner was giving me a raw deal, and they decided I needed the best lawyer in town.

"That's me," he had said smiling.

He took a personal interest in negotiating with Powers, the SEC, and even Banner, but his investigation seemed to go nowhere. Hank had kept me out of jail and the poorhouse, but he couldn't seem to find the guilty party.

Hank didn't have good news for me. "Powers won't let you take out bankruptcy," he said as he pulled the cart up to the second tee, a three par with water on the right and in front of the green some hundred and thirty yards away. "If you do it; they'll bring criminal charges against you without hesitation. They want you to liquidate and sign over the proceeds to them, then promise fifty percent of your income until the remaining money is back in their hands. They also want ten percent interest."

I picked up my ball and headed for the clubhouse. Hank followed.

Inside the lounge in the men's locker area, we sat at a small table. The place was empty except for a foursome playing poker in the far corner.

"You okay?" he asked. I wasn't. I felt like throwing up, even though I was glad, deep down, about the bankruptcy.

"Now I know what a condemned man feels like when the governor refuses a pardon and sends him to the electric chair. Fifty percent and ten percent interest! I might as well go to jail. At least that way it would be over in a few years."

He rolled his fat cigar to the other corner of his mouth, deepening the frown. "At this minute they are attaching liens to all your property—stocks, bonds, cars, art work. You name it."

The depression was complete. Frustration burrowed into the lining of my gut. "So. What next? Do you have any particular tall building selected from which I should do a jackknife?"

He smiled. "If you had picked up your messages, you would know that Dick Sellars' secretary has tried to get ahold of you."

I sat straight up. "The guy who heads your investigative division? Has he come up with something?" I asked, scratching for hope.

"Calm down. I wouldn't get my hopes up if I were you."

"When did you put Sellars on the case?" I asked.

"He took up the gauntlet about a month ago. Roger Seamons is a good investigator, but Sellars is the best. He wants us to meet with him tomorrow. He'll fill us both in." He paused. "Until we see what he has, let's don't jump to conclusions. There is a lot of evidence against you, and it will take some pretty straightforward, foolproof information to bail you out, and don't forget that.

"Which brings me to another point. Are you aware that you are trustee over an account at Valley Bank with better than a half-million dollars in it? A half million that showed up the day the two and a half million left the Powers account? In fact at exactly the same time that other ten percent found its way into your personal account?"

My jaw was dragging on the floor again.

"I thought not. Sellars found that too, and if Powers finds it, or the SEC, they'll nail your coffin shut."

"But . . . how . . . ?"

"All part of the puzzle, my boy, all part of the puzzle," he said, lighting the smelly Cuban cigar but being kind enough to blow the smoke over his shoulder. "Someone out there wants you out of the way, broken and beaten to a bloody pulp. My guess is they are waiting for the right moment to make an anonymous phone call to the SEC, *if* they even need to. I don't think they want to use that avenue unless they're forced. They may even want to get the money back."

"Then we—"

"Could watch the account and follow the trail? Yes, maybe. You should understand that because of the way money is transferred nowadays, we may never know it's gone until it's too late. Whomever we are dealing with here is smart enough to get at the money through methods we would have a hard time tracing. Sellars has someone at the bank, watching the account, discreetly. We'll have as good a chance as there is to follow it, but . . ."

"Hank, you're a wonder."

He sat back and took a big puff on his cigar. "Yeah, I know. Too bad you can't afford to pay me anything. Just pray we can get something more concrete before you're on welfare. By the way, how much do you want for the Chevy?"

"If you get me out of this, consider it a down payment on your fee!"

"Good enough for me. Shall we finish our game?"

3

The answering machine reeled off four messages, one from Sellars' secretary, one from Jan, one from a lady from the SEC named Freeman, and one from Danny. Jan's voice was tinged with optimism, and I silently wished her luck.

The autodial on the den phone rang Danny's number. I asked him if he'd been able to find out anything about Jan's problem. He told me Jan wasn't in as serious a situation as it might seem. TriStar, he said, is a company involved in drilling in questionable ground in western Wyoming, near Jackson Hole. They bought leases from the government in areas where the chances for a hit are next to none. The stock had jumped on a leak that big money was involved, then began a dive when people found out where they were drilling. Apparently the rumor had been going around that TriStar had struck a rich well further northeast in the Powder River Basin area, to which they aren't even close.

"But what are they trying to accomplish?" I asked. "An operation like that must cost millions, and they surely must know their drilling will give them nothing of value."

"Patience, Captain. Let me finish. Tomorrow or the next day TriStar will be taking two new businesses under its well-financed umbrella. Rumor has it they will do wonders for the stock over the long haul. I haven't found out who the businesses are yet, but we're working on it."

"So you're saying that TriStar's drilling operation is simply a front for someone attempting to get what they really want?"

"You see it all the time. Big money that can't use the normal channels without being asked to pay exorbitant amounts for what they want, so they go a less-obvious route. That's how it looks."

"Hmm . . . So she should hang onto it?"

"I would," he said. "Look, I'll keep an eye on things and let you know. Is Kirk still controlling Jan's account?"

"Yes, and I'll call him," I said. "I have a bone to pick with him anyway, about putting her in such a deal without knowing what TriStar . . . but then maybe he did know. Didn't you say Kirk has been selling a lot of that stuff?"

"As near as I can find out, he's purchased nearly two million shares for clients."

"That much!" The surprise was genuine. Kirk and I didn't usually deal in over-the-counter speculations. "Anything else?"

"Yeah. You owe me one, right?"

"Right. But go easy. I'm broke, and I have already given the Chevy you've been lusting after for years to my attorney as part payment of his fee. I need the Cadillac until the Powers people come and get it, and the house is sold. I do have several pair of socks with only one hole and a couple of dark business suits I probably will never wear again. Those good enough?"

"Real funny, Jer. No money, no car, no decent socks—and no sense of humor. But I don't want that stuff anyway. All I need is a place to stay for a few days that has ramps and private butler service. Your place fits the bill."

The house had been fixed for wheelchairs when Liz was too weak to walk but still wanted to get around. "You're coming out here? What for?"

"Comic-book convention at the civic center," he said.

"Be serious, please. When did you take up collecting comic books?"

"Lifelong hobby; I just never talk about it much. Can I stay or not?"

"You know you can, but Liz won't be around here to settle arguments you have with Jan."

"She's staying there is she? Well, I'll keep to my end of the house if she'll keep to hers. I'll be there tomorrow afternoon. Does the key you gave me still work?"

"Should. What about transportation from the airport?"

"I got the same guy to help me this time as last. Everybody needs a full-time bodyguard, don't you think?" Danny had hired a male nurse to drive and to take care of him. He didn't like the word *nurse*. I didn't blame him.

4

The lady from the SEC had said it was urgent and I was to call her night number. My first instinct was to ignore it altogether. The SEC had been ruthless and didn't deserve the time of day from me. But, at that moment, the phone rang and I answered it.

"Mr. Daniels, I now have your case. Mr. Belmont has been promoted to other things. I think we should meet so we can iron out a few details and set a date when payments to Powers will start. When are you available?"

"Uh, Ms. Freeman, isn't it?" I asked, wishing I had never picked up the phone. "Well, Ms. Freeman, my attorney, Hank Butcher, of Butcher, Clemens, and McCloud, is handling this, and I think it might be better if you called him."

The reply was right out of the handbook. "I appreciate the fact you have an attorney, but I really think we need to have a face-to-face conference. This looks pretty cut-and-dried to me, and Powers feels the same way. With your license revoked and criminal charges pending, I had hoped you would be more cooperative."

"It isn't that I'm not being cooperative," I said in a voice tinged with anger. "I've done my best under circumstances I find disagreeable, and more like a lynching than a legal process. I think if you will look at the record carefully you will find that I have stated my innocence, and I continue to do so. It is not my intention to give up what few legal recourses I have left so you can ram demands down my throat and further ruin my life. Now, I suggest you call my attorney. His number is 878-5900. He is there from ten o'clock to four o'clock each day, or they can find him for you. Goodnight, Ms. Freeman."

I sat back in the couch and let the steam rise from under my collar. The phone rang again.

"Mr. Daniels? Please, don't hang up. I apologize for being overbearing, and in all honesty I didn't read the entire file. I'll read the entire case history tonight if you will let me buy you lunch tomorrow and discuss it with me further. I'll let you tell me your side. You can even bring Mr. Butcher to represent you. I just want to do my job in the best possible fashion. Can we meet? Please?"

"Is this the same Ms. Freeman who just called? Or do you two work as a team?"

The laughter was refreshing. "Same one."

"I'll tell you what. We'll meet without the attorney, but no dates are to be set. I would like your opinion about what you read in that case file, and I would like to tell you a couple of things you may not know, which may enhance your perspective. Deal?"

"Deal! Tomorrow at noon. Where?"

"There is a little out-of-the-way place with the best south-of-the-border menu anywhere. It's called Bordertown, and it's at forty-three hundred West Charleston. A friend and former client of mine owns it."

"I'll be there."

"Good."

Curious. Six months of dealing with Hank and now all of a sudden a new opponent. A very anxious new opponent, coming directly to me. Trying to impress the boss with a quick kill? Probably. But, at least lunch would be free.

Tony Manza came to this country from Mexico, gained citizenship, fought in Korea, and gave two sons to Vietnam. One of them was my gunner on the Sikorsky. I carried his personal belongings inside my briefcase on my return to the United States for surgery. Las Vegas was a bit out of my way, but Jimmy had been on the chopper for longer than most and saved my life too many times to count.

Tony and Maria Manza had shared their grief with me while showing concern for my eye injury, then heavily wrapped in layers of white gauze. Their compassion and concern had helped a lot with the guilt I felt for losing their son in the storm of battle.

The Manzas and I became friends and kept in touch during the year and a half of my recuperation in the East. When I moved to Vegas a few years later and went to work for Banner, we set up a retirement program for him and his wife.

His restaurant was strictly down-home. His wife cooked everything with fresh vegetables and meats. Nothing frozen or boxed, bought or sold by the truckload. Of course, the proof was in the taste of Maria's cooking and never left you wondering.

The place looked like the movies version of an old Mexican restaurant, with heavy dark wood paneling and imposing pictures of bull-spearing matadors and flamenco dancers with rose stems between their teeth. Thick red and white candles stood in dishes on the tables of high-backed wooden booths padded with thick red tufted leather.

Tony did the greeting, seating, and some of the serving while discussing different topics with his customers. He was just finishing with a foursome when I walked through the door, and he greeted me with the usual warmth and concern. We discussed his account at Banner and when I was going to take back the reins from that young upstart who called too often. I assured him Kirk was a competent broker, everything was okay, and his money was safe. With an unsure grin he left me and went to seat other customers.

The tables at Bordertown were always filled, yet it was never noisy and confusing. Tony didn't allow wall-to-wall seating, which created wall-to-wall people. If there wasn't a table you waited. You knew it would be worth it.

Ms. Freeman was a pleasant surprise; she didn't fit the picture of the typical government employee I had stamped on the judgmental side of my brain.

Tall, about five feet ten, slender, and well endowed with a full figure properly presented in a modest business suit of light tan, she had most of the male business-lunch crowd staring. As Tony brought her to my table I found myself looking more carefully. Well tanned, with curly black hair cut shoulder length. Perfectly straight teeth set in a pleasant smile, and deep brown eyes that made you want to look into them. The guilt of a once happily married man laced my appraisal and made my face turn the color of ripe tomatoes.

Tony gave his sign of approval as she slid into her side of the booth. He placed a menu in front of each of us as I made the introductions, trying to regain my composure.

"Well, Ms. Freeman, I hope you had no trouble finding Tony's place."

Her eyes smiled. "No trouble. I'm just glad . . . well, I was just a little concerned you might not be here when . . ." She looked around. "This is a pleasant place, isn't it?"

"The food is even better. Allow me to order?"

"Yes, as long as there is plenty of it. I'm starved!"

I waved to Tony's son Benito, who took our order and brought us freshly cooked flour tortilla chips, along with his mother's special salsa. The chips were hot and didn't cut the gums like the corn chips used by most Mexican restaurants.

We made small talk, then I dived into what I thought might be a cold sea. "Ms. Freeman, I—"

"Please. Just call me Mike. Short for Michaelene. Does Mrs. Manza give out the recipe for this salsa?" She was finishing off the last tortilla. A smile on my face, I waved for Benito to bring more.

"Nope, but you can buy a bottle or two on your way out. What on earth are you doing working for the SEC, Mike?" My amazement was genuine.

She dabbed her mouth with a napkin, tilting her head quizzically. "Why do you ask?"

"Well, my apologies if this sounds a little forward, but you just don't look like someone who would get trapped in a dead-end government job. I—"

The warmth left her eyes. "Mr. Daniels, government work, especially in the securities business, is not dead-end. I am there because I choose to be. I have a degree in law from Harvard, and I worked for two years for a firm like your Mr. Butcher's before I realized I hated defending crooks." She leaned a little toward me for emphasis, then said, "Now I put them in jail!"

The glint in her eyes softened the blow a little, but I got the message.

"However," she continued, "I usually try to give the rabbit a chance before I snare him."

"Well, as a struggling rabbit with a wish to be free of the net, I thank you for that."

She laughed the same way she had the night before, and the air cleared between us.

"Did you read my file?"

"Yes. And frankly it looks like the net is pretty tightly sprung."

"So it would seem. Would it do any good to shout my innocence from the top of Las Vegas's newest hotel?"

The dark brown eyes had a talent for measuring a man. "Legally no, but I told you I'd listen."

"And buy lunch," I said, smiling.

I told her the story. How I had come to the office one morning after it was discovered that the Powers account had been tampered with over a two-week period, and all fingers started pointing in my direction. Then, about my world collapsing around me—Banner firing me, the SEC sanctions, the Powers demands, my fall from social grace, and my desire to kill the person or persons who did this to me when I finally found them. By the time we finished our meal I had told it all, and she *had* simply listened.

"Can you explain yet how your signature got on those sell orders and where the rest of the two and a half million dollars went?" she asked.

"Not exactly," I said, frowning painfully. "I just know that very convincing scrawl is not mine, and I don't have the money. Somebody set me up and . . ." I saw the hardness return to that beautiful face.

"How do you explain the trustee account with a half a million at Valley Bank, then? The one you supposedly control for your long ago deceased father?"

Hank was right. The final nail was being placed in my coffin. I leaned forward and turned my voice to iron. "Ms. Freeman, my attorney's investigators just found out about that account two days ago, and I can't explain it. Your perspective may be aided if you answer a question for me. How did *you* find out about it?"

She returned the cold stare. "An anonymous caller . . ."

I gave her a smile. "Anonymous, you say? Isn't that interesting?"

"It is not unusual for information to come from people anonymously. Fear for their jobs, even their lives, often keeps them from revealing their identity."

"What do they have to fear from me? I'm not in a position to take their job, and if they ended up dead, surely there's no one for the police to accuse but me. And after revealing their information, if I were really guilty, what good would it do to kill them? Isn't there enough evidence anyway?"

"Yes, but . . ."

There was a crack in her conviction. I decided to wedge it further open. "Look, Mike, you have no obligation to pursue this further. The evidence is certainly incriminating. But doesn't all this seem rather pat to you? Do I strike you as a person who is stupid enough to leave a trail leading right to my own doorstep? You know the securities business well enough to know that if I really intended to steal I could have done it a thousand other ways without taking a chance on losing every possession I have ever owned. No, there may be several accusing fingers pointed in my direction, but I didn't commit this crime."

"Why does someone want to do this to you, then?" she asked calmly. "What enemies have you made? Who inside the business could do it?"

"I'm lost on that. I simply don't know. Hank Butcher is doing his best to find out." Then I remembered my meeting with Dick Sellars. "Tell you what. Hank and I are meeting with his investigator this afternoon. He thinks he has something. Wanna come?"

Her face lit up. "Yes, but . . ."

"Worried about appearances, Mike?"

She smiled. "My question is, Why didn't you report the Valley Bank account discovery to us?"

"That's a fair question. Hank and I decided not to because it would do no good. In fact, Belmont might use it to put me away. Frankly, he wasn't the least bit concerned with questions, only with overpowering evidence." I smiled. "We thought the person or persons who put the money in that phony account didn't really want to use it unless absolutely necessary and might try to get it back. If they did Hank thought they might leave a trail, and we could follow it. We were wrong. Apparently they don't care about the money, only about making sure the case against me is so overwhelming that no one could save me."

"So it seems," she said. "Too bad if you're innocent. Downright damning if you're guilty." She looked at me with those pools of brown over the top of her glass. A final assessment, getting ready to render her verdict.

"I'll go with you to your meeting this afternoon. You don't fit the picture in your file, at least not exactly, but the jury is still out. If I see anything that would raise questions I feel need pursuing I'll buy a little time for you. If I don't you must agree to the settlement terms I decide. Did you sign the papers for the sale of the house?" I gestured in the negative. "Good. You are to sell nothing for the time being, and you are to stop bankruptcy proceedings. Can you live with those terms?"

The Harvard law student was efficient. "Yes."

I liked this lady. But I also knew that if I didn't come up with something tangible her skills would dig the hole extra deep and bury me. Permanently.

"Now," she said, "what time do we meet with Mr. Butcher? And what address?"

5

One-hundred-ten-degree heat hammering the inside of your car is a paradigm of living in the desert. You need gloves just to keep the steering wheel from giving you first-degree burns.

Once the air conditioning had frozen the sweat to my forehead, I picked up the phone and dialed my old private line at Banner.

"Kirk, what do you know about TriStar Oil?"

"Uh . . ."

"You know, the penny stock that has dropped better than a full point in the last three days?"

There was a distinct pause and a heavy sigh. "Has Jan been talking to you?"

"Yeah. With good reason. Jan's financial condition right now makes a typhoon look like a pleasant day. Putting her into penny stocks is an act of negligence, Kirk.

"What was the price of TriStar at the close of the market?" I asked, cutting him a little slack.

"Up fifteen cents and climbing, slowly. Bad news about drilling efforts in Wyoming gave it a setback, but it seems to be recovering, Jerry. I think—"

"Somebody propping it up?" I interrupted.

Another pause. "Could be. How much do you know about this stuff anyway?" he asked harshly.

Then followed an explanation of my conversation with Danny. It always bothered Kirk that Danny wasn't as affable with information for him as he was with me, but he came to understand when Liz explained what Danny and I had experienced together in Vietnam.

"Then Danny thinks we should hang on?" he asked. "Then why so upset about Jan's having the stock?"

I took a deep breath. "Kirk, at the first sign of trouble you get to Danny and get Jan out, first, *before* any of the others you've put in! And that seems to be a substantial number."

"All right! But . . . "

"But what?"

"Nothing," he said coldly.

Speculating on penny stocks was worse than gambling. Good for commissions, good for brokerage firms, good for the company they represented. Disaster for the investor. Kirk knew it and yet saw these stocks as a way to branch out and let investors use spare money to have "fun in the market." But speculating was like a fever, and it wasn't just fun money that ended up lost. Looking for the big kill, people mortgaged their homes, used their rent money, hawked jewelry and furniture—anything to play the market. It destroyed more financial security than the tables of Vegas, more lives than could be counted.

"Jan is at my place, Kirk. Call her. Tell her you and I have discussed this and you are on top of it. Tell her that for now she should hang on to the stock."

"Did it occur to you, Jerry, that maybe she didn't want me to know about her visit to you? She could have come to me about all this."

"Yeah, it occurred. Did it occur to you she may have lost confidence in your ability because you put her last savings into pie-in-the-sky?"

There was silence. Time for a change of subject.

"I'm meeting with Hank Butcher's investigative attorney this afternoon. He seems to think he has something for us. A Ms. Freeman from the SEC is willing to come to the meeting and give me a little more time if it proves informative."

"You'll be coming back before you know it," he said. "I could use the help." I sensed the insincerity.

"What time will you be available this afternoon?" he asked. "Is this guy you're meeting with in town or what?"

"Same building you're in. It's Dick Sellars, remember, the manager of Lifeline Investigations we've tried to meet with for six months? Hasn't he talked to you about my case?"

"Oh, that guy. A tough nut."

"But very good at his business. The meeting will take an hour, so about five o'clock we should be through."

"Well . . . good luck, then.

"I think we should buy some oil futures in the joint account. This thing in the Middle East is heating up, and good old West Texas crude will be worth a lot more a month from now." He hesitated. "At least, that's the analysts' viewpoint."

Good ol' Kirk. He never gives up. Futures could be worse than penny stocks.

"How much cash in the account?" I asked, surrendering.

"Forty thousand dollars."

"All right, Kirk. You can speculate with our money, but please, lay off the clients!" I said as lightly as I could.

"You made your point, Jerry."

6

The office complex at Rancho and Charleston housed a number of small suites where businessmen with a need for low overhead could operate. The office had a mailbox and a secretary to take calls, whom I shared with four other small-time operators and has-beens.

Jan had called several times, and a message from my eye doctor reminded me it was time for another refit of my glass eye and to call for an appointment.

When I dialed home Jan was relaxing by the pool and seemed a little more upbeat. Kirk had called and filled her in on the stock, and the dinner appointment last night had held some promise of a contract, even though only a minor one.

"Where is your agent in all this?" I asked.

"Delfont Modeling and I have gone our separate ways," she said, bitterness edging her voice.

"Want to talk about it?" I asked.

"Maybe later. Suffice to say I wasn't willing to give what Hiram Delfont wanted. Hiram doesn't touch the money girls, but when one falls from glory he tries to play her for *all* she's worth. I'm not that desperate."

"Good for you."

"Jerry, thanks for the run of the house. I needed this."

"You're welcome, but you might not thank me much longer." I told her about Danny.

I could sense her shrug over the phone. "I owe him an apology. I'll try to be nice."

After I finished my conversation with Jan I called Hank at

his office and verified that we were still on for four o'clock with Sellars; then we talked about Ms. Freeman and her deal.

"Finally a heart inside of government? Maybe. We'll see." His skepticism had come after years of court battles, negotiations, and attempted intimidations.

After discussing the anonymous phone call on the Valley trust account, he agreed we had no choice but to do it Ms. Freeman's way. Even he appreciated her straightforward honesty about the account, but he wondered if it was a good idea to have her meet with Sellars.

"Why not?" I asked.

"Well, he may not be as willing to talk about what information he has. Sellars recently retired from government intelligence, and doesn't trust anyone he can't kill." We laughed.

"My choice?" I asked.

"Yes, I suppose so, but—"

"Let her come. I think she can help."

"Are you thinking with your head?"

"My head, Hank? Come on, give me a break. I just met the lady."

After I had called the eye doctor and a few others it was nearly three-thirty, and time to head for the appointment.

Hank and his partners had two offices. The main one was in the Valley Bank building downtown. He housed himself, his partners, and all attorneys directly involved in litigation there, along with a string of secretaries, aides, and runners, who carry paperwork to attorneys and judges.

The other office was two floors below my old suite in the Pincock Center, just off Sunrise Boulevard. Hank kept his investigative division there. The hard-nosed work, undercover jobs, wiretapping, photography, and other "clandestine" operations asked for by clients were under the direction of this office. Few people knew it was Butcher, Clemens, and McClouds' private subsidiary. That's the way they wanted it.

Dick Sellars, the number one man, managed the business affairs. Sharp and disciplined, he had an ingenious mind that worked overtime. His past government experience gave him connections invaluable in his profession in the private sector. The competition's best were in awe of his uncanny ability to find answers when no one else had a clue.

It seemed strange to be looking for an empty visitor's slot in the parking garage instead of my old leased one. But Hank's was empty. We had used it on a previous visit to Banner. I hesitated momentarily, thinking about what the extra steps going to the next level would mean, then watched as another vehicle pulled out only two cars away.

Walking through the breezeway, I saw Hank's personal toy, a Corvette Stingray, pull up to the garage gate. On time, for a change.

The elevator quickly arrived at the tenth floor, and only a few steps away was the outer office of *Lifeline Investigations.* Mike was waiting, her appearance adding a few extra numbers to my blood pressure.

The receptionist broke my reverie with her greeting. "Mr. Daniels, Mr. Butcher will be here any minute." She checked her watch and looked askance at the door to the left. "Mr. Sellars hasn't arrived yet, but I expect him any moment. He . . . just went down to the bank offices on the first floor. Something about a mix-up on yesterday's deposits. I'm sure—" Hank Butcher walked through the door as the phone rang. As I turned to greet him the receptionist screamed, making me whirl. I jumped to catch her as she fainted. Mike was quickly on her feet, helping me lower the girl clumsily to the plush carpet, while Hank captured the phone.

"Mike," I said, "can you get something from the bathroom? A cold cloth or something?" She was on her way before I had finished speaking. The secretaries and other office personnel began to gather round.

Hank swore, slamming the phone on the receiver, his face pale and wrinkled with concern. He leaned on the desk for support. "It's Sellars. They found his body in the private elevator. He's been shot."

"What? Who . . .

He shrugged as Mike came back into the room, the cold, wet cloth in hand, listening. The look on her face was one of disbelief. Shaking her head lightly and kneeling by the girl, she placed the cloth on her brow.

My knees went weak and forced me to a chair, Mike's eyes searching mine. I looked away. I had no answers.

Three hours later we sat in Sellars' office. A police detective by the name of Carone questioned each of us and all the office staff. Finally the place was quiet, everyone gone but the three of us.

Listening had taught me a little. The person who killed Sellars was someone he knew. Someone who stood next to him in the elevator, placed a small caliber pistol against his head, and pulled the trigger, all without a struggle.

A key-operated private elevator should narrow down the list of suspects, but Pincock's management was caught with that part of their security in serious disarray. A mistake for which someone's head would surely roll.

There were nearly one hundred and fifty keys out, and employees had access to nearly every one of them. Over the last year fifty had been reported stolen or missing. No one had changed the lock and given out new keys.

Mike sat with her legs crossed, fingers playing with the trim of the stuffed chair, deep in thought, a worried look on her face.

"Well, Ms. Freeman, I'm at your mercy. It seems my last hope just went down as another statistic in the world of murder and mayhem. Where do we go from here?"

She looked at me, then at Hank. "Mr. Butcher, Mr. Sellars' case files, where would they be?"

He hesitated, then pointed at the desk drawer. "The most recent ones he usually kept in there. Bottom-left-hand side. There will only be the briefest of information, though. The more critical material is kept in his computer. Everything is coded, but possibly his secretary knows how to get in. I sent her home, but I'm sure we can get into the computer tomorrow." The ordeal was taking its toll on Hank. He seemed nervous, anxious, as if he had a lot on his mind.

Mike opened the drawer and went through several Pendaflex folders. "Here's Jerry's file."

Hank and I moved to the desk as she spread out the sheets. There were a number of notes—hours spent on the case, names and addresses, and a short journal account of each phone call or visit.

She began turning sheets over. "These mean nothing, at least as far as what we're looking for is concerned." There were three sheets remaining. One was the journal entries; another, addresses and phone numbers; and the third, a list of apparent stock symbols running across the page, spaces between each individual set. There were a dozen lines, more than a hundred stock symbols in all.

"Jerry, you're the resident stock specialist. See if you can find a pattern in it. Hank, read these journal entries, will you? See if there is anything that strikes you as odd. I'll take a look at this list of names and addresses."

For the next five minutes we each did our thing. Nothing strange about the paper full of symbols, but I wondered what the list was doing in my file. Hank read the journal a half dozen times, and Mike checked the names and phone numbers.

"Well," she said, disappointed, "not much here, but let's go over it. Hank, what are your observations?"

"Nothing odd. Just a summary of meetings with me, Jerry, his partner, Belmont, and half a dozen others involved in the case. Looked like one dead end after another. Most of it in the previous investigator's handwriting. Nothing new. No hints at all!"

"Same here," Mike said. "The only unfamiliar name on the list is a Mrs. Samuel Harrison, Sahara Country Club estates."

"Is there a reference to her in the journal, Hank?" Mike asked.

Hank looked a minute and then responded. "Yes, here." He lay the papers in front of Mike and pointed to the spot. "He just says that he attempted to contact her but had no luck. Looks like . . . six times."

"How about you, Jerry?" she asked. "Can you see any connection to your case in that sheet of symbols?"

"Some of these symbols I recognize. But I'll need some time and my computer before determining what they all are. Powers is here but with seventy others, and I haven't a clue why they're in my file."

"Doesn't seem as if Sellars had much to say, Jerry. No new revelations, I mean."

"No, it doesn't," I said, discouraged.

"Listen, you two," Hank said. "I have to meet my wife at Betty Sellars' home in half an hour. Can we finish this tomorrow?"

"Go ahead, Hank," I said. "Mike and I will take these and put our heads together. Maybe we'll come up with something."

He looked at me funny.

"You don't mind, do you?" I asked.

"Oh no. That would be fine." He fumbled in his pocket, taking out a set of keys and removing one and handing it to me. "Just lock up when you're finished, and I'll meet you back here in the morning. You won't be long, will you?"

"No. I've had enough for one day, and I'm sure Ms. Freeman is ready to finish up as well." She nodded.

"Okay, then I'll see you tomorrow," Hank said. "I'll need to be at this office for a few days."

I watched as he left and closed the door behind him. His huge frame seemed less imposing, his color pale.

"This will take its toll," I said.

Sitting down on the sofa, I blankly looked around the office. Expensively done, but discreet. Original artwork on the walls, depicting scenes from everyday American life. One of the trading floor of the New York Stock Exchange hung above the couch. The chaos it depicted was nothing compared to that which seemed to plague my life.

Mike, sitting at the desk, deep in thought, sensed my eyes boring holes through her. She looked up and forced a smile.

"Would it help at all if I told you I believe you?"

I smiled. "A bunch."

"I need to freshen up a bit," she said. "May I use his private bathroom?"

"You may. *If* you will let me buy you dinner."

"Are you really up to it?"

"Borderline, but the knot in my stomach demands immediate attention."

"I have a better suggestion."

"I'm listening."

"Let's go to my place and I'll fix us something."

I hesitated. Nearly two years since Liz died, and yet—

"All aboveboard. Just dinner."

"How can I refuse my jailer?" I said.

She stuck her tongue out at me as she disappeared through the bathroom door.

I went to the desk. The papers sat there, glaring at me. Was there something important in those pages? It sure didn't look like much. If Sellars had answers they had to be somewhere else. I began to open the desk drawers. It wouldn't hurt to do a little search of my own.

The usual desk and office supplies were evident. Pencils, pens, paper clips, clip notepads—odds and ends but no miracles.

Mike came out of the bathroom, makeup redone and clothes neatly smoothed. A beautiful woman.

With effort I forced the thought from my mind, knowing

the direction it was headed could only lead to complications I didn't need.

Gathering the papers, I shoved them into my briefcase and then walked to the computer. The IBM sat on a table behind Sellars' desk. Flipping on a fluorescent lamp, I sat down and punched a key. The screen came alive. "It was still on. Maybe he was doing some work before he went to the bank."

Mike came and looked over my shoulder. The Word Perfect format on the screen revealed nothing. I hit F7 and went back to the main menu, checking to see what other programs he might have. There were four. Word Perfect, a spread sheet, an accounting worksheet, and one named CONCIA, which I had never heard of.

I punched it in.

The computer hummed, displaying the auto-dialing system. CONCIA was held in another location, probably in a much larger system. A common practice when you have gobs of information to store or need a lot of memory to do the work.

USER NAME?

 SELLARS.

PASSWORD?

I punched in his first name.

ACCESS DENIED. PASSWORD?

"What are you doing, Jerry?" Mike asked.

"Look at this file name. It connects him to another computer somewhere through the autodial program. I tried to get into it, but I don't know his passwords, and without them the computer won't access me."

"What did you just type in?"

"His first name. Just a stupid guess. Didn't work, but a lot of computer operators use things simple like that so they don't forget their passwords and lock themselves out of their information."

"What could he have used?"

"Anything between one and eight characters long. The longer, the harder to break. A random selection of letters just six figures long could take as much as a thousand years of constant work to decipher. But that kind of password is hard to remember, so most people either write them down and hide them someplace or work with easier, more familiar names. Something in the room, a family member's name, a hobby, something like that. If Sellars used the last method, which most people do, we should be able to get in. Eventually. If he used a difficult one he may have written it down and hidden it in his desk or around the room somewhere. Will you look while I do a little fiddling here?"

She started going through the drawers, his day planner, then she moved to the file cabinets. I started thinking. If Sellars' files were stashed in a protected computer somewhere, and I could get into those files, I might find what he had discovered about my case. Then again, I could be in big trouble if I played too long with the wrong words. Big systems either lock you out after one or two attempts with incorrect passwords or they trail you along until they can trace your phone number. But traces take time, and warrants are necessary to come after us. By then we would be long gone.

I punched in half a dozen possibilities—Pincock, the building we were in; Crystal, his secretary's name; tennis, his favorite sport and hobby; and Butcher, his boss's name. Then I started using the names of articles in the room. Nothing.

"You find anything?" I asked.

"Not yet. You?"

"Nope. It isn't going to be easy."

My eyes bored a hole in the screen as I tried to think of other possibilities, then I decided on another tack.

"I'm going to send all this stuff to my computer at home. Breaking his code will take a lot of time, if I can do it at all, and I want to go through the files he has parked in the Word Perfect memory here as well, but I'm too tired and hungry to do it tonight."

Going back into the main directory, I called my computer on the modem then had it start copying all of Sellars' files and directories. There were gobs in his memory alone, and it would take a while. I shut the screen off, swiveled the chair around in Mike's direction, and looked at my watch. "Probably no chance of breaking into the files he has housed elsewhere, but it's worth a try. It's nearly nine o'clock," I said. "The offer of food still good?"

She sat on the couch, smiling. "Are you kidding? I'm starved, and the only way I know I'll get enough is if I cook it. Come on." She picked up her valise. "You can follow me up the hill."

7

Michaelene Freeman's place "up the hill" was a three-bed-room home on the east side of the city at the foot of Sunrise Mountain. An impressive view of the city of lights was at her front door, while the temple stood as a beautiful sentinel at her back.

On the way there I thought about Sellars. His past government intelligence experience and a password with the letters CIA made me wonder if the mainframe computer his autodial was set up to call had anything to do with the government. Maybe a coincidence. Maybe he was still working for the government. The question, how to find out?

The matter of his death had me confused, and apprehensive. The only person wanting him dead because of my case would be the one who framed me at Banner. That thought gave me goose bumps.

How to get in those files?

Luck . . . and time enough to try every combination possible! I'd be old and gray.

After arriving at Mike's, I washed up in the guest bath, then headed for the living room.

Mike had changed into white cotton knee-length shorts with deep pockets and a cotton blouse the shade of pink roses, her hair tied back with a ribbon of the same color. I watched her from the living room couch as she prepared dinner, the soft music on the Technics stereo system relaxing my tired mind. I decided to shove Sellars and the whole business of Powers aside for the rest of the evening. There would be time enough tomorrow.

Mike's home was decorated modestly—modern and warm. Off-whites accented with mint green and salmon-colored pastels. She and Liz were as different as day and night in some ways, but they loved the same colors and styles—Southwest.

We ate on a patio facing northwest and near the pool, the lights of the city stretching south to our left. With the house between us and the temple, I could see only the tops of the spires and its many lights reflecting in the dusty air above it.

"You live well," I said respectfully.

"I bought the house at an auction. The people who lived here trashed it when the bank foreclosed. It was beat-up and run-down, and with no other bids I got it for a prayer. It took me six months to clean it up, repair it, paint it, and make it what it is. But I enjoyed every minute of it. Except for the home I was raised in, this is my favorite place. I wish I could spend more time enjoying it, but my job takes me back to Washington much too often."

"You did it alone?"

She laughed gently. "No. One of my brothers, as yet unattached, spent his weekends this winter with me and did the hard stuff. That was his bedroom and bath you used."

"Where is he now?"

"He teaches at the University of Wyoming. Geology. He's really my adopted brother."

She pushed her plate aside and lifted the glass to her lips. "What do you think of the view?" she asked.

"Almost as good as mine," I said, smiling.

"Oh, really? Where do you live?"

"Almost straight through, on the other side of the valley. Actually I have no view at all, except of my neighbor's high walls and rooftops. With both of us working we thought it best to buy a place in a protected housing area." I took a drink, eyeing the bottle in the middle of table. Clearly Canadian sparkling water. Cherry flavor. Very tasty stuff, and no alcohol.

"I like our house," I went on. "Roomy but not too big. I did a few electronics to it and some remodeling in the den and upstairs studio, which are kind of my retreats. One for business, one for pleasure and maintaining my equilibrium."

"Studio?"

"Yes. I oil paint landscapes and historical personalities."

"What do you mean 'historical personalities'?" Her smile was catchy and made me feel like talking.

"Mostly my feeling about Indian life as it was years ago. The hunt, the battle, the survival among tribes. And mountain men. I have done a few of those as well. I love nature, and spend some of my summer each year back in Teton Valley, Idaho, where I was raised until I was twelve. I draw scenes of historical places, do research on faces and people who lived back then. Then I paint. It gives me some relaxation."

"You're from Teton Valley?" She reached her hand across the table. "Shake, neighbor, I'm from Jackson."

"Jackson Hole, Wyoming. Gateway to Teton and Yellowstone National Parks. Nice coincidence. Just an ol' country girl, are you?"

I started to put two and two together. "Freeman. Senator James Freeman. Democrat from Wyoming. Independently wealthy, owns a big cattle and horse ranch, among other things, northeast of Jackson. Chairman of the Senate Committee for the Interior. Sits on the Senate Select Committee on Intelligence. Personal friend of the Republican president. Any relation?"

She blushed. "My father."

"I'm honored. I don't have much respect for men in Washington. Your father is the exception."

Senator Freeman was a courageous politician who didn't take bribes and nailed those who did. He hated corruption in Washington and said so with actions, not words. Retired from the navy, he had served aboard the battleship *Arizona* until she was sunk at Pearl Harbor. He had been on leave at the time. He was decorated for his actions at Midway and several other major sea battles, and he hated war almost as much as he hated crime. He wasn't a bit shy about doing something about it, either.

"Has he recovered from that sting operation a few years ago?"

She smiled. "But those around him won't let it drop. Gets tons of invitations to all the big social events. Others see him as the man to have at your party. It seems to be unusual in Washington for a senator to demand being used to uncover corruption in high places."

"How did he find out Senator Grisham was on the take?" I asked.

"Grisham turned up at work with a new Porsche 944 and moved into one of Washington's nicer sections without any apparent source of additional income. Just three months earlier he had come to Dad asking for a loan to keep out of bankruptcy. Dad, always a soft touch, had given him what he needed under exceptional terms but mentally had written it off as a bad debt. Grisham just hadn't had any way to give it back."

She leaned back in the chair. "But Grisham did pay it back and bought those toys before the ink had dried on the agreement with Dad. So"— she smiled—"he tailed Grisham."

"He tailed him? You're kidding!"

"Uh-uh. He tailed him and got lucky, called the FBI, and the rest was in the newspapers. Dad loves being involved. Sometimes it's scary how much he loves it."

"A trait you seem to have inherited."

"Thank you. I think. Tell me more about your painting."

I let myself get comfortable in the thick cushions of the couch. "I'm part Shoshone Indian. That's some of the reason for my interest in the people I paint, I suppose. My grandfather was dedicated to his Shoshone heritage, even though he was partially integrated into the white man's society. He used to take us hunting and fishing in wilderness areas, where we learned to live off the land. Then he taught us how to dry the fish, make jerky and pemican, tan the hides of deer and elk, and make clothing using every inch of the skin. At night, as we worked around the fire, he told us great stories about our ancestors. A lot of my pictures depict those events.

"I was just starting sixth grade when Dad and Mom moved to take better jobs and I was forced to leave the valley. We went back in the summer for a few years, then it just sort of tailed off as I got older.

"My roots are pretty deep in the valley, and some of my relatives still live in Tetonia and Victor, but I was raised in white society and lost track of the other side of my heritage."

I decided to change the subject. "The meal was excellent." I stood and started to clear the dishes.

"Now," I said. "I insist on cleaning up."

"I'll let you."

"Good."

She stood in the kitchen and dining room doorway, her arms folded, shoulder against the frame, watching me, "Jerry, will you tell me about your eye."

"Not much to tell. I lost it in Vietnam. Our chopper, disabled by missile fire, went down. Everyone was killed except me and my copilot, Danny Trevino. While we were trying to get back to friendly territory, a landmine got us. It could have been worse for me, but Danny took most of the blast. I carried him another ten miles before a bunch on reconnaissance spotted us and came to our rescue.

"But his spine was cut in half, and my eye was gone. Two years and three plastic surgeries later they gave me glass as a substitute. Danny's paralyzed from the waist down. Does my eye bother you?"

"Not at all, anymore. When I first met you I noticed it didn't move quite like the other one, and it didn't dilate. I figured it was glass."

"Liz, my wife, was the one who fixed me up." I finished putting Crystal Clear soap in the dishwasher, dried my hands, and turned and faced her, placing myself against the counter. "It took some getting used to, and it's hard to play some sports, but golf is okay as long as someone spots where the ball goes when I hit it."

She looked at me, never changing expressions. "Do you play chess?"

"Yeah, a little, but I'm no grand master. Are you setting me up, here?"

"You'll have to play me to find out."

After four games in one hour, and one win to three losses, I swore never to play her again. Then, while she was getting something in the kitchen, my mind changed. Study. That's what it would take. Next time—

She returned with a plate of cookies in her hand and a couple of glasses of milk. She sat down on the couch, with her legs tucked under, facing me. I found myself feeling guilty about wishing she would sit closer.

"Can I ask you another personal question?" she asked with her mouth partly full of a cookie.

"I suppose, but why the interest? I'm really quite a boring person."

She smiled that infectious smile again. "I like to know all I can about a condemned man."

"That's real comforting, counselor." I took a bite of my cookie and chewed it to pulp. "Talking about Liz is still . . . uh, a little uncomfortable, but other than that . . ."

Her eyes went soft but were short of pity. "I know about Elizabeth Dellingham Daniels. And I know about your rare love affair. It was the kind of thing really good movies are made of. I respect that and won't tread on sacred ground. Tell me about the rest of your family."

"Thanks," I said, wondering how she knew but letting it slide. Probably in some government report. "All my immediate family is gone. I had only one brother. He was killed in an F-15 a few years back, in 1978.

"My parents died of natural causes after a nice retirement in St. George, Utah. My life is my work, which I don't have right now, so I don't have much of a life." I reached for another cookie, controlling the anger that gnawed at my stomach. "I live on the quiet side and avoid the renowned Las Vegas nightlife."

"Did you really hate Vietnam?" she asked sincerely.

"Vietnam," I said, sighing. "Yes, I hated it and what it did to thousands of young men and women, and to what was a beautiful country. I was one of the lucky ones, really. I got out without too much damage, and, I found Liz. Not many found anyone like her. She gave me a lot of reasons to live, and the ability to work my way through a tortured mind."

"Do you hold a grudge against those who started it all?"

"And who would that be?" I sat back in the couch, pausing a moment.

"Mike, there were thousands responsible for what happened over there. It started with Kennedy. Do I blame him? Maybe Lyndon Johnson? He escalated the war without much concern for life. Or how about one of hundreds of generals, colonels, and politicians who played games with our lives? Maybe I should blame the American people who acted as though they were ashamed of us, when all we did was fight as we were told, supposedly for them. When it comes right down to it they were the worst to deal with."

I took a deep breath. "I'm sorry. One thing I have never been able to shake is a degree of indignation. I quit trying to find people to blame years ago. I couldn't stand the hate it was making me feel."

She inhaled. "Would you do it again?"

I couldn't believe the question, but tried not to let it show. "No . . . and yes. At first I fought for my country. When I decided my country was wrong and wasn't going to do anything about it I fought to save as many lives, including my own, as I could. I'd drop kids off and watch them disappear into the jungle, knowing only half would come back, sometimes none, but I'd do everything I could to save those who desperately needed a way out. I never turned my back on any of them, though ordered to on several occasions. I was good at what I did and seemed able to do things with my chopper that others couldn't. I used that the best way possible." I paused.

"Yes. I'd fight to save others. Always!"

"What if we go to war with Iraq?"

I paused. Where was this leading? "You think we might?"

"Very possible. Would you consider it the same as Vietnam?"

"I don't have enough information to decide that."

"But from what you know, is it the same?" she pressed.

"No. The Vietnamese didn't control what Iraq's Hussein could in the Middle East. Control of the region by one of the world's megalomaniacs would be asking for Armageddon."

She got to her feet and followed me into the kitchen. I wanted another change of subject.

"What about you?" I asked. "Your family, I mean."

"I mentioned the adopted brother who's a geologist. His name is Robert Doolittle. He came in from a frozen marriage that created a nonexistent home life. We had a warm fire, and he just stayed. My older brother, Bob, is a vet like you. Army Special Forces. He married a local girl, and they have twins. He is the man who runs the ranch, quietly.

"Dad lost Mom a few years ago to early Parkinson's disease. It took him about a year to bounce back. They were an incomparable couple. He is a cowboy at heart and would rather be on a horse than at a desk, but he felt an obligation to do more than gripe about how Washington was handling our public lands. He's been battling for them ever since. At first he didn't know how to negotiate, so he bulled his way with spit and grit, as he called it. He didn't seem to make much headway, but he won a lot of respect that paid off as he learned to deal with the Washington mentality. Now he's powerful enough that people listen carefully when he talks. They know they can trust his viewpoint."

She paused, thinking, then decided to go ahead. "I understand your pain, Jerry. I was with Mom most of the time when she was sick. My own private assignment, I guess. As strong as Dad is he couldn't take watching her die by inches, and he knew she didn't want him to. She didn't want me to, either, but I didn't leave her any choice."

Others had tried to say they understood what I was going

through, tried to think they did, anyway. All their efforts were appreciated, but empty. "Begging your pardon, Ms. Freeman, but I don't think so." I said it a little more coldly than I had intended, but she had been asked to avoid the subject."Watching Liz die was something no one could understand unless they stood in my flesh and felt what I felt. There is love and then there is love. I watched both my parents die, and it just isn't the same. Sorry. I appreciate your effort, but it doesn't wash."

We put away the plate and glasses. "I'm sorry," she said. "It was foolish of me to say. Can we still be friends?"

"Do you think your boss will appreciate your fraternizing with a condemned man?"

She took my arm, and we walked through the dining area toward the front entry. "I am the boss. Belmont worked for me."

I bowed exaggeratedly. "I am honored that you would consider me worthy of your time." She poked me in the stomach. "Ugh. Careful, that's dinner."

My hand went to the doorknob, then I turned to face her again. "I apologize for—"

"Please don't." She put her finger to my lips and moved a little closer.

"Well, then, thanks for a wonderful evening. I appreciate your steering clear of my financial problems. I needed to relax. I cringe even now when I think about facing them."

"We'll need to meet tomorrow about those, Jerry," she said. "How about lunch again? You've got me hooked on good Spanish."

"You're on." I extended my hand after wiping the sweat on my pant leg. Her closeness made me tingle while making me feel . . . nervous? I clumsily opened the door and stepped out.

"Goodnight, Mike." I walked toward the car with her watching from the porch. I turned and waved as I opened the door of the Eldorado. She was special. But, not yet . . . not now. My life was too much of a shambles, and . . .

I got in the car and turned the key. And? And what? I asked myself.

And, you're still too much in love with Liz. *And*, no one could ever replace her.

And, this lady is out to nail your hide to the wall!

I hated *and*.

8

After locking up the house and turning on the alarm, I went for another cold shower, then lay on the bed to think while listening to CNN. The news summed up the problems in Kuwait and showed Iraq's Hussein smoothing everybody's feathers while amassing troops at the border. A classic case of talking out of both sides of one's mouth. Would we go to war? More fighting, dying? I rubbed my arms to make the goose bumps go away. How many would die this time? I shook it off.

I went to the den and flipped on the computer monitor. The transfer of Sellars' accounts was complete. I opened and formatted a fresh package of disks, then made a floppy backup while the high-speed printer spat out a paper copy. I labeled the disks with phony names, slid them back in the box, then placed them on the shelf with several dozen others. It was nearly three o'clock when I smoothed the bedding out and slid between the cool sheets, the printer still clicking away down the hall.

A disturbing alarm in my mind warned me to shake off the sleep just as two bodies dressed in black with ski masks to match pinned me to my bed.

They said nothing, but while one made me breathe from the barrel of an apparent sawed-off shotgun, the other went through my briefcase. He took the Sellars case file, placed it on the dresser, and looked through it under the beam of his flashlight. He then closed it and, placing it under his arm, strode down the hall toward the den. When he came back he had the stack of computer paper from Sellars' files and quietly closed the door behind him.

He came over to me, flashing the light in my face, momentarily blinding me. I heard the click as the other man cocked the gun, and realized they intended to take more than the Sellars papers. My muscles tensed and prepared for a last-ditch attempt at escape.

The knock on the door came with a voice, Jan's voice. "Jerry, are you there? Is something wrong? Jerry?"

I felt that panic between them as well as in my own heart. If they shot her . . .

The man with the gun released his grip, half turning toward the door. My arm struck out, hitting his gun hand and sending the weapon clattering against the wall as my leg slammed into the midsection of the other assailant, consigning him to a sitting position against the wooden frame of the patio door, gasping for air.

Rolling from the bed, I grasped for the handle of the drawer holding my .45 caliber Colt.

"Jan! Run! Get the police!"

My hand was on the pistol grip as the first man in black slammed the drawer on my wrist while shoving his fist into my empty eye socket, banging my head against the side of the bed. The pain was excruciating, but I swung where I knew his crotch must be, connecting dead center, forcing him to the floor doubled up and hurting. I clawed at the drawer, freeing my hand, the pain shooting through my brain. The door flew open, the light from the hall streaming in.

The second assailant stopped in midstride, changed directions, and ran for the patio door, the first assailant hobbling after him, needing help as they went over the railing and into the bushes and disappeared beyond the fence and into the darkness of the neighboring subdivision.

"You all right, Jerry?" she asked calmly. "Should I call the police, still? What . . . who were they, anyway?"

"I'm . . . I'm okay. Turn on the light, will you?" I got up and sat on the bed, thankful I slept in pajamas. "No, don't call the police. Those two are gone, and it would mean no sleep until noon tomorrow." I gingerly touched the bruised and slightly torn flesh of my wrist.

She sat beside me, close enough that I could feel her softness against my shoulder. "Let me see that," she said, grabbing my arm roughly.

"Take it easy! They almost cut it off. I don't need you to finish what they started!"

"Oh . . . sor . . . reee!" she said mockingly. "Not broken, but a nice red-and-blue mark. You'll heal." She touched my eye socket. "I've never seen it without the glass. It'll swell. Now, who were they?"

I shrugged my shoulders, leaning away from the pressure. "I . . . I wish I knew! I think they might have taken life this afternoon and somehow thought I had evidence against them. They took a file that belonged to the dead man."

"Since when did you start playing with such rough characters?" she said as she went into the bathroom. "Where do you keep the aspirin? You'll need a couple."

My heart calmed a bit. "Uh . . . behind the mirror. Top shelf." She was right; it hurt like the dickens.

She had two pills and a glass of water in one hand, a wet, steaming cloth in the other. "Who knew you had the file?" she asked as she placed the cloth against the tender tissue of my socket.

"No one I don't trust. The burglars in black must have found out some other way."

She shrugged her shoulders. "As they say, your funeral. Goodnight, tough guy." She headed for the door. "I'm glad I was in the next room."

"I thought you were staying in the guest area down by the pool?"

"Nah, I put Danny in there," she said. "He needs more room and everything on one floor, remember?"

"Jan . . . uh . . . th—" She poked her head through the opening. "Don't say it. Just pick up that gun and unload it. I can't touch 'em. They make me physically ill." She smiled wryly. "Goodnight."

I smiled back. "Goodnight. And thanks, even if you don't want to hear it. I'm glad you're a tough kid from Idaho."

"Hah. It's New York that made me tough, not Idaho!" She shut the door.

The attacker's weapon of choice was a sawed-off Remington twenty gauge with double barrels. I removed the shells, throwing them into a dresser drawer, and put the gun on the closet shelf behind some boxes. Turning off the lights and locking the patio door, I stood and watched from the shadows, waiting for the adrenalin rush to subside.

Closing the curtains, I took the .45 from the drawer and put it under my pillow.

Then I lay awake.

Only Mike and Hank knew I had that file. Mike was out of the question. She had nothing to gain, but then neither did Hank. I didn't know many men in Las Vegas who controlled more personal wealth than he did. Besides, he had followed me into the parking area and had arrived on my heels at Sellars' office, from the direction opposite that of the private elevator.

Mike was already in the office when I got there. She could have killed him before, but she had no access to the elevator and didn't know Sellars, by sight, anyway. At least I didn't think so. I couldn't get comfortable in the bed, my brain thinking until it hurt. There had to be another answer if I thought it through long enough.

At five A.M. I fell asleep.

The pain in my wrist and socket woke me. The clock said 8:00 A.M., and the sun was forcing its way into the room, casting a hazy orange tint on the mint green sheets. Struggling to my feet, I went to the bathroom and surveyed the damage. The socket was bruised and swollen, tender to the touch. I was grateful the glass had been resting in its velvet box.

After splashing my face with cold water and putting a cold cloth on the now black-and-blue eye, I filled the sink with steamy water and soaked the wrist. Then I called Hank on the bathroom phone.

"This is Hank Butcher."

"Morning, Hank. This is Jerry. How are things this morning?"

"Morning, Jerry. Not real good. Someone was kind enough to break in last night. Made a mess of Dick's files, and—"

"I thought they might have. They came calling here last night."

"Are you all right? Why would they come to your place? What—"

"I'm going to dress and come down. We'll hash it over then. Don't let anyone touch Dick's files or, more particularly, his computer. They may have missed something."

"His computer? How—"

"I'll explain when I get there."

47

After taking a quick shower, I threw on some Levi's and started to shave when Mary started calling for her lambs again. I grabbed a robe, heading for the door, swearing I'd have that noise replaced before the day was over. The eye patch slipped into place over the swollen eye, and I toweled off the freshly applied lather as my feet stumbled downstairs toward the entry.

Jan was punching the numbers on the alarm system and opened the door as I threw the towel into a corner and tied a knot in the robe sash.

"Good morning," Mike said, eyeing Jan's loose-fitting silk robe.

"Uh, good morning, Mike. Uh . . . this is my sister-in-law, Jan Delling."

I always hated the fact that Jan had shortened her maiden name for purposes of modeling. She said *Delling* was more poetic than *Dellingham.*

"Jan, this is Michaelene Freeman with the SEC. She—"

"I recognize you, Ms. Delling. Anyone would who reads women's magazines while under a hair dryer. I'm pleased to meet you." She stuck out her hand. Jan took it.

"Ms. Freeman. Shall I let her in, Jerry, or punch her out?"

They laughed as I opened the door in astonished invitation.

"If you two will excuse me," Jan said. "I'm making breakfast for another houseguest, and under the best of circumstances I usually burn it." She disappeared with a "caught you" look on her face, but a pleased "caught you" look, I thought. Till then I hadn't noticed the smell of bacon cooking.

"Who's the other guest?" Mike said.

I smiled. "Her archenemy from a previous visit. It shouldn't be long before he's up and about. Maybe I can introduce you."

"Archenemy?"

"A story for another time," I said, adjusting the patch.

"From the looks of your face you didn't sleep very well." She touched the patch and began to lift it. "Naughty, naughty," I said, grabbing her hand gently. "It isn't polite to undress a man in public." She smiled, taking the hint.

"What happened, Jerry?" she asked, a little more shocked as she looked at my wrist.

I told her.

"But there was nothing important—"

"More bothersome questions are who it was and how they knew to come to me. Only you, Hank, and I knew I had that file."

She frowned, measuring me again, trying to decide what to say. The hair curled around her face, framing it. She looked businesslike and yet very feminine in a gray skirt and a silk multi-colored blouse.

She walked into the living room, smiling at the decor.

"Jan's idea of what's good in New York," I said in explanation.

"Which side of New York?" she smiled. "Jerry, sit down. I have something to tell you."

She put her briefcase on the coffee table and sat down in the overstuffed chair opposite me. "I am with the SEC, and I am investigating your case, as any good SEC officer should. But I am also investigating a much larger one, involving international markets and money—something that may jeopardize the free-market system we use in this country. We think what happened to you at Banner is related to that."

My jaw was playing tag with my toes. "I suppose you're going to explain what you're talking about."

She opened her valise and pulled out a folder containing pictures. She lay the first one in front of me and pointed to a man sitting at a large desk. "Do you know who this guy is?"

Maneuvering around my shattered ego, I leaned forward and looked carefully, shaking my head in the negative.

"Here's a blowup," she said. "That's Fillmore Duquesne. A very rich and powerful man, and a very dangerous one."

"Everybody in the business world knows about him," I said, "but his picture isn't seen much. This one looks pretty old. Does he still look this young?"

"Hardly. It was taken twenty years ago.

"As you know, then, he owns Duquesne Industries along with a dozen or so other businesses. Word is he's involved in Middle East politics, buying and selling governments so his petroleum, airfreight, shipping, and a few other interests can operate more effectively.

"We believe he was helping finance terrorism and drug activity until about three years ago, when he pulled back to prepare for something we have come to believe is much more dangerous."

"Who's the pretty lady with him?" I asked.

"Jerisha Salamhani Duquesne, his wife. Her family immigrated when she was just a baby—1949, I believe. Her family is Palestinian and was forced to flee from Israel after the partitioning. Her father was injured but was able to amass a small American fortune despite his handicap, and, according to our information, he kept his connections in Israel. Jerisha may have used those to give her husband an inside track with some Arab leaders over there."

"What kind of connections?"

She shrugged. "Duquesne moved his base of operations to Tunis ten years ago. Since that time he has been seen with Arafat, Hussein of Iraq, Assad of Syria, and half a dozen others. Our sources say he has been generous in his donations to them."

She pulled another folder from her valise and slipped two more pictures out of it. "These are blowups of two of his men. This is Jason Winters, Duquesne's vice-president of special operations. He runs Duquesne's less-publicized businesses and sits on the conglomerate's board of directors. His rise to prominence with Duquesne is rather amazing and, we suspect, a cover. The committee is trying to dig up more information on him and the next man you will see. But so far this next man's cover is deep enough we can't find much. As with Duquesne, consider him dangerous."

She pointed to the other picture. "Here he is. This is Court Owens, Winters' assistant. He's as cold as steel at thirty below, and he's ruthless in his, shall we say, enforcement of policy. When someone gets in the way he moves him. Or eliminates him." She pulled out some three by fives that made my stomach churn. "These are a few glossies of what is thought to be his handiwork. The last two were brokers like yourself. All of them are murders clothed in accidents, but one member of the president's task force is working on placing Owens at the scene of this last one. He may have been one of your unexpected houseguests last night. Winters may have been the other. They both live in Las Vegas and are here right now."

"But how could they have known?" I asked, a little edge in my voice.

She took a deep breath. "After you left last night I called some people in high places. You were right about the CONCIA file. Sellars was still working for the CIA."

She put another photo on the coffee table. "This was taken in the Middle East by one of Sellars' agents in 1987. The man sitting in the big chair that's only partially visible is a well-known military leader."

"I recognize him. The Stalin look-alike."

"The man with his back to us, the one with the bald spot, is Fillmore Duquesne. We have identified four of the others, all Middle East businessmen, rich, powerful, and very political."

"And this man sitting next to Duquesne, who is he?"

She handed me a magnifying glass. "There's an identifying mark on his hand. A rather nasty scar. Take a look at it."

My heart dropped into my shoes.

"You know him, don't you, Jerry?" she asked.

I nodded. "I worked with him every day for the last few years. That isn't a scar you could miss. That's Ben Stevenson, branch manager at Banner, Stutz, and Milligan, Las Vegas." I sat back in the soft cushions of the couch and looked at her, hard. "But then, you already knew that, didn't you?"

9

Mike sat in the overstuffed chair, her arms in her lap, hands clasped together. Waiting.

"Quite the little investigator, aren't you?" I said.

She looked down at her hands. "I know what you're thinking, Jerry, and you're partly right. I asked for the luncheon appointment with ulterior motives. Ben Stevenson is involved in some serious illegal activity, and it's our job to go after him. Others in the firm may be involved as well. We don't know for sure. Because you were thrown out of Banner and eliminated as a possible suspect I decided to come to you. We need your help."

I stood up and walked to the window. I couldn't think clearly when she was close to me. "You must have known Sellars was involved . . . yesterday . . . when he was killed."

"I didn't. Until you pulled up that password on his computer. Even then I wasn't sure how it fit together. I had never heard of Dick Sellars."

She came to the window. "As I told you, I made a call last night and screamed until Washington told me what they could over the phone. I'm meeting with someone this afternoon who's supposed to finish filling me in."

"What government agency is running this show?" I asked sarcastically. "One of those groups with three initials? Or is it some specialist military death squad inside the Pentagon?"

She hesitated a moment.

"You're closer than you think. Four years ago, under the former administration, it was decided that terrorist activity was becoming a major threat to United States concerns here as well as abroad. Several different groups, including the CIA, the FBI, the NSA, the Department of Justice, even the SEC because of the terrorist connection to illegal funds used for investment purposes, and representatives from each of the branches of the armed services—these were all brought in to form a game plan to significantly reduce the threat. At first it was more of a think tank than anything else, but after about a year they decided that more had to be done. They expanded with a few other groups and, with the president's blessing, initiated a plan of action."

She had my full attention. "It was decided to hit them on two fronts. The first was military. That's being coordinated with Israel in the Middle East; government leaders in South America, Britain, and a dozen other countries; and police and government organizations at home. You've read in the newspapers about a lot of what they are doing, but believe me, it goes much deeper than that. We're making inroads, but that avenue will never stop them. They have too much support, and too much money to buy what they need. And frankly, the world isn't ready, and neither are we, to declare complete war on them. That time may come, but for now it is not viewed with any degree of sincerity.

"The second is to hit them where it really hurts, in the pocketbook."

"You mean destroy their financial base?" I asked. "But how can you? Don't they get most of their money from donations by wealthy patriots, even governments? How can you stop that?"

"They used to. Even the United States government has made that mistake, only to have it blow up in their face. Events in Panama are a good example of it. But in recent years most of the big organizations, like the PLO in the Middle East, have become self-sufficient. We think that group alone has a financial base stronger than many Third World countries. Nearly ten billion dollars in cash and investments in banks and brokerage houses around the world. Many of them in the United States. The interest alone keeps them going from year to year.

"They have moved from the grenade throwing, money begging murderer to the respected business arena in a little less than a decade. They are very well organized and have learned hard lessons about relying on financing from political leaders and individuals whose loyalties change with the wind. They can now be compared to a multinational corporation, something governments in the West have been unwilling to accept because they're stuck to the old idea of terrorists being a bunch of fanatics who hijack airplanes or attack innocent people in airports. Terrorists now hire those sorts of things done by butchers who can't live without shedding blood, while they themselves maintain a politically safe distance.

"Even the simplest decisions about whether to launch an attack on an American, European, or Israeli target go before the board of directors, who now consider economic and political repercussions, as well as the pros and cons of the targets, over the military and psychological value to their cause."

"Is that true of all terrorist organizations?" I asked.

"No. Not yet, anyway. But some are headed in that direction. The PLO has set the standard, showing others how to use the capitalist system to get their way. That group now finances new terrorist activity by fanatics they think will help them reach their goals, making their wealth more effective while their leaders can maintain that they have no direct involvement in the killing, giving them a somewhat respected position in the world community and effectively blunting any action against them.

"Other groups are now following suit, or attempting to, and are thus becoming more dangerous."

"But how can they be more dangerous?" I asked. "It seems to me that negotiations and less killing would lead to better relations by all those concerned. And, if the killing stops entirely, that has got to be a move in the right direction."

"I wish it were so simple, but it isn't. With money now available to bargain with, groups like the PLO are buying a place in world affairs while still financing covert operations. They still kill people, but more efficiently, without the stain of direct involvement. They have political clout and are gathering support from around the world. Like the Mafia, they deal in killing, and every other negative, while showing a respectable front. We believe they finance terrorist schools and labs for the development of biological and chemical warfare that will soon be used on the terrorist level. They are getting to a point where we cannot stop them if we don't get it done soon."

"Gadianton's band," I half mumbled.

"What?"

"Nothing. And you?" I asked. "How did you get involved in all this?"

"I volunteered," she said, smiling, "Actually, I got assigned to the committee about a year ago. Since then my small group of specially assigned SEC officers and I have been looking for investments in the United States held by terrorist organizations."

"Any luck?" I asked.

She smiled. "Yes. We have been able to pinpoint a number of banks and brokerage houses that launder and invest terrorist money, both from the Middle East and from South America. The South American connection, with its drug-related aspects, is being dealt with by others. I concentrate on the Mideast and, at the present, on this group in the photograph.

"They are relatively new in the arena of direct terrorist organizations. Sellars ran into them back in 1987 and, from what I am told, has been tracking them ever since. They are concentrating on economic and political change and have completely exorcised themselves from volatile fanatics and mainstream terrorism."

"Same year you said Duquesne withdrew from active involvement with mainstream terrorism," I said.

"Yes. And, the money I'm after comes from them. They are using it to control, or buy outright, a large number of American businesses. We don't know all the hows, we can only guess at the whys—to weaken us, even cause financial collapse."

She paused and went back to the couch. "They must be as computerized as any corporations in the world. We just think we have a line on how they get the money into the country, and then we lose the paper trail. They are much too fast, and we can't pin them down."

She took a list from her briefcase. "We have identified what we think are a few of the accounts they control, but at this point we don't have enough to take to any courts or freeze any assets. And frankly, the way they work they could have the money moved before we could serve the court order, plus they have the attorneys to keep us from getting results for years.

"Jerry, it's frightening to see how many billions of dollars are in our system but owned by them."

She put the list on the coffee table, leaning forward, her

forearms on her legs, her fingers wrapped around one another. "I need proof. Ben Stevenson is a definite link to this group and may hold the key to finding out which assets are theirs and what their intentions are. I need your help."

I went back to the couch, thinking. "That picture of Ben Stevenson, the one with Duquesne, when was it taken?"

"March 1987. Why?"

"Ben Stevenson went on vacation that month. Four weeks in Europe, Israel, Egypt, and half a dozen other spots. I was acting manager at the time. Why wasn't your agent able to tell you who he was?"

"Our agent was only at this meeting, and names were never mentioned. We got the impression that the man you've identified as Stevenson was strictly there to get instructions dealing with only a small part of the entire operation; he is not one of the major players."

"Then how did you identify him?"

"A year ago I decided to take a shot in the dark. I made blowups of the papers on his lap, the ones you can just barely see over his shoulder. It's Banner's logo, and the scar on his hand gave me something physical to look for. I started an investigation of Banner's personnel and came up with Stevenson. I transferred here and have been trying to figure out a way to get to him, while continuing the national investigation of the entire group. My devious mind told me I might be able to get you to cooperate."

She smiled. I didn't return it.

"Dick Sellars," I said. "Ex-CIA comes to Las Vegas, supposedly retired from government service and looking for work. But, it's all a cover. He's very successful managing Lifeline Investigations for Butcher, Clemens, and McCloud, but his real work is still in the Middle East. He's getting close to Duquesne when he takes my case from a going-nowhere investigator. I assume, then, that you also believe Sellars was going to tell Hank and me a part of what he had found out about Duquesne. The part that would clear my name. Someone killed him before he could, then came to my house and collected Sellars' computer files and that stock list. Is that right?"

"Yes. I think Sellars knew about Stevenson's relationship with Duquesne because of the information I had sent back through channels. He saw your case as a way to get closer to his real target without raising suspicion."

"What did he find out about my case?"

She paused. "I think he found out that Powers Limited is another company controlled by this group."

My body stiffened. "What?"

"Some of my people spent the night doing more thorough research on Powers and a Mrs. Samuel Harrison, its major stockholder. A sweet little old lady, who suddenly comes on the scene two years ago, buys controlling stock in Powers, moves to Las Vegas, and disappears. Her neighbors say she travels a lot. We don't think she even exists anymore, if she ever did."

"A front to hide illegal purchases of controlling interest in Powers stock?" I said, not ready to believe.

"Yes. Harrison controls Powers through voting rights. You did Powers' investing for their pension plan. Someone decided you were getting too close and—"

"Ben Stevenson!" I walked back to the window. "Ben has a policy of reviewing corporate accounts with brokers, looking for new money we can go after, better ways to help them, that sort of thing."

"When did you have your last review with Stevenson?" she asked.

"A year ago. I said I was going after Powers' major stock-holders as clients. We listed them, and he gave me permission, notifying the other brokers in the firm that they were mine to harvest. I worked profitably on two other smaller accounts, then went after Samuel's Shipping, the major stockholder. That is when my world fell apart."

"Samuel's Shipping, Box 1900, Downtown Station, Las Vegas, Nevada 83101, is, as near as we can tell, a shell created to buy Powers stock. It looks good on paper but has never physically existed.

"Stevenson probably watched every move you made, and when you were considered a risk someone gave him the order to put you out of business. Who got control of the account when you left?"

"Huh! Guess! Stevenson brought a letter from Powers to Kirk and me the day I was cleaning out my desk. It insinuated that Kirk was guilty of negligence even though I stole the money; he should have been aware of what I was doing. They demanded that Stevenson take the account. There was nothing we could do."

"When you were looking at that list of stock symbols last night you said Powers was on it. It's a guess, but I'm pretty sure that list had the names of companies controlled by Fillmore Duquesne and his group. How much more Sellars knew is anyone's guess, but I think it may have been substantial."

She paused again. "I called Officer Carone, the one who is investigating Sellars' murder. He says Sellars was booked on a flight to Washington at seven o'clock last evening. He must have had something pretty solid to want to deliver it personally and endanger his cover, and his life."

"Are you saying that list of symbols was enough to kill Sellars for?" And, to try and kill me for? I thought.

"Yes, along with the computer printouts. At this point those who came here and took those papers last night have to be our major suspects."

"How did they do it? Outsiders don't have access to the private elevator." That was weak. I knew how many keys had been reported stolen and missing. "And how did they know I had Sellars' file?"

She shrugged her shoulders. "Stolen key. You heard what Carone said. Fifty lost or stolen over the last year." She was playing with the ruffle on the couch pillow. "Jerry, do you trust Hank?"

I had to admit it was a fair question. "I saw Hank's Corvette pull into the parking garage on my way in. He didn't have time to go to the elevator and still get to Sellars' office only a few minutes after I did. Besides, the elevator isn't accessible from the main hall, and he came in from the main hall."

"I have to be honest with you, then, Jerry," she said. "I don't know how they knew you had it. A mystery to be resolved, but in my mind's eye this group is at the top of our list."

"Hmm. Question. CONCIA. It must be in a government-controlled computer. Your people in Washington can surely access that computer and get the information he filed there?"

"*CONCIA* is only a name Sellars used to dial up whatever computer he was using, remember? You couldn't get in because you didn't know the password. Washington doesn't know it, either, and there are literally millions of such passwords kept in the government's mainframe. However, they are looking, and I'll have more information on the odds later today. For now, not much hope."

She lay her head against the back of the couch, frustrated. "He must have had the answers, keeping them in his computer files in the government's mainframe. From the look of things he was headed to Washington to reveal them. Once in the president's office all he had to do was pull up information from the mainframe, print it out, and hand it over. Now, unless we get mighty lucky, it's probably so well hidden it'll take years to find it, and would mean reading every single report and file held by the government. Literally billions of pages."

"That's why I'm here. Sellars found what Stevenson was doing, and it led him to what information he had. You know Stevenson better than anyone does. You know Banner, inside and out. We need your help."

"Whoa! Slow down, Mike! I'm not the guy for this! I don't know the first thing about spying on people, and those connections you speak of have closed up since the SEC revoked my license and made my name a swearword."

She leaned forward. "The chairman of our committee wants your cooperation, Jerry, and he will do whatever it takes to clear your name and get things right financially. Call it a retainer for your services."

"You're not serious, are you?" I said, surprised.

"Yes. Second, we only ask you to use your expertise and your remaining contacts to help us. We'll do the spying." She smiled. "This may sound bad, but we are desperate and running out of time."

I returned the smile. "All right. On two conditions."

"What?"

"I get the full story, nothing held back, no secrets, no lies. If I suspect I'm being led down primrose lane I'm through."

"Okay. What else?"

"You fill out the paperwork necessary to clear my name, now, before we begin. One copy for me; one for my attorney. It has to be something I could use in a court of law and in the newspapers."

"It's all in there," she said, taking an envelope out of her valise. "If what I've written isn't satisfactory we can amend it."

She looked at the front of my loose robe, then at my bare feet. "Even as poorly dressed as you are for this interview you're hired."

I started toward the entry and the stairs beyond. I was in. How bad could it be? I thought. Ben Stevenson would be easy to nail, now that I knew what to look for. He had left a trail once; if Sellars found it, I could. After that the big boys take it, my name is cleared, and I can go back to Banner, even take over as manager when Stevenson comes tumbling down.

Hope. There was an old spring in my legs as I took the stairs three at a time.

Pride cometh before the fall.

10

We went to the den. Mike liked the house and said so. "Maybe now you won't have to sell it," she smiled, as I opened the door for her.

"Maybe," I responded.

I took the disks from the shelf and loaded them into the computer's memory, then hit Shift-F7 and one for a printout.

Mike tore the sheets along the dotted lines and started laying them out on the floor. By the time the printer finished we had hundreds of sheets involving more than two hundred different cases of both companies and individuals. Some were names of well-known locals. Corruption and immorality all around town.

"Here's the Powers file," she said.

"I don't suppose the stock list is attached," I said. "Do you see anything in it you didn't already know?"

She thumbed through several sheets. "Nothing."

We divided the cases into people, corporations, and miscellanea. Then we began looking through them by group, people first. We discovered the names of several of the members of the group who had their picture taken with Duquesne. I was amazed at what Mike knew about Duquesne's group and how quickly she picked out his accomplices and who she thought to be potential accomplices.

"Besides the four in the picture we've already identified, along with Ben Stevenson, these six are definite possibilities," she said. "Nothing revealing about them, though."

"Read me their names," I said. "I'll start a list."

"Al Hassani Salah, from Jordan; Abul Gussani, from

Saudi Arabia; Sabri Kwaseini, from Saudi Arabia; Baruch Al Banna, from Iraq; and Hana Saiqa, from Yemen. Umm . . . the last one is simply 'Royalty.' "

"Code name?"

"And no new intelligence whatsoever," she said, disappointed.

It was quickly added to the list. "I would bet Sellars' CONCIA files contain a hoard of information we haven't been able to get to. The list we have here is for keeping track of these people."

I started through the corporate papers. Each corporation was on a separate set of forms listing all pertinent information one might want to know if looking seriously to invest hard-earned cash.

"Well, well. Duquesne Industries." My eye wandered over the six pages. "Nothing you couldn't read in a Standard and Poor's list of corporations. Same facts and figures." Then I saw it. "Look at this, Mike. In caps, right there next to *R* and *D*, the word *TERROR1*."

"*R* and *D*, Research and Development?" she asked.

"Something planned for the future. Maybe it has something to do with their past covert operations in the terrorist world. You said he used his companies as cover for terrorist activities."

"Hmm. Maybe."

I went to the computer and typed in CONCIA, then TERROR1.

ACCESS DENIED.

"What did you do?" she asked.

"I thought it might be Sellars' password. It's not, but it sure looks like a password." We went back to looking through the stacks, the word sticking in my brain.

Each company had similar information. Stock float, debt and what kind, locations of assets, profits over the last ten years, and on and on. Some had listings under *R* and *D* but had much more orthodox words in the blanks.

A pattern emerged. All companies on file were directly or indirectly related to the oil business. All very prominent worldwide and all very American.

"Looky here. TriStar Oil."

She looked at me quizzically. "What do you know about TriStar Oil?"

"Not a whole lot, except that Jan bought fifty thousand shares and afterward it went way down. She wanted me to help get her out because of some financial difficulties. Danny said something strange was going on, but his gut feeling was to hang onto it, so she is. Why? What does the SEC know about it, if I might ask for insider information?"

"The SEC, nothing. But you remember my brother I told you about? The one that helped with the house? He's a geologist and was asked to do an independent survey for a new company that had leased some government lands southwest of Jackson Hole."

"TriStar Oil?"

"Yes. He called me about it the other day and asked if I knew anything about the company. He seemed a little edgy at the time, but indicated he was just curious. I told him I would get back to him. I assigned it to one of my aides and then completely forgot about it until I got this note."

She grabbed her valise, pulled out an envelope and handed it to me. "Read it," she said.

Mike,

Anything on TriStar Oil? They are drilling for oil where there isn't any. Something strange going on.

Tried to contact Dad—no luck. I'm staying at the playpen. Please come up or let Dad know.

Love, Dooley

"What is the 'playpen'?" I asked.

She smiled with the memory. "A box canyon where we used to play when we were kids. It isn't far from the ranch, about two hours by horseback. He's been staying there the last two summers while doing some research for his doctorate." Her brow furrowed. She looked at the TriStar file, then read it out loud. "TriStar Oil, founded August 1987 as a subsidiary of Drymount, Inc., a well-hidden, Duquesne-controlled enterprise. TriStar won the bid on government-leased lands in Bridger-Teton National Forest in 1987 when all other companies 'mysteriously' withdrew at the deadline. TriStar began drilling in the summer of 1989." The rest was all facts and figures.

Mike stood up and walked to the den window overlooking the pool and deck area. "Dooley would only go to the playpen if he wanted to stay away from civilization. If it's part of the Duquesne group's investments it could be trouble of some kind."

She paused. "I have tickets on an afternoon flight to Jackson." She left the room and went down the hall toward the bedroom. A few moments later water was running in the tub. My watch said it was almost noon.

I tried to concentrate on the papers, listing the last few companies and going through the miscellanea section. There was nothing to add. When she came into the den dressed in my robe and combing out her wet hair, I'd finished and had packed the papers into my briefcase.

She smiled. "There wasn't enough time to go home. Anything else in that stuff?"

"Nope. Sellars was too smart to leave anything really important out in the open. CONCIA is my guess. But, I need more time to read them all carefully. I see the pattern. Oil-related companies. Not a bad area for men from the oil-rich Mideast to control. Scary."

She stopped brushing her hair. "I want you to come to Jackson with me for a few days. I'm meeting with my father. It's him you'll want to talk to to get your full story." She was mocking my earlier words.

My lungs began pulling for air. "Your father? What has the senator got to do with this?"

"You'll have to come and find out. He's the one who has to fill in the blanks."

"You're working with your father, a United States senator, in covert operations?"

"Who else?" she replied.

"Yeah, who else?"

"Very nice," she said, standing close to one of my paintings. "Does this picture depict any particular event?"

"Yes. That's the signing of a treaty between a tribe of Shoshone and the soldiers who tracked them down. The chief is a man by the name of Sun Who Never Sets, my great-grandfather. He saved the lives of his people with that treaty, but he died a broken man on the Indian reservation at Fort Hall, Idaho. See the other paper in his hand? That depicts a map he made to get several small groups of his people through some pretty rough country south of Jackson, hiding them from the soldiers until he thought it was safe to make a deal."

I took her hand and walked across the room, stopping in

front of a sheet of old paper hermetically sealed in a wooden frame.

"Are you going to tell me about your father?" I asked.

"No, you can talk to him."

I did need the information. Probably best to get it from higher up the totem pole, I thought.

"This is the map. My grandfather had it framed in this air-tight case a long time ago. He gave it to me before he died."

She looked around the room at the other pictures. The sweet smell of perfumed soap softly scented the room.

"These pictures depict your heritage, don't they? They're all pictures of relatives in different historical settings."

I nodded, wanting to put my arms around her.

"You must be proud of them."

"I am, but I haven't shown it very openly, I'm afraid. I was raised in the white man's world, and my Indian blood has been relegated to pictures on my wall. I don't know if they would think much of me. When you compare my deeds to theirs I don't hold up very good.

"That one is of a dream I've had many times," I said, pointing at a gold-framed twenty-four by thirty-six.

"A rather gruesome dream," she said, looking at it carefully.

"You see those Indians jumping him? They kill him in the dream, after he gets four of them. The boy, a Shoshone of about fourteen years old, killed the Blackfoot Indian he's standing over, just after the Blackfoot put a knife between the dying mountain man's ribs. The last one, there lying beside the body of the mountain man, was killed by the woman, the wife of the mountain man. She used a rifle she took from one of the first Blackfoot killed. Every little detail is etched in my brain."

"What does it mean?"

"I wish I knew." The tan collar was pulled tightly around her neck and ears, her body snuggled inside the terry cloth robe. We were only inches apart, she in front of me looking closely at the picture. I backed away, looking at my watch, diverting my mind.

"You through in the bedroom? I have to throw a few things into a suitcase . . ."

She took a step in my direction, a sly grin on her face. "All through." Her hands moved down the collars to the sash as she started to take off the robe. I gasped, turning away.

She laughed. "Here. Put this away. I was cold after washing my hair."

Danny had whistled when he was introduced to Mike, but seemed to be enjoying Jan's attention too much to talk. It couldn't last. Before long they would be at each other's throats. Two different backgrounds, two different worlds. The beautiful model, who loved the jet set—well maybe that had changed. But they were still two different, very different, people.

As I pulled out of the garage my mind wandered back to all that Mike had said. One piece wasn't fitting well with me—Ben Stevenson.

"You're deep in thought, Jerry," Mike said as we drove down Rancho toward West Sahara. "Care to share?"

"Just thinking about Ben. His involvement is a little shocking, I guess. He's a forthright family man, dedicated to Banner. Comfortably wealthy. It just doesn't strike me right." I slowed the car down to make the turn east. "I guess I find it hard to believe he would try to destroy my life. One or two others in that office, but not Ben." There had to be a reason.

"He was probably in too deep to have a choice. Can I use your car phone to call my office to see if there are any messages?"

"Be my guest. Still worried about Dooley?"

She nodded. "With good reason, I think."

I agreed.

She hit the buttons like a pro. Probably had one in her own car. When she finished we had turned down Paradise toward the Pincock Center. She half turned in her seat, placing her arm over the back.

"What are you thinking?" she asked.

I shrugged a little. "I'm having a difficult time putting you in the role you seem to be playing."

"Because I'm a woman?"

"No. I'm not a male chauvinist. At least, I don't think I am. It's just that it's all so covert. Something you'd read about in the news or a novel or something. I saw intelligence operations in Nam when I was there. I know how rough it can get, and I don't think terrorist-types play any nicer."

"They're worse. Concern is warranted. Duquesne has no morals whatsoever, and Winters and Owens are killers that are of the terrorist mold. We must be careful. But I don't think they know what we're doing. That gives us an advantage we need right now."

Hank was waiting in Sellars' office. He looked up from the desk, giving us both careful examination.

"Well, Jerry. I've never seen you with a patch before. Rather becoming."

"I only wear it for special occasions."

The office was a mess of strewn files and papers. "You should be a little more tidy in your work, Hank. A man of your stature. Tsk, tsk."

"Yes. Well, I'm just waiting for the custodial service, and now that you've arrived will you move ahead? The party was well attended; everyone had fun; but oh, the mess they made!"

I smiled. "What have you made of all this?" I looked around.

"No damage, but as you see, the file cabinets have been emptied on the floor, folders and their contents spread everywhere. It'll take a while to put everything back. The desk was ransacked, and the photo files in the adjacent office look like these."

"And the computer?" I asked.

"I can't say. Never use one, even though we have them on every desk. Too complicated for my old mind."

After I punched the keys, the screen flashed on. I typed the current time and date and watched for the main menu. When it came up I hit the number for Word Perfect and then the F5 directory key.

"Whoever was here knew exactly what they were doing," I said. "All Sellars' in-house files have been erased." Hank looked bewildered.

"After you left, Mike and I got into them. Apparently somebody came in after we did and erased them. Did you come up with anything new this morning?"

"Nothing yet, but I don't really know what to look for," he said.

"Don't let it worry you much. I have an idea that Dick was too careful a man to just leave important information lying around in hard-copy files. I'll bet my last nickel that everything we want to know is locked up in computer disks and memory. Have his secretary go through his floppy disk files and see what she can find for you, and see if she might know the passwords he used to get into other systems. I doubt it, but it's worth a try."

He jotted down several notes.

"Mike and I are flying to Jackson, Wyoming, for a few days. She wants to go over my case in detail and try to help.

"Here's a number where you can reach us anytime. Jan Delling, my sister-in-law, is staying at the house, along with Danny Trevino from New York. He is a paraplegic, and she's here trying to get her life straightened out. They might help one another, but then, they might kill one another, too. Would you have that cute little runner of yours—Maggie I think is her name—check on them, see if they need anything? While I'm gone I'll make a decision about what deal we'll make with Powers and let you know."

"Okay. Anything else I can do for you?" he said wryly.

"Yes, just one." I smiled. "Lease me the Lear for a week."

11

We drove straight to the Hughes Air Terminal instead of International. Her fear didn't show until we pulled into Hank's hangar and parked the car. She stared at the Lear, pale as a ghost. She hated flying, she said, but small planes—they scared her to death. I could see from the goose bumps and ashen skin she was telling the truth.

I tried to explain that I had been flying since I was a kid and had only crashed twice, both in Vietnam. She held tighter to the Eldorado's door strap. Telling her about the Lear's record, unblemished or unmarred by anything other than pilot error, was wrong again.

Finally my cajoling convinced her just enough to get out of the car and walk around the plane, touching it as she would a new pet Doberman. I took her inside, showing her the miracles of modern technology. She loosened up a bit when told the Lear had a better record than the big DC-10 she would have flown in to Salt Lake City.

Mel Skipson, Hank's personal mechanic, got our luggage out of the car and secured it in the luggage compartment while Mike and I buckled in and I checked everything out. After I had gone through the mental list twice and revved the engines to clean out the cobwebs, we taxied from the hangar and to the head of the runway to wait for our turn to take off.

She seemed to be doing a little better. We moved into place at the head of the runway, a big Federal Express jumbo taking off in the slot ahead of us. Clearing with the tower, I pushed the throttles forward and felt the thrust of the Lear's powerful motors as she sped down the runway.

Mike passed out.

When safely in our flight pattern, I reached over and adjusted her seat so she could rest comfortably, then went over the charts while following instructions from the tower to go north and then east around Nellis Air Force Base. Normal procedure. I obtained permission to climb into an assigned lane. I switched on the autopilot with a flip of the wrist just as Mike came around.

I had considered going back to the galley to get something cold for her but thought better of it, picturing her waking up in the clouds with no pilot. The laugh was hard to stifle.

"Oh!" she said. "How could I have let you talk me into this!" She lay looking up at the ceiling, her hand across her forehead.

"Ladies and gentleman, this is your pilot speaking. We are presently cruising at fifteen thousand feet. Our destination is scenic Jackson Hole, Wyoming, gateway to Teton and Yellowstone National Parks. Time of arrival, approximately eight o'clock this evening. The temperature outside is a balmy 105 degrees in Las Vegas and a cool but cloudless—I repeat, cloudless—80 degrees in Jackson. We expect no turbulence"—the plane suddenly jumped and Mike grabbed the armrests as if her life hung in the balance—"except for an occasional down draft created by masses of cold and hot air duking it out in the heavens."

"Just what I need," she said, "a pilot trying to be a comedian! I think I'm going to be sick."

I handed her a bag. She felt a little better afterwards. There was a mental note to be made. She hates flying, but she's pretty. Even with her head in a barf bag.

An hour and a half later we were touching down at Jackson Airport. Her color had returned, and she had actually talked to me without growling.

The plane dropped through a wisp of clouds onto the runway at Jackson, the Tetons looming sheer and massive to the northwest, light, fluffy clouds snagged to their granite tops. I had always been amazed at the impact those mountains had on me. Even though they were smaller than many other mountains in North America, there were no foothills to soften the look or get in the way of the sheer thrust of the solid granite from the valley's floor. As a kid I had visited the valley many times with my family, especially my grandfather. We walked many of the range's deep and shadowed canyons and blue-green forests, and we even did some swimming in the icy water of crystal-clear mountain lakes that reflected the tall peaks in their bluish black waters.

As the plane taxied to a parking area my eyes focused to the south, where the sharp-spined Hoback and Snake River ranges were shrouded in blue-gray haze.

Grandfather had talked about his people and how that part of the valley had been one of the best hunting grounds in the West and one of the last places the "white man" took from them. And how his people had struggled to survive before their leader, Sun Who Never Sets, my ancestor, led them to safety by a trail only he knew. It was cold in winter, with freezing temperatures as late as June and as early as August, and they were caught in early storms as they fled from a cavalry set upon destroying them.

We rented a Ford Bronco with four-wheel drive, threw our luggage in the back, and drove onto the main road going south toward Jackson, the Gros Ventre and Washakie ranges in the distance on our left, their gradually ascending slopes covered with a forest of lodgepole and quakie, a contrast to the starkness of the great Tetons opposite them.

We turned at a sign that said Kelly, and Gros Ventre Slide Area. "I remember coming this way when I was a kid to see the slide that happened long before I had even been a thought. It was 1925, wasn't it?"

"Yes," she said. "Heavy rains and a tremor from the Teton fault along the west side of the valley sent a mile-long section of the north face of Sheep Mountain into the valley and river below. Fifty million cubic yards of shale, sandstone, and limestone deposited, damming the river and creating Slide Lake."

The lake was dark blue in the late evening light, the scar left by the slide still ugly on the mountain above.

After traveling to the end of pavement, we continued for several miles, finally coming to her father's ranch, a modest but well-kept mass of white buildings, fences, and a large log ranch house with three vehicles parked in front. Two late-model four-wheel-drive, short-bed Chevys and an older-model Lincoln Continental in immaculate condition. Looked like a complete restoration.

There were half a hundred horses feeding on tall grass in the pasture surrounding the ranch and several well-bred quarter horses in a corral next to a large white clapboard barn. It was dusk, and several lights shone through windows in the big log house and further along in a smaller one, apparently the bunkhouse for ranch hands.

I had just turned into the lane when several people came out of the house, standing in the dim light of evening and the shadow of the large porch. Mike jumped from the Bronco as it came to a halt next to the Lincoln. She embraced her family while I removed the luggage from the back seat, feeling strangely like a college kid who had just come home for the first time with his best girl.

"Jeremiah Daniels, this is my father, James Freeman."

He reached out to shake. His grip was firm, his large hand enveloping mine. He had dark brown eyes, not unlike his daughter's, set in a face with a somewhat flat nose and square jaw. A striking figure of a man who exuded confidence and could easily intimidate with his six-foot-three frame and estimated 220 pounds, firmly rooted in a pair of brush-leather, beat-up cowboy boots.

"Jeremiah, welcome to our home."

"Thank you, Senator."

Mike went on. "This is my older brother and his wife, Robert and Charla."

Charla was a handsome woman, middle thirties, blond hair cut very short, tanned. Wearing Levi's and a western work shirt, she fit in with the scenery and comfortably beside her husband. He wore a well-maintained mustache cut at the corners of his mouth. He was two inches shorter than his father, but had very powerful shoulders under a flannel shirt.

"Dad, I don't think I know this gentleman," Mike said. He was standing near the door in a blue pin-striped suit and red silk business tie, a leather briefcase dangling from one arm. He stepped forward, reaching for Mike's hand.

"Ms. Freeman," he said overpolitely. "My name is Dutton. Willmore Dutton. I'm here from the president's office on business. Nice to meet you." His hand reached for mine. "And you are . . ."

I shook, already knowing I didn't like the man. "Daniels, Jeremiah Daniels."

He smiled, measuring me, then turned to the senator. "Senator. The president thought you should know." He looked at his watch. "One of your men can drive me to the airport?"

"Yes. Bob will you take care of it? Dutton, appreciate your delivery. Give my thanks to the president." The senator's son and Dutton started down the steps. I smiled at the thought of his stumbling over his ego, but, no luck.

"Well, Jerry, Mike has told me a little about you. We have you a room, and a late dinner is on the table. Won't you come in?"

The dinner was Charla's specialty—charbroiled marinated tenderloin strips, whipped potatoes drowned in gravy, beet greens, fresh peas, and a fruit salad. Fresh made raspberry pie finished it off and filled me to bursting. The talk was friendly as I got to know the family and talked of some of my past.

Senator Jackson asked Mike and me to join him in his den, where a large picture of a beautiful lady, who looked much like Mike, hung above and behind his solid-oak desk. Still his companion, even in death, she was a remarkable-looking lady. The room was large, well furnished in a manly sort of fashion, with several large windows looking out into the dark night. The light came from lamps strategically placed next to the desk and near each of the leather chairs and the sofa. This was his domain.

"Mike has filled you in, I assume?"

I looked at her quickly. She didn't look back.

"Uh, yessir. On a few things. But until a few hours ago I didn't know you were—"

"I'm not. At least, not officially. Mike called last night and filled me in on you, Dick Sellars, and Hank Butcher. I called people in Washington and got permission to bring you in on this. Dutton had to deliver some information on another matter but brought this as well." He shoved some papers toward me. "We need your help. You will find there a check for your services and a letter from the president asking for your cooperation. An item he and I agree on."

"Excuse me, Senator, but is this going to be a political game with me in the middle?"

He frowned but maintained control. "I can see your thinking. A Democrat who serves on two very influential committees going after a Republican president. But no, I'm not out to get him. Not this time. This is way too important to be fooling around, playing political games."

I remained silent, unconvinced. He leaned forward, putting his elbows on his desk and fiddling with a paper clip. "A few years ago my wife and I were traveling in Europe. While I was getting tickets for a return flight to Washington a bomb went off at the other end of the airport in Rome, killing and maiming a couple of dozen people. My wife was a nurse by profession and did what she could, which wasn't much under the circumstances. Several died in her arms, including one small child.

"We managed to keep our part out of the papers, for safety reasons, but on the way home we talked about what had happened, and the fact that the child could have been ours. I've been doing what I could against that menace ever since. I don't like terrorists more than I don't like Republicans, by a long shot, son, and I hope you won't forget that. Second, the risk to our economy and way of life is extreme. If we don't get some answers soon it won't matter who belongs to what party. We'll all be out of work."

"Yes, Senator, I won't forget. On either count."

"Now, any update, daughter?"

She filled him in with a report on the day's activity. I brought out the briefcase and showed him the papers and the disks. "I think, Senator, some of these files are CIA related. Would you like to fill me in on Mr. Richard Sellars?"

He leaned forward again. "Dick Sellars was a good man. His death may be our fault; we don't know yet. Let me tell you a story.

"Dick Sellars publicly left government service in 1987 when more than a million dollars turned up in a briefcase he was told to deliver directly to the president. The person giving him the instructions was a trusted agent within the government of one of our wishy-washy allies over in the Middle East. After he boarded the flight for home Sellars happened to discover the contents of the briefcase and a letter which indicated the money was to go to the president for services rendered in securing weapons for a country that to you shall remain nameless. This was their way of showing their appreciation.

"Needless to say, Sellars saw the implications and knew what it meant to both him and the president. It didn't take a brainchild to figure out that someone unfriendly to the president would be waiting when he arrived in Washington, on an anonymous tip of course, to look that briefcase over.

"He went to the rest room and ate the letter, then went back to his seat. He thought about flushing everything down the toilet but knew that whoever was waiting would force the issue and make the airlines conduct a meticulous search. He began looking around, thinking he might be able to switch the case for another one similar in size and color, but there was nothing even close. He was probably being watched anyway, and no matter what he did his guardian angel would probably undo it. There was nothing for him to do but play it by ear when he got off the plane in Washington, D.C."

"Who was waiting?" I asked.

"An influential senator from the East who received that anonymous call and thought he now had information that would win the next election for our party by putting the Republican president in an extremely bad light. When he opened the briefcase, with Sellars' permission, which shocked them all, he found the money, but not the letter. Of course Sellars' responses to questions were most unhelpful and only increased the senator's embarrassment in front of a few invited members of the press."

"What explanation did Sellars give?" Mike asked.

"It was a personal loan from a friend in the Middle East, a man, by the way, whom Sellars knew would cover for him if necessary. It got him out of the airport and to the White House, where he called the Middle East friend and solidified his story, told the president, and handed him the briefcase." He smiled. "Of course the president refused to take it; after all, it was a loan to Sellars, therefore his money. Sellars took it to his bank and deposited it. Most of it ended up being used to finance the building of a new science lab for his old alma mater."

"Education at the expense of the bad guys!" Mike said. "Can't beat that."

"Only one problem. In the process of all this his deep cover was blown, and he became an easy target. One picture reached the newspaper, and that was all it took."

"That's what you meant by publicly leaving the CIA," I said.

"Yes, and that is when Sellars took the job with Hank Butcher's firm."

"Then Dick Sellars isn't his real name."

"No. He went undercover again, for protection this time. We knew there was a price on his head for the damage he was responsible for to several Middle Eastern countries." He chuckled. "He had infiltrated some rather high places.

"Anyway, he kept his connections over there open. After he had gone to work for Butcher his main assignment was to track down who had set him and the president up with the letter and money, and to continue work on the very new Duquesne file, two of his pet projects.

"To my knowledge your friend, Hank Butcher, didn't know who Sellars really was. No one outside knew. His new identity was all taken care of in-house, and the cases he was working were kept in the tightest security classification."

"1987? The Contra mess?"

"Yes."

"Whew! The president taking a bribe. That could have been a political bombshell!"

"The Contra affair was a case of several overzealous high achievers who got in over their heads. The money in Sellars' briefcase was a carrot his Middle Eastern enemies thought would bring everything down around the president's ears. Sellars was a pawn, but, fortunately for the president, a very sharp one.

"As an important part of his cover Sellars took the job with Hank Butcher because he knew Butcher's firm was involved in international law and represented a number of clients in the Middle East and their business affairs in the United States. Some of these clients Sellars needed to contact. His job with Butcher gave him continued access to that area of the world under a different name, different circumstances, and, incidentally, an altered identity."

"You mean a face-lift?"

He smiled. "That description will do. He was able to travel to the Middle East often and kept his deep-cover contacts intact. We think that, a little at a time, he'd been putting together the information they fed him and the pieces of what Duquesne is up to."

"What do you mean, you think?" I asked.

"Sellars' contact was by a system called TITAN. He had direct contact with only one person in Washington, for reasons of safety for him and his family. What that individual has received has been insignificant, until last week, when Sellars broke silence and contacted him directly. Sellars' message indicated that he had been sending him much more important information than he had actually received. Information about what Duquesne was up to *and* about who had set him and the former president up."

"Someone was intercepting his messages?"

"We think so."

"Who?"

"Royalty," said Mike.

"The name in Sellars' file? But I thought you didn't know anything about—"

"It shocked me to see the name there. Only a limited few are supposed to know about him."

"In defense of my daughter, Jeremiah, she was under strict instructions about that name."

"I understand that, but I want what you have on this guy. Now!"

"Calm down. She told you I could fill in the blanks, and I will. Just understand, she couldn't."

"Okay. Let's hear it, then."

He looked at Mike and nodded the go-ahead.

"We've sprung a very big leak in our little ship, and we don't even know where it is," Mike said.

"You mean a spy?"

"Maybe more than one," she said. "We don't know. But it's suspected at least one is very close to the president."

"Washington knew about Royalty for some time previous to Sellars' message. We set up several traps to catch the traitor, or traitors. We were unsuccessful. Shortly thereafter, critical information discussed only at the White House level found its way to the Mideast and seriously hurt our relationship with several countries there. The president was forced to put an intelligence blanket on all operations. Needless to say, it seriously hampers the White House's ability to make important decisions and carry on business."

"How did you get involved?"

"The president and I are good friends. We know we can trust each other. He needed someone outside his immediate people whom he could trust. He came to me. I asked for clearance for Mike because of the obvious reasons of trust, and she was already involved and doing quite well, I might add, in discovering the depth of what Duquesne was doing in the financial area. Several others have been added; now we've included you."

"What others are involved?"

"I'm not at liberty to say, but we are severely hampered. We don't know who to trust."

"The intelligence establishment has become untrustworthy?"

"Not all of them," he said, irritated. "Not by a long shot. But we have been very selective, and all of us have to be very careful about using standard channels, for now at least. Those pictures of accidents you were shown were some of our people lost over the past two and a half years. We think Royalty was at least partly responsible, and now that we have narrowed down where he might be we can't take those chances anymore.

"This operation is probably the tightest circle in history used for such a major problem," said Mike.

"I apologize for my flippancy, Senator. I see the problem.

"Correct me if I'm wrong, then, will you? All this means Sellars' CONCIA files may contain extremely sensitive materials, or nothing at all if Royalty got his hands on them, and Royalty probably has gotten his hands on them, correct?"

He took a deep breath. "Jeremiah, have you ever heard of TITAN?"

"No, sir, I haven't. What is it?"

"*TITAN* is the code word for the government's mainframe computer and intelligence-gathering system. Every major organization plugs into it, feeds data, uses data, and trades data. Not the least of which are senators who have proper clearance. TITAN code words are changed daily, and TITAN computers are set up on voice-identification systems, with several dozen safeguards. When I am in Washington I can access TITAN."

"So you can get the information in Sellars' files by accessing TITAN?"

"Not quite *that* simple. There are other passwords necessary to operate in other areas. For example, the NSA can't get into CIA files without proper passwords, and the CIA can't get into FBI files. And senators are limited to their own respective areas. Each effectively locks out the other."

"Then how—"

"One man has total access to TITAN."

"You mean the president?"

"No. This man's code name is WASHINGTON, and he is responsible for TITAN. Very few know who he is, where he is, or how to contact him. He runs the government's computer, keeps it operative, changes the passwords, and monitors everything coming and going for potential computer viruses, hackers and the like."

"A systems manager!" I saw the question on Mike's face. "A systems manager is the man responsible for any mainframe. He has complete responsibility and access.

"This guy has to be the most trustworthy man in America!"

"There're checks and balances on him, but I don't even know what they are. The point is he can get us what we want."

"When?"

"He's working on it now, but it won't be easy. Millions of files all have to be looked at, one at a time."

"But Sellars would only be in the CIA section of TITAN, wouldn't he?" I asked.

"Ordinarily, yes, but Sellars was cleared for other areas because of his assignment. He could have put the file anywhere."

"Does Royalty have that same access?" I asked, incredulous.

"We don't think so, but apparently he was intercepting Sellars' messages in the computer's bulletin board. If Royalty had found a way into Sellars' files, and Sellars knew it, it's doubtful he would be foolish enough to put the file in the same place. We think they're as inaccessible to Royalty as they are to us."

"Your systems manager, WASHINGTON, is watching, anyway, isn't he?"

"Yes. If anyone crosses unauthorized lines or uses bad passwords in an attempt to look around he'll be on them like bears on honey."

He leaned forward again. "Jeremiah, there's something else you should know. Mike." He motioned for her to begin.

"As near as we can tell, Duquesne is trying to create, through a dozen different methods, a financial octopus whose tentacles reach deep into America. Without a lot of detail, they're trying to control the oil-related segments of American industry. If they're successful, life as we know it could change, drastically."

She pulled a paper from her valise. "We have identified these companies as Duquesne Group Investments. We believe these are completely controlled by Duquesne through management, majority stockholdings, or outright ownership. You will see Powers on there, and you will see Duquesne Industries itself, along with a couple dozen other companies. All of these are on the list you got from Sellars' computer. You'll notice there're only thirty. As near as we can tell he'd pretty much uncovered the same ones we had.

I read the list and almost went into shock. "They *control* these companies?"

"Yes. Through means it would take years to follow up and

dig out. How many were on the stock symbol sheet those two guys took from your briefcase?"

"At least a hundred."

"Then we've barely scratched the surface."

The senator continued. "Stocks, bonds, investments. Shell games, hidden assets. Reliable sources abroad indicate that somewhere in the vicinity of thirty billion dollars has been invested by Duquesne's special little group over the last two years. Mike's list represents ten billion. The top third of the iceberg."

I sat back in my chair. "I see. Mike, why didn't you tell me this back in Vegas?"

"Too many ears," she said. "Someone killed Sellars, or had him killed, who knew him and who knew what he was doing. We couldn't take any more chances."

The senator leaned back. "Overwhelmed?"

I looked up. Then smiled. "Perceptive. Or do you read minds?"

He smiled back. "No, but that's how I'd feel if I were in your shoes.

"We need you for two reasons, Jeremiah. First, your expertise and connection with Banner, which honestly, at the moment, is our only real solid lead which might get us into what is really going on. And, second, you're not part of the establishment in Washington. Frankly, you can be trusted."

"How do you know that?"

He handed me a computer printout lying on his desk. "Jeremiah Daniels. Helicopter pilot in Vietnam. Recipient of the Purple Heart, the Medal of Honor, and a couple dozen other citations for bravery and going beyond the call of duty to save the lives of numerous fellow soldiers. As a pilot of a Sikorsky chopper, you had a life expectancy that was less than six months in war conditions. You lasted nearly two years, and were dedicated to saving people, not injuring them.

"And, your life and career since that time. You were considered one of the few really honest men in the brokerage business, trusted by clients around the world in all walks of life. Very successful, but not at the expense or the welfare of others. A former bishop in your church, at a very young age, I might add. People have a high opinion of you; you exhibit great judgment under pressure, and you're resourceful under conditions in which most men give up. And, you married well. Liz Dellingham wouldn't take just anyone."

"You've done your homework," I said, trying to control my swelling head. "You know my wife?"

"Almost as well as I know you," he smiled.

"I don't know whether to be embarrassed or upset. No, I'm upset! I keep running into a government that doesn't have a whole lot of regard for my privacy, and the privacy of others, and I don't care for it much at all."

"Calm down, Jerry. Let me ask you a question. Before you were hired at Banner did they ask you personal information? Don't you have to sign something that said you hadn't committed any crimes, never been involved in any illegal activities? Isn't there a complete background check run on you before they give you a license?"

"Of course, but that's different."

"How? They checked you out just like we have, because they have to know they can trust you with their money and the money of people who put their trust in the firm. They don't hire crooks, or derelicts, or people who don't have incentive and drive! Why should the government be any different? We are placing our country in your hands, and we'd better know who you are and whether you have what it takes. The only difference is we got it before you gave your permission, this time. And, most corporations do the same thing, by the way. We compiled it on short notice, after Mike's recommendation last night. Now get off your high horse and be proud of the fact that you've led the kind of life that you can be called on.

"The financial welfare of this country hinges on what is happening here. We have a few trusted individuals informed and working outside of the three of us, looking for answers, trying to make the pieces of the puzzle fit, but we have to be very selective. We need your help, not your self-righteous indignation!"

The blood had turned his face beet red, but I wasn't about to let it go at that. "You're right. I'm indignant with every right to be so. This country's covert operations are out of control, in my opinion, and need to have their horns cut back . . . But you've made your point. I'll help. Because you, Senator, are one of the few people in Washington I consider trustworthy, in spite of having to work covertly. Both of you've been straight with me." I paused, sitting back in the chair. "But mostly, because I like your daughter, and I figure this is how to get in with the old man."

He smiled, I returned it, and Mike went into shock.

12

When my mind snapped awake I was thrashing at the blankets, sweat clammy against my skin. The mountain man had returned, the dream so real that the burning powder from rifles hung in my nostrils and mingled with the sweat of fear.

Forcing my feet to the floor, I put on a robe and went down the hall to the bathroom, flipped on the light, and looked in the mirror. The swelling in the eye socket had gone down. It would probably be okay to wear the glass eye tomorrow. The wrist was still sore but not a big bother.

Drinking directly from the tap, I thought the water was as good as any ever tasted, even though the cold made my teeth hurt. I splashed it on my face and wet a cloth and pressed it against the empty socket, then I hit the light switch and walked as quietly as possible back down the hallway.

Mike stepped out of her bedroom as I got to my door.

"Are you okay?" she asked, genuinely concerned. "I heard you . . . a minute ago."

"Just the dream."

She looked at the cloth. "How's your eye?"

"Black-and-blue, but the swelling is down," I said. "Probably won't need the patch tomorrow. Are you tired?"

"Wide awake. Want a snack? Mrs. O. makes a mean oatmeal and honey cookie." I went in my room just long enough to put the patch in place, then she took my arm and went toward the stairs.

"Who's Mrs. O.?" I asked.

"Our housekeeper, Mrs. Olafson."

Mike was as comfortable in the kitchen as behind the desk of a high-powered SEC attorney. Even in the middle of the night, no makeup and hair undone, she was beautiful. Liz would like her, wouldn't she?

She placed some cookies and milk on the table and poured some milk for both of us.

"Good," I said, savoring the sweet taste. "Tell me about Charla and your brother; they're an interesting match."

"I will if you'll tell me about your dream."

"Deal." It was a fair trade. I needed to talk about it, if for no other reason than to assure myself I wasn't crazy.

"Charla was raised in Jackson Valley like the rest of us. The difference was that she was raised on skis. By the time she was sixteen everybody thought she was headed for the Olympics. She was on the junior national team and top point getter. If you know anything about skiing you know what that meant.

"One day she was doing a downhill at Aspen, Colorado, and fell. The nets weren't used then, like they are today, and what snow fence there was did little to stop her momentum. She broke her back and was paralyzed from the neck down."

"But—"

"Yes, I know. She's as healthy as you and I. Rides horses, ropes, works hard right alongside Bob. She even skis for fun. Some call it medical genius . . . others a miracle." She paused, her brow wrinkling a bit. "They performed several surgeries in New York. She went through three years of intensive rehabilitation, and gradually gained back the use of her body above the waist, but that was it. They couldn't explain why her legs didn't come back; they just didn't, so she came home.

"She and Bob had known each other since childhood. They did everything together. When she got back from New York Bob was waiting for her at the airport. He hadn't seen her in four years.

"He boarded the plane, by permission, knelt by her seat, and asked her to marry him. She and thirty or forty other people were stunned, but she said yes, to a backdrop of rather embarrassing applause."

She filled her glass with a second helping of milk, enjoying the memory.

"Two years later she and Bob were driving to town in a storm. You know that kind of steep place just after you come past Slide Lake? They were going down that and slid into a snowbank in the old pickup Bob used to own. A '50 Chevy, all spruced up, restored, but only two-wheel drive.

"Bob was able to rock it back and forth until it moved away from the bank a little, but no further. He got out to look over the situation, not realizing he'd left it in neutral. He put his body between it and the icy snowbank and pushed a little, causing it to roll and pin him, almost crushing him against the bank. He passed out.

"Charla screamed and tried to reach the clutch with her hand and shift into reverse. She couldn't. A half an hour passed, and she knew she had to do something fast or he would freeze to death. He had moved, even tried to speak to her, but she couldn't hear him over the wind. Desperately she tried again, crying out for help. She said she felt something in her legs and forced herself to lift first one then the other over the hump, then slid into the driver's seat. She was able to push the clutch in, put it in reverse, and pull away just far enough that Bob forced his way free and struggled into the passenger seat with broken ribs and a punctured lung. She worked with the gears, rocking back and forth, back and forth, until she finally broke free. Then she drove him to the hospital. She has been well ever since. Slow at first but, as you can see, no side effects.

"Bob adores her and she him. And the twins came to add to their joy. She had been told she could never give birth."

"Tough lady."

Mike finished her milk and took the dishes to the sink. "Jerry, do you believe in miracles? I mean, like that. Was it a miracle?"

She had her back to me, washing the glasses. "Yes. But I don't think every time something is unexplainable it is, quote, unquote, a miracle."

"You mean it isn't always an act of God?" she asked.

"Yes. Because I don't think God interferes in men's lives as often as some like to think."

"Why not?" she asked sincerely.

"Life is a time of growth *because* of hardship, not by escaping it. If God used miracles to come to our aid every time we ran into trouble, it would stunt our growth and, more important, take away our free agency."

"I don't understand that. How could healing someone do either of those things?" she asked with an edge on her voice.

"It seems to me that if there really was a God, and if he really loved us, he would be there when we need him most."

"He's always there, Mike, just not always in the way we would like him to be. His perspective and our free agency prevents it."

She waited. I was trying to find just the right words to explain a difficult belief. Liz had been able to put it in words. Simple, straightforward, understandable. Until now I hadn't realized what a talent that had taken.

"Mike, I believe in a longer period of existence than most, a life before this one, a life after. In the one before, I made decisions that impacted this one. In the one coming up, my decisions here will have an effect. God sees me in all of them and bases his decisions to interfere in my life on his view of that wider perspective. So when I scream for help because of pain while I'm here, his answer—and he always answers—is based on what he sees. Lots of people have very short mortal lives, or very miserable ones devoid of anything but pain, but that's far from all there is for them. When they die their mortal experience is valuable to what is yet to come. They learn, grow, experience things in a different sphere, in ways I never will *because* of what pain they suffered. Good things, blessings, if you want to give them a name.

"God could prevent death, pain, sorrow, suffering. He could interfere in everything we do. But he won't because in our former life we committed ourselves to accept those things as a part of the larger picture, the future opportunities. We understood it wouldn't be easy, but we accepted it as a necessary part of the experience by which we can return to live with him and . . . even to be like him."

There it was, the doctrine that set us apart from other beliefs. The doctrine that made all the difference, really. If you didn't believe you could become like God, then you looked at him as a kindly father who should always come to your rescue instead of a god who is schooling you for the opportunity to be all that you can be, even as he is.

"I believe in a different outcome for us. The very best outcome. And I believe in a God who guides and directs, but who schools—and who waits so that I can have that outcome. I can't be like him without pain and growth and lots of experience that I've been getting first in the life before, then now, then in the life after this."

I was beginning to like that wrinkled brow that always came when she was thinking deeply.

"Liz and I wanted a miracle, very badly. We were both active members of our church. Both had seen miracles, the real kind, from God, and we knew he could grant us one. We prayed, we begged for one. It seemed she didn't deteriorate as fast, but she didn't get better, either, and the pain was unbearable. The drug dosages got higher and higher, and I watched her become a zombie, wasting away."

I took a deep breath. "One night, after finally getting her back to sleep with three times the normal dosage of morphine, I went into the den and yelled and screamed and cursed. Then I pleaded and cried and pleaded some more. Then I demanded, made deals, promises of a perfect life, anything he wanted."

I paused again, gritting my teeth against the pain of those endless hours of confusion and misunderstanding. "After four hours I was exhausted and sat down in the overstuffed chair, still frantic. A thought came to my mind that I didn't like much, but it stayed, and I couldn't get rid of it, so I thought it through. Who was being hurt the most by my hanging on to Liz? Why was I being so selfish? The answer was that because I loved her and I would never stop loving her, I couldn't stand to see her suffer, couldn't stand the idea of being without her. Why couldn't God see that? Why did he refuse to help her, and me? Why?

"The answer came. It was not his will that she suffer. It was not his will that I suffer, or that anyone suffer. It was our choice to experience this life, because we knew that without that experience we could never learn compassion, and pure love, and sacrifice. And all the things it takes to become like him. If, now that the experience was hard, he interfered, what would that do to both of us?"

The tears welled in the corners of my eyes, the pain in my gut hard and relentless. "Then came the miracle. The peace of soul I needed to hold her, to touch her and comfort her, to be a strength instead of a burden. I think Liz knew all along she wasn't going to get over it, but she didn't want to leave me angry, and fighting. She was more worried about me than she was about herself."

The tears flowed. I tried to wipe them away with the edge of my finger. "She changed after that. Even the color returned to her cheeks. The pain went down and the morphine with it.

She died comfortably and contented, and I handled it better than I would've otherwise."

Mike was holding my hand, crying with me. We laughed a little and dried our eyes as quickly as we could, a little embarrassed.

"Sorry," I said. "A tender spot in an otherwise ruthless heart. But I learned firsthand that God is always there, always trying to help in the way he *can,* without hurting us in the long run. When we're healed, or when he interferes in some other way in either our own lives or in history in general, it is always for the greater purpose of bringing to pass the immortality and eternal life of mankind. He saved the children of Israel from the Egyptian pharaoh for that purpose. He had Lazarus brought back from the dead for that purpose. He helped the Allies fight World War II for that purpose. And, he helped me deal with Liz's moving on for that purpose. They are all miracles.

"It takes nothing but a loud voice to demand that God give us what we want. It takes real faith to accept what comes to us as a part of a life we agreed to in the first place. And my religion teaches me that the development of faith is one of the major reasons why I've come here to this world. It isn't easy, and I struggle along with a lot of others with the pain and the sorrow, but I'm learning."

I took a breath. "Mike, I consider the atonement of Jesus the greatest miracle ever to occur. The miracle was in that suffering, being able to have angels visit him and strengthen him, because he was willing to do what was needed, not what he wanted. Liz's dying was like that. She received peace because she was willing to suffer, without complaint, that which would help her fulfill her mission. She suffered, in a minor way, as he suffered, to become like him."

She smiled, thinking, then got up and went to the sink, looking out of the window. It struck me odd that I could feel something of her indecision and pain, sensing a need to change the subject.

"Want to hear about my dream?" I asked.

She turned and faced me again, the shadow disappearing from her face. "Please."

My watch dial indicated 2:00 A.M., but this part I needed to talk about.

"For several months now, I've had a dream about a mountain man, a long-dead forefather of mine.

"It really isn't a dream. I mean, it's not all jumbled around with junk thrown in that nobody will ever understand. It's almost a clear reenactment of an event I'm pretty sure took place a long time ago."

"But why is it so deeply planted in your mind that you would dream about it constantly?" she asked.

I shrugged. "Maybe it has something to do with the research and reading I do for my paintings, or maybe it's too much pasta before bed. I don't know, but it's driving me crazy!"

She looked at me, genuinely concerned, then reached out and put her hand on mine again. "I read once that the subconscious triggers information into the brain when it's needed. Information learned a long time ago, even when a child, that is critical to something happening in your life at the moment. Do you think you might be remembering something you were told, possibly by your grandfather, a long time ago?"

"I don't think I've ever been told about what actually happens in the dream. But, maybe, a long time ago."

"Who do you know in the dream?" she asked curiously.

"The mountain man, I think, is my great-great-grandfather, Finan Daniels. He died in this valley, but until the dream I didn't know how."

"You mean you think what you saw in the dream really happened?"

"Yes. I don't know it up here, in my head; I know it down here, in my gut! That's why I painted it."

She sat back. "You're an intriguing man, Jeremiah. He must have loved them deeply. Most of the stories you hear about mountain men say they dumped their Indian wives when they got tired of them or they proved to be a burden. Finan sounds like a rare specimen of that period."

"According to Grandfather, he was."

"But I thought you said your grandfather never said much about him."

"Just about the facts of his death. Finan Daniels is a legend in our family. Quiet, but forceful, he never killed unless he needed food or was in the act of protecting others. He said God 'ordained it thusly.' I agree with him. There are things to fight for and things to give up. You fight for family, country, and freedom. Grandfather used to tell us that Finan would say, ' 'Taint but three things to bleed for, love of God, love of freedom in a good land, and love of them that loves ya!' "

I looked at my watch again. "What time does this ranch roust out the hands, ma'am? It be three in the mornin'," I said in mock-western form.

She laughed. "In two hours, cowboy." She stood and pulled me to my feet. "Come on. Time to get some sleep."

She hung onto my hand as she shut off the light, and we walked through the dining area and hallway. When we reached her bedroom door I squeezed then shook her hand, bowing to kiss it. "Ms. Freeman, your knack for listening bodes well for a long and enduring career in law. Thanks."

She put her arms around my neck and pulled me close. I found myself resisting, my body stiffening even though my brain wanted the feel and touch of her lips.

She felt the tenseness, hesitated, then touched my lips lightly with her own. Then again, breaking down the barriers.

I pulled her close, feeling her softness through the terry cloth robe. My tenseness was replaced with a gentle desire, my body relaxing, my arms enveloping her.

"Umm . . . Mr. Daniels. I'm glad I pressed the point." She kissed me gently again, then slipped through the door and closed it softly behind her.

I took the few steps to my own door, my mind in a euphoric haze. As I slipped between the sheets I found it impossible to take my mind off what had just happened. Was I ready for what I was feeling? She's young and beautiful, intelligent, full of life, and very desirable. Only a man out of his mind wouldn't be attracted to her, but it couldn't be permanent. Too many differences, too many . . . We came from two different worlds, didn't we? Besides, there was . . .

It was too soon. That's all.

I rolled over, pulling the pillow around my head, trying to shut out the feelings as one shuts out the noise of traffic in a New York City hotel. It was just too soon.

Wasn't it?

13

I awoke to the sound of voices in the yard. Light was just beginning to touch the top of the mountains on the west side of the valley no more than a mile from my window, mountains covered with tall pine and capped with the blue-white of yet unmelted snow. It seemed like a magnificent day, bright and beautiful. The smell of fresh morning dew on grass mingled with frying bacon and pancakes.

From the window I could see the barn where men saddled horses for the morning's work, ribbing and joking with one another but doing their work with no wasted movement, the slap of saddles against blankets and the clink of spurs sharp and clear in the cool morning air.

Bob and Charla came from the back of the house and mounted two almost identical working quarter horses. With a signal to get going, everyone eased into saddles, reined their horses, and rode through a back gate and off into a distant pasture, finally disappearing from view in an even more distant canyon. The younger hands were left to feed the stock and clean up around the ranch. I counted three. With the seven that rode away with Bob and Charla, that made ten hands. Not a small ranch. I wondered how many head of cattle they ran and what chore waited for them in the hills beyond my view.

I was in the process of finishing dressing in designer Levi's, Nikes, and a Polo shirt when a knock came at my door. "Mr. Daniels, breakfast is ready. Will you be coming down?" It was the housekeeper's voice, heavy with a Nordic accent.

"Yes. Almost dressed, Mrs. O. Be there in five minutes." I wouldn't miss it. My taste buds were already drooling, even with only the smells to work on.

The glass eye felt tight, the still-swollen skin pushing against it, but it fit, and the patch was something I only used if forced to. Vanity.

There was no one in the dining room and no settings on the large dining table, but voices trickled through the door to the kitchen.

Mrs. Olafson was at the stove turning pancakes, while Mike and her father were busy feeding two small children at the table. As the door swung closed behind me all motion seemed to stand still, eyes glued on my person.

Finally the senator spoke. "Mike. When you two take me to the airport, stop in town, will you? This man needs to be properly outfitted. That shirt, and those shoes . . . Jerry," he said, feigning disgust, "you look like a darn tourist."

Mike pointed at an empty chair while she shoveled a spoonful of mush at a child's closed lips. "Never mind Dad, Jerry. He thinks anyone not in cowboy boots and faded Levi's ought to be thrown in the county jail." She cajoled the baby, pushed with the spoon, cajoled some more. Finally he opened his mouth, took the mush, and summarily spat it at her.

"Good shot!" I said. He smiled; she glared.

"I suppose you can do better?"

"Maybe. Spoons make good airplanes if you just add the right sound effects." I showed her. His mouth fell open and in went the mush. He stared at me, but his little mouth worked, and then he swallowed it. The grin I felt cross my lips was satisfying, so, another spoonful found its motorized way in the direction of the other boy who was giving his grandpa similar fits. It lasted all of five bites, but it was worth it.

Mrs. Olafson placed a big plate with ham, eggs, and pancakes with gobs of butter in front of me. I devoured it all, while sneaking a bite or two to the kids. We were instant friends.

After clearing the dishes Mike and I went to the den to make some phone calls. Hank wouldn't be happy for a call at 6:00 A.M. Las Vegas time. But . . . If we folks in Wyoming could get up with the sun, so could greenhorn lawyers in the big city.

" 'Lo?"

I cleared my throat. "Morning, Hank! You up for all day?"

"Jerry! What are you doing calling me at . . . at six in the morning? I'll have your hide hanging on my wall when you get back here!"

"So nice of you, Hank. I'm honored."

He mumbled. "This had better be good."

"I talked to Senator Freeman." I told him about Sellars' still working for the CIA and possibly keeping files, including mine, in the government's mainframe. The rest he wasn't to know. "He'll be on his way to Washington shortly and may be able to get us a copy of my file."

"The senator is a powerful man. If anyone can help you he can, but getting into government files . . . ? Has he told you how he plans to go about this little coup?"

"Yes. But if I told you I'd have to kill you."

"Jerry, you're starting to sound like a bad movie!"

"Yeah, too many super-tech novels. Anything happening on your end?"

"Nothing. Sellars' secretary has no idea about his passwords. And none of us knew about his continued dealings with the CIA. Is the senator sure about that?"

"Yes," I said. "How about Mrs. Sellars?"

"Nothing. Jerry, I have to leave town for a few days. A client in LA goes to court, and, as his attorney, he thought it might be nice if I came along."

"Will I be able to reach you?"

"Just leave messages with my secretary. I'll get back to you.

"What are your plans for the next few days?" he asked.

"We wait for the senator and we visit a place called the playpen and talk to a guy by the name of Robert Doolittle. Probably this afternoon."

"What is this . . . this playpen? And who is Robert Doolittle?"

I laughed. "Mike says it's a canyon where she and Doolittle used to play as kids. Like a box canyon, I guess, just a few miles into the mountains west of here near a place called Crystal Lake. Doolittle is an adopted brother."

"When will you be back?"

"I don't know. Do you need the plane?"

"No, my client is sending a plane and two aides to pick me up. By the way, I checked on your two houseguests. If you ask me, they're getting along a little too well."

"How's that?" I asked.

"Sitting by the pool, reading to one another from some novel. Sipping Cokes and being polite. Married stuff."

I laughed. "Odd, all right. Keep in touch, Hank." We hung up.

I called Kirk and checked on things. I didn't like the feel of world events. The market was getting volatile, and if things happened based on the senator's scenario they could go completely sour. I put in several sell orders.

"You know something I don't?" Kirk asked.

"I don't like the feel of what's going on in the world, that's all. But the oil futures are a good move. Hang onto them."

TriStar was up .35 cents since yesterday morning. Some big buyers getting in at the low, he thought. It smelled as rotten as a pair of two-year-old tennis shoes. TriStar seemed to be working its unwelcome way further into my life on several fronts, and it felt uncomfortable.

I gave him the number where he could reach me in Jackson but told him to keep it to himself.

"Just a bit mysterious, aren't you?"

"A bit. I'm on vacation, and I don't want vultures roosting in any nearby trees, that's all."

"I've heard of Senator Freeman's place up there. Runs a bunch of cattle, two thousand head, I think. Just northeast of Jackson, isn't it?"

"Yeah. You planning a visit?" I asked jokingly.

"Sorry. Not my life-style. I'll be in touch."

"Okay, but remember, TriStar gets dumped out of Jan's account at any sign of problems. Got it?"

He sighed. "Okay, okay. But nothing can go wrong. Word on the Street has it that they are adding a couple of subsidiary companies to it, to enhance its value."

"You've piqued my curiosity. Go ahead, what companies?"

"Next you'll want some for your own account. Maritime Properties and Haschal-Bowen Drilling."

"They're involved in a lot of Midwestern drilling and oil and gas pipelines, aren't they?"

"Two of the biggest. HB has just bought property that looks to produce big-time, but gas and oil prices will have to go up significantly before they can become profitable. Maritime is the holding company for gas and oil pipelines that distribute crude from wells to refineries and then to holding areas. They're big."

"How good is the rumor?" I asked.

"Danny's secretary verified it this morning when I checked on TriStar."

I thought about that. It fit with what else they were doing. If the news from the Middle East was right and Iraq was planning to attack Kuwait, there would be a substantial price rise in any oil-related stocks. If they had an idea of capturing the Middle East it was even more a possibility. A corner in oil there and here in the United States. Neat.

"Okay. Hang tight, but at the first sign . . ."

When I got off the phone Mike and I compared notes. She called another number and verified heavy action against the stock of Maritime, and a large buy-out offer for HB, which was privately owned. Speculation was five hundred million, and the present owners could still keep thirty-five percent of the stock. The families were probably going to take it.

"Another thing, Jerry. My people say that they think Fillmore Duquesne is meeting with his group in Los Angeles."

"Doesn't meeting like that, especially here in the United States, strike you as a little odd and a whole lot dangerous?" I asked.

"Very. It must be important."

"Yeah, critical, I would think. That worries me. Any way to bug the place?" She knew I was joking.

Her look of shock was fake. "Jeremiah Daniels. Your government does not, as you say, 'bug' people!

"Actually," she went on, "I was told it was considered, but Duquesne's henchmen do a mechanical sweep for bugs on an erratic schedule; they don't allow outsiders in for any reason without a guard holding their hand. They meet in a place where you can't get close enough to use scanners or other electronic surveillance equipment. Impossible."

"Mike, how did you know all that stuff?"

"Trade secret."

"How!"

She took my half-hearted anger in stride, and with patience in her voice responded. "Dad mentioned that others are involved. Other groups, Jerry. I appreciate your naivete, but covert operations—wiretapping and invading the privacy of suspected crooks—is a real part of this world.

"Each other group that's involved reports to the president just as we do. The nice thing is, at least for the present, he has them sharing what they learn."

"Good for them." I stood and walked to the window. "Do you know how this sounds?" I turned and faced her. "I don't believe this covert garbage should go on, even if it does. Listening at people's windows, sneaking into their houses and bugging them, looking through their records via computer. It's all so . . . so—"

"Illegal?"

"Yeah, and frightening. Governments like ours speak about freedom while picking locks and invading privacy. Somehow that does not compute."

"I agree. I find myself finishing a phone call and waiting for the other party to hang up, then listening a little longer to see if there is a third party on the line, a bug that goes click. I hate it."

"Then why do we do it?"

"Well, in the first place we don't break the law. We would have the legal papers necessary to bug the place if we thought we could do it, but, in answer to your question," she paused, "we are in a time when our democratic system, our open borders, and our tolerance are being used by our enemies against us."

"So we get down in the gutter with them?"

"That's one way of putting it," she said, exasperated. "Jerry, society as a whole has changed from one in which most people have morals and concern for human life. Under that system if you didn't hurt someone they wouldn't hurt you. That doesn't hold true anymore. Now groups are organized to hurt, destroy, and enslave by the use of force, justifying their killing in the name of a cause. You can't stand face-to-face with them and talk sense and reason. You give them what they want or they kill you. Our nation, in order to follow its constitutional mandate to protect its citizens, must use every means at its disposal to stop these people before they kill. We can't do that using methods that might work with someone who has morals. These people use your very goodness against you, get the advantage, and before you know it, destroy you, others, and your freedoms."

I shook my head. "It's just so unreal."

"Actually it's what is real, and we've got to accept that and deal with it, or the bad guys win.

"Why did you decide to help us, Jerry?"

"I suppose because I was spitting mad. They tried to wreck my life. They, whoever they are, took away my job, destroyed what reputation I had, and had me walking a thin line between 'should I live or should I die.' "

"They invaded your privacy and your right to live without fear of them sneaking into your bedroom at night and taking your property and your life. What motivates you right now is what motivates a man in the big cities of this country to buy a gun. Fear and a strong desire to cling to his freedom.

"Even in your dream your mountain man grandfather killed, and then was killed, trying to get back that which others took from him. Those Indians invading his privacy stole that which was precious above everything else, and he had to act or lose it forever. I think that's what we've come to in this country. Gangs in the streets trying to take away life and the rights of others, dealers of drugs doing the same thing, power groups and political organizations doing it as well. Who's going to stop them if someone doesn't tell them to keep their crooked hands off?" Her voice raised an octave with the passion of her belief.

Gadianton's band, I thought. *They were the real enemy to the Nephite nation, the ones responsible for their eventual destruction. They caused the wars, the hatred, the greed, and the lust for power. They worked to overthrow governments and destroyed anyone or anything who opposed them.*

"Sometimes," she continued, calming her voice, "to catch them we have to do things we'd never have considered ten years ago. I hate admitting they've won by forcing us to come to their level to fight them, but I refuse to let them just run over us, enslave us, deny our children and grandchildren the chance for freedom that we enjoy."

"It's hard to admit you're right, Mike. It means the wicked of the world are getting a pretty solid foothold."

"But if we don't draw the line now," she said, "they will conquer our mountain. All we can do is use every tool at our disposal to dislodge them."

Fillmore Duquesne, a modern-day Gadianton. Why should I be surprised? How many times have we been told that Gadianton's band would return and create chaos and war? Trying to gain power so that evil could destroy good.

"You're right," I said, "but it makes the hair on my neck stand on end! How can we possibly stop all of it? Duquesne, war in the Middle East because of greedy, power-hungry leaders, the cartel in South America, the Mafia here and in about every other nation, the gangs. It seems hopeless."

She walked over and put her arms around me and lay her

head on my shoulder, calming my gut-felt anger. Something only Liz had ever been able to do.

"We fight. We let them know they can't have what they want. We make changes in the law to protect the innocent, and not the criminal. We get indignant and let them know they can't scare us into submission, and we won't lie down and play dead!"

"And we pray."

"Yes, that too. A righteous man availeth much."

"Where did you hear that?" I asked.

"Dooley. He is a Mormon like you. Jerry, good people make a difference, but they can make a bigger difference in this period of our history if they pray like everything depended on God, then work like everything depended on them." She smiled. "Another one of Dooley's masterful little sayings."

She pulled away, taking my hand. "Come on, city boy, let's take Dad to the airport and then get you to town and buy some decent clothes before one of the ranchers around here mistakes you for a tourist and shoots you." She looked at my clothes. "You're definitely in danger."

14

The big buckskin was built for the mountains. Strong and surefooted, but with a gentle disposition that responded well to the touch of spurs and rein. The day was a record-setter for Jackson, soaring to near ninety degrees in the lower elevations. But the shade of the tall pines in the high mountains made the ride better than comfortable, almost exhilarating. After the earlier stop at the clothing stores in Jackson I wore a cool cotton western work shirt with long sleeves for protection against early morning chill and afternoon sunburn, Levi's and a straw hat fashioned in what Mike called the bull rider style. I had left the new boots at the house, thinking blisters on my seat would be enough without blisters on my feet. I was already regretting the decision. The higher-topped boots would have prevented the sores I felt on the inside of my calf, and my foot would have stayed in the stirrup better because of the higher heel.

I was glad I had taken Mike's advice about gloves. The split cowhide kept blisters from developing on my soft city-slicker hands.

Michaelene sat on a sturdy Appaloosa she had owned since it was a colt, an animal with the powerful hindquarters of a sturdy working ranch horse. The faded Levi's and worn, roughed-up leather boots were a world away from the trim silk blouse and knit suit she wore when I first saw her, but they didn't detract from the natural beauty that emanated from her and pulled at my still-reluctant heartstrings.

We followed a game trail over a couple of ridges and through a valley thick with pine until we reached a silver-blue lake. It was surrounded by mountains laden with thick pine and was smooth as glass, inviting the thought of rock skipping. The water looked cold, but the moose on the far side stood knee-deep in the marsh of what must have been an inlet, his head raising just long enough to acknowledge our presence, then returning to the business of filling his large frame with fresh, green shoots of grass in the inlet's shallow water.

Pulling up, we cooled the horses before letting them drink—and then only sparingly. Mike tied the Appy to a small tree then went further up shore, dropped to her belly, and drank deeply from a small spring in the midst of sandy bottoms and deep grass a few paces from the lake. The human mind forgets the simple pleasures and peace that nature can offer, but the taste buds and other senses nudge us gently into pleasant memories. I drank deeply of the cold, pure wilderness nectar, and jammed my brain with moments so deep in the past that I had nearly lost them.

The calico hanky Mike had stuck in my pocket served as a napkin for my wet face as we sat on some large rocks and took in the beauty.

"The man in my dream would be real comfortable here."

"Describe him," she said curiously.

"What you saw in the picture is pretty accurate. About my height. Tanned, leathery skin. Reddish brown hair receding at the sides of the forehead but long on top and almost to his shoulders in back. Clean-shaven. Probably weighs . . . two hundred pounds. Muscular, thick through the chest and shoulders. Wears a leather outfit, darkened by wear and weather. Moccasins, but high, about halfway between ankle and knee, tied with leather laces. There's some fancy bead and quill work on the sleeves and a few long leather strands hanging down from the arms. He was carrying a Hawken rifle, at least fifty caliber."

"Buffalo gun."

I nodded. "He's determined, but his eyes are sad. Greenish eyes, alert, edged with crinkles from squinting, I suppose. At times in the dream I'm so close I can smell his breath and sweat and see the freckles on his nose."

"Your great-great-grandfather?"

"Yes, I think so, in all his glory, and darned annoying, I might add!"

"What do you know about him?"

"Not much beyond what I already told you."

"Nothing written?"

"You have to remember I come from Shoshone blood. Our history is handed down father to son, orally. The father makes the decision of what and when to tell and to teach the son."

"What about your father? Didn't he know? Couldn't you have found out from him?"

"My grandfather was not pleased with my father. Dad was against Indian ways and wouldn't listen. The pressure was from a dozen sources for him to be "white." Grandfather spent a great deal of time with his Shoshone people. When his son refused to go along they went their separate ways."

"What about your grandmother?"

"She died when Dad was just a kid. He was mostly raised in the white world with white people. It was almost like . . . he was ashamed of the Indian blood and heritage. Probably because he was raised with families who didn't understand the Shoshone people, and he married in the white world and has lived in it even more than I have.

"When I was born my grandfather showed up again and stuck pretty close. From the time I was small I remember him coming and taking us to the mountains, where he would teach us the wilderness stuff. Dad came along once in a while and seemed to make amends with Grandfather, but it was never a close relationship."

I shifted on the rock, releasing the pressure of Levi's on saddle sores. "Grandpa was my best friend when I was young. I spent more time at his cabin in the mountains than I did at home in my own bed. It was a choice time of my life.

"I remember when we left Teton Valley. I thought my heart would break as I watched him out the back window of the car, standing in the middle of the road. I promised him I'd come when I could, and I did. But when he died . . . well, I kind of lost interest. I quit going back at all until I got back from Nam." I paused.

"He taught me many things about being an Indian, being proud of it, letting my Indian blood guide me. He taught me about instincts, and measuring men. How to think and hunt, how to outsmart an enemy and how to kill if the enemy threatened me or someone I loved. More than once his training saved my life in Nam.

"He taught me a lot about believing in myself, too. I've always thought about what he'd want me to do, and how he'd feel about what I was doing in any situation. That saved me from the other side of Nam, the moral diseases and the drugs."

I paused, thinking. "In some ways I haven't been a good Indian—you know, stayed close to it, the way he wanted. Always something forcing me into that other world, but I've tried to remember who I am. I've always tried to honor him and the blood he gave me."

"What did you admire most about him?"

"This is going to sound crazy, but I was awed by his reverence for nature. He was one with it. I remember when I killed my first elk and he taught me to be thankful for the elk and its willingness to give its life so that we might eat of its flesh and live. That night as we cooked the meat over an open fire he thanked the Great Spirit and asked the spirit of the elk for forgiveness. Then he taught me many things about the animals, and that I should never take the life of one of them needlessly, or any life, for that matter. Only when I needed food or clothing, or if they threatened me or my family."

"He must have been proud of his heritage."

"It was almost sacred. Everything to do with the mountain man and his wife, Blue Dove, seemed too sacred to talk about, except under special conditions. But when it came to his father, Sun Who Never Sets, the stories never stopped."

"Do you think it was because he was not proud of the white blood of the mountain man?"

"Uh-uh. It was sacred, all right. Grandfather had some of the mountain man's things that he kept in a trunk. One of the rifles, a greenriver knife, a pistol, and a few personal items in a set of homemade saddlebags. I saw how he treated them, with awe and reverence. I have them now, back at the house in Vegas."

I took a deep breath. "After seeing what happened to the mountain man, the way he died trying to save his wife and son, I believe he deserves that respect. Without his sacrifice our family would've been over. Sun Who Never Sets, who saved his people from destruction at a later time, would've died that day."

She took my hand and drew close. "Something you ought to consider, then."

I looked at her quizzically. "What's that?"

"Your ancestors may be trying to get through to you for some reason."

I grimaced. "Thanks a bunch."

She stood and looked at the sun, now on the western side of noon. "Don't force it. Don't analyze it. If there's something there it will come.

"Come on. We'd better get moving. It's not much farther, just at the end of the lake."

We mounted up. Then she spoke again. "When it comes it will be important; even I can feel that." She spurred the Appy and headed up the trail, leaving me with a new respect for her perception, and a chill running down my spine.

At the end of the lake she left the well-traveled trail and went into tall, thick timber, wending her way along a path the untrained eye would never have seen. The path ended in a cut in the mountain leading into a canyon, hidden from the unfamiliar eye in heavy timber and underbrush. We rode between sheer walls a hundred feet high, our horses in water to their knees. A couple of hundred feet in, the crevice opened into a box canyon. The stream meandered through marshy grass, willows, and a few large pine left standing after someone, many years ago, had cut timber for a now-rotted cabin, whose remains lay in a tangle of trees near the far wall. Toward the north end a grove of quakies and pine protected a pond, beyond which was a waterfall, only partly visible.

We entered through sheer granite cliffs, their brows leaning toward us, ominous and threatening. The far side of the canyon, similar in spots, but less eminent, displayed occasional steep, grass- and shrub-covered pockets, good nests for high-flying eagles. The other two sides a person could climb, but with his nose against ground most of the distance, having to go around a number of large, weathered pines. Heavy brush ensnarled root and branch in a maze few squirrels would get through.

Dismounting, we led our horses to an old corral of interwoven, decaying logs, half hidden in trees and underbrush a hundred feet from the old homestead. She then led me along a scant trail that ended further up the canyon, at a cave. Man tracks showed a light boot imprint and signs of recent activity.

"Dooley, you in there?" she yelled.

She bent over and walked into the opening, stopping long enough to retrieve an old kerosene lantern hidden on a ledge above eye level. Holding it out to me and taking a book of matches from her pocket, she lit the wick, then slid the glass into place, lighting the heavy pungent darkness.

"The cave is wide enough you can walk beside me."

We came to Dooley's bedroll lain out on soft, sandy soil. Against the back wall rested a backpack, some canned goods, matches, and neatly stacked firewood. The fire ring in the center of the room was neatly prepared with bark shavings and kindling, as though he had been interrupted when about to start a fire. Against the far wall stood a man-made tripod on which hung a quarter of meat, giving reason for the heavy smell that now mingled with that of burnt kerosene.

Finding no sign of Dooley, and no note, we went back to the mouth of the cave, deposited the lantern, and went outside to find a comfortable place to sit and wait.

"Where would he be?" I said, trying to remain casual.

Mike answered. "I don't know. He must have gone into town for some reason, or down to the hunting lodge to send another message. Hard to tell. He'll be back soon." Her voice lacked conviction.

"What did you find out about TriStar this morning?" I asked, attempting to get her mind off her fears.

"Sellars' report was correct. It's Duquesne's, and completely legal. My aides are looking to see if any others of his little group are involved.

"I also found they have a rather large security force at the site. Thunderbolt Security is responsible for it. They're a highly trained group of ex-psycho-vets who can't get killing out of their system or who have some fantasy to fulfill. Duquesne has used them before—often, particularly in South America. The head man is a guy by the name of Babcock."

"Walter Babcock? Mike, do you know who he is?"

She nodded. "That's what has me worried. If Dooley didn't know anything about these guys he would be in over his head without even realizing it."

Walter Babcock, ex-commando, ex-human being. Forced out of the service because of his part in the killing of more than a hundred civilians in Nam, some of them tortured for information. The government kept it under wraps because they had decorated him with every medal ever made. Another one of the inconsistencies of war.

"I heard from a friend of mine that Babcock was in South America," I said. "Now he's back in the United States. What for?"

"Why Thunderbolt Security at two oil wells in Bridger-Teton? That's what scares me."

I tried to put her mind at ease. "They sold stock in this company. It's a new well, a new venture. If someone got close enough to see what they're doing he could make a lot of money. If the well is a bust, gushing water all over the place, a speculator could sell the stuff short. If it looks like it might come in, buy low and wait for it to hit big time. A lot of companies have security like that to keep the wrong information from getting into the wrong hands at the wrong time. With TriStar, a possible shell for buying other, more important companies, the security would be heavy to keep people from discovering TriStar. Alone, it isn't worth the price of the lease."

"I suppose."

She paused and then continued. "If Dooley doesn't show, tomorrow we'll go into town, take a look at the forest service lease papers, and see if anyone can fill in some gaps. I just don't like the idea of Dooley being out of his element."

I didn't say it, but I agreed. Anyone would be out of their element with Babcock and his security operation.

She set her hat aside and lay back, hands behind her head for a pillow, trying to be unconcerned.

"I'm looking forward to meeting Dooley," I said.

Sliding closer to me and turning on her side, she laid one arm across my chest while the other cushioned her head. The clouds moved swiftly across the blue sky, and my system felt content to be lazy and soak up the afternoon sun. It had been a long time since I felt anything but empty.

I awoke with a start. She was gone. I stood up, my eyes shifting from place to place as I called her name. Nothing had changed. The horses were both still in the corral gnawing at grass, their tails swishing flies. I had started for the cave entrance, when the lantern came my way out of the darkness.

"You scared the daylights out of me!"

She looked at me, pleased. "I left Dooley a message to come to the ranch when he could. We've got to get back. I used to travel these hills at night, but that was a long time ago. I don't trust myself as much, especially with a greenhorn in tow!" She walked off toward the corral.

"Who you calling a greenhorn?"

She laughed lightly and slowed to let me walk with my arm around her waist. "Nikes," she said, pointing at my feet. "The sign of the greenhorn."

As we mounted and walked the horses back through the canyon and to the lake, she lapsed into silence.

"You're still worried about Dooley, aren't you?"

"I can't help it. If something happened to him because I didn't warn him—because I was too busy with . . ."

The tears welled up, and she spurred the horse ahead of me, heading swiftly down the mountain.

I thought about it a minute and then decided this was not the time to talk about the blood on the corral post. Anyway, it probably belonged to the animal whose last quarter hung in the cave. Rankled by my own words, I loosened the rein on an already anxious buckskin.

15

We arrived back at the ranch about the same time as everyone else, just before dark. I had two things no one else seemed to have: Nikes, and saddle sores the size of watermelons. The saddle sores made me sit a little high and, along with the white Nikes, made me the center of attention. I tipped my new hat to all as the buckskin stopped, ready to be unsaddled. Most just shook their heads and looked at each other as they removed the gear from their own horses. Charla and Bob smiled a little too pleasantly, and Mike put her hand to her mouth to stifle a laugh. As unhappy as she had been when coming off the mountain, the smile was worth the embarrassment.

Dismounting with as much aplomb as possible, I removed the Tex-tan saddle and took it and the blanket into the tack room, where I deposited it on an inverted V-shaped stand running the length of the room. I found a halter, returned to the buckskin, exchanged the bridle for the halter, and led the horse to the corral gate, where I undid the halter rope and let him free with a healthy slap on the hindquarters. I then returned to the tack room, where I hung up the bridle and rope. As I sauntered toward the house, bowlegged from necessity and my Nikes kicking up dust, a tall cowboy, cigarette hanging from his mouth and an old beat-up straw hat gracing his narrow face, began applauding. The others joined in, and I turned, bowed, and then continued toward the house and toward relief from the searing pain in my upper legs and buttocks and along the inside of my calves. Closing the screen door behind me, I began to walk as carefully as I felt I needed to.

Taking the stairs slowly, I went to my room, gathered my bathrobe, towel, and shaving gear, and headed for the bathroom. After I had suffered the initial sting of the searing water, my tired muscles relaxed. When I had finished I noticed a new tube of Diaparene someone had slid under the door. I applied the fishy-smelling substance in several layers and felt better, while renewing my compassion for babies with diaper rash.

"I called a friend of mine, Mike," I said. We relaxed in the front porch swing as I tried to recover from too much steak and potatoes. The two layers of sheep's wool covering the pine seat boards, along with the Diaparene, eased the pain in my buttocks.

"The one who was in Vietnam with you," she stated, matter-of-factly, chewing the last remnants of a thick slice of hot homemade bread smothered with butter and honey.

"No, another one, who handles analyses of new stocks coming to the market. Mrs. O. outdid herself with that meal tonight. I'm going to be twenty pounds heavier when I get home." Mike gave me a bite of the bread. "You've got to quit putting this stuff in front of me. I'm a weak man!"

"You could use the extra few pounds." She tried to find an extra inch to pinch in my midsection. I was quietly proud that she struggled.

"You were right. TriStar is completely legal, all their paperwork is in order. Every *T* crossed, every *I* dotted, nothing left to chance."

"Sounds almost too good," she said.

"Yeah. That's what worries me. Are we still going to check with the forest service tomorrow?"

"Yes. Did you find out anything about Stevenson?"

"Danny's secretary in New York snooped around and found out that Ben put in twenty-five trades today. Most of them oil futures, all of them in accounts he trades on a regular basis. Each one of those accounts has the same amounts of the same oil stocks, western technology stocks, and the stocks of oil and gas pipeline companies."

"He's trading exactly the same stocks in each account?" she asked.

"And exactly the same amounts. By the end of the day the accounts are all equal."

She stiffened. "All in phony accounts, I'd bet."

"My guess, too. The clincher is that he traded more than

ten million dollars in securities today. Most brokers don't see that in a year. No wonder he's top broker month after month." I took a piece of paper from my pocket and handed it to her. "Those are the accounts and their numbers. It might be a good idea to have your office check into them and see if they're phony."

"If Ben spent ten million today for his accounts I wonder if each other broker Duquesne uses did the same?" she asked.

"You say they own enough stock in each of the companies you showed me on that list last night to control them. To do that without raising suspicion, you would need at least ten to twenty brokers involved, each using a dozen separate accounts. If the *same* client account were used—say this one of Ben's, Jonathan Rayburn, Inc.—at five different brokerage houses, and they tried to buy six percent of, say . . . IBM stock, J. Rayburn, Inc., would come under immediate scrutiny. They must have hundreds of accounts, at a lot of different brokerage houses, to control it all without being discovered. I'd say you're looking at better than five hundred illegal accounts and at least fifteen to twenty brokers, maybe more."

"I'm glad we hired you."

"I haven't really done anything, just verified what you already knew, and found out for myself that Ben Stevenson is a rat!"

"You don't like it, do you?"

"I hate it. Having people spy on him made my skin crawl, but when I found out he was really in this deal up to his bulging little eyeballs, I felt angry, then cheated, then even more angry!" I stood and leaned against the porch wall. "It's the pits when you know you've been betrayed, and I'm going to get the little worm, stick him on a hook, and feed him to a school of hungry fish!"

She stood and put her arms around me, from behind, shivering a little in the cool night air. "The Las Vegas sun has thinned my blood out. I can't handle the cold like I used to," she said.

We stood quiet for a minute or two, both immersed in our thoughts and the warmth of each other.

"What now?" she asked.

"I'm working that out. We don't want to spook anyone, but we do need to talk to Ben. The size of this operation indicates a huge accounting problem for Duquesne—keeping track, watching the money, deciding what stocks to buy, when to sell, how much. He can't get the brokerage house confirms sent to him because they would lead the authorities to him as well."

"You mean the confirmation for each account showing the trade, its cost, the date, and all of that. The client's copy?"

"Yes," I said. "If those confirmations all ended up at one address, any suspicious office manager could follow the trail, and the SEC would for sure. He has to be keeping track of everything some other way, probably a super computer like TITAN. If that's the case, Stevenson, and every other broker, must have access to it to deliver their daily trade record to Duquesne and pick up instructions from him. Duquesne probably has a message center, a complete financial worksheet of investments, maybe more.

"Duquesne could control everything from his office in L.A., or anywhere. With a computer center and a communications hookup. He could reach it anytime with a lap-top computer and a modem phone hookup. That way he would know what was going on at any given moment, keep complete control even while traveling."

I sat down and looked at the notes from my call to New York. "Danny's secretary says Stevenson has traded a lot of futures lately. That worries me. As unsteady as futures on oil are, it isn't a place to play around with large amounts of money."

"They know something." She looked up at me. "The Middle East."

"Yes," I said. "What would be the key to victory if Iraq attacks its neighbors? Are there any of them that could resist effectively?"

"None. Hussein's war machine is the biggest and the best in the Middle East, except Israel's. Syria might give him some trouble, but other than that he could control the area in a relatively short period of time."

"What about other countries outside the area? Will any of them come to the rescue?"

"None, outside of the United States, have the courage under present conditions," she said. "Iraq has everyone believing they are keeping a balance of power in the area."

"But the United States will?" I cringed at the thought of another possible Vietnam scenario. No, this was different. Vietnam was for no reason other than the egos of leaders and professional soldiers who liked playing army with other people's lives. Too much was at risk here. Iraq was a threat to the world's economy and peace that the Vietcong leadership could never have dreamed of being.

"The president said he wouldn't hesitate to move against Iraq, that we're the only chance, unless something unforeseen . . ." She stiffened. "Is that what you're getting at? If they could put us out of the picture he could do as he pleases?"

"Couldn't he?" I asked. "Suppose we were in the middle of the biggest financial failure in the history of this country? That somehow they were able to put us into a major tailspin? How many citizens would support a troop movement into the Middle East under those conditions? How many leaders?"

"I see what you mean," she said. "So that's what our agent in the Mideast meant. Iraq's attack there hinges on something about to happen here? Could they do that? Financially, I mean."

"Yes. Remember October 1987? A sell-off in the market feeds itself and creates panic. Only level heads kept that one from going clear back to a thousand on the Dow. They closed down the market and shut off computer trading, and companies bought back their own stock. A bunch of stuff. I remember the lethargy, the fear that one created. If they could duplicate it, *and* create a worse panic, you'd have people jumping off high buildings by the thousands, not to mention the unemployment it would create, and the worldwide repercussions economically and politically. Our own people would lose total confidence in our government, and so would everyone else. It could be done, all right, but I think they're waiting for something to set it off, so it can be done naturally and will look totally innocent. If it looks like a manipulation, Wall Street generals will shut it down. It has to be precipitated by something."

"Give me a worst case scenario of what would happen if they were able to control the Middle East," she said.

"Disaster. We would manage, but most European countries would be devastated. They rely heavily on Mideast oil. Japan almost sixty-five percent. The price of oil to run factories and transport goods would double, maybe triple, causing prices for goods to skyrocket. World consumers would be hit hard on that front while having to carry the burden of increased prices for gas and oil for cars and homes. Some economies won't be able to handle the strain. "In addition, those who control oil prices could have a very strong voice in world affairs, a sort of blackmail to sway economic and political opinion.

"But worst of all, a man like Hussein would be able to use his new-found wealth to build a formidable military machine with extensive chemical, biological, and nuclear capability. In his hands every one of his neighbors would be in immediate danger, the rest of the world in at least desperate straits, Israel on their way to Armageddon."

I felt the chill go through my own bones, and I pulled Mike closer. I was overwhelmed by my own words. Could they be stopped? What were they up to? When would Duquesne move? Did we have enough time? Any time? How far-reaching would it be?

A shot in the dark. All we had was a shot in the dark. "Anything from Washington on Sellars' files?" I asked.

"Dad called while you were soaking in the tub. He met with the man responsible for TITAN. It's an impossible job of going through all the files in such a short time, but they have started. If we could just come up with a password!"

"Did anyone look through his wallet, briefcase . . ."

"Officer Carone was told what to look for. Nothing."

We were quiet with our own thoughts.

"Jerry, if you were working on this from Sellars' standpoint what password would you use?" she asked.

"Good question. Maybe Duquesne's name or the name of the committee itself. Does it have a name that you know of?"

She shook her head. "Nope."

It was quiet again.

"Little chance, but you might have them watch for anything with *terror* in it."

"Terror. Why terror?" she asked.

"Remember the word in Sellars' files next to Duquesne's name? TERROR1. I'm sure it's a password."

"But it didn't work when you tried it the other night."

"Not in that form, but maybe a derivation." I sighed. "At least it will give them a place to start."

She took my hand and started for the door. "Come on. I'll make the call. You can make a fire. It's getting cold out here."

16

The next morning Mike said she hadn't slept any better than I had. We were frustrated by too many missing pieces and the size of what we were dealing with. Both of us accepted the idea that Sellars knew what they were up to, but finding his files was a big question mark. The people in Washington appreciated our suggestion, but their tone said "Fat chance." We had to find another way.

And Dooley still hadn't shown up. No calls, nothing. Mike called everyone she could think of who might know where he was or might have heard from him. She paced the floor, wrinkles of concern etching her face.

I tried to put both our minds at ease with encouraging words, but as the early morning slipped by, she paced, called, and questioned more. I made plans to drive to town to see the administrator of Bridger-Teton National Forest. At least it would occupy us.

She handed me the keys to her father's 1990 Chevy four-wheel-drive pickup with a license plate that read SENATE. Deep blue with dark-tinted windows and leather interior, it was fully loaded with all the latest gadgets. Folding the seat forward to stow my jacket, I saw a rack for weapons, a sleek 30-06 with cherry-wood stock and a Marlin automatic .22 varmint gun resting in felt-covered slots.

"You'd be surprised at the kind of dangerous animals you might run into around here," she said, smiling.

The drive to town took about forty-five minutes. The skies, overcast and cool, were a sudden change from the heat of yesterday. We both reached for the heat control.

Mike made a joke about the smell of fish, and I reminded her the Diaparene was her idea. "Us cowboys usually settled for bar grease." She rolled down her window a couple inches. I responded by turning up the heater. She called me a city slicker with a wimp complex. "And you, young lady, need to have more respect for your father's houseguest!" I said, with half a grin.

After a moment's silence I sprang it on her. "Mike, I need another player."

She looked at me, measuring, gauging her reply. "You know the circle is small, and you know why. You wouldn't ask, I suppose, if it wasn't important."

"It is. I need someone to invite Ben Stevenson to a private place for a long talk."

"Kidnapping?"

I smiled. "Technically? Yes." I had thought about it all night. If we confronted him openly he might mince the truth and head for Duquesne, blowing any chance for information. I had to isolate him and get his cooperation.

"Duquesne has a computer keeping track of the finances. He has too big an operation to do it any other way. Ben has some passwords, hopefully enough to get us into Duquesne's system so we can dig out some answers. If Ben is approached any other way we take a chance of blowing the whole deal and losing what trail we have.

"With computers, once they discover even a hint of our being on their trail, they have the ability to lose us simply by locking us out of their system or completely destroying what records I know are being kept. Our only chance is secrecy. That means taking Ben aside and getting his help."

"Who is it you want?" she asked.

"His name is Trayco. Kentucky Trayco."

"Wow! You don't go small-time, do you?"

"You know his reputation. He has the best personal security service in the country. He has the contacts, the personnel, and the method to do what needs to be done, legally—if possible . . ." I paused. "I can trust him."

"How do you know him?"

"Trayco was forcefully inducted into the marines a lifetime ago at the beginning of official combat in Vietnam. Fighting was right up his alley, and he had put several adults in the hospital in the streets of LA. The judge gave Trayco a choice, probably thinking he wouldn't come back.

"Kenny was what you might call a quick study. He learned to sneak into a Vietcong emplacement and destroy key enemy gunners, spotters, and the like slicker than anyone in the service. Then he taught his skills to a select few, and he was given command of one platoon of what was rumored to be a group of hard-nosed soldiers—all smart, all seasoned—called Red Five. They did a lot of nasty work very effectively, and saved a lot of American lives. He got enough decorations to paper a good-sized wall, but never got promoted past sergeant because he bucked leadership who were trying to kill Americans with their stupid military objectives. He was in the brig more than once for decking such fine idiots."

I took a deep breath to calm my emotions. There had been so much stupidity in Vietnam. Gung-ho lieutenants willing to send anyone anywhere just to conquer an objective that meant nothing but commendations and personal advancement in their professional careers.

"Danny who was my copilot and I ran into Kenny's group while we were running away from Vietcong after our chopper had crashed and after we'd been nearly slashed to pieces by a landmine. We were both about half dead, and when Kenny, knife in hand, sprang from the swamp like some reptile from hell, I thought it was over.

"He and his men carried us safely back to a pickup point. Then he personally escorted us by helicopter to a field hospital. He saved our lives."

I paused. "With my eye gone I didn't see any more action. Instead I came home for surgeries and an attempt to put my life back in order. Best thing I ever did for another human being was tell Trayco thank you and that anytime he needed a return favor to call me in Vegas.

"When he came home it was to the same depression—probably worse—and the same dislike we all did. He knew nothing else but weapons and fighting, and he couldn't find a decent job. He had a lot of offers, all from the wrong sources. Mafia, as a hit man; paramilitary groups, which he despised; and private businesses, as a contract killer. He turned them all down, but he was floundering and got into a little trouble. He found me in Vegas, and I got' him an attorney."

"Hank Butcher."

"Close. Rod Clemens, Hank's partner. I didn't know Hank very well then; that came later when he took my case.

"Anyway, Trayco's medals and Clemens' connections and ability got him a reprieve, his fairly clean record still intact. He was released into my custody, and through a client I got him a job as a guard for VIPs at one of the major casinos, and the rest is a history of growth and success."

"His reputation is well known, especially in Washington," she said. "The president would certainly approve."

"Yes. But several others in high places would not, and it would be better if we kept it quiet."

"Like who? Why?"

"Willmore Dutton, for one."

"The man—"

"Yes, the man we met yesterday. Your father's guest. I've always wondered what he looked like.

"Anyway, he was Trayco's former commanding officer, and he's never forgiven Trayco for making him look like the fool he was over in Nam."

She laughed. "Dad calls him one of the world's ten best-dressed idiots. What did Trayco do to him?"

"Dutton was a climber. Always volunteering his troops for action he would never see. Trayco got tired of watching him put his troops in stupid, deadly situations so he could get a few points with the boys upstairs. So Trayco forced him out, at gun point, to go along on a dangerous mission that Dutton had just commanded them to do. Dutton was scared to death. He would run for cover whenever a twig would break, couldn't load his gun and use it properly, and nearly got himself killed through sheer stupidity. Kenny brought him home safe, but the word was out among the men that he was a coward. It destroyed his ability to command, but the big boys didn't know what to do with him, so they busted him into command headquarters and out of everybody's hair."

"Amazing, isn't it? How one person can louse up so many times and still end up on top of the heap just because he knows how to play politics.

"Okay! If Trayco will come I'd like to have him along just to keep you out of trouble." She smiled.

"Oh boy! Thanks."

She slid closer and nuzzled my cheek and neck with her lips. "Careful. Your dad wouldn't appreciate me smashing up his favorite rig."

She kissed my neck again, snuggling closer. "It isn't his favorite. The Lincoln is." She turned my head with her hand and kissed me gently on the lips while I tried to keep at least one eye on the road.

"Mike . . ."

"What?" She smiled, then laid her head on my shoulder.

"Nothin'. Now." I smiled back.

I had seen the red Bronco when we had first left the Kelly cutoff. It was still in the rearview mirror—one car with Colorado license plates between us—as Mike and I passed the elk refuge coming into Jackson. The Bronco was beginning to make me nervous.

We ran into some construction work on the street by the visitors information center and had to pull up. The Bronco's windows were heavily tinted like ours, and you couldn't see anyone clearly, but it looked like there was only one man. The state roadworkers moved us through the construction, and we made a left-hand turn across the lane and into the Bridger-Teton forest administrative complex. The Bronco kept going.

We entered the reception area, where two young rangers were stationed behind a half-moon counter answering the questions of two sets of tourists. Next to the counter was a rack of information pamphlets, and on the wall hung some maps with small price tags attached. Two of the pamphlets interested me, and I picked them up, along with a map of the Bridger-Teton forest and one of the park. When one of the rangers, a Chinese American whose nameplate read "Chen," had finished we stepped to the counter and, while I paid for the pamphlets and maps, asked if we could see the administrator. He gave me my change and asked us to be seated. He said he would check. A few minutes later he came back and waved us down a hallway that was to the left of the counter and then into an adequate office on the right. There was no desk. Instead there were two drafting-type tables with lamps; maps hanging on the walls next to bookshelves containing binders full of information; and an array of odds and ends—from coffee cups to hats with the forest service emblem—hanging from nails on the wall. A working environment.

A man busy at one of the tables stood and introduced himself as Sam Danson. He apologized that the administrator wasn't in but said he would be glad to try and help us. He was medium height at five feet ten, tanned, with a beard and mustache containing a few gray hairs in an otherwise black mass. He had the look of a man used to the out-of-doors.

The Chinese American seated us and offered us a cup of coffee. We thanked him but declined.

On his stool Danson sat facing us with his arms propped on the table behind him, his expression friendly and cooperative.

Mike introduced herself. He immediately recognized the name and stiffened a little.

"Mr. Danson," I began, "you let out bids on oil leases on the Bridger-Teton in 1987. The successful bidder was TriStar Oil. For openers, could you show us on a map where their leases are?"

"Sure." He stood up and went to a colorful map on the wall. Reds, greys, golds, browns, and blues, with little letters and numbers that meant nothing to me. He pointed to four numbered sections: 24, 25, 32, and 33. "They successfully bid these four areas."

"Excuse my ignorance." I said, "but what do these numbers represent? And why all the different colors?"

He gave a tolerant smile. "The numbers simply represent sections and are used for bidding purposes. The colors are the important thing. You will notice that section 25 is mostly gray with little dots. That indicates that most of the section is too steep for drilling or the soils are technically unsuitable for drilling. Then there is a fringe of red with the letters NSO on the west side of the section. That has been set aside as No Surface Occupancy territory as well, because it is used to fulfill other objectives set by the government."

"Such as . . . ?" I quizzed.

"Such as campgrounds, prime animal habitat, threatened species and forests. That sort of thing."

"Are you saying that because of your restrictions this gray area without the dots is the only area where drilling could be done?" Mike asked.

"That's correct."

"And all these other areas that TriStar purchased have similar restrictions?"

"Yes, ma'am."

"Are they presently drilling?" I asked.

"Yes, sir. Approximately . . . here . . . here and . . . here."

"All are within the law . . . I mean within your restrictions?"

"That's right. Why do you ask?"

I ignored his question and went to another of my own.

"Has anyone been up there lately? I mean, do you ever check up on them to make sure they aren't drilling in the wrong areas?"

He looked at me as if it were a rather dumb question, but he answered anyway. "They must obtain drilling permits and turn in a stack of information a yard deep before drilling. Before they ever begin we send inspectors to the site they wish to drill. After that, they drill. There is little we need to check. Besides, in these areas there are only certain locations even suitable for drilling. Most of the terrain—as the color code indicates—is way too steep for drilling rigs to even get close. There are no roads, and the geological formations are solid granite ten feet down, maximum. They also have to get an independent geological survey. We have received it, and it has been cleared without a problem."

Mike looked thoughtful. "I've been there, Jerry. He's right." Then she looked at Danson again and asked another question. "Were there any other leases sold in this area?"

He looked at her curiously. "No, ma'am. In fact, all the other bidders withdrew at the last minute. It surprised everybody, but it's happened before, they say. Just seemed curious at the time. Actually, on this lease offering we didn't expect any bids at all. Drilling in these locations is extremely difficult and very expensive. The chances of hitting oil of any profitable amount have been determined to be one chance in five hundred. Not very good odds. TriStar was a surprise, and their bid unbelievably high."

"I don't suppose you could give us that figure?" I asked.

"I don't have the exact figure, but it is a matter of public record and available if you want—"

"Just wondered. It's really not necessary."

Danson showed no sign of nerves. Whatever TriStar was doing, it wasn't with his knowledge and/or permission.

"One last question, Mr. Danson," Mike said. "Do you see any danger—any danger at all—in TriStar's attempts to drill oil in this area?"

"Yes, ma'am, I do. I think it's absolutely idiotic to endanger the lives of good men who have to drill under those conditions at those odds. They've already brought one body out, and—"

My head jerked in his direction, and Mike's eyes went big as dollars. She beat me to the question. "Who . . . what body? What happened?"

Our surprise set him back a moment, but he went on. "They brought a young man out of the area this morning. It was an independent geologist they hired. Word is he was getting samples and slipped on a steep sidehill. He has been several days at another site TriStar had asked him to look over, I guess. He must have gone out there alone. They say he battered his head on the rocks so badly you couldn't hardly tell who—"

Mike turned on her heel and left the room. I thanked him, his mouth still hanging open, and quickly followed. She was standing by the pickup throwing up.

Dooley was gone.

17

The shock hits you in the stomach first, then the heart, then the head as reality collapses around you, squeezing—painfully squeezing—forcing the tears, then the words. At first it is words of disbelief, then wishing words and words of denial. Finally words of anger.

Mike was in my arms. I held her tight as I tried to protect her somehow, to ward off the anguish I knew was there. It had been that way with Liz's death. It hurts, and hurts some more. Then you get numb. Then, slowly, you adjust, trying to fill the emptiness, to block out the loneliness. Later you cling to the memories even though they still hurt, afraid you will lose even those. Mike was only in the first stages of hurting.

When she finished crying and blowing her nose into my new red-checkered hanky, she sat back against the high-backed leather seat and looked blankly out of the front window. "Why, Jerry? Why did they need to kill him? He . . ."

I looked at her, not sure if she really wanted an answer or just wanted to ask the question and vent her feelings. I decided to wait. Even in my own mind the idea that they had actually killed him hadn't fully sunk in. Why would they? What did Dooley know? What was so important to an oil-drilling operation that they would take a human life?

After a few moments she went on. "I'll have to make plans for the funeral . . . Dad and I . . . and Bob . . . we were the only family he ever really had." The tears flowed again, but just gently down her cheeks. More time passed.

"Take me home. I need to talk to the family."

I started the engine and backed out. When I pulled onto

the highway past the construction, I saw the red Bronco again, parked at a Chevron gas station across the road.

Mike slid over next to me, putting her head on my shoulder. My arm went around her and pulled her in close, my heart aching for the pain I knew she felt.

I watched the rearview mirror, but the Bronco didn't come onto the highway. I relaxed a little and tried to concentrate on lifting some of Mike's grief by holding her tighter.

Senator Freeman got back in the late afternoon. On his employment and various other forms, Dooley had listed the senator as next of kin, and the sheriff had notified him personally at his office in Washington. When the senator entered the house his face looked ashen and gaunt, his eyes filled with a fear that was unnerving.

And it was gone in a moment as he summoned up the strength he would need to pull his family together and make the necessary decisions. Everything else could wait.

As they were closing the den door against the outside world I started to walk toward the kitchen. Mike grabbed my arm before I got to the dining room.

"We'll need your help with this, Jerry," she said, urging me toward the family enclave. Mystified, my mind searched for an explanation.

The senator was near the fireplace, busying himself with paper and kindling for a fire to take the chill off a rainy day. Mike motioned me to the couch, next to her. The four of us waited in silence while he finished gathering his thoughts.

"Jerry, Dooley was an active member of your church. Will you advise us on how he would like to have this done? We want to do it right." He was standing, his eyes on the new flames engulfing the paper. "He was a returned missionary from Brazil, if that makes any difference, and he'd been to your temple. I have only been to one other Mormon funeral, and . . . well, what should we do?"

His voice broke, and Mike stood and went to his side, putting her arms around him.

"Do you know who the bishop of Dooley's Jackson ward is?" I asked.

"Bruce Klingler," Mike said stiffly. "He's new, but Dooley liked him."

"Charla, could you get his number. We'll need him out here right away." She went to the phone book. "Senator, the bishop can take care of most of the details once you make a few major decisions. Which mortuary will prepare the body?"

Bob spoke. "He was taken to Williamson and Harris. Dad is good friends with True Harris, and True knew Dooley. True is a member of the Church."

"Good. Then he'll know the appropriate burial clothes. He and the bishop will be able to work out all the details without much trouble. Where do you want the service?"

The senator spoke. "Is it okay with everyone if we have it in the yard here, same as we did with your mother?" They all nodded, then looked at me. "We have a private burial plot on the knoll up by the mouth of Crystal Lake canyon. I want him buried there."

"Bishop Klingler is on his way," said Charla. "He works for the forest service and was on his way back from Jenny's Lake. They reached him on the radio." She looked at her watch. "Should be here in about half an hour."

The senator paced his way to the couch. The strange look—almost a fearful look—was still etched in his face. Something deep was bothering him.

The talk centered on arrangements for someone to dig the grave, and Bob was given the assignment to call a man with a backhoe who had done it before; then how many to plan on, which was tabled until they could talk to the bishop; then who needed to be notified, and the senator was assigned to call the university and Mike to call friends she knew and the newspapers.

When Bruce Klingler arrived I watched a young, nervous, and tenderhearted bishop put together his first funeral. Dooley had been his friend, he said, his face lined with the fresh shock of loss. All of us ignored his nervousness, and soon it was done. He had discovered funerals were not easy, physically or emotionally. For a bishop they were almost always for someone known and loved.

The bishop would conduct the meetings and arrange for two special musical numbers. Charla would give the obituary, and the senator would be the only speaker, the bishop giving a few comments. The senator had balked at having to speak, doing everything he could to get around it, but the others had insisted. I noticed how his anguish went deeper, and he became more troubled.

They asked me to dedicate the grave. It sobered me as I remembered the last one. Liz's.

Bishop Klingler handled himself well, and the family was impressed. The two of us started for his pickup.

"The family will need some chairs brought in for the services," I said, filling in some blanks. "It would be appreciated if the Relief Society would take care of the arrangement of the flowers around the grave. Could they do that?" I asked.

"You've done this before, Mr. Daniels," he said respectfully.

"Eight times while I was bishop of a ward in Las Vegas. Six were members of my ward; two were indigents, street people with no one else to take care of it. Finding their families was the hardest part. Funerals aren't easy, but I found nothing more rewarding than helping people do it right. You did a good job, and I personally appreciate it. Those are good people in there, and right now you're doing the best possible service for them. Thanks."

"You're welcome, but you should know they're not new to the Church. The senator's wife was a member, although semi-active, and both children were baptized and used to attend once in a while when they were young. Michaelene attended with Dooley quite often."

My face must have showed my confusion. "I saw how you looked at the senator's daughter." He smiled. "Just thought you'd like to know."

Blankly, I watched his forest-service green pickup disappear down the dirt road. Mike must have her reasons for not saying something. The obvious one was she didn't care for the Church. But then neither had I not long ago. Liz had been patient. Now I understood how scared she must have been that I wouldn't see the Church for what it was.

Returning to the kitchen, I found the mood quiet and somber. I sat down and concentrated on my meal, deep in thought.

I couldn't escape the fact that my feelings for Mike were deep, but I still wasn't sure. Liz and I had something special, unreplaceable. Liz had been my anchor through everything since Vietnam, saving me in more ways than one, giving me a desire to live, putting doubts about God and religion forever to rest.

The knife clattered on the hardwood floor as it slipped from my hand after an overzealous and frustrated stab at buttering a slice of whole wheat bread.

"What's the matter?" asked Mike.

"Huh? Oh, nothing." I picked up the knife and went to the drawer to get a clean one, then returned to the table. I smiled, holding up the knife, then sat down and busied myself again.

I love Mike, I thought. *At least, I think I do. No, I know I do. It's different than it was with Liz . . . and yet . . . it's not different.*

I looked across the table at her. Dark curly hair, tanned, tall, and well proportioned. A woman that didn't seem to ever be concerned with her weight. Physically different than Liz. Both beautiful. One light complexioned, one dark. One, strawberry blond, one, curly black hair.

Yet . . . the eyes. That was it. Not the color—Liz's were green, Mike's dark brown—but something inside those eyes.

She caught me watching. "What's wrong, Jerry?" she asked.

I noticed that everyone else had left the room. Even most of the dishes had been cleared away. She sat with her arms folded and lying on the edge of the table, her body leaning slightly toward me.

"Hmm? Oh, nothing, just admiring the scenery." I smiled.

She blushed a little. Then spoke. "Thanks for your help with the arrangements." That stiffness still evident.

"No problem." I looked at her, hoping she would say more. It wasn't to be. Not yet, anyway. Patience, Jeremiah!

"Where is everyone?" I asked.

"Dad and Bob are out telling the hands about Dooley—he was one of them in a lot of ways—and giving them instructions about getting things shipshape. Charla is putting the twins to bed."

We stood, gathered up the remaining dishes, and took them to Mrs. O.

"I need to make some calls," I said. "Can I use the den?"

"Sure. I'll join you in a few minutes." She took the steps two at a time. Yes, they were a lot alike. It was the energy, the love of life, the genuineness. Loving Mike would be easy because she was so much like Liz, but the Church . . . I shook my head, trying to rid it of the confusion, the emptiness that comes when you wake from a nice dream and get hit between the eyes with reality. The world seemed darker again.

Trayco was in his car, as usual, and over the phone I brought him up to speed on what had been happening, then told him what to do about Stevenson.

"It'll be in the next few days, and it has to be very private,"

I said. "Use my place, but seal it off. I don't want anyone know-ing we're there."

He asked me why the delay.

"I don't want Stevenson out of circulation until I know I can be there. If he disappears for too long Duquesne will have a big reason for concern and might lock him, and us, out of his mainframe."

"Mmm. I'll find him and put a tail on him."

"No rough stuff, Kenny. I want him scared, but in good voice."

"Jerry, when you invest my money, I give you instructions, and then I let you do the job and don't mess with you like an old mother hen." He hung up. The smile came automatically. He wouldn't mess him up, but he would sure scare a few years off!

With Jan and Danny the inevitable had happened, and the two of them had mentally split the house in half, refusing to cross the line, which complicated life because Danny owned the kitchen and Jan was the only one who could cook. They were both threatening to take the next flight out, even though neither had made a move to do it.

"What's the problem?" I asked.

"He's getting on my nerves with his chauvinistic garbage! Ever since I made him a meal, he's wanted me in the kitchen, like I was some sort of maid, or slave or something."

"She's like all women nowadays" he said. "Ya can't live with them, and if you try to live without them they never leave you be! And talk, talk, talk. All the time."

My arm stiffened, putting the phone a few inches from my ear as they erupted into wild incriminations. Finally I whistled as loud as I could to get their attention. Their noise changed to a low but steady murmur.

"Listen, you two, you're *both* my guests, and I don't want to find *my* house torn apart when I get back, *understand?*" I paused. They mumbled something about being sorry, but it was clear they were sorry only to me.

"I'm going to need the place for a few days—a week," I said. "Will you two do me a favor?" They mumbled again, but both asked what. "Danny, take my sweet and beautiful sister-in-law up to the condo in Deer Valley, outside of Salt Lake. It has two sections with separate living quarters. I'll call and have both refrigerators stocked. It's cool enough to take the heat out of the both of you, and there is plenty to do there."

There was silence and then Danny spoke. "All right. Banner told me to stay away for the whole two weeks. I guess I can keep in touch from Utah as well as I can from Nevada. But I'm only doing it as a favor to you, Jerry."

The phone erupted again as Jan said, in no uncertain terms, she wanted no favors from him and he didn't have to go on her account. She was completely capable of taking care of herself, she said, and she would get there on her own without so much as a finger being lifted by him. And on and on.

I whistled again, trying to stifle the laughs. "Then you'll both go?" I asked.

"I'm not due for my next photo session for another week, and I need the rest. How do I get in?" Jan said.

"Just go to the clubhouse for the key. I'll make all the arrangements." Then I added, "No offense, you two, but don't let anyone hear you fighting like that; they might think you're the world's best version of a marriage."

They erupted again but were united in their efforts against me. I said good-bye and hung up the phone, laughing.

"What's so funny?" Mike said, coming into the den.

"Oh, just two friends back home who are madly in love."

After I called Deer Valley we went into the yard and walked in the dimming light of late evening, the sun out of view to the west but still glistening off the snow in the high mountains to the east. The clouds had gone, but the smell of new rain was sweet to my senses. A few of the ranch hands were putting away the gear for the day, watering and feeding stock, or just standing around smoking and quietly talking. They moved toward the bunkhouse a few at a time as the shadows deepened.

"I knew something was wrong when we were at the playpen." She paused, her feelings close to the surface.

"Dooley and I spent tons of time there when we were kids—dreaming, making plans, deciding how we would solve the world's problems. When he went away to college I still had a year of high school left, and I would go up to the playpen when I missed him. I always felt comfortable in the quiet calm and memories. Not this time. I knew something horrible had happened." She choked on the words.

"Like a premonition?" I asked.

"More like a . . . like a message. I just knew we wouldn't be together anymore. My heart just broke, and it was all I could do to shove it aside, shake it off." She shuddered as if a chill wind had blown. She put her arms around my waist, placing her warmth against me. My arms started to go around her, then pulled away. Instead I took her hand, walking as I cleared my throat.

"The sheriff will turn something up. They'll find out if it was murder."

She looked at me a little confused. "Maybe. Jerry, is something wrong? Ever since—"

"No, nothing's wrong. Just tired, aren't you?"

"A little, and don't lie to me," she said, stopping and folding her arms adamantly. "What's wrong?"

I took a deep breath. "All right. Why didn't you tell me you're a member of the Church?"

"Ohhh, I get it. The good bishop fill you in, did he?" she said, almost angry and walking away a few feet, her back to me.

It took a minute before I realized she was crying.

"I gave up on God and the Church the day Mother died."

Too shocked to move, I watched her disappear into the house.

My eyes were fixed on the shadows above the ceiling fan of my room. I was trying to concentrate on figuring out the Tri-Star-Dooley connection, while haunted by the bitterness of Mike's last words.

The red numbers of the digital alarm read 12:10 A.M. I wondered if Mike was having trouble getting to sleep in the next room.

My stockinged feet found the floor as my fingers fumbled to find the switch on the table lamp. Just as well get up and do something constructive for an hour. After putting my glass eye in, I opened the top drawer of the dresser and took out the Colt .45 and stuck it in my belt at the small of my back. Bob had surprised me by bringing it to my room earlier in the evening. "Dooley was no accident" was all he had said. He was right.

Many chopper pilots used a similar weapon as a side arm in Vietnam. Piloting a chopper didn't leave a person free to use large weapons, and the side arms had saved more than one life—including my own—while we were trying to dig soldiers out of tight spots.

The thick carpet on the floors made it easy to slip down the hall quietly and the steps carried my weight without more than an occasional light squeak. After I had closed the door to the den and turned on the desk lamp my mind ran quickly through the numbers Mike had given me for the safe.

I quietly laid Sellars' computer files out on the desk. My eyes passed over them, looking for the information about Tri-Star.

Dressed in a bathrobe, the senator appeared in the doorway, his hand gripping something inside the right pocket.

"You couldn't sleep, either," I said.

He shook his head as he fell into the big leather chair next to a reading lamp, clicking it on. "Nervous. Even though I don't think Dooley's killers would come here, it's better to be cautious." He laid a nickel-plated Colt .45 on the end table. I smiled inwardly. Two paranoid peas in a pod.

"I got a call from Washington," he said.

My back stiffened. "The CIA files?"

"No, but just as good." He took a piece of paper out of his bathrobe pocket and handed it to me. "WASHINGTON—code name for the man in charge of TITAN—gave me this number."

I looked at the post-it note.

"The number is only a temporary one. It'll be changed—put completely out of circulation—tomorrow. We'd better use it now and see what he has to say."

He made no move to the computer, his face lined with concern. He seemed to have aged a few years over the last twenty-four hours. "Jerry, we could stop now. These boys are playing rough, and I don't want anyone else to get hurt. They, Washington, could find another way."

"We're just getting a line on these guys. No time to quit now." I smiled, trying to put him at ease.

"They've killed, Jerry. They'll kill again." He paused, his shoulders slumping, making the chair loom large.

"I've always liked to be in the center of things," the senator said, "an active part of the solution. When I heard about Sellars' death, even though I knew him I put it off as a normal casualty in a hard and desperate business. When I heard about Dooley it hit a little closer to home."

"You think they've connected you to Dooley?"

"I don't know, but it scares me. If Royalty knows of my involvement he may try to eliminate me and in the process hurt more of the people around me."

It suddenly dawned on me. "Did you have something to do with Dooley going back up to TriStar?"

He got up and walked to the big picture window, the anguish filling his face.

"But how . . . I mean . . . Mike didn't know about TriStar until we were going through Sellars' papers. How could—"

"I kept it from Mike, and I didn't tell Dooley enough. I'm responsible for his death as sure as I stand here."

Not wanting to believe what I was hearing, I sat back in the chair. He turned and looked at me. "Like I said, I've never been one to sit back and watch others solve problems. This time it cost me a son." His voice was low and edged with pain.

"But why *didn't* you warn him, or at least fill him in?" I asked, trying to control the heat in my voice.

"Because I was an old man playing in covert operations for the first time, and my dime-novel knowledge caused me to make a bad decision. I even used the term *need to know!*" His voice raised an octave with disgust. "I'm in over my head, Jerry, we all are, but I got Dooley killed because I played games with his life. Games that seemed exciting, but never deadly. I kept him in the dark because I was playing spy, enjoying the power and the danger, like some idiot in the movies."

He was right. "You couldn't have known they'd kill him," I said feebly.

"I shouldn't have used him without filling him in completely and giving him a chance to understand the danger. Instead I let him walk in there thinking it was just another company I wanted to look at for a personal investment and needed him to report anything he saw that wasn't right.

"Dooley sent me a message in Washington. He said he wanted to meet with me as soon as possible. That's one of the reasons I came home and told Mike to come here from Las Vegas. He was going to come to the house but never showed up. When Mike told me about the note I wanted to die on the spot. I sent out the word in Jackson to locate him, but no one did. Not in time. I prayed you would find him at the playpen; but, deep down, I knew you wouldn't.

"My playing games cost him his life."

"How did you know about TriStar?" I asked.

"Another source in our covert little community," he said sarcastically. "I had a man in the Treasury Department do some research through tax and business records and put together a schematic of Duquesne's personal holdings. TriStar's name was included in the list but seemed to be a rogue company. It just didn't fit everything else Duquesne did, and it was located in my state—even at my doorstep—so I decided to look into it.

"That's when I found out TriStar had asked Dooley to do an independent study. The rest is easy to figure out. The old man uses his son for his own selfish reasons." He choked on the words.

"It was natural to ask him. But you're right; you should have told him everything up front. He needed to know the dangers. But in all fairness, Senator, you couldn't have known they might kill him. As yet even I see no reason for it, and I'm—"

He held up his hand. "I had already received the report on their security. I knew who Walter Babcock was and his reputation. That kind of protection has a purpose. I just took it too lightly, telling myself that Dooley was better off not knowing what was going on, that he might give himself away. I was wrong!"

There was a long silence. Again, he was right; it was his fault. He would suffer for it until the day he died and made it right with Dooley.

He went on. "I don't want to make that mistake again."

"Have you kept anything back from Mike and me?" I asked candidly.

"I haven't told Mike what I just told you, but other than that, no."

"I believe you. Look, Senator, bad judgment is a weakness common to all of us. We live with the mistakes the best we can. In this case there isn't much leeway for error. When we make them under these conditions they cost more. You're right; you should have told Dooley, but Mike and I have our eyes wide open. Have you filled Bob in? Do it!"

Dooley was dead. Nothing was going to change that. I knew I could still trust the senator—maybe even more than before.

The clock on the mantel said 1:00 A.M. "Now, we had better make that call." He wiped some tears from his eyes before he turned to join me at the computer.

"Is the president on our side?" I asked.

"Yes, but the reality is that he can't let this erupt into another Contra affair, or Watergate. If this gets out and we can't get proof, I will be hung out to dry as a meddling senator who aspires to take over the country."

"Lovely portrait," I said.

"Yes, well, it would be for some, but worse, it would send the whole mess into a whirlwind of controversy and political name-calling that could allow Duquesne's group to accomplish their purpose."

The IBM had two 40-megabyte hard disks, a high-quality modem, a couple of floppy disks, and the power to move through files at ultra speed. "Where did you get this baby?" I asked, waiting for the C> prompt.

"Your tax dollars at work."

I entered WASHINGTON's number.

WHO ARE YOU?

"Type in SILO; that's my code name," the senator said.

WHAT CAN I DO FOR YOU, SENATOR?

"Tell him to give us the information in Sellars' files," the senator said.

I did so.

WAIT.

I watched the screen, biting my fingernails, my right leg twitching. I checked the printer to make sure it was ready to give us a hard copy. This could be the answer we were in need of.

INFO TO FOLLOW!

The high-speed printer hummed to life.

I typed.

▶ ANYONE ELSE ACCESS THESE?

NOT SINCE I TALKED TO THE SENATOR EARLIER TODAY. WE'VE BEEN LOGGING AND WATCHING ALL USERS.

▶ HOW DID YOU FIND THE FILES, SUPERMAN?

YOUR CLUE LOCATED THEM. FILE IS CALLED *TERUN*. IT IS A FORM OF FRENCH FOR *TERROR ONE*. NOT MANY KNEW SELLARS' REAL BACKGROUND. HIS PARENTS WERE RAISED IN FRANCE. HE SPOKE THAT AND SEVERAL OTHER

LANGUAGES FLUENTLY. PASSED HIMSELF OFF AS A FRENCH BUSINESSMEN AS HIS COVER IN THE MIDEAST. TWO AND TWO MAKES FOUR.

▶ THANKS.

WELCOME. NEED ANYTHING MORE, THE SENATOR KNOWS WHO TO CONTACT FOR MY NEW NUMBER. AS OF THIS MOMENT THIS ONE IS NO LONGER USABLE. SENATOR, SORRY TO HEAR ABOUT DOOLEY. GOOD LUCK.

The C> appeared, but the printer was still filling paper. We waited, hopeful that Sellars had some answers.

"How did Sellars use TITAN's bulletin board?" I asked.

"Simple. He would dial up TITAN, use his password, and then go to the bulletin board program and leave a coded message for his contact."

"Does everyone have access to the same bulletin board?"

"Yes, but all messages are encrypted."

"What?"

"It's too complicated for my small mind, but I'll try to explain. A message is made unintelligible by changing it according to a specific method using numbers for letters. It's made intelligible again by reversing the method on the receiving end. Call it scrambling, coding messages—whatever you want. The point is that only the sender and the receiver know what the message says because only they have computers that have their specific encrypted code."

"Sellars was sending to a specific contact, right?"

"Yes."

"Who actually received the message, though, after it got to TITAN's bulletin board? WASHINGTON?"

"No. It goes automatically to the computer on the contact's secretary's desk. She decodes it," he said, pausing. "I know what you're thinking. She can be trusted, Jerry."

I decided to pursue it. "Who had access to her computer, then?"

He looked puzzled. "Just she and her boss, Sellars' contact . . . I think."

"Find out, will you? Somebody got to those messages and sent altered ones as well. It had to be someone who had access to the encryption/decryption codes in the computer. That may narrow down our list of possible traitors."

"I'll do it first thing in the morning," he said.

The printer stopped its mechanical chatter. I appreciated the fact that it printed single sheets instead of the type hooked together. No delay for ripping them apart and tearing off tractor-hole attachments on each side.

"You going to tell me who this contact is?" I asked.

"Can't. Not yet." He smiled. "Need to know."

"Need to know is baloney, Senator."

He shrugged. "I was told—"

"No matter, let's get this done; it's getting late."

We split the stack and read for thirty minutes, each making notations of what to share with the other. Most of it we put aside as irrelevant—dealing with other personalities, cases, and times. I made up my mind to return to it sometime just for the interesting reading it might make. It was all definitely highly classified shredder fodder.

I finished the last page and organized what I wanted to keep, taking a minute to go to the fridge for a couple of glasses of orange juice. We needed at least another half hour before I could allow the senator to collapse into his bed. When I returned, drinks in hand, he was finishing up.

"Interesting reading," I said.

"Even things I didn't know were going on. The president and I are going to have a long talk about some of these operations when this is all over. What do you have?"

"I defer to the senator from Wyoming," I said as I handed him the juice.

"I'd put a little vodka in this if I weren't in mixed company," he said with a wry grin.

"I'll bet. What ya got?"

A half hour later the senator was finished. I picked up the paper I'd been making notes on and read back the pertinent points. I added mine as *C* and *D*.

"*A*. Duquesne tried to frame Sellars with the million dollars. They discovered he was a CIA operative who was getting too close to their little group. Duquesne thought they could get him out of the way without a lot of ruckus and they could embarrass the president at the same time. They were only partially successful.

"*B*. By intercepting Sellars' messages, someone in Duquesne's organization was kept informed by Royalty of Sellars' progress.

"Sellars gets wise to it, circumvents the message system, goes directly to his contact and asks for a meeting, and then hides his records inside TITAN. Sellars ends up dead. Unfortunately he doesn't include any information about who Royalty is."

"That worries me," the senator said. "If I knew who the enemy was and that my life was in danger I'd get it down on paper."

"He probably didn't know who was intercepting, only that it was being done. He may not have thought his life was in immediate danger." I shrugged, feeling uneasy.

"Point C.," I went on. "Everything else in Sellars' files reports greedy, power-hungry people trying to control the world's oil. Sellars knew about all the ones involved. The names in his file coincide with yours, with the addition of two new players: code names, Defender and Commandant. Not much is said about them except that one is an American money man working to bring on board more dollars from interested American sources. He also seems to be pointing Duquesne in the direction of possible participants they might be able to involve through blackmail.

"The other, Commandant, is an American military leader who believes in the Arab cause and hates Israel," I said. "Any ideas?"

He sat back in the leather couch. "One or two. But neither Defender nor Commandant seems very involved in the planning. They must have come aboard later."

"Maybe. Better have WASHINGTON start using TITAN for possible candidates.

"Point D. TriStar is right in the middle of all this. Sellars didn't know any more about how Defender and Commandant were involved than we do, but he confirms the involvement."

"Dooley knew something," the senator said. "He must have seen something. But what?" He got to his feet and went to the window.

"I intend to find out, Senator. Another question. Anything new on Kuwait and Iraq?" I asked.

"Iraq is making gestures of peace. They told Mubarak of Egypt that they had no intention of attacking Kuwait. Same with Jordan's King Hussein. It's all a smoke screen. Iraq is massing troops on the border."

He took a breath. "I read the last communication from our

agent closest to leadership in Iraq. He sounds almost desperate and very concerned. I'm afraid he'll give away his position if he's not careful."

"Senator, did we make that monster?" I asked.

"We helped when Iran was the enemy with full intentions of destroying its neighbors and controlling the Middle East through its so-called Islamic state. Hussein made a good bed partner."

"Why did we need a partner?" I asked angrily. "Why not just stay out of it altogether?"

"Jerry, the Middle East is in the process of extreme change. Some Arab leaders want to bring all Arab nations under one flag, with one leader. They feel that's the only way of ever pulling all Arabs toward total unity. They haven't been able to accomplish it with political negotiations, so some seek to do it militarily. Khomeini of Iran saw himself as that leader. Now Hussein has the same delusions. Both have shown themselves willing to do anything to reach their goals.

"Many Arab people want no such form of government, but they're weak militarily and will be quickly forced into submission unless someone comes to their aid. Kuwait is the most notable. The richest per capita but the weakest militarily. In truth, they are a spoiled, rich society, and under normal circumstances I wouldn't go out of my way to help them cross the street, but Iraq is intent on taking their wealth as a first step to conquest. We have no choice. The oil fields of Saudi Arabia are next, and with the newly acquired wealth he can build his military machine and complete his nuclear and chemical arsenal and solidify his position by paying his debts and buying new friends.

"At that point those who won't kiss his boots and accept his leadership will be overthrown militarily, unless someone mounts the cavalry and comes to the rescue."

"Our job?" I asked.

"Everybody's. Trouble is it won't be as easy then as it might be now. And many will refuse to participate because Hussein will control their oil."

I leaned back in the chair. "We fight alone, from further away, with no land base from which to operate, and against greater odds. We have created a monster."

"With no respect for human life," the senator said. "He has stated openly he wishes to destroy the Jews of Israel. He was creating a nuclear bomb just for that purpose. Said he would drop it on Israel then rebuild the holy city on top of their bodies, more beautiful, more wonderful than ever before."

"Another Holocaust?" I said.

"That's one name for it. Israel is very high on his agenda, as is continued expansion. Nebuchadnezzar was the king of ancient Babylon. Babylon controlled the known world of its day and defeated the Jewish nation soundly, destroying Jerusalem and taking most of the surviving Jews captive into Babylon, in present-day Iraq. Hussein sees himself as the modern Nebuchadnezzar."

"Then this is not a war for oil."

"It's a war to stop the second Hitler, but oil is very much a part of the equation, as you can see."

"But the Arabs—they seem to like Hussein."

"Some, but only because they hate us and Israel worse. Some Arabs have been raised since small children to hate. When a leader like Hussein comes along and threatens Israel's destruction while standing up to a world power, those who hate feast on his every word. But the majority of Arabs are very sane and reasonable people. They understand very well what a future under Hussein would mean, and when push comes to shove in the next few weeks they will work for his destruction before it's too late."

"Senator, you're making the hair on the back of my neck stand on end. I shrink at the thought of another war like Vietnam. Isn't there any other way?"

"In the first place it won't be like Vietnam. We may make mistakes, but we won't make the same ones again. Second, we're doing all we can to get him to back off. He's not listening. We've already begun secret discussions with every other nation we can, and they are applying pressure, but frankly, they are hard to convince that he is this kind of a threat. Once he moves on Kuwait they will be ready to help us. The writing will be on the wall. Then we will exhaust every possibility—using sanctions, under-the-table negotiations, everything. But you have to understand, Jerry, we can't give him what he wants, and we can't allow him to keep Kuwait. That would be a show of weakness, and to his mind a sign of weakness is the same as permission to carry on. He must be stopped, without a victory."

"War."

"He won't back down; we can't. Way too much at stake. Yes, we'll have war. But this time we'll give our troops everything they need to win, and thousands of other men will be with us. And once the people of this nation see what Saddam Hussein is really like they will support our troops."

"How do we get ourselves into messes like these!" I half shouted.

He sighed. "As long as there's evil in the world someone will have to fight it. You asked if we created the monster. Greed, avarice, the fight for power and money—*they* created him. We supported him as the lesser of two evils. Now he is the remaining evil, and we must deal with him."

"Someone else will take his place," I said.

He looked tired, drawn, and pale. "Yes. The indication is that Assad of Syria already is making plans.

"I don't know, Jeremiah. We live in a wicked, greedy world of our own making. Man creates his own enemies and then has to go to war to keep that enemy from destroying him and others. I wish . . . I wish I could go back to change things, but how far back would I have to go to find a time in which we could eliminate the evil in men's hearts? Isn't that what it will take to end the possibility of war?"

We sat silent. I stared out of the window. Beyond the darkness man sat plotting the deaths of others, playing their games, using the lives of men like pawns to be sacrificed to protect them and their desire for power and money. Turn the other cheek? Love your fellowman, even those who despitefully use you? Watch as they destroy, kill, and maim? If you did that, only evil would remain. Not a world I wanted for my children. And yet stopping these evil men would mean killing them.

For my part I must find another way.

18

Outside the dark of the bedroom a full moon caressed the landscape, producing eerie shadows around trees and buildings, adding to my empty feeling. The senator's words had sobered me: war; casualties. Déjà vu.

But I was beginning to see the full picture. A frightening fulfillment of scripture through real events that could explode into Armageddon in any of a dozen different ways.

Or could stop it from erupting and even open doors for changes that would end up saving millions of lives. Such prospects could only be handled one day at a time.

My watch illuminated 3:30 A.M. A half hour for things to settle down, and I'd be on my way. Thirty minutes to concentrate on the task at hand.

Sellars had been thorough. He had a good grasp of what was going on, and he knew TriStar was in it to the top of their shiny red rigs. He just hadn't figured out how. The only thing I had come up with was a front for some sort of terrorist operation involving a nearby military facility of some kind. A center to gather terrorists as they sneaked into the country for a large operation was possible, but what could the target of such an operation be? Missile silos in the Dakotas, possibly even closer? I'd need to check on exact locations and potential threats under terrorist control. Denver and Las Vegas munitions storage facilities? Possible if they're looking for a big bang in a populated area, but too far from Jackson, Wyoming, and definitely a political mistake if they wanted to maintain no involvement. Maybe they didn't.

Hill Air Force Base and the F-15s based there? Another political problem. Maybe later, if we went to war, but as a prelude to war? Doubtful. Same with Nellis Air Force Base's secret Stealth-testing center, which wasn't so secret anymore. None of it fit. Too military and too political! Whatever their scheme, it had to connect with their financial operation, and it could not carry earmarks of terrorism!

Frustration!

I looked at the time again. 4:00 A.M. Time to go. Taking a deep breath, I slipped out of the door and down the hall. Remembering which stairs squeaked helped me clear that obstacle without a sound. The back door in the kitchen would be best for an exit. It was furthest from the sleeping area of the house and nearest to the rented Bronco. What I was doing was at least mildly dangerous. Having others along would only complicate and multiply that danger.

As my hand clutched the cold chrome handle of the Bronco door, the grip of a calloused and hardened flesh encircled my wrist. Another vise-like hand grabbed my arm and held it steady, an inch away from the gun I struggled to get. He pushed me against the Bronco as I braced for the blow to come.

I was flipped around, the shadowed face of my attacker relieving my suddenly racing heart. He let my gun hand go and put his finger to his lip, calling for quiet. He smiled, then gestured for me to follow. Slowly the strength came back into my shaking legs as Bob led the way up the lane toward the main road. "Wouldn't want my sister's boyfriend to get lost in this wilderness," he said. "She'd never forgive me."

We climbed into the pickup. "How'd you know I was—"

"Simple matter of deduction. According to Dad, TriStar is smack-dab in the middle of somethin' shady at best. He figured you'd be goin' out for a look and told me to load up a couple horses and baby-sit you."

Bob pulled onto the road and checked the trailer in the rearview mirror. "I know what's happenin', Jerry. I usually mind my own business when it comes to Dad and Mike, but when Dooley . . . well, ain't no use you tryin' to keep me out."

There wasn't anyone I'd rather have along.

We passed through the center of Jackson. It appeared foreign early in the morning with only a few cars parked in the central square, and hardly a soul in sight. Bob waved at the deputy behind the wheel of a four-wheel-drive Bronco with Sheriff written on the side and asked if I wanted to invite him along. I declined. "Maybe another time." Stores were locked, and tourists were all in bed, the dimly lit streets quiet.

We headed south, turning left at Hoback Junction. Having hunted the area dozens of times, Bob said he knew a way that would get us pretty close to the rigs before we had to unload the horses. He suggested we pass ourselves off as hunters preparing for the fall by scoping out the best spots. "It ought to keep snoops from puttin' a gun to our heads," he said.

"Those new boots and clothes will give you the look of a greenhorn hunter. I'll be the guide you're hirin'."

We talked about possible clues and what had happened to Dooley. Bob's face went hard as granite, his hands punishing the steering wheel.

"Dooley was a good kid. Wouldn't hurt nothin' or nobody. Went to church every Sunday and even got me and Mike to go sometimes. I never could sit still that long; seemed like there was just too much to be doin' back at the ranch."

He paused, handling a hard memory. "Church was okay, just not for me, I guess. Seemed to make Dooley come alive. Dad paid for him to go away on a mission for a couple of years for the Church, and when we said good-bye at the airport in Salt Lake City he was as excited as a kid in a toy store. Went to southern Brazil." He breathed deeply. "Came back twenty pounds heavier, full of the Lord, and rarin' to get married and move on with his life." He thought a moment more before continuing. "He asked Mike."

He noticed my body stiffen and laughed.

"Face it, Jeremiah, you ain't the first to entertain that idea. She's been asked more 'n once." He went serious again. "She turned him down, as you guessed, with a reason she thought was a good one. She only thought of him as a brother and that would never change.

"Nearly put him away right then. Moped around for a week, thought it through, and then returned to his old self. He went back to the University of Wyomin'; she to Harvard. She can tell you the rest of her life's story, but that's Dooley's in a nutshell." The face went hard again.

"He may have been as ready as any man I know to die, but he didn't deserve it!

"These people are mean, Jeremiah. Cold-blooded killers. I

saw a few like them in Nam—on both sides of the battle—and they gave me goose bumps."

"Vietnam turned a lot of good people into killers," I said. "Some got over it; some didn't."

"Which were you?" He looked at me quizzically as he turned onto a dirt road.

"I don't know. Most of the time I feel cold inside about all of that. I block it out when it comes roaring back in the middle of the night. Flying a chopper in that mess, pulling people out of hell, I got more than my fair share of shots at the enemy. I didn't enjoy killing them; it was just automatic. I saw them; I shot. I watched them die, their guts splattering with the impact of the 50mm machine gun we carried. Like everybody, I steeled myself against it—blocking it out to keep it from driving me crazy. Until I got home. Then I had to deal with it."

He pulled the outfit into a small, grassy spot next to the road and turned off the lights, then the ignition.

"Charla helps me through a lot of bad nights. Without her and the kids . . . well, a lot of vets . . . some of my friends . . . they quit livin'. I might have too. But the dreams still come, and I still feel it overpowerin' me sometimes."

"Killing someone—even in war—gives mortals a lot of guilt to deal with, Bob. It takes time."

We had the horses out of the trailer, saddled and ready, just as the first light of dawn touched the horizon. Bob gave me a sheepskin to put in my saddle. "Save you from makin' those saddle sores worse," he said, a knowing smile on his face.

As the horses pushed into the hills I thought about what Bob was feeling. What I felt for so long. The Atonement had finally done it for me. I'd have to explain that when the time was right.

The sun glistened in full glory when we reached the top of the first ridge. The sweet scent of pine and morning dew on grass was in the air, and the birds sang into a gentle wind. It was a beautiful, magnificent morning that was clear enough to see the majestic Tetons to the northwest, beyond the Gros Ventre range.

After a breather for both animals and riders we descended into the next canyon and then climbed another ridge. The area was primitive, steep, and the last place I would have looked for an oil rig. I was glad to have the big buckskin under me again, his strong legs making the steep climb seem easy.

Two hours later we gazed down on a narrow canyon with steep slopes on three sides, a dirt road at the northeast end. In the center of a spot slashed out of the mountain by D-10 cats stood a red oil rig. A number of small buildings dotted the landscape, and a chainlink fence surrounded the approximately five-acre operation. I swept the length of the galvanized links with my binoculars.

A camouflaged gun emplacement, two men with a .50 caliber machine gun, its ugly nose sticking toward the gate at the lower end. After learning of Thunderbolt's role, I should not have been surprised. But surveying the length of its barrel and perceiving the destruction it could do constituted a stark contrast to the peace and serenity of pine-covered mountains.

I continued my search and found additional units, all carefully placed and hidden from the untrained eye. "I have three emplacements, two men at each, and an additional four men roaming the perimeter. All dressed in green and brown camouflage, all well armed. Trained professional mercenaries, it looks like."

"I have the same on the other side. And . . . inside the fence I spot another six men dressed as rig hands, but they're packing weapons. A tarped trailer sits in the middle of the compound, and I'm bettin' that underneath that tarp is a weapon of considerable size. Why all the fire power? Don't see nothin' to warrant it." We both lowered the binoculars and sat back on our haunches. "I'd bet if some federal government official turned up in this valley for a short visit or inspection, those guys down there would disappear in a hurry.

"Let's see what else we've got here." The oil rig was some distance off, and men looked like ants as they climbed and worked on the platform and in the mud surrounding it. A diesel-powered generator posed to one side of the rig itself, plus numerous hoses like snakes out in the sun. Two pumps, stacks of pipe, and other paraphernalia were crammed into the minimal space cleared directly around the rig.

Dug around the one-hundred-square-foot drilling platform was a twenty-four-inch trench filled with liquid sludge. The trench reached down the canyon and fed into a freshwater stream, polluting it. It seemed to be runoff from water being used to soften the ground as they drilled, or possibly to get rid of water they hit in pockets. We scanned each foot, each inch, looking for something that deserved the honor of such military attention. There was nothing out of the ordinary. An oil rig doing what oil rigs do. Bob took pictures with his telephoto while I retrieved a map from my saddlebags.

"That's where we are," I said. The other two rigs are located about equidistant from this one, say five miles by horseback, one to the east, one to the west."

I looked through the binoculars again, frustrated. "Bob, what in the name of death and destruction are they so protective of? I haven't seen this kind of protection for a compound since Nam!"

Bob looked through the binoculars again, and then he walked to his horse and mounted up and placed his binoculars back in his saddlebags. "I'm thirsty; wanta drink?" He reined his horse toward a trail that led into the canyon.

I hesitated, then shrugged my shoulders and followed. *Take the offensive. Strut right down there into the lion's den, so she won't think you're there to harm her. Why not? We'd at least get a closer look. I have lived to a ripe old age, haven't I?* I swung my leg up after putting the .45 pistol in my belt at the small of my back, covering it with my shirt, and snapping up the light Levi jacket.

We hadn't gone a hundred yards before two men—unarmed—stepped into the path from behind heavy bushes. I had sighted their first gun emplacement about fifty feet further down and closer to the fence, hidden in a pocket of small trees and shrubbery.

Both were dressed in camouflaged field uniforms, military boots, and dark green berets. One was blond with a heavy, waxed mustache pointing toward his ears. About six feet, with broad shoulders and a flat nose, he looked like a man to avoid.

The other was dark complexioned, short, and solid. His boots showed a good attempt at a spit polish scuffed by rocks, shrubs, and a light layer of dust. His uniform was pressed with a crease you would cut your fingers on. Attached to their sleeves both wore a round emblem with a gold star in the center that was crossed by a white thunderbolt. A matching patch was on the beret. The heavier man, with the handlebar mustache, had two bars underneath his emblem, an apparent sign of rank. Because his hand was behind his back I figured he wasn't as unarmed as I had first thought. He smiled and spoke with an accent I couldn't place. "You gentlemen realize this is privately leased property?"

Bob answered. "Figured it was, inside the fence. Didn't know *this* was. Just thought we'd be sociable, and water the horses." Bob's face didn't reveal any animosity, but I noticed he had released the thong from his holstered pistol.

The waxed mustache responded with a wry grin. "I think not. The boys down there are too busy to do much socializing. What're you doing out this far, anyway?"

Bob lifted his leg up and hung it over the saddle horn. "Spottin' elk for the fall hunt. I work as a guide, and this feller's payin' my fee. We like to know where the animals are hangin' out before we wander all over tarnation lookin' for 'em. Seen any?"

"Saw a few east of here." He was measuring us with his steel-gray eyes, a look I had seen more than once. Modern-day guns for hire are as ready to kill as any that drew a gun in a western movie. "Not many, though. If I were you I'd try to the south." It was more of a command than an offer of help. "We've been hired by a large international drilling firm to keep people clear of this area. There has been a threat of industrial espionage." He smiled. "People just can't seem to get along nowadays."

Bob tipped his hat back on his forehead and looked thoughtfully into the distance, as if deciding about the steely gray eyes' suggestion for direction. Then he put his foot back in the stirrup and prepared to ride. "Thanks for the help. Best way to get past this fence right or left?"

The foreigner answered coldly. "Back the way you came."

The other nudged him and faked a laugh. "Left, down the canyon, but my friend is probably right. The *safest* way is that way." He pointed in the direction from which we had come.

Bob touched his hat. "Much obliged." He turned his horse and headed back up the trail. I gave them one last look. Definitely the type to bash a man's face in. I reined the buckskin up the trail.

Though we didn't see them, they followed us for some distance. We had both been in the service long enough to feel an enemy presence. Their smell choked the air.

We pushed south a few miles before thinking it safe enough to change directions. It took us another four hours to get to the next rig, but number three well wasn't any different than number one. Same fence, same armed guards patrolling, same gun emplacements but in different locations, same hoses only without a stream. These hoses poured their refuse into a large tanker parked a hundred feet from the rig. When full, another took its place. They were extracting a lot of water, two tankers every three hours.

We were careful to keep out of sight. Paramilitaries such as the two we had run into were efficient. They would be in touch with all units under command. Our presence had been duly noted and logged, and being seen again could mean serious trouble.

It was frustrating. The evidence was real enough. Something heavy-duty was going on. But what? You don't hire gorillas like these for "potential" industrial espionage. There was definitely more to it than the surface appearance. "Could be an artillery stash," said Bob. "They have enough weapons around here to make that believable."

"Yeah, but for what purpose? No offense, Bob, but Jackson Hole isn't exactly located near any strategic sites."

"One, Idaho boy, and you should know it better than I do. The Idaho Nuclear Testing Laboratory. If someone needed material to make a bomb, or needed to steal a device to hold the government hostage, that'd be a likely target."

"Hmm. Could be. We'd better have the senator check out what's going on out there." Somehow I wasn't convinced. Why here? Why not get closer to the target, in the Sawtooths maybe?

It was too late to get to the last rig, so we hung around to see if anyone familiar popped in for a visit. Nothing. The sun began to close in on the ridge to the west, bringing an evening that was calm, cool, and beautiful.

The night shift arrived in a van and replaced the day crew. Lights flicked on and dimly illuminated the rig platform and surrounded work area and the front hallway in the main building. The rest of the compound receded into darkness.

Bob made no effort to head in the direction of the trailer and pickup. Instead, after taking care of the horses and hiding them in a nearby heavily forested ravine, he settled into a soft spot hidden from view by fallen logs and fell asleep.

I found a spot of my own and began to check the inside of my eyelids for leaks. We would need to be rested.

Bob gently shook me awake. It was well after dark, and the lights of the rig down in the canyon could be seen clearly, but the clatter of metal was muffled by the heavier night air.

Bob pulled three tins of camouflage face paint from his saddlebags, along with a couple of dark-colored stocking caps

and sweatshirts. "In Nam I always did my best work at night."
He smiled.

I applied the paint liberally, which evoked thoughts of training I had some twenty years earlier in night maneuvers. Every pilot went through it because every pilot was in danger of needing it. I had used it twice.

"You ready?" Bob asked.

"Poor choice of questions, captain, I . . ."

"Havin' second thoughts?" he asked without accusing.

"Aren't you?"

"Yeah. Come on, let's get it done and see if we can make heads or tails of this." He edged into the darkness.

We picked a blind spot between emplacements and then concentrated on getting past the fence. It looked even more formidable when lying twenty-five feet away in thick brush. We searched for a spot where there might be a depression in the ground large enough to slide under without being seen by guards. Nothing. The top was heavily ornamented with circles of razor-sharp wire and was fully visible from any of the four directions. Definitely out.

Bob signaled for me to follow. Withdrawing into the thick forest, we worked our way to a vantage point a short fifty feet from the gate.

"I clocked those trucks earlier," he said. "They come through here about every two hours, and one is due anytime. A bump another hundred yards down the road will slow them down considerably. That's where we'll get on."

"But the shine of the stainless steel tanks in the light from the rig! We'll stand out like bugs on flypaper."

He shook his head. "Next to the wheels, inside above the axle, each side. Grab hold and hug up tight. The duals will block their view unless they check awful careful, and I haven't seen them do it all day."

"Yeah, but that was day." My heart was pounding, the adrenaline shooting through my brain, creating an excitement mingled with fear I hadn't felt in a long time.

The clamor of an approaching truck sent us hustling further down the canyon and through the trees. Bob pointed at a spot for me to wait, then he darted across the road and hid himself in deep grass. The truck rounded the turn and slowed for the bump, the driver concentrating on the gate. I ran for the rear wheels, forced my body into the slight cavity under the tank, and hung onto the rods that were welded to the axle.

The truck was cleared through the gate as I strained to look for anyone coming my direction. Suddenly the trailer shuddered at a missed gear, and I lost my hold, my upper torso banging into the dusty road below, my legs straining to hold me from falling altogether. I grabbed for the rod above me, but it was too far away. Straining my body upward with the only leverage of my legs, I almost tore my taut stomach muscles in two. My fingers caught hold of something, and I pulled upward and flattened myself in the cavity just as we passed the guard closing the gate behind us. The dusty sweat covering my face and caked in the corners of my eyes and mouth precipitated a cough. I stifled it, knowing the noise could be fatal.

Bob signaled to release, and we rolled clear, hiding ourselves in the shadows of a stack of pipe.

"Jeremiah, you scared breakfast out of me. You all right?"

I spat to clear my mouth of grit and dust. "Okay. what now?"

"You check out the main buildin'. I want to get a closer look at the rig. Watch for other emplacements, and see if you can see what kind of communications system they're usin'."

"Gotcha."

I wended in the general direction of the main building and stopped at the pump house, which ran from a diesel-powered generator some hundred yards away and which was doing its job nicely. Nothing suspicious.

Creeping closer to the main office, I tried to stay clear of light falling like nets through the windows.

"Good evening. May we be of help? Or do you think you could find what you're looking for on your own?"

I froze, cold steel pressing against my spine.

19

Owens smiled in the dim light from the rig, then used the gun to give an "after you" gesture in the direction of the office door as he slipped the .45 from my belt.

Winters posed at a large metal desk strewn with papers and flanked by our newest friends, the two paramilitaries we had met earlier in the day. There were no signs of recognition. The camouflage paint . . .

Owens pointed to a chair against the far wall. "Sit!" he said. He walked over to the mustached soldier, whispered something in his ear, and received an affirmative nod. So much for paint.

"Would you care to give us your name?" Winters asked. I remained silent, looking the office over carefully. He continued. "I thought not. Never mind. It doesn't matter. Why would a hunter be skulking around in the dark on private property, dressed like this? We have nothing to hide, and—"

There was movement at the door as Bob was shoved through the opening, a sniper's Remington 40xB with 12x Redfield scope attached pointed at the small of his back.

Owens motioned with his gun for Bob to join me. He took a stance leaning against the wall. Like mine, his gun had been taken.

Winters smiled again. "Now, as I was saying. We have nothing to hide here. You would have been welcome to look around all you liked if you had come to our main office in Afton. As it is I'm afraid we must decline you hospitality. However, if you wish to have someone else come and look at our operation you may do so. Through proper channels, of course."

He looked at us confidently. Up close his pocked face resembled small, dirty-looking craters. His mustache thinned to accommodate the extended scar in the flesh below the cheekbone. But it was the eyes that bothered me most. They were empty of life, like cesspools in which only death lingered. They caused me to shiver.

Winters spoke, looking at Bob. "This is very disturbing to us, you must understand. We're involved in very important drilling operations here upon which TriStar stockholders are placing a good deal of money. We can only assume that you are involved in industrial espionage of some kind. I think you understand the consequences of such charges?"

Rock and a hard place! A comment my father always used in situations my brother and I fell into in which there was no way out without at least some pain.

He went on. "However, we are willing to allow you to leave here without calling the authorities if you will give us some idea of who you work for and what their intentions are." He smiled with the warmth of a dead man.

Are they playing us along? I thought. *Surely Owens knows who I am . . . and yet . . . maybe he wasn't at my house.*

Bob spoke. "No offense, Mr. . . . ?" Winters just stared at him, still smiling. "Our reputations wouldn't be worth much if we did that, would they?"

Winters' smile was still painted on, but the eyes were definitely thinning into slits.

At his side Owens tensed as if a big cat ready to pounce for the kill. Winters put his hand on him. "Let's stop playing games, shall we?" He looked hard into Bob's eyes as he stood. "I don't know who you are, but I will." He turned to me. "As for you . . . Mr. Daniels . . . My rather anxious friend here says he knows you well, having been a . . . shall we say 'guest' in your home?"

The belly does strange things at times like these. In an effort to keep things under control, your mind tells you to move around, and this makes the men with the guns nervous, making you start the cycle again.

"With a sawed-off shotgun up my nose I didn't have a choice, now did I? My 'guests' are better behaved and much more talented than this fleshy piece of evidence for the theory of evolution." Now I was being sarcastic.

Owens was turning white with anger. "Mr. Daniels," Winters went on, "you seem to have a talent for getting in the way.

"But, your presence is a nuisance at best. It's not really important that I know your reasons. In a short time it will make no difference, anyway." My stomach did more flip-flops when he let go of Owens' arm and nodded. I didn't like the signal and firmed my posture as Owens, taking a rather wicked-looking buck knife from his Levi jacket, came my way.

"We have it from good authority, Daniels, that you lost an eye in Vietnam. How unfortunate for you." He placed the knife against my cheek, and I reacted with a cringe. "With the flick of this blade *I* can take the other." He inched it toward the socket, and I winced, fear inside my chest.

Winters spoke. "The message should be clear to you, Mr. Daniels." Owens backed away, an evil grin on his face. My stomach felt like vomiting on his shoes.

Winters stood and went to the small window and looked into the dim light emanating from the rig. His posture indicated careful thinking, planning his next words.

"There's nothing any of you can do to us. We are beyond the point where flimsy attempts like this could keep us from our goal." I felt the coldness of his voice. "No one will stop us. No one. Others have tried; they have failed." He turned and focused his satanic stare on the bridge of my nose. "Go to Europe, Mr. Daniels. Stay for a few weeks. Take Ms. Freeman. Enjoy her presence while she's in the world." The threat wasn't even cleverly veiled, but it had its desired effect— standing the hair up on the back of my neck.

He looked at Bob. "And now I know you as well, Mr. Freeman. How silly of me not to realize! You should be glad I have. It's saved your life, for now.

"As you both can see, Mr. Owens and his friends would love nothing more than to kill you. Now. But I am of the opinion that the senator knows of your whereabouts and would have operations put to a halt here until your bodies were found. I cannot allow that." He smiled wryly. "I must consider the stockholders. We've promised them . . . well, Mr. Daniels, you know how stockholders are when companies don't meet their expectations."

He continued arrogantly. "Now, is there anything else you'd like to see here? Mr. Owens could certainly show you around. I think you'll find everything in order." He laughed. "No? Then I think it's time for you to return to your horses. Mr. Owens, will you act as escort? We don't want them to get lost in the dark, now do we? The senator would be most upset." He paused, then turned directly to face Owens. "And do not damage them or give them any legal reason to return. Do you understand?"

Even Owens was afraid of Winters. In this case I was grateful.

"Now then, gentlemen. We have noted with the sheriff's department a threat of industrial espionage. You have been duly photographed near this complex giving false information about your identities, and now breaking into it covered with that ridiculous paint, and carrying concealed weapons. Should you return we will identify you and have you hauled to jail, if we do not shoot you. We're legal here, even if a little overzealous in our choice of weaponry for our self-protection. By the way, your camera and maps have been confiscated by my men."

Definitely a rock and a hard place, I thought.

"Should you go to the authorities with your story, we'll know, and we'll take proper steps to make you look foolish before we identify you as industrial agents." He gestured toward the door with his hand. "Get them out of here. And gentlemen, give the senator my best." His laugh filled the suddenly cold night air.

20

We were back at the trailer about 4:30 A.M., bushed, frustrated, and angry. Had they just happened to be at the rig, leaving Duquesne's side long enough to come and check out operations on an insignificant oil well in the mountains of Wyoming? I doubted it. Security was tight. Even two hunters had demanded immediate attention. Something was happening, all right, something they didn't want seen. TriStar was the link, and TriStar was now the focus for us.

We had been lucky. They were dangerous, and another confrontation could be fatal. They had been forced to let us go because they knew who we were. Not so with Dooley. They hadn't established that connection to the senator and had felt no reason to be cautious. I decided their reluctance to kill us on the spot meant they didn't want trouble, and our disappearing might force a shutdown of the entire operation, whatever it was! At this point they couldn't afford that.

More frustration!

He knew who and where we were. Mike, the senator, all of us were in danger. How? Royalty? Had to be, didn't it?

I felt exhausted and found it almost too much to load the saddles, rifles, and other gear in the tack compartment at the front of the trailer, to put the horses in their stalls, and to feed them the hay we had brought along.

By the time we were headed down the steep canyon road my eyes were drooping shut and my mind was a fog.

Half asleep, I felt Bob shove on the brakes, hard, and heard the pedal slam against the floor. My eyes popped open as we lurched around a switchback turn, out of control. He shoved again. Nothing. He shifted the five-speed down to third, but with the weight of the trailer behind us we kept picking up speed, forcing the motor to high enough RPMs that it was within seconds of blowing apart.

Bob manhandled the rig down the dirt and gravel road, the trailer swaying and swinging around curves at better than fifty miles per hour. I pulled my seat belt tighter, then pushed hard against the floorboards with my feet, and the too-thin roof with my hands, bracing for what would come. The pickup slammed against a tree that was too close to a corner, then another, but somehow Bob kept control. I glanced toward the trailer and watched it jerk onto one wheel, tipping and causing the pickup to jackknife. Bob tried to adjust, but without brakes the next corner was on us before the rig was steady.

We almost made it.

Mike filled my mind as the pickup and trailer spun around me, the hard, cold metal grabbing at my flesh, the glass shattering toward my face. I saw a flash of dark blue as the trailer careened past us, the pickup rolling completely once, brutally banging my head twice and sending me into the black abyss of unconsciousness.

It rushed into my mind. The carnage and the burned-out Indian camp where his wife and son had been taken prisoners by the Blackfoot raiding party. Crossing the raging spring runoff of the river even though unable to swim. Then finding his family. Attacking his enemy in a desperate attempt to free them from sure and terrible death. He filled my head, haunting, the pouch and its contents glaring at me, the pouch stained with his blood as his wife and son stooped over him, her hands pressing into the wound trying to stem the flow of his life. The face of the young man who had killed his father's assailant seconds too late blazed into my mind as he stood over his mother and the lifeless body of Finan Daniels, a defense against anyone else who might come against them. The pouch. Opened. The bloodstained document carefully slipped into its opening. A document whose signature I could see clearly for the first time.

I fought to be free of it, to struggle back to the world I knew still existed for me just beyond the darkness, just beyond the dream. Laboring under the pain in my chest and arms, I fought my way back to reality, the dream the focus of my desperate desire to be free.

Now, a new stench. Gasoline mixed with hot antifreeze and oil. I focused on it, trying to be free of the other smell. The smell of blood and burnt powder. My hand swept my face like a tentacle from some foreign body, then fumbled to my chest and down to my legs, which were bound by twisted, cruel metal.

My chest felt crushed, my right arm strangely numb. The darkness. Why the darkness? Night. No, it was near morning. There should be some light. I panicked, the thought of blindness slapping against me like waves, my hand striking out to be free.

"Take it easy, Jerry. I . . . I'm almost free," Bob moaned, his coarse voice filled with the pain as he worked against the crushed and torn wreckage that held us trapped. I attempted deep breaths to get control of the horror that gripped my senses.

"Ugh! That's it. I'm out."

"How bad are you, Bob? What about the gas? Any fire?" I asked desperately.

"Broken arm, bleedin'. Ribs, maybe somethin' internal. Head, full of cotton, and I'm dizzy. Maybe some shock." He paused to get his breath. "There's gas on the ground, but no fire." He coughed deep in his chest. "No time to take up smokin'. How about you?"

"My right arm feels numb, and . . . and I can't see."

"Take it easy. I'll get you out. He stumbled around the front of the pickup to my door. He pulled on it, trying to wrench it free. I felt the pain in his efforts and in his labored breathing.

"Won't budge," he said. "I'll try to get you free . . . from my . . . side." He paused, getting his strength.

"We're lucky, Jerry. The pickup . . . looks like it took a direct hit . . . from a 125mm M1 tank shell."

Fumbling around in the back, clanking metal tools. "I've got a crowbar . . . I . . ." I felt the impact as he struck the pickup and fell to the ground.

"Bob? Are you okay? What happened? Where are you? *Bob!*"

The uninvited anxiety crept back into my brain and tightened across my chest muscles, cutting my air off and forcing me to hyperventilate. Deep breaths! Try to get control! "Relax. Got to relax. I'll be of no help to myself or Bob if I don't relax. Got to think!" More deep breaths.

My free arm reached, felt, became my eyes. The dash pressed against my chest, and I lay half slumped in the seat, legs crammed against the floorboards. My numb right arm was pinched tightly between the smashed door and seat. Slowly I began working it free with my left arm, allowing the blood to flow and the feeling to return, bringing some relief to my anxiety.

Reaching where I thought the steering wheel must be, I found it mangled and facing upward. Bob's seat cushion was wet and sticky. Blood. The amount frightened me.

I used my legs as leverage to force the dash away from my body, simultaneously pushing forward with my good arm and up with my legs.

Nothing. Filling my lungs with air, I pushed harder. Pressure released just slightly across my midsection. I tried to slip sideways. Still no go.

As I repeated the performance the weight of the dash relented. Grabbing the steering wheel, I pulled while pushing with my legs again and again, finally slipping free.

The exhaustion raked my body, sending pain through every muscle. Forcing myself through the twisted metal of the driver's door, I propped myself against the pickup and gently rubbed the injured arm for signs of a fracture. Bruises and pulled muscles kept me from raising it more than inches from my side.

The sweat dripped out of my hair and from my chin and down my neck, even though the early morning air was cool. I fell to the ground, dizzy, exhausted. *No more! I need to rest.*

My fingers fearfully touched my good eye, exploring for damage from a splinter or a sharp piece of metal. The fleshy skin around it was sore and bruised, but the eye itself was intact. Vision wasn't totally gone as I had first feared, and I wondered how much was due to blindness and how much due to the darkness of night. I tried to focus, to stare at the pickup only inches away, then at more distant trees. I caught only glimpses of light enshrouding objects not clear. I remembered how hopeless I had felt when the other eye was gone, and how for weeks I had had nightmares of the doctors removing the good one while I watched.

Get control! You're not blind! Get control!

Reaching toward the ground, I groped for Bob. I felt the warmth of his breath before actually touching him, then I gently probed his body, searching for injuries.

His arm was cleanly broken and bleeding badly. With effort my fingers searched deeper into the wound, feeling the intermittent pump of the sticky liquid near my index finger. Pushing on it, I was able to stop the flow. When I released pressure it began again. An artery.

Holding the finger in place, I ripped my shirttail, momentarily forgetting the injured arm. Pain shot through my chest, taking my breath away.

After a moment I shoved the cloth in the bleeding hole. More cautiously, I tore more cloth and wrapped a tight bandage around the arm, cutting off the flow.

I slid my palms over his legs and torso. They seemed okay, but he was in shock and shaking. Something warm was needed to cover him. My jacket came off first, and I laid it across his chest. It wouldn't be enough.

A sudden thought jarred me, and I stood. I must find the horse trailer. My fingers located the back end of the pickup. It was mashed in on the driver's side clear to the rear. A flattened and disfigured tire. No fender—and the trailer was gone.

Holding my breath while funneling all sounds into my brain, I listened for breathing or the kick of a hoof against the trailer. It had to be close by.

A dull, metallic thud. Something struggling, downhill, below the pickup. The blue of the trailer going past us during the crash flashed in my mind.

Carefully—both hands in front of me—I picked my way through underbrush, jamming a finger as I stumbled over a large piece of metal.

Pushing it aside with a frustrated curse, I searched again, stumbling, groping, listening.

My shinbone hit it first, then my hand was against the cold steel of the trailer. As I called to the buckskin, hooves danced nervously. He was still standing!

My fingers found the latch as they groped the surface. A moment later the gate swung open—unevenly and with effort, but open. My voice broke the still air as I talked to him, calming him, afraid he might kick me clear into the next canyon. Picking a moment, I eased my body in, keeping my back against the trailer, and began working forward, petting, talking, and easing his tense muscles with my hands. By some miracle there was no serious damage.

Finding the halter rope, I quickly untied him and eased him back and out of the trailer and tied him to the gate. The other side of the trailer, solidly ensconced in trees and shrubs, had taken the direct hit of two large pine trees that stopped the downhill plummet, killing the bay mare.

Resting, taking deep breaths and working to get more oxygen, I felt nauseated and dizzy. My bones ached clear to the marrow, and my head felt as if little men were pounding at the inside of my skull with miniature jackhammers.

I forced myself up and worked the jammed access door of the tack compartment with a rock, hammering the latch until it slipped free. Using a stick I pried the door open enough to get an arm inside.

The saddle blankets were there, flung over saddles, and still wet on one side from the lathered horses. Clutching them, I struggled uphill to Bob and covered him, hopeful it would be enough. I collapsed at his side, laying my head on the cool but soft and inviting grass.

"Jerry . . . you got out? How . . . Jerry, wake up."

His voice sounded distant but forced me to open my heavy eyelids. I wondered how long it had been since I had passed out.

"Is it really dark out here? I can't see a dollar's worth of light," I said.

His cough sounded congested. "Dark, but first light is on the horizon. Not enough to see much, though. Do you feel as bad as you look?"

"Worse." I pushed myself against the pickup. "Careful of your arm if you have a mind to move around. It snapped right in half, sticking through the flesh about where your bicep used to be. You won't be lifting much for a while. Is the bleeding still stopped?" My body tried to get to its feet.

"Yeah. Hurts like crazy, though."

"Can you get up?" I reached down and gave him my good hand. The buckskin danced a little as we trudged in his direction and away from acrid gasoline and untidy wreckage.

"Wow! How did you get him out of that mess, Jerry?"

"The trailer is that bad, huh? Hard to tell using my hands. Are we where you want to be yet? Any further and it's going to cost you triple, or you'll have to carry me!" I said weakly.

He let go and eased himself to the ground. I reached out, found a tree, and did the same. After a long pause to catch our breath I apologized. "Sorry for being so stupid."

"Me too. One thing for Winters, he's a convincing liar. I

didn't even consider somethin' like this. They were way ahead of us. Makes you wonder if they'll be comin' to check their work."

"Yeah, give me a minute to get enough strength to survive what we have to do," I said, placing my bruised skull against the rough bark of the tree trunk. "When you think about it this was really their only choice. Having us arrested would be time-consuming and would draw a lot of attention to themselves. This is simpler, and it would take a lot of convincing to make anyone believe they were involved." I shifted a little. The pain in my arm forcing the adjustment.

"The few questions that might be asked by authorities could be handled from their Afton offices. I think we made them nervous."

"Yeah, nervous," he said. "We'd better get out of here, Jerry."

"What's your plan?" I asked.

"The buckskin, double. They gave you back your gun, didn't they?"

"Yeah, but no bullets. I stuck it behind the seat. Better forget it. Come on, let's get the buckskin's reins and a rifle out of the trailer compartment."

The reins were out of reach, but the 30-30 slipped through the opening. "Be a challenge to try and shoot, won't it?" I said. "Me holding and pointing, and you telling me which way."

He laughed until he coughed that congested cough again. "Knock it off, Jerry. You tryin' to kill me?"

I rigged the halter by Bob's instructions, then gave him a leg up. He maneuvered the buckskin over to the trailer, where I was able to get high enough to mount without trouble.

With me hanging on, Bob guided us through thick trees, telling me when to duck. We had gone three or four hundred yards when we heard a vehicle climbing the road below. In a matter of moments it stopped at what must have been the crash site. Two doors slammed. It was followed by a string of cursing.

Slipping from the buckskin, I helped Bob down. He led me and the horse into thick brush, hiding us, coaxing the nervous animal into silence. We listened, waiting. Bob had the rifle and handed it to me. "Get behind me and put it over my shoulder. I'll direct your shot right or left, and then you fire when I tell you."

As we maneuvered I was thankful to hear doors slam again and an engine start up, I silently celebrated the sound of wheels peeling against gravel.

Bob crumpled to the ground, passing out in the grass. I slipped down beside him, checking his pulse. Weak, but even. I lay down again. Too tired. I fought unconsciousness, but lost the battle, finally letting the waves of blackness overwhelm me.

The voice in my dream drew me. Was it Liz? The words were gentle and soothing, her touch cool to my brow.

"Jerry? Can you hear me? Can you wake up?"

My mouth was dry and full of cotton, my voice refusing to respond.

"Jerry? Can you hear me? Jerry?"

"M . . . Mike . . . How . . . ?"

"Thank heaven! Dad!" she cried. "They're here. Hurry!

"You're okay now. Lie still."

"What about . . . Bob?" I asked. "Is he okay? I . . ."

"He's right here. He's breathing, but he's unconscious. Don't . . ."

My body felt like lead, but I tried to force myself up, only to fall back.

Someone pushed through the willows. "How bad, Mike?" the senator said. I thought of our conversation the night before about Dooley and wondered if he was ready for this new shock.

"We'll need stretchers right away. Bob . . . has lost a lot of blood. He's unconscious and has a very weak pulse."

I heard the senator scramble through the bushes yelling at others. My mind was a haze, darkness beginning to collapse into it again, snuffing out the images and the dim light overhead.

21

A gentle breeze blew across my forehead as I said the last words of dedication over the grave. Mike held my arm, and I placed my hand on hers, her slight weight heavy against me.

Peace had come to my troubled mind as I sat in the funeral, peace that had made dedicating the grave easier. The anger had been real enough—the frustration almost overwhelming—while mending in the hospital. Good people had died because of the greed and power hunger of a few. How many others would suffer? Who else would have to die?

Bishop Klingler had stopped in just before I checked out of the hospital to come to the funeral. I had asked him for a blessing, hoping to shake off the hate and anger.

The walk back to the house was a short one, the sun warm as it beat down on my dark pin-striped suit. I loosened my tie and took the jacket off and flung it over my shoulder cautiously, the battered arm still painful.

Some had driven their cars the short distance from the house to the grave site and were standing about visiting. Some approached us giving their condolences to Mike and the senator. I felt out of place.

"How ya doin', cowboy?" Charla had come to the rescue.

I smiled. "Okay. You?"

"Better. You look good in dark glasses, but in that suit, well, the Mafia came to mind." She smiled.

"The hospital called just before the funeral. Bob's itching to come home. Somehow he convinced the doctor to sign a release. You didn't leave him a gun, did you?"

"No." I chuckled under my breath. "But he did have one

good arm." The three days of recuperation had been the longest of my life. All I could think of was TriStar, Duquesne, and what they were up to. The delay might leave them free to accomplish their goals. The frustration of lying helpless, waiting for the whole thing to collapse around our ears before we could figure it out, nullified the doctor's orders to get more rest.

And Mike. I felt the love, and I saw it as my vision began to return. It was in her voice, in her touch and her kiss, in her concern; but the hardness returned, thrusting itself between us when—as a matter of events—the Church was mentioned. I attended sacrament meeting in the morning before the funeral—alone.

The senator had been busy reading Sellars' reports, gleaning further information from other sources, and putting together a few missing pieces. The financial scheme was becoming more clear by the hour, thanks to Mike's SEC assistants and what Sellars had revealed. There was nothing like it in past history, and nearly thirty billion dollars had been pinned down, most of it in the United States. Approximately seven hundred false accounts had been identified. Duquesne's group made the ten largest insurance companies look like petty cash.

In the Middle East things had fallen into place as the senator had predicted. He showed me some confidential reports that confirmed what he had said, making an attack on Kuwait not only imminent but brutal. I began to gain a different perception of one man's evil nature.

"Are you seeing any better?" Charla asked.

"Up close. I can see the new worry wrinkles around your pretty eyes, but distance is still blurred a bit." She poked me in the ribs.

I thought of the doctor's words. Shock. No real damage. Give it some time. "You're a lucky man, Mr. Daniels," he had said. He didn't know the half of it.

Charla reached through my arm as Mike let go, saying something about final arrangements. She pulled me away in the direction of the house.

"Bob told me about what happened up there. Thank you." She paused while I worked my way up the front steps onto the porch. The bruises and sprains, cuts and scrapes made moving difficult.

"I'm glad you were together. You make a good team."

"How long before he's back to full steam?" I asked.

She laughed lightly. "Tomorrow probably. Stubborn as a mule. One good thing is that the cast will keep him partially sidelined; he lost a lot of blood, so he'll be weak for a while. The worst thing is . . . he will be pure misery to live with."

Most everyone had returned the short distance to the house. There were cars pulling away down the lane, the slamming of doors as others prepared to leave, and the low rumble of funeral talk nearby as people said all the wrong things for all the right reasons. To the left I could hear Mike's voice—tired, trying to respond to the same words over and over, but seeming to hold up well.

"How many were here?" I asked.

"A couple of hundred. Dooley was a well-liked young man."

We sat quiet, emotions close to the surface, thinking our own thoughts. Pain, I decided, was a relative thing. My body ached from the physical punishment of the mangled pickup, but somehow it seemed insignificant to what all of us were feeling inside.

"Are you really okay, Charla?" I asked.

"Yes. When the senator first told us about sending Dooley up there blind I wanted to flog him with my bullwhip. But how can you punish a man who is hurting worse than anyone else for that mistake? Your prayer helped too—at the grave, I mean. What was it you said . . . that he would come forth on the morning of the first resurrection? I believe Dooley will, and knowing that helps a lot.

"The Church people are here to pick up the chairs and tables. I need to thank them. Will you be all right here?" she asked.

I nodded. "Tell the bishop to see me a minute, will you?"

The banging of chairs, intermingled with the echo of departing cars and subdued voices turning to lighter subjects, lifted a little of the sullen mood that's always present at funerals. "Are you okay, Jerry?" Mike asked, coming up the steps.

"Hi. Yeah, I'm fine. How about you?"

Mike sat down in the swing, snuggling close, laying her head on my shoulder. "I'm glad it's over."

"Frustrated?" I asked.

"They have taken away something very dear to me and to my family. I feel helpless. Like a victim, I think.

"Then when we found the pickup and the trailer . . . then the mare . . . I nearly went to pieces . . ." She struggled to control the tears.

I put my arm around her and pulled her closer. It had been a rough three days for all of them. After Bob had recovered somewhat, the senator pulled them all together and told them about Dooley. Mike had taken it the hardest, and after we were alone she vented her feelings through a torrent of tears.

Later that night, just before they left Bob and me to go home, the senator had tried to convince us to back out and turn this one over to trained professionals. After a small argument everyone agreed it was too late for that. We must take precautions and be less foolish in considering what they might do, but we owed it to Dooley.

We had decided to notify the sheriff and enlist his "off the record" help. Once he heard the story he gave us full cooperation, setting up around-the-clock surveillance at all three wells and using his best deputies, experienced in Special Forces training from Vietnam, and hunting techniques gleaned from years in the mountains. We also requested a tail on Winters and Owens. He obliged, giving us twenty-four-hour reports of where they were, which helped us all sleep better at night.

Since the moment Bob and I had checked into the hospital the ranch hands had been kept busy close by the ranch house. All of them had rifles close at hand, and most carried side arms. Open fields surrounded the ranch house, simplifying efforts to watch it. A watch was also placed on the side of the mountain to the east of the house, where the valley could be seen for a couple of miles in both directions. When unknown vehicles ventured past Slide Lake Park and the boat dock they monitored every move.

At first it had given me the jitters. Cowboys with loaded guns—some just out of high school and still shaving only once a week—might get the feeling of the old West and do something stupid, like shooting each other in the darkness. They surprised me by taking it seriously—no stupid talk.

"Mike," I said, leaving my thoughts. "I had the dream again. The one about the mountain man."

"And?" she asked, that slight stiffness in her voice.

I ignored it. "This time everything focused on a document in a leather case he wore around his neck and arm. I saw it up close. It was written in longhand, and was hard to read. You know, fancy circles on the *T*'s and *L*'s.

"In the other dreams he always tried to tell his wife and

son of the document's importance, but they couldn't understand. This time I understood. It was a land grant giving them deed to property that was to become their home."

"A land grant? Come on, Jerry. If what you have told me about this mountain man is true this area didn't even belong to the United States when he lived. How could he be granted land?"

"Look, I don't understand it either, but that's what I saw. A presidential grant for land. Ten thousand acres of it. Signed by President Millard Fillmore and, I quote, 'given for services rendered to the United States of America between the years of 1810 and 1815, to become effective on the first day of the first year in which said land is part of the territory of the United States,' unquote. It had the seal of the United States in the lower right-hand corner.

"Finan Daniels could settle his family on that land, knowing no one could ever take it away from him if or when it became a part of this nation. He could build a future without fear."

"What happened to it? Did they bury it with him?"

"The son dug a grave with his father's knife, wrapped the body in a buffalo robe, and buried him overlooking the valley. I could find the spot, I've seen it so many times. But then he gathered his father's belongings, including the pouch and document, and left with his mother. According to my grandfather's oral history they found the tribe and remained with them, the son eventually becoming their chief."

"Then what did happen to the grant?" she asked, frustrated.

"I don't know."

"You mean it just disappeared and hasn't been found since? Lost . . . forever?"

I nodded. "But it seems to me—if it's real—a presidential grant like that should have been recorded somewhere, shouldn't it?"

"Yes, but what difference does it make?"

"I can't answer that. I just feel it's important and I have to find out, that's all." I paused to move away from her and to the porch rail. I hadn't felt such tension between us before. I didn't like it.

After a moment she moved to my side. "I'm sorry, Jerry. I know it's important to you. Dad's aides in Washington can do some research. If it exists they'll . . ." Her body stiffened, and she moved away as Bishop Klingler came up the walk, her mood returning to cold toughness, arms folded, face firm.

He looked at her, confused, but went ahead. "Dooley had some personal things in a locker at the club. We played raquetball when he was in town. I'll see that you get them."

"Thank you," she said, reaching out with a stiff arm, shaking, then pulling back.

"Jerry, Charla said you wanted to see me before I leave?"

"Just to thank you. For everything. Especially the blessing this morning. I feel . . . a lot better." I wanted to say more, but Mike was making it so . . . uncomfortable.

"You're welcome. Be seeing you. Good luck." He walked away toward his pickup.

I turned and looked at Mike. "What was that all about?"

"What?" she said defensively.

"The chill you just sent through both of us was enough to freeze the warmest heart, Mike."

"I'm not feeling anything I shouldn't."

"Then why treat him that way?"

"I hardly know him."

"Hmm. Then it's what he represents?"

"What's that supposed to mean?"

"The Church, Mike. He represents the Church."

"That's not it. Not all of it."

"Then what?" I asked.

"He represents God, and I've been let down enough by God lately, thank you."

There it was. Old wounds, new wounds. Inactivity since her mother's death. Cold to his representative.

I waited. It was silent for long minutes.

"You explain something to me, Jerry. Why does God get away with it?"

She caught me off guard. "What?"

"Why does he get away with it?" she said adamantly. "Mom dies, Dooley dies, Liz dies, and we still give him our allegiance. If you had allowed Liz to die you wouldn't have gotten away with it. You would have been punished."

This was all new, and my head was swirling.

"Dad was partially at fault for Dooley's death because he didn't warn him. He'll go through hell for weeks, years, maybe the rest of his life, but not God. He doesn't stop it, and we not only don't yell at him—we thank him!

"When we catch Dooley's killers they'll be punished. That's

the law. What's the law when God fails, Jerry? More devoted worship?" The words were like knives—sharp, painfully cutting, and thrashing, trying to hurt.

"You expect God to rescue everyone from pain?" I asked.

"No. God doesn't exist." The words were cold as an icy wind, each emphasized separately.

"You're right." I paused, letting it sink in. "The kind of God you're talking about doesn't exist. If he did, mankind would have been annihilated ages ago and you and I wouldn't be having this conversation."

She sat in the big porch swing, her face set in concrete, looking out on the lawn.

"If God stopped killers, and dying, and accidents, and disease, and famine, and pestilence. If he stopped every individual from doing that which caused such things, he would interfere in our lives almost by the minute. To stop drunk drivers from killing he could grab their hand as they went to take a drink and then throw them across the room to teach them a lesson. Of course, some kind of lesson, forceful lesson, would have to be taught because they would just do it again. Or, maybe he should punish the real culprit, the president of the brewery. That's it, he could annihilate him and prevent drunk drivers by getting at the very roots, where the stuff is made.

"And what about abortions, Mike? Instead of man being able to make that decision—by fighting for or against it—he could just prevent it by saying anyone who did it will be ashes! And stealing, he could stop stealing, and immorality, and abuse, and . . . you name it, he could stop it!"

"He could," she said.

"Yes, he could," I replied quietly. "But he won't.

"That's not God, Mike. That's a dictator. I don't believe in dictators, earthbound or in heaven."

I turned and walked down the steps and toward the barn. It had been a few days since I had seen the buckskin. Now was a good time.

22

When the senator came into the den after dinner he went to his desk and began shuffling papers while watching me from the corner of his eye, debating, then sitting down, shrugging his shoulders as if deciding not to pursue what he was thinking.

I spoke first while handing him some papers. "I just finished reading what you compiled from the rest of Sellars' files. Not much new. Anything from WASHINGTON?"

"Nothing, yet. He says that to come up with the names of Defender and Commandant with such limited information is a thousand to one shot."

"I think we're running out of time," I said.

His eyebrows wrinkled. "Yes, Iraq's troops are in place, but they seem to be waiting for something else to happen. Something, I'm afraid, meant to hurt this country badly.

"What is the latest from your sources in Banner?" he asked.

"Nothing different. Duquesne's brokers, at least the ones we've pinpointed, aren't trading a thing! No buying, no selling. Just waiting."

"Our source in Baghdad has dried up altogether. Either scared, or dead. We haven't heard anything for four days. Needless to say, Washington is worried and even more adamant about keeping things out of normal channels. They're afraid the wrong word in the wrong place will somehow set things off, and we're not completely prepared to stop the end result. Frankly, I've never seen them this concerned."

"Senator, I've got another problem I'm a little confused about, and I need your help." I told him about the dream and the document. "Do you think you could get some of your aides to do some digging? I've got to get this thing off my mind!"

"I'll call in the morning." He smiled. "Sorry, but it sounds like a story right out of a mystery magazine, or the twilight zone."

"Thanks a bunch! I hope that's all it is."

"What next?" he asked.

I leaned forward. "It's time to pick up Ben Stevenson and have a little heart-to-heart. I had hoped for more from Sellars or maybe a revelation out at TriStar. Now . . . now I think our only chance is Duquesne's computer. Unless I miss my guess, Ben has the passwords to get us in."

"When?"

"I'll leave for Vegas tomorrow afternoon. Senator, doesn't it strike you as odd that Dooley would get onto something and not leave some sort of mesasge?"

"More than odd. Dooley was a very organized person. So much so it used to drive Bob crazy. The tack shed used to be a pile of saddles in the middle of the floor with a few bent nails for hanging ropes, halters, reins, and the like. Until Dooley organized it the summer of his senior year in high school. Now it's rows of saddle mounts, with names, numbers, boxes, all painted, a clean floor—the works."

"I can't help but think he left something at the playpen. I'd like to go back up there tomorrow before flying to Vegas."

"Fine, but I want a couple of my men to go along."

I agreed.

Mike was in the kitchen finishing up the last of the dishes. It was Mrs. O.'s evening off. I sat down at the table and watched her hazy form move around in front of me. "You're beautiful even when you're hazy, do you know that?"

She laughed lightly while continuing to mop up the counter with a dishcloth. "Thank you, I think," she said.

"Mike, we need to go for a ride in the morning, early."

"Do you think you're up to it already?"

"Yeah. I need the fresh air. So do you. But there's another purpose as well. I want to go back to the playpen."

She stopped. "Why back there?"

"I think Dooley may have left you and the senator something. There hasn't been anything turned up at your office, the house in Vegas, your dad's office in Washington, or here. He had to leave something somewhere; I can just feel it in my bones."

"Probably just the painful aftereffects of the accident," she said. I returned the smile.

"If he went to confront them after he sent that message to you—and I think he did—he must have been pretty sure of his ground." Her movements stiffened. I went on. "From everything I understand of Dooley he would have left you something pointing the way."

She was standing at the counter, silent, thinking, a sad look on her beautiful face. "Yes, you're right. And the playpen would have been the safest place."

"Yup." I hesitated, then went ahead. "I think TriStar is the key, Mike. Dooley got too close, so did Bob and I."

"What about the land grant?" she asked, shaking her head as if to brush aside an unpleasant thought."

"I told your dad about it after dinner and showed him on the map. He said he would have some of his people get on it first thing in the morning. It shouldn't be all that hard to find unless it's all a figment of my imagination.

"Do you want to go?"

She sat down at the table. "Yes. I'll go."

"Good."

"Jerry"—she touched my hand—"I'm sorry about . . . about this afternoon."

I grabbed her hand and held it tight. "Don't be. You're not the first to have feelings like that. I went through the whole thing. If ever there was a doubting Thomas, you're looking at him."

She grinned. "You don't mind if I cling onto your faith for a while, do you?"

I smiled back. "Nope." *Thanks to Liz,* I thought, *I've got enough to share.*

"Good, but I still apologize for my bitterness. It has been a long time developing, I guess it's a lot to expect to just start believing again."

"What do you mean?"

"I watched you today, and the last few days. You were as angry as I was. As upset about everything. But you handled it. You found some sort of peace. I tried to feel what you were feeling, but there was only anger, and more frustration because I couldn't. Why can't I, Jerry? Why can't I believe anymore? I used to. But those feelings are gone. They started to leave before Mom died, but when she didn't get well I started to blame God, and the Church, and even Dooley because his blessings wouldn't work. I wanted a miracle, and God refused me and took her away . . . and I . . . we needed her."

Tears filled her eyes and started to flow down her cheeks. "Oh, Jerry, I want so bad to feel different. To feel at peace about things . . . about Mom and Dooley and . . . God. I want to feel his comfort, but I can't! Why, Jerry?" She began to sob.

I stood and pulled her to her feet and embraced her tightly, trying to absorb some of the hurt. After more than five minutes I pulled my hanky from my pocket and dried her eyes. Then I kissed her forehead.

"Mike, your mom is fine. It's good that you miss her, but you'll be together again. She'll bring you up to date on what she's been doing, and you'll do the same. It'll be an exciting moment in your eternity." She held me tighter.

"You make it sound so . . . right. Maybe I've known it all along, but the bitter feelings are just getting in the way. I don't know." She looked up at me.

"Give it time, Mike. He is there. Give him a chance."

"Jeremiah Daniels, could you ever love me like you do Liz?"

It took my breath away, but I already knew the answer. "Yes. I think I already do in a lot of ways. You're different people; that's for sure, and yet the same determined, loving individualists that make my world go round. I do love you, Mike." I decided to go on. "But I worry about how you feel about Liz. She's still a very real part of me and always will be. Do . . . do you resent that?"

"No, and that's the amazing thing, I guess. I don't resent her at all." She smiled. "Anyone who could put up with you for ten years has got to be special."

She leaned forward, soft against me, her lips caressing mine gently. "I love you, Jerry. I've been waiting these twenty-eight years for you, and now I've found you. In that alone I see a miracle." The next kiss was longer, harder, and full of the need for each other, fanning old embers into a renewed flame that warmed my whole soul.

23

The 4:00 A.M. call to Trayco had been short and simple. They would invite Ben for a short stay at my home later in the afternoon. The operation was set up to take place in the parking garage of the Pincock Center. That was the good thing about Ben—he had no vices like golf and tennis after work; he just went home and played in the garden, while thinking of ways to make paupers out of guys like me.

We left the ranch at sunup. It had been three full days since the accident, but my vision was still a little blurred. Having only one eye plagued me on the best of days. Now, that reduced vision made me forget breakfast, leaving an unsettled feeling in my gut.

We each carried a holstered pistol that was tied down, thong in place, and a sheathed lever action 30-30. The two ranch hands who volunteered when the senator had put out the word were Luke Shievers and Hal Barton, the old man who had applauded me earlier in the week. Hal seemed to be half asleep in his saddle the way he rode, but for a reason I only felt, I trusted him. Shievers was the newest hand on the ranch, a young buck who broke horses for a hobby and chewed tobacco with relish, spitting his leavings at anything that moved. He seemed a nervous sort and kept to the rear, apparently checking our back trail.

We started early, to beat the late July heat and to save wear and tear on the horses and because I wanted to get to Vegas by late afternoon. If Dooley had left something that filled in some blanks about TriStar I wouldn't be going after Duquesne totally blind.

When we arrived at the canyon about midmorning, Luke suggested that he and Hal station themselves near its mouth, where they could keep an eye on things. I watched as they tied their horses and positioned themselves hidden near the canyon's mouth and then reined the buckskin through the crevice and to the cave beyond.

Lighting the lantern, we went back into the coolness of the cave, the smell of the now rancid meat heavy in the cool air. The place was untouched from our previous visit, Mike's note still lying on top of his bedroll.

We searched each item carefully, looking for even a scrap of paper with a message. Nothing. The lantern ran out of kerosene, the light flickering out as I put a match to the already prepared fire, the dry grass immediately leaping into flame and setting shadows dancing off the granite walls.

The smoke rose to the ceiling and disappeared into some large cracks, a natural ventilation system. By firelight we searched every nook and crevice, but still found nothing.

I crouched by the fire and added a couple of sticks. Mike stared blankly at me from across its flames, the fire reflecting in her eyes.

She shrugged her shoulders in frustration. "We've looked everywhere I can think of!"

"When you were kids, did you have a special place where he might put something for you?"

She bit her lip and thought, her eyes falling to the fire.

A flash of memory crossed her face, and she got to her feet. "Come on."

Having to kick dirt on the fire as she headed for the light of day, I hurried to catch her at the cave entrance. She took the old path and strode quickly away from the cave and toward the stream. Then we followed it up the canyon and into the trees to a pond whose source sprang from a waterfall that literally poured from the rocks fifty feet up the canyon wall. A beaver dam held back the water at the point where the stream began to meander through the canyon, then exited at the crevice and into the lake beyond.

The pond wasn't large, but crystal clear enough to reveal grass and rocks in its first steep ten feet. On the far side stood a large cottonwood tree, a frayed rope hanging from a limb extending out over the water.

I followed her along the trail at the pond's edge until we came to the waterfall tumbling into the shining depth of the gentle little swimming hole, creating a mist that filtered onto surrounding grass, flowers, rocks, and trees. I pictured Mike and Dooley as children on a hot summer day, swinging out over the pond and dropping happily into the cold water.

Stopping, she stared across the pond, deep in her own thoughts, a tear trickling from the corner of her eye and down her cheek. I pulled her to my chest and rubbed her back. "I'm sorry, Mike. I shouldn't have brought you back here so soon."

"No. I'm glad. The memories hurt, but they're good memories, and the bitterness is gone. I can feel him here, Jerry. I'm so glad I can feel him here."

She paused a moment, wiping the tears. "Come on," she said. "I think I know where he may have left something."

She took my hand, squeezing it gently, and led me to the waterfall. On the right, hidden in the tall grass, were rocks that formed a series of steps that ascended the hill.

Climbing past the first slippery steps, we passed between two large boulders and into a hidden crevice whose upper end came out just above the falls.

Next to the fall's edge someone had placed a five-by-five flat rock on which several people could sit half hidden and look upon the pond and trees below. I stood on the edge, wondering if the water was deep enough to handle a dive from that height. "Our robber's roost," she said. "When we brought friends here this was our way of escaping them, disappearing into the mountainside then watching from up here as they tried to find us." She smiled. "Only a few ever knew of it."

She knelt down on the rock's upper edge and, taking a stick, pushed the tall grass to one side, then poked it into a cavity underneath, feeling and listening. "Dooley and I found a rattler in there once. Luckily he sank his fangs into my lunch instead of my hand."

The stick hit something solid. She jumped off the rock and reached directly into the hole, her arm going in clear to the shoulder, her face alight. She grabbed something and yanked on it. The handle appeared, then the whole briefcase. A battered, well-used leather one. She put it on the rock, and we both fell to our knees beside it. We looked at each other. "It's your prize," I said. "Go ahead; open it."

She wiped her hands on her Levi's then flipped the latches. The lid sprang open, revealing a stack of papers inside.

The top one read, "Independent Geological Survey. TriStar Corporation, 1990. Contents confidential."

We looked at each other, both smiling.

"He did leave us something," she said.

We sat down and began reading through the papers. She read then handed me the sheets, one after the other. "Look at them for any immediate red flags," I said. "Something that might tell us what's going on at those rigs."

An hour slipped by. Each minute dragged my hopes further into discouragement. When the last one was laid aside we had found nothing. Bureaucratic mishmash, red tape, forms, charts, jargon!

She put the papers back into the briefcase and shut the lid, then pulled her knees up to her chin and wrapped her arms tightly around them.

"Disappointed?" I asked.

"Very. I thought sure . . . I mean, why would he leave this here, hidden, if it wasn't supposed to give us something important? Nothing but a standard geological survey, with its substantiating charts and letters of verification. I'll bet the Forest Service alone has half a dozen copies."

I opened the briefcase and looked at the stack of papers.

"Let's look at it from Dooley's eyes. He made this report. Something in it concerned him enough to bring it to TriStar's attention and to leave a copy here.

"Suppose it wasn't anything so obvious that to laymen like us it would stick out, but to him it was at least worrisome enough to start asking questions and to try and get TriStar to stop drilling. After your dad brought it to his attention and he did a little looking around he got even more nervous. He couldn't reach the senator, so he came to you concerned about the company, but not running over with dire predictions or angry denunciations. At that point I think it's safe to assume he didn't really have proof that anything was going to go badly wrong. It was just his suspicions."

I took a deep breath. The sun high in the sky beat down on my back, sweat trickled down my forehead. I took off my hat and wiped my forehead with a handkerchief and then the inside of the imitation leather hatband.

"Then you think he started watching TriStar, and his worst fears were confirmed," she said. "Being innocent enough to believe they were just ignorant oil drillers he confronted them, and considering him a risk, they killed him."

"That's right. He probably made some excuse to go up to the drilling site, confirmed his concerns at close range, and threatened them. Too many witnesses at the site, so they let him go, then followed him. He must have known they were after him, so he hid this, hoping you would get the message."

"Then the blood on the corral post is his," she said.

"Yes, I think so. We can have tests run to find out for sure. I had hoped you hadn't seen it. They took his body from here and made up that cover story Danson heard."

She picked up half of the papers. "Then we have to read it as if we were geologists to see what he saw. You're right, Jerry. The clue is here; we just have to dig it out." Her lips were pulled tight across her teeth, determined.

I put my hand on the papers. "No offense, Mike, but do you mind if we find some shade before we settle into being bored out of our minds a second time?"

She laughed lightly, putting the papers back in the brief-case and snapping down the latches. "Come on. It's almost eleven o'clock, anyway. We can do this better back at the ranch."

She stood, grasping my hand. I picked up the briefcase, and we started back through the crevice and the path beyond.

I heard the thunk and saw the dirt fly before the resounding whack of a high-powered rifle split the air. Mike was leading the way and instinctively jerked my arm toward her, pulling me quickly in between the large boulders.

The next shot careened off the granite, ricocheting and planting itself in the soft earth further uphill. Then another hit, and another. I pulled her down, covering her with my body, putting the briefcase over both our heads and praying that the flattened lead of a ricochet wouldn't find any vital organs.

The shooting stopped. I lifted my weight from her soft form, afraid she might be hit. "*Mike!* You okay?"

"Yes! I'm . . . fine. You?"

"Petrified!"

We lay in the dirt and wet grass, waiting, listening. Then I pulled myself into a kneeling position, hugging the slightly rounded side of the boulder. I took off my new straw hat and lifted it slightly above the rock while unholstering my gun. Watching old westerns on TV late at night when sleep hadn't come did have its advantages.

No shot was fired. "They must be moving to get a better angle," I said.

We knelt in the confined space, peering into the trees around us, looking for movement.

"Considering the point where those shots hit the boulders," she said, "I'd say they had to be up on that ridge over there. Lucky. The trees between us and them probably threw the shots off a few inches."

"See anything?" I asked, squinting to get my eyes focused over the longer distance.

"Nothing. Wait! Something . . . someone, up there, on that hill." She was pointing, but I couldn't see beyond the blurred images of trees.

The sound of horses splashing through the stream in the canyon entrance echoed loud off the granite walls. "Hal and Luke heard the shots," she said. "As they say in the movies, 'Cavalry to the rescue.' "

There was a shrill whistle, then a yell. Hal came into view as he maneuvered his horse through the trees.

"Whhht!" came the whistle again.

I whistled back and pointed toward the ridge. He had reined his horse and slid easily from the saddle to take up a firing position when I heard another shot, a small caliber from behind Hal. I watched in horror as he was thrown to the ground with the force of the bullet. We ducked as two more shots jumped off the surface of the rock.

I turned to find Mike hugging another boulder, pistol in hand, looking through a crack.

"See anything?" I asked.

"Just Hal. He's alive. I can see him moving his arm, trying to reach his rifle." She turned and faced me. "Where's Luke?"

"Up there somewhere is my guess! Getting into position to shoot at us. Hal was hit from behind. Somebody bought Luke! Where did the other shots come from?"

"That same ridge across from the playpen. There's an old logging road that runs from here to the valley below Slide Lake."

"Okay. Let's get back to the crevice. Better protection!"

My right hand closed around the handle of the briefcase, sending the pain through recently torn muscles. My left hand gripped the six-shooter. "Go!" She ran across the short open space while I pointed the pistol in the general direction of the ridge and fired. No shots were returned. Either they hadn't seen her or, now alerted, they were ready for me. My lungs sucked in all the air they could, and I threw myself across the space, my heart bucking into my throat.

Still no shots!

The air escaped from my lungs in a flood, and my knees were suddenly weak. "Keep to the walls; Luke may already be above us," I said, looking up at the streak of blue sky.

We inched forward, she watching our backside while I tried to focus on the open space that led out to the top of the falls and the stream beyond. The light, unusually bright, hurt my eye, and I rubbed it, trying to focus better, to adjust.

The few small trees and underbrush in the distance provided little cover for both of us.

"I'm going up there and see if I can get a look." A small pocket where the wind or water had eroded the face of stone stood near the floor of the crevice. "Push yourself in and keep an eye on the way we just came. Wait for me!"

She started to protest, when the sound of muffled, distant voices reached my ears. They seemed to be higher, by the waterfall, or maybe further, up in the trees. I pushed her down and gave her the briefcase, then molded my body against the sides, listening harder.

There it was, the sound of a horse, fading in the distance. One rider. Where was he going? To get behind us? To get help? Were there others?

"Stay here."

She nodded with reluctance, sweat soaking her hair and face. I moved slowly forward, peering through the opening, listening. Where were they? I forced my mind to concentrate, taking deep breaths and holding them and letting them out quietly, focusing on any noise.

Think.

They both carried rifles. Luke had a lever action 30-30, the other had sounded like a high-powered hunting rifle, a 30-06, probably with a scope, considering the distance from which they must have fired. An outsider and not that good with a gun. I wiped the sweat from my forehead and noticed my hat was missing.

If one of them was circling behind us we had little chance of escape. Had it been stupid to pull us into the crevice? Reacting to the thought I ran back to Mike. "Come on." She jumped to her feet as I grabbed her free hand, and we ran back toward the boulders, bolting from the opening and through the rocks. I saw him coming up the steps from the pond, his face filled with shock, but quickly bringing the rifle into firing position. Remembering the training from high school football, I used my crossbody to send him reeling down the steps, his rifle flying into the pond.

"Mike, watch out for the other one," I yelled, jumping after Luke, trying to pin him down before he could get away. I reached him about the same time he made contact with a small group of boulders at the bottom, his head crashing into one and his body going limp.

Mike was right behind me, grabbing my hand as we ran toward Hal, terrified, expecting lead to pierce both our bodies and stop us cold.

Nothing.

When we reached Hal he lifted his head and pointed his gun toward the far hill with barely enough strength to keep it off the ground. My head jerked in that direction as Mike fell behind a fallen tree. I flattened myself next to Hal, taking the rifle before realizing my eye didn't see what his did, and cursing under my breath.

Still no shots.

Empty lungs pleaded for air; my body ached. *Get control.* I had to get control. My mind began to slow down, letting me catch up. "My eyes are no good for anything over fifty feet. Can you see anything?"

I looked at Hal's face. His eyes had closed, and the pale skin had turned yellowish. My heart sunk as I placed my finger on his neck, looking for a pulse. None. Then it thumped gently against the tip of my fingers, weak, but pumping. "Mike, he needs help, fast. Any suggestions?" She still clung to the briefcase for dear life, her knuckles white with the effort. I almost laughed.

"What are you still carrying that briefcase for?"

She looked down at the white knuckles of her hand and stared unbelievingly at the case.

I smiled at the look on her face. We were both scared out of our wits!

"Mike, we've got to get out of here before whoever is up there works their way behind—What was that?"

"A motor. From a car. Up there on that ridge where the old logging road is. She stood up, half bracing herself with the tree, checking in the direction of Luke. "He's still out," she whispered.

I peered in the direction of the ridge, seeing only a glint of sun and blur of red as a vehicle careened out of view.

"A Bronco," she said. "A red Ford Bronco."

24

Mike and I sat on the couch listening as the sheriff asked his final questions and filled out his report. A short, stocky bulldog of a man, he wasn't happy about keeping things under wraps any longer, but had already made the commitment and would stick by it.

Mike and I had taken a chance by loading Hal on his horse and bringing him out, but he had lived and was rushed to Jackson's hospital via helicopter within half an hour after our horses had seen the ranch and bolted for home.

The sheriff had sent a team back for Luke, but found nothing but a warm trail leading higher into the hills. Two men had followed, and we were hopeful they could dig him out. It might take some time.

Hal had no family except for the senator's and the ranch hands, most of whom were shocked and angered at Luke's betrayal. Charla and Bob gathered them together and fed them a few of the details. Several volunteered to go after him, but were told that there was greater need at the ranch and that the sheriff would take care of Luke.

After the senator had seen the sheriff to the door he came back and sat at his desk, pale and drawn, thinking. More near casualties. He couldn't do it much longer.

I pulled the briefcase onto my lap and opened it, taking out the papers and laying them in front of him. "That's Dooley's survey. The answer for what TriStar is doing is on about page forty seven under 'Methods of Drilling.' "

I had figured it out on the way home. Dooley was a geologist. He knew a bad drilling operation when he saw one, and he had written everything into the survey. I just had to look through his eyes.

The senator found the page. "Notice under method three he talks about using water pressure as a method of liquifying oil."

"That's not uncommon. In good wells it isn't necessary, but where you have high density oil, sticky stuff, it's done."

"Yes. He says that in the report, but notice he strongly opposes the method in this case. The reason is on page seventy-three under 'Seismic Activity.' "

The senator's back straightened as he turned the pages.

"I'll save you the trouble, Senator. He says that TriStar is drilling on a very dangerous fault line where numerous seismic activities have been reported. He knew that drilling with water pressure would upset the balance and create a dangerous earthquake situation.

"Now put the two together, and I think you'll have the answer. When Bob and I saw the drilling at TriStar we saw a lot of water. Then I thought it was being pumped out of the hole, or just being used in drilling. The trucks were full of fresh water, not dirty water. The hoses led to a pumping shed, probably where the water is heated then pumped directly into the holes."

"But wouldn't an inspection turn up what they were doing?" Mike asked.

"With the flip of a switch the pumps could be reversed. If an inspector showed up it would look normal. Water being pumped into the ditch, or into the trucks. Inspector leaves, reverse the pumps and get back to business.

"Dooley knew the problem before you asked him to look into TriStar, but apparently hadn't caught them doing it. The more he learned, the more the danger level went up in his mind. He may have confronted them, without realizing who they were, and how dangerous. I would say that he wrote you, Mike, just prior to that confrontation."

"Let me get this straight," the senator said. "You think they are trying to create an earthquake along the Teton Fault?"

"Yessir. You said they were planning a diversion. I think that's it."

"But what damage could it do?" he asked.

"I can answer that, Dad. The Teton Fault is attached to the

Yellowstone Fault on the north, and the Wasatch Fault on the south, the one that runs under the most populous centers of Utah. It could be devastating."

"Senator, I need your permission to get a professional opinion of what might happen if I'm right," I said.

"Who?"

"His name is Phillip Perrigrine. He's a seismologist at the University of Utah. He was a client of mine, and I think he would have some answers."

"Call him," the senator said.

"Before I do we need to discuss Luke."

He looked at me quizzically. "What about the—"

"He wasn't hired by Winters or Owens, and I'm not sure why he was hired, but I think we've got another player."

Mike sat rigid, the senator suddenly alert. "Go on," he said.

"Not much to go on about, but you said it yourself that Owens uses accidents. Dooley was an accident, and Bob and I were supposed to be. Sellars wasn't, and neither was today. If what I'm thinking is happening at the rigs, I would think Duquesne would be particularly careful right now not to bring down your wrath or anyone else's on their heads by hunting us down with rifles. They could have killed Bob and me at the rigs. They made it very clear that they are legally within their rights, so why raise undue concerns? It doesn't fit. Someone else wants to stop us, and *they* aren't particular about the method."

He thought about that, then nodded agreement. "So what do we do? Who could it be?"

"Someone with a lot to lose if we break this deal up. Any ideas would be appreciated."

We all sat silent, thinking it over. I had a couple, but I wasn't ready to say. Not yet. I thought the senator might have one or two himself. He didn't say, either.

"As for what to do, we watch our backside, stay close to home, and call in some help as soon as we decide what to do about TriStar."

They nodded agreement. I called Phillip.

I had run into Phillip when he came into some property in Las Vegas after his father had passed away. He had dropped into my office out of the blue with a letter of recommendation from a mutual friend. I advised him to hang onto the land. It was the best investment around. Five years later it had tripled in value. He sold it, and we invested his money in solid stocks and bonds.

I looked at my watch as I listened to the ring. Nearly five o'clock. Should be home from work. I switched to the speaker-phone, so everyone could hear.

"Hello."

"Hello, Natty. This is Jerry Daniels from Las Vegas. Is Phillip there?"

"Hold on. I'll get him."

"Hello? Jerry? What's wrong?" The reaction my calls made on clients, particularly after hours, never ceased to amaze me.

"Nothing. Everything is fine with your account, but I need some information, and it's important. I'm in Jackson Hole, Wyoming. We've felt a few tremors here the last few days and wondered about them." No reply. "Are you familiar with the fault line down the state's western border into Utah?"

"Yes. We call it the Wasatch Fault on this end. One of the biggest and most dangerous. We're just waiting for it to leave us mortally wounded. The one you're talking about is well connected to this one and is called the Teton Fault. It's connected to one on the north that goes into Canada."

"If there were a quake anywhere along that line, a major quake, say eight or better on the Richter scale, how far would it reach in every direction?"

He seemed suddenly alert. "That's not a very comforting question, Jerry. Eight to ten would leave the Wasatch Front in a shambles and would be felt south of us a good hundred miles. North? All the way to the border and beyond. Yellowstone would never be the same. You could have a domino effect there that might explode into severe eruptions of that whole system. New volcanoes are even a possibility.

"East? If my memory serves me right there's a minor fault connected to the upper Yellowstone area that goes from the northwest corner through Wyoming to the southeast corner. A major quake would definitely have an effect on oil production—breaking pipe, destroying rigs, shutting off present wells. Complete chaos.

"West? All the way to central Idaho. The Idaho Nuclear Energy Laboratory would be in danger. It's only 150 miles away. Jerry, what is going on? You're talking serious problems here."

I ignored the question. The senator was pacing the floor in front of the wall map. "What have been your readings in the

Jackson Hole area lately? Any unusual activity on the read-outs?"

"In size? It's reaching the high end of its historical record, but nothing like you're talking about. The frequency, however, has been unusually high. Very heavy.

"Now! What's going on?" he asked adamantly.

I looked at the senator. "Ready to add another player?"

He took a deep breath and nodded.

"Phillip, is your government clearance still good?"

"Uh . . . yes . . . but—"

"Good. I'm with Senator James Freeman, and we need your expertise. Will you help us?"

It was silent. "Yes. What do you want me to do?"

"We want you to do a hypothetical. If an earthquake epicenter in the area southwest of Jackson Hole, along the fault, were to reach ten on the Richter, what would the loss of life, damage, and economic repercussions be?"

"Jerry, you're scaring ten years of life off me. I—"

"You have to trust me, Phillip. I'll call you back tomorrow at four o'clock. Wait for my call at the office. Will that give you enough time?"

"Yes." There was a pause. "If what you're saying has the potential of happening we'd better be ready. Do I have permission to notify a closed circle here?"

I looked at the senator. "Dr. Perrigrine, this is Senator Freeman. You do not have permission. It must be kept extremely confidential. National security and the lives of a lot of people depend on it. I want no mention of this conversation to anyone even remotely connected to the press. Will that hamper you too much?"

"No, sir! I just thought—"

"I know, Dr. Perrigrine. You must trust us. We will let you blow it wide open if we confirm any potential earthquake.

"Now, one more question. Strictly confidential. Has anyone ever started an earthquake?"

"Yessir. Back in . . . 1962, I think it was, at the Rocky Mountain Arsenal northeast of Denver. They were manufacturing weapons. One of the by-products was contaminated water, which was pumped down a deep well of about 3670 meters. It was injected under pressure."

"How severe?"

"Sir?"

"The quake. How bad was it?"

"Wasn't just one, but more than seven hundred epicenters ranging from .7 to nearly 5 on the Richter scale before they got it stopped."

We inhaled all the air in the room.

"But how can that happen, Doctor?"

"The increased water pressure at the well produced a flow of ground water into crevices and cracks already in existence in the faults. The increase in pore pressure led to a reduction of the shear strength of the rock material. In layman's terms, Senator, the water acted as a lubricant along the fault, causing it to slip. How much it slips is determined by the pressure the fault is under."

"Okay, last question. Could man control or time an earthquake if he could control the pressure?"

"Yes. In fact it was done a few years back by the U.S. Geological Survey at the Rangely Oil Fields in Colorado. They wanted to see if they could control the pressure, releasing it slowly, and effectively diffuse the possibility of a bigger quake along a fault line. They found they could manipulate seismic activity by an increase and decrease in water pressure. Of course, you have to know what you're doing—Hey! I just remembered. A young geologist from Jackson was present on those experiments at Rangely. Robert Doolittle. He would know everything about it."

We gaped at one another, shocked.

"Could you get us the names of others who were in on it? It's quite important."

"Sure. I'll have them for you at four o'clock tomorrow."

25

"A 'natural' catastophe like this would be listed as an act of God," I said, "a diversion that fulfills all a terrorist ever dreamed of. Little danger of discovery, even after the fact, and destruction and death in imperialist America. Follow up with economic turmoil by putting the market into a tailspin we might never pull out of. All it would take is a heavy sell-off in a portion of those companies on your list, and the market would turn into a cat trying to eat its own tail. It all fits."

"The investments even make more sense now," Mike added. "As the market nose-dives, companies will be begging for financial help, some ripe for takeover. Foreign money could move in and buy up more of American industry, giving them a stronger voice in what we do."

"With a catastrophe like that our congressional leadership would never allow our country to become embroiled in the Middle East," the senator said. "Never. Duquesne's group *could* change a very delicate balance of power. Israel would be in serious jeopardy."

"Senator, I need to get to Vegas. Tonight. I need to leave within the hour. Can you arrange it?"

"I'm going with you," Mike said.

I turned to her quickly, relying on the senator's support. "No, you're not, Mike. I need you here to be my attorney."

She looked at me, baffled. "Your attorney? What—"

"I need you to start proceedings to get an injunction to stop TriStar, legally. They're on my property." I smiled.

"You mean the document?" She sat straight up. "But that won't hold up; you haven't got any evidence."

"Yes, he does, Mike. My aides went to the national archives and got this for us." He pulled a fax copy from his desk. "I showed it to Jerry while the sheriff interviewed you."

She took the paper. "Then the dream . . ."

I nodded. A shocked smile creased her lips.

"That's a fax copy of the records, showing the grant was made for ten thousand acres of land to one Finan Daniels in 1850," the senator said. "The coordinates are given as well as the information indicating stipulations, chief of which was that the territory had to be added to the United States. The attorney general says it would be looked upon favorably by the courts and should at least give us an injunction until the matter is decided."

"I need you to get that injunction," I said to Mike.

"Any attorney in Jackson can do that. I'm going, Jerry."

The senator leaned forward in his chair. "Mike, he's right. You're the only lawyer in this room. He's leaving tonight. Power of attorney must be given tonight, to you."

Mike looked at us, scanning for cracks in our argument. Then her shoulders slumped, and she gave in. "All right, all right. I'll make out the papers so you can sign them before you leave."

I breathed relief. "Can you get me there, Senator, incognito?"

"I'll call the airport and ask for a priority flight. You'll take my plane and use my pilot, Bill Blaznack. Anyone who cares will just think it's another crisis trip for the overworked senator from Wyoming. When you get over the Wind River Mountains you can change course to Las Vegas.

"I'll have Cal Burkhart fly his tourist chopper out here to pick you up. It's only ten minutes to the airport that way. We'll dress you in my clothes, and in the dark no one will know the difference. Will that do?"

"It's nice to have friends in high places."

"I'll need to contact my people in Washington about all these developments," he said.

"I can't afford leaks, Senator. Give me eight hours?"

He nodded. "Eight hours, unless you can make it sooner."

Quickly tossing clothes into my suitcase, I stopped to answer the quiet knock on the door. Mike stood there, still in Levi's and a western shirt I had admired all day for fit, but she wore a new set of mascara-smeared eyes.

I closed the door as she seated herself in the antique rocking chair. Tense silence loomed as I continued packing.

"I'm scared for you, Jerry."

I sat on the edge of the bed, facing her. "I'm scared for all of us, Mike, but this has to be done. I must persuade Stevenson to spell out what he knows before you slap them with that injunction. If I don't they could still hurt the economy very badly."

"The government. They could stop Duquesne. You don't have to go back there. I think you underestimate them."

"Maybe. But we can't afford to overestimate, can we? You're the one who told me about their in-house fighting and game playing. While they're jawing about possible solutions and who gets the credit for the bust, lives could be lost and Duquesne could pull this off."

She sighed deeply. "Do you remember the feeling I had when we were at the playpen looking for Dooley the first time?"

"You mean the one about Dooley never coming back?"

"Yes. I have it again." The tears trickled down her cheeks through streaks of mascara.

I reached, took her hand, and tried to pull her into my arms. Instead she pulled away and went to the window. "I couldn't stand to lose you. Don't you understand how much I love you? How much you mean to me?"

"I'll have Trayco with me."

"I want to be with you."

"Mike, you've brought new life to me. I don't want to lose you, either. If anything happened to you because I endangered your life I would never forgive myself. I don't know what to expect back in Vegas. I don't know who's watching. I do know you'll be safe here. It has to be this way. You must understand that!"

She walked to me, drying her eyes, smearing the mascara further across her face.

"Here, let me do that." I took the hanky and rubbed away the black marks, making them brown smears. She put her arms around me and pulled in close.

Touching her cheek with my finger, then pressing my lips against hers, I kissed her long and gentle. "I love you, Michaelene Freeman. I'll come back."

Her hands slipped behind my neck and pulled my lips to hers. The kiss was hard, shooting passion through me, exploding into the strength of my arms.

She clutched me tightly, laying her head on my shoulder, pressing her softness against me. "Come on," I said. "This is no time to be in a bedroom!"

She pulled gently away, a smile on her lips. Then she kissed me again. "One day . . . soon, we'll finish this!"

"Promises, promises," I said, grabbing for the suitcase with my free hand. "Forty-eight hours, Mike. It'll be over in forty-eight hours. Then we can get back to our lives."

We walked to the door and switched off the light. Somehow I couldn't envision it.

26

The plane banked to the right as it climbed into the darkness above Jackson Hole. I could see Jackson in the distance, the lights bright against the dark backdrop of the ground, the full moon highlighting the mountains beyond.

The pilot was a lanky kid of no more than thirty, who chewed on cheroots and wore a baseball cap with the words *Pilots Fly High—Naturally* written on it. His eyes were almost perfectly round, set in a thin face that reminded me of Jeff in the old-time comic strip duo, "Mutt and Jeff."

He knew the senator's twin-engine Cessna Citation like the back of his hand and flew with the confidence of a cocky fighter jock.

"Five minutes to the Wind River Range," he said. "The senator told me you would set a new course at that point. You want to give it to me now?"

"Las Vegas. But I want you to land at the North Las Vegas Airport instead of International or Hughes. A friend will be waiting for us there."

He chewed the cheroot a minute, a hesitant look on his thin features, then decided to go ahead.

"The senator said I should wait for you. He said twenty-four hours."

I smiled. "That's correct. Any problem?"

"No! Waitin' for twenty-four hours in Las Vegas will be a lot of fun compared to flyin' tourists over Yellowstone and the Teton Range spoutin' memorized propaganda about the wonders of nature!" He looked at me quickly. "Uh . . . don't get me wrong. I love Jackson Hole, but a little high-class nightlife, well, it'll be a nice change."

"Mmm. There's plenty of that in Vegas." I looked out of the window at the sharp and rugged peaks of the Wind River Range. "Flying for the senator, you must have friends in responsible places."

He laughed. "Actually, just plain dumb luck. Since I got out of the air force I've been movin' around. I spent some time with American and Delta airlines, but I didn't like their regimentation. Too much like the service. Flew a crop duster for a while until I piled up the boss's new plane. Hit a darn tree and landed in a farmer's private pond. I started driftin' again and ended up in Jackson a few summers ago. Worked at the Bar J feedin' tourists for a while, then got a job flyin' for Scenic Tours when one of their pilots got fired for buzzing a herd of elk so a bunch of prima donna tourists could take pictures. The senator uses our choppers to get from his ranch to the airport fast and easy. I met him on one of those runs. When his pilot went to Alaska lookin' for more money, I got hired. The rest is history, even though I worried some about passin' government inspection."

A young, talented pilot drifting from job to job. It was evident that he and the air force had parted under strained relations, but I thought I'd ask to be sure. "Did you bail out of the service or were you asked in a nice way to find other employment?"

"You sound like you've been there." He looked at me with a wry grin. "I bailed out, but they opened the door real wide. When the senator got the report he let my little faults slip through the cracks. Nothin' that would keep me from flyin'." There was a coldness in his tone, even bitterness. I decided I was too tired to pursue it.

The rest of the flight was spent in the main cabin going over Sellars' papers and trying to get a little sleep.

I awoke as he brought the jet up to the hangar where Trayco was waiting. Trayco used his car phone and made arrangements to have Blaznack put up at Caesars Palace, then he called for a taxi.

When he had finished telling Blaznack names and places he turned to me. "Jeremiah. Get in the car. I don't like being out in the open."

He went around and got into the driver's seat. I slipped into the passenger side, leaving Blaznack waiting for his cab.

I filled Trayco in as we pulled onto North Decatur and headed for my house. "Any problems getting Stevenson?" I asked.

He smiled. "None." He was proud of his work.

"Can you stick around for another few days, Kenny? I think I'm about to pop somebody on their blind side, and they aren't going to like it. Anyone watching the house?"

"We've taken all the precautions. There was a house for sale behind you. We're set up there and can get you into your place without a problem. Your windows have been blacked out. No one will know you've come back."

"How much is this all going to cost me?" I asked.

"I needed the house. Good neighborhood, good investment. The black plastic for the windows came to twelve dollars plus tax. No offense, Jerry, but you don't have anything I want, except two or three of your paintings. And a '56 Chevy." He smiled.

We pulled into my former backyard neighbor's garage. When the door was closed one of Trayco's men stepped from the house and gave his boss a status report. We were escorted through the flower beds to a new hole in the concrete wall and then into my yard and on to the house. There were eight men. Security was tight, a Trayco business trait.

"Have you seen any sign of my sister-in-law and Danny?"

He pulled an envelope from his pocket. "Just this." The letter said they would see me in a week. Both had signed it. They had left together. One never knew. I smiled, wadding the note and tossing it into the wastecan.

"What's next?" he asked.

"I want you to put your people in Los Angeles to work. Find Duquesne and put a tail on him. We need to know where he is and what he's doing every minute for the next eight hours. Is Stevenson here? He might be able to help us with that." I walked to the den wall and took down the picture.

"In the spare bedroom, under guard."

I began taking the screws out of the sealed frame. When it was dismantled I took the map out and turned it over.

Trayco came to the desk. "What's this?"

"That, my friend, is going to be instrumental in stopping Duquesne and his partners."

I looked down at the document. There it was, Finan Daniels' grant for ten thousand acres of land. His son had used the backside of the only paper he owned to make a map to save his people while they were running from soldiers bent on their destruction. For more than a hundred years it had been in my family, and no one had ever made an attempt to use it. I doubted if my parents even knew it existed. Even I had never been told directly. It was only as I lay entangled in the wreckage of Bob's pickup, unconscious, the dream vivid and detailed in my mind for the hundredth time, that I remembered grandfather's words to me when he gave me the framed and sealed map.

"Jeremiah," he said, "you are descended from a noble people. They sacrificed much. Now it is for you to carry the burden of their sacrifice. They watch you. I will watch you."

He had handed it to me then. "This saved many lives of our people. It is yours now. Use it wisely, and it will save again."

Did he know what the document would do? Did all of those who had gone before understand the great good it must do sometime in the future? Is that why it hadn't been used? Why my ancestors had not laid claim to their rightful property? The exact piece of land we needed to have in order to stop the rampage of men gone mad.

I shook my head. My mind couldn't explain it, reason certainly didn't apply, but there it was, intact 100 years after saving many of a historically obscure Shoshone tribe in the fargone past.

For the first time I realized why my grandfather had been so careful to teach me of my heritage and the greatness of those who had gone before.

"How, Jeremiah?"

"What?" I said, coming out of deep thought.

"How is that going to stop Duquesne?" he said impatiently.

"It proves that TriStar Oil is drilling on private land. Land belonging to my family. I can stop him with an injunction."

His look was one of confusion. "How—"

I put up my hand. "Don't ask! It would take hours to explain what I know, and then we'd both still be in the dark. There it is. A real, tangible, and legal document. Right now that's all that matters. Sometime, when we have a few days, we'll all try to make sense of it. Right now"—I sandwiched the document between two pieces of vellum paper and placed it inside an empty leather portfolio case—"we have other things to do."

27

The phone system in Trayco's new house had a scramble device called a TI-5000. Even when tapped, the words sounded garbled and made no sense to interlopers. The only concern was a tap on the other end. I took the chance and called Mike, telling her about the document.

"When did you figure it out?" she asked.

"I don't know. I guess after the dream at the accident. Even then I wasn't sure until I actually had it out of the frame."

"Is it readable?"

"Like new. Very clear for as old as it is. They took very good care of it."

"But why didn't they use it?"

"That's the million-dollar question. They had every reason to, considering the way they were treated. Maybe they were afraid it would be taken away from them. Indian property rights are only part of the last twenty years. Had they used it they might have been accused of stealing it after killing the white owner. I have an even deeper respect for their wisdom and good judgment."

"This is all so odd, Jerry. A document that has been out of circulation for 100 years suddenly surfaces when it's needed to save lives?"

"Spooky, isn't it?" I said. "But, like I told Trayco, we can worry about the hows later. Right now we have it, and it's the real thing. That's all anyone needs to know in a court of law. It's all we need to put an end to drilling at TriStar."

"Agreed," she said. "When can you have it here?"

"Will the information from Washington get the injunction?" I was thinking of Blaznack.

"Yes, but we'll need your document for the actual court case. For now a copy by fax would be nice."

"Consider it done. I have a copy machine here, and a fax. It'll be on its way in half an hour."

When it was done I went into the kitchen and inhaled a sandwich and several glasses of cold milk while I parleyed with Trayco. Then it was time to talk to Stevenson.

Stevenson sat on the floor with a blindfold strapped around his eyes and a nylon cord binding his feet. My conscience bothered me for all of ten seconds. Just long enough to remember my wrecked career, the deaths of two good people, the attempted murders of four others.

"Hello, Ben," I said, closing the door behind us.

"Jer . . . Jerry . . . is that you?"

"Yeah, it's me. Uncomfortable?"

He nodded.

"Untie him, gentlemen, and take the blindfold off."

He rubbed his arms and blinked, adjusting his eyes. His grayish blond hair was mussed, and his tie was off to one side. I had always hated his yuppie suspenders.

"What . . . what's going on?" he asked, looking around.

"First of all, understand that Trayco here doesn't like you much right now because he doesn't like your partners and what they're up to, but he has promised he won't break every bone in your body, only those necessary to get you to tell us what we want to know."

His face grew hard. "What are you talking about? I don't know this . . . this black lackey from the wrong side of town, and I don't know what—"

Trayco was on him like frosting on a cake. I grabbed Kenny and pulled him back. He resisted just enough.

"You know him by reputation." I kept my voice even. "Any second now and you're going to know him by experience."

We moved a few steps back, and Ben unfolded himself from the protective fetal position he had taken.

"This is Kentucky Trayco." Recognition was evident. The blood sunk from his face, magnifying his fearful expression.

"Now, Ben, do you want to play games? Or do you answer my questions?" He was beginning to sweat and wiped it away with the sleeve of his initialized shirt.

194

"This is kidnapping."

"Maybe, but it could be worse." I walked over and put my face up to his. "Now answer my question, you treasonous waste of human flesh, or I'll personally break your manicured fingers." My sincerity scared even me, and I didn't like the way it made me feel. How did people who did this for a living stand it?

"They'll . . . kill me, Jerry!"

"They don't have you; I do. If you get with it and cooperate, Trayco will keep you out of their hands. If not, you're probably dead anyway. These nice folks you work for don't like loose ends." I told him what they had done. He went from pale to ashen. "What . . . what do you want to know?"

I was glad I knew the man and his weakness. "Good. Trayco, sit him in the overstuffed chair, then have one of your people make him a sandwich and bring him something to drink, will you? Mr. Stevenson is just about to turn back to a good guy, and he's going to need all the energy he can get."

"What about my family, they'll—"

"Are they in town or at the beach house in Newport?"

"Here."

I dialed the number; I knew it by heart. His family didn't deserve to be in the way. "Marg? Jerry Daniels. Don't ask questions; just listen to me. Ben is okay, but he's in a little trouble with some rough clients. We're keeping him out of their way for a few days. He's afraid they might, well, harass you and the kids. I'm sending a couple of men to escort you to the airport. He wants you to spend a few days at your sister's in New York. Will you do it? Good. Yes you can talk to him; he's right here."

"Watch it, Ben. They don't deserve trouble of your making. And believe me, they are in danger."

He did it right, and then hung up.

"All right, Ben. Two people have died. Two good people who didn't deserve to die. Two very dear friends and I have almost been killed, and frankly I'm sick of the whole mess. You did your best to put me out of business, and my name is spoken only in jest, so I'm just a little ticked at you and your group for that as well. I intend to put you all out of business, but I have to get straight answers. They have something planned that we need to know. Any information may help, so clear your mind and pay attention. Understand?"

He nodded.

"All right, then. First of all, what's going on at TriStar?"

"I . . . don't know."

I scowled, tensing, ready to knock some sense into him.

"Wait! I swear I don't know! That part of the operation is unknown to anyone but Duquesne, Winters, Owens, and the people from the Middle East. My group and I are only concerned with the money. I swear, Jerry! I don't know!"

I sat down in my chair. "All right, I'll give you another chance. Who's Royalty?"

His voice, subdued and anguished, displayed some conscience. "I told you. My group and I only deal with the money. I don't know who's involved. Duquesne keeps each part of the operation separate from all the others. I have never met with more than five at ony one time, and those five are the committee who makes the financial decisions, who tells the committee of brokers what to do, when, how much—all that! I know the name, but I've never met the person."

It had been worth a try. "How many brokers are involved and what do you estimate was invested?"

He gulped. "Twenty. A minimum of one-and-a-half billion each. Some of us who can deal in futures have more."

I was stunned, and it took me a few seconds to get my breath. The senator's information was right, but until that moment I hadn't really let it sink in. "That's at least thirty billion. No wonder you have such great commissions!"

He smiled, just a little. I handed him a piece of paper and a pencil. "I want you to diagram your organization. I want your procedure jotted down, and passwords if there are any. I want it all, Ben," I leaned close to him, "You're going to prison, Ben, but if you screw this up, I'll see that you never get out! Don't fool with me by writing down something that might lead us astray. Even if you stopped us, Senator James Freeman and others know of your involvement, and they'd nail you. Your boss, Duquesne, also may know we're after him. If we get word to him that you've turned, your usefulness is over, and he'll create an accident just for you. Your only way out of this is to play ball on our team. Got it?" I said.

Shrinking into the chair, he nodded in the affirmative. "Yes . . . I . . . understand. But I can't remember all that. I . . . I have a ledger. I'm not supposed to keep it, but there were so many different accounts, and I started fouling them up. I was warned, so I started keeping journal entries and—"

Another lucky break. "Where is it?"

"At the office, in the safe of my desk."

"Has the combination changed since I filled in for you while you were in . . . where was it . . . Iraq?"

He didn't smile. "Yes. It's a special lock. You can't even turn it without voice activation."

"Nice touch." I turned to Trayco. "Make arrangements for transportation, will you? That journal is critical."

He nodded and left the room.

"Ben, are the stocks and investments you're responsible for listed in the journal as well?"

"Yes."

"And what's the point of all these investments?"

"I only know part of it, but I think I can guess the rest. Most of the investments are in companies dealing with industry, mostly oil. They control pipelines, drilling companies, and five of the top ten oil producers in America. When Iraq invades Kuwait they're in a position to make major profits in oil futures, stock options—you name it. If you control the future and know how the market must go you can't lose. I think they'll drive oil to a hundred dollars a barrel and gas at the pump to at least five dollars a gallon in the United States alone. I project profits of thirty billion over the first month. When the big panic comes and people sell off, they clean up again, using their profits to buy up companies who can't pay their debts. The group steps in and buys America and the rest of the world dirt cheap, while demoralizing our system and creating financial collapse. They don't want the average company to survive. By precipitating a stock market panic, they succeed at destroying the companies. But they want oil to skyrocket. War and then control of Arabian oil accomplishes that. It's simple."

I couldn't believe my ears. "And your cut?" I asked angrily.

"Five million up front and twenty-percent commission on buyouts, takeovers—everything that I handle. All business would eventually be channeled into two newly created firms in which the involved brokers have been promised major positions. The income is endless."

"Maybe. Until they decide you're not needed anymore. Did that ever occur to you?"

"Never." He convinced neither of us.

"At least you got a hefty price for selling out your country. Were Sellars and Dooley worth it? Was the attempt on my life and the lives of Michaelene and Bob Freeman worth it?"

"Hold on, Jerry. I know nothing about those killings, or the attempt on the lives of anyone. I told you; Duquesne kept each operation separate. I . . . I didn't know what they were up to, or how they planned to bring it all about, until you told me a few minutes ago. All I know about is what goes on in the financial end of things."

I wasn't convinced. "And I suppose you didn't know anything about the sellout of Powers and the nightmare I've been through for the last six months."

His eyes went to the floor. "I knew, but I did try to stop it. They wouldn't listen. You were getting too close, they said, and they talked about an accident. I came up with an alternative." He looked at me, his eyes pleading. "I intended to send you a part of the profits and clear you later. I had it all worked out, Jerry, I . . ."

I stood and walked to the window. "Some of us aren't interested in blood money, Ben. You knew about the takeover of Kuwait. You knew people were going to get hurt. But your greed got the best of you. Admit it."

I turned and looked at him. "You're going to help us get in that computer, Ben. I haven't got all the pieces to the puzzle yet, and I need the financial statement and accounts ledgers for the whole operation."

I walked over and put my hands on the arms of his chair, mad at blurred vision and aching muscles, mad at greed, and mad at traitors like Ben, and especially Duquesne. "Then, my greedy little friend, we're going to pop your little balloon, take it all away from the lot of you." I punched my finger at his chest, emphasizing each word. "Every last dollar is going to disappear into thin air."

28

It was 3:00 A.M. when we pulled into the Pincock Center parking garage, the desert temperature hovering at a pleasant eighty degrees. It was as cool as we could expect before sunrise, only two or so hours away.

The Center was Las Vegas's entrance into the "new breed" of office complex, an attempt at pulling businessmen together in an environment that was exciting but comfortable, fast paced while still giving the impression of control. A person could talk to any of a number of industrial, technical, and financial world businesses without ever leaving the main tower, then have lunch—a fine gourmet meal in one of three over-rated restaurants—and then work it off in the health gym.

The two-story breezeway, with a clay tile floor and tinted glass walls, housed palm trees and exotic plants both inside and out and gave one the immediate feeling of spacious comfort.

At the far end of the breezeway, gold-plated doors reeked of wealth and power. The doors were the Center's main thrust, letting clients and businessmen know it was first-class all the way.

As the huge doors closed behind us with no more than a whisper, we walked past huge original oil paintings, a glass-enclosed atrium four stories high, and a lobby the size of a basketball court. The lobby was furnished with only the best in Southwest furniture and art. An environment intended to make wealthy men feel wealthy and poor men want to stop being poor. The great and spacious building redefined.

The guard stood at his unobtrusive, well-designed work

space, a quizzical look on his rough, mustached face. Even his immaculate Pincock Center uniform spoke money. His gold badge, braid, and trim stood out against the deep blue color of his well-filled shirt.

"Mr. Stevenson, Mr. Daniels." He looked at Trayco curiously. "Early, aren't you?"

"Some new evidence in Jerry's case has come to light, Bill," Ben said calmly. "This is Mr. Trayco, a private investigator. We'll be meeting for a while, then we have a phone conference to New York. Jerry will be coming back to the firm soon."

"Mr. Daniels," he said in his well-trained and controlled manner, "we congratulate you. Welcome back." He reached out and grasped my smaller hand in his powerful grip, cognizant of his strength, being cautious not to offend me.

I smiled and said thanks. It was nice to know that Ben's revelation was at least partly true.

We took the cherry-wood-paneled elevator to the twelfth floor foyer. Ben used his magnetic key to unlock the door in full view of the cameras. I knew the guard was watching carefully on one of a dozen monitors.

It seemed Ben was walking a little taller, and the color had returned to his face. The change of the penitent, I supposed.

The large, expensively decorated office complex of Banner was empty and could remain so for at least another two hours, the time when Larry Rawls, a commodity broker, usually began his day. I looked at my watch, figuring quickly in my head. If we could break into Duquesne's system with only minor delays it should give us enough time.

Ben's voice-activated key slid aside a wall panel behind his desk. Another activated the combination. In a matter of seconds the safe door popped open, and Ben handed me the journal.

I thumbed through it, my mind racing to keep up with the figures, the names, the companies. I realized this was just a tip of an iceberg set up to bring down the U.S. economy like the Titanic.

"You kept good records." I withdrew a letter stuck inside. "What's this?"

He hesitated for a moment. "A . . . letter in case of accidental or unexplained death."

"So you did know you were dealing with killers."

He shrugged. "I knew the way Duquesne did business with the brokers, that's all. It was enough."

"Why did he choose you, Ben? Why does he trust you?"

"He doesn't trust me." He took a deep breath. "He's black-mailing me." He walked to the full wall of windows and gazed out on the lights of the Strip, only a few blocks to the west.

Though I shouldn't have been, I was surprised. "How?"

"Does it matter?"

"No, I don't suppose it does."

"He was going to see that I rotted in prison for something I did while a marine. Something very stupid. He brought the evidence to me in 1987 and invited me to Iraq. How could I turn down such a wonderful offer?

"That was when I met the other brokers. Duquesne singled me out as a sort of liaison between the grunt brokers and the financial bigwigs. As heady and ridiculous as it sounds right now, it made me feel . . . powerful. The other brokers relied on my information, at least to some degree. I sat in some big meetings, talking about billions, controlling companies I had always been in total awe of. The money, the power! It was like a drug." He shook his head. "When it came down to it I was nothing more than a glorified executive secretary, kept under surveillance like everyone else. I didn't care at the time. The money, the giddiness of power—they became all-important. The gods of Benjamin Franklin Stevenson." His voice was filled with sarcasm.

"Anyway," he said, shaking his head and turning to face me, "we all report our accounts directly to Duquesne through the mainframe computer. Each of us carries separate code names and passwords, although I suspect each of us operates on the same principle. Each morning we call in and receive the information for our particular accounts. Each afternoon we send them back with the day's additions and deletions. I spend the hour before the market opens making out orders—as per his instructions—for each of the accounts I control at Banner. Considering the buys and sells I have in a day—all done in manageable, unsuspicious lots—I'm sure Duquesne must stay up all night writing out instructions."

"Maybe not," I said. "From what we've been able to find out, each broker has identical accounts, under different names of course, but the same amounts. The same buys you make each day seem to apply to all the other brokers; it's the same with your sells. Once he has programmed one broker's work, the other's could be easily duplicated. Any exceptions can be handled on a need basis.

"I suppose he has a similar hold on the other brokers?" I asked.

"You mean blackmail? Yes. I've had a chance to broach the subject with a couple of the others I knew before we got into this mess."

"He'll crucify you, Ben, if he ever . . ."

He turned and looked back toward the Mirage Hotel on the Strip. "I knew about the takeover of Kuwait. I justified that as inevitable anyway; I was just a broker taking advantage of world events. I suspected he killed two brokers who had turned on him or had tried to get out, but I wasn't sure. I didn't know about his planned diversion in Wyoming, or the geologist, or Sellars, or you and the guy that was with you. I won't be a party to cold-blooded murder." He turned and looked at me. "As hard as it may be for you to believe, I do have some moral fibre left."

I looked at my watch. "Okay, let's get to the computer. You said he has his phone line open as early as 3:30 A.M., right?"

"Yes. Especially now, with things at their peak. He wanted special vigilance, and brokers on the East Coast need access that early." He scratched his stubby whiskers. "Duquesne hasn't done anything lately—anything major that is—and yet he acts like something could hit anytime. I just put it down to caution. Now I'm not so sure. After what you've told me, I think they're probably waiting for things to happen at Tri-Star's wells, and they don't want any of us falling asleep at the wheel."

"You said Duquesne would know if someone tried to get in that shouldn't. If I use your passwords—the ones written here in this journal—how could he know?"

"The passwords are jumbled. That's the part of the journal that's legal even in Duquesne's eyes. See the list? Each one begins with the first three letters of the day *prior* to the day they're to be used. Also, the last letter changes each time you use the word. The first time I used the Monday password I used the word SUNCO, Sun being the first three letters of the day prior to the day of use, then I added the letter A, or SUN-COA. The second time I used the password that day the word was SUNCOB. The first time I used the Tuesday password, MONTE, it was MONTEA. If you use any of the others his computer picks it up and won't let you in."

"Hmm. Tricky. Without the journal anyone onto them would have little chance to get through this or any other terminal, unless of course they got very lucky. With some fifty passwords on this page, and no indication you're to add a letter of the alphabet, the chances would be remote.

"Do these marks by each password indicate how many times you have used that word?"

"Yes. I couldn't keep track."

"No offense, Ben, but you're their weak link. If they caught you with this journal they'd pulverize you."

"It was either that or have them beat me to a pulp for making mistakes. You remember that day I came to the office with two swollen eyes and blamed it on falling while being drunk?"

"No fall, huh?"

"No fall. That's when I decided I'd better take precautions. They give no second chances. Like I said, I've seen two new faces at our meetings over the last two years. The old ones died rather suddenly."

"I thought you said you were never in danger," I said with a wry grin. "Duquesne must print out a daily report for safekeeping." I mused. "Just in case."

"He does. Then he shreds it when it's replaced. When we met in New York with the finance committee I saw the brokers' reports come in. He took the old one out of a briefcase chained to one of his bodyguard's wrists, shredded it along with a backup disk he had made, then put the new list and the new disk in the briefcase.

"I also know he sends the entire report to another computer somewhere. Probably in the Middle East."

"Hmm. Thorough. Ben, we have firsthand knowledge that anyone close to his operation like you are has been eliminated. Except for the members of his main group."

He nodded. "I'm depending on you to keep me alive until he's out of the picture."

"We'll give you that much."

Trayco was looking out of the window and into the private drive below. "You two had better move it fast. Only an hour and a half before we get company. If we're lucky."

I sat down at the computer. "Okay, Ben. What do you think will happen if I begin a search for information other than your financial records. Will he know?"

He bit his lip. "I don't know. He isn't at his complex in LA; he's here, at the Mirage. I met with the financial group and him the other day. If he has people monitoring the system they may not be as vigilant while he's away."

"Did you hear that, Trayco?" I asked.

"Yeah." He took a phone from his pocket, switched it on and made a call. There was no need setting up surveillance in LA if the man we wanted to watch was staying here.

"By the way, the meetings taking place here end tomorrow, I mean today," he said, looking at his watch. "Then Duquesne goes back to Los Angeles."

"Okay, here goes. Maybe he'll monitor us; maybe he won't. We have to get those records, so that doesn't leave us a lot of choices."

I pushed the keys to dial.

The prompt came on the screen. "What now, Ben?"

He took a deep breath. I didn't blame him. He was about to cut himself off from five million dollars, and a seven-figure income for the rest of his days, while putting his life and the lives of his family in danger.

"Type in JERISHA."

"That's original. His wife's name, isn't it?" My fingers hit the keys.

"He wants all of us to be able to get in, so he made it fairly easy, I guess." USER NAME came on the screen. "Type in BEN."

PASSWORD?

"What now?" I asked.

Ben looked at the journal and gave me the proper coded password.

PLEASE WAIT. DOWN LOADING BENS THUDD.

"It won't take long. I don't know what you've got up your sleeve, Jerry, but you can't get into the other compartments of this computer without passwords."

"Just a hunch. That's why I'm getting the financial records first. If I blow it, at least we'll have the latest info in your accounts, along with his orders for the day."

"Peanuts," he said.

LOADING COMPLETE.

The C> prompt came back on.

"You're out. Now you have to go back in. Type in JERISHA again. Now type in BEN and hope there's no way to monitor what we're doing."

PASSWORD?

Sweating profusely, Ben removed a handkerchief from his pocket and wiped his brow while Trayco moved from the window and leaned over my shoulder. My pounding heart alone could create tremors through the seventeen floors of the glass tower.

"This is it," Ben said. "I hope you know what you're doing. You'll never get back in if you don't."

I thought about that. We would need to get back in. But if Sellars' message was right . . .

I typed in TERROR1, holding my breath. Waiting for what seemed like long minutes but was only seconds.

PLEASE WAIT. LOADING.

We exhaled together, filling the room with the scent of raw onions mixed with minty toothpaste. No monitor called a halt to our entrance. The password had worked.

"Jerry, how did you know the password?"

"A friend left me a message."

"What do you mean?" asked Trayco. "What friend?"

"Dick Sellars."

"But—"

"A story for another time." We waited as the computer dumped in the files. I crossed my fingers, hoping Ben's system would have enough memory in its 80-byte hard disks.

LOADING COMPLETE.

The C> prompt appeared again.

My lips went to a broad smile.

"You have what you want," Ben said, leaning back in his chair. "Now what?"

"Now we send it all to my computer at home, were we can work without interruption." I dialed, thanking heaven above I had added another 40 bytes to my computer only a month ago. It quickly downloaded the material into its memory. I noticed that my hands were shaking. "I'll leave your computer tied into mine. That way if Duquesne or anyone else comes into the system to check on what you're doing it'll come straight through to us at the house. Any problem with that, Ben?"

"No. I do it sometimes so I can work at home." He looked at his watch.

"All right, Ben, here's another critical question for you. Can he monitor your trades? Does he know what you're doing?"

"He can break into my computer anytime and take sections of the information, look at it, and put it back. He does sometimes when he wants to check a trade he ordered, seeing if it was executed, in which accounts, how fast—that sort of thing."

"But if we never change anything in the computer and just work from the journal, would he know he was being sold out?"

Ben thought a minute. "He might. Once I forgot to put down a million-dollar stock trade, and his assistant called me on it within the hour."

"So he has some sort of check system," I said. "How could he do it?"

"The only thing I could ever figure out was some type of connection to the telex so that when the order was placed he would be notified. Bought our operator or her counterpart in New York. I don't know."

"But he couldn't monitor the other houses that way. There isn't any way he could buy the operators in twenty brokerage firms!"

Trayco spoke. "He's bugged the telex machine."

"What?"

"He's planted bugs on the machines and wired it directly into the computer," Trayco said. "The computer then sorts out the proper account numbers, amounts, and such, makes the comparisons, and prints out those that don't jibe at the end of each day."

Trayco must have seen the puzzled look on my face. "Look, you had my account when you were an honest working stiff. One of the things I liked was that you could give me an almost hourly update of my account. As soon as you put in a buy or a sell order over the telex and it was accomplished in New York, Banner's mainframe would sort it out and credit or debit my account and send out the confirms. All you had to do was look up my account on your monitor, and you had the updated info at your fingertips. Right?" I nodded. "Then if they tapped into the telex lines and monitored all trades, programming their computer as to what to look for, it could pick them up and do the same thing. An unpublicized way of making sure everyone stays honest."

"That must be some computer," Ben said.

"Like TITAN," I mumbled.

"What?"

"Nothing. You're right; it has to be big. Not necessarily for storage, but for its ability to do many things at one time. No matter how they do it, we at least know they do."

"First thing we do is check for bugs, just to be sure," Trayco said, standing. "Where's your office telex?" He was already going through the office door.

"That machine behind the counter, the big one," I said as we followed him out. He knelt down and followed the heavy wire, first to the bottom of the machine, then to the wall. Pulling a small kit from his pocket and selecting a tiny flatnose screwdriver, he removed the wall plate. No bug.

Four screws secured a plate at the bottom of the machine. He removed them and inspected inside with a pocket flashlight.

"What on earth do you have in that kit, Trayco?"

He smiled. "Look what we have here."

He pulled a small box from inside the machine. Black with an antenna attached. The lead telex wire entered it and then came out the back side.

"That, white boy, is what we're looking for. The antenna is wired into the telex and sends a signal to a transmitter somewhere close by. It beefs up the signal and sends it to an antenna that is probably attached to Duquesne's computer. He can keep track of every transaction.

"How can we shut down twenty of those babies in twenty different locations without anyone noticing?" Trayco asked. I could see the wheels of his devious mind delving into inventive gray matter.

I looked at my watch. He was right. Shutting them all down would be impossible, and this confirmed the difficulty of selling their securities out from under them. Using TITAN remained paramount.

"I think this had better be a discussion for another time," I said. "It's late—or early, depending on your perspective—and time we got out of here." I switched off the computer and stretched. Bone weariness was fogging my brain, and I didn't care to tackle another problem until I could clear at least a few of the cobwebs. "I'll have to think this one through." I handed Trayco the journal. "For now, Sergeant, see that this doesn't fall into enemy hands."

Ben used his keys to lock the safe and to slide the false panel back into place. Then, flipping off the lights, he hurried to catch up with us at the main doors of the office foyer. Using his magnetic key to lock things up solidly, Ben turned and pushed an elevator button. Trayco eyed the floor designator lights above the shining stainless steel doors. Two of them were flashing. Both elevators were stopping at our floor.

29

Before I could take a breath Trayco manhandled me around the corner and into the dim light of an empty hall.

"What the . . ."

Trayco had his gun out and used it as a finger, bringing it to his lips and signaling for quiet. The rasping voice coming from the direction of the elevator was unfamiliar, cold, and carried a slight accent.

"You're wanted at the Mirage."

Ben responded calmly but an octave higher than normal as his chest tightened with fear. "Fine. But what for? I've just tied into the system so I can go home and work today. The market will be open soon, and I need to monitor—"

"It will wait. He wants you, *now.*"

I tried to move, to help, as I heard the elevator doors close, but Trayco held me tight.

"Jerry, if you don't knock it off I'll pistol-whip you! Now, do exactly as I tell you, or you'll get Ben killed. Understood?"

His face was hard, his eyes boring holes through the back of my head.

"Stairs!" I pointed. "Come on!" He jerked me by my jacket collar.

We crashed through the door and bolted down the steps, my mind racing ahead to find a plan. Ben may have given me a lot of grief, but if anyone was going to beat the hay out of him it had to be me, not a couple of muscle-bound, brain-dead messenger boys sent by Duquesne, a man I had come to despise more than America's role in Vietnam.

The new Walther .38 that Trayco had provided was out of

my belt and in my hands, a shell quickly injected. I had to take three steps at a time trying to keep Trayco's long-legged six-foot-four frame in sight. A door with a large number one on it suddenly appeared, and Trayco turned the knob while waving his gun for quiet.

Trayco was quick to assess the situation. Gun in front, he slipped through, signaling me to follow. We were hidden in the small hall behind the elevators that put the stairway access out of view from the lobby and breezeway entrance. The thump of leather heels on ceramic tile and the dull thud of oak doors closing signified their entrance into the breezeway at the far end.

Trayco peered around the corner at the guard desk. Then he straightened.

"The guard's down." He looked again. "They're going into the parking garage. Any shortcuts from here?"

I felt the sweat rolling down the back of my neck. "None. If we try to take them now, Ben may be in the way."

He nodded agreement. "We've got to beat them to the Mirage."

He slipped into the lobby, watching the garage exit through tinted windows, and took up a position behind one of the expensive couches. We didn't dare go through the breezeway until they were in the street beyond the Center's covered main entrance and out of sight.

I checked the guard! He was alive, but he had a nasty bump on the back of his head. I dialed 911 and requested an ambulance, then placed the receiver in the guard's hand.

A moment later the Lincoln limousine drove by the big lobby and turned south into the lit street at the front of the Center. We would go down Paradise to Flamingo, turn west to the Strip, and then go back north to the Mirage's main entrance. Wider streets and less traffic, it was usually the fastest way.

That left us the shorter distance, but it had too many red lights and the intersection funnel at Desert Inn and the Strip—a bottleneck that usually backed traffic up even in the early morning hours.

We raced down the breezeway and into the garage. We had parked on the second level to keep the car out of sight. Now it was a good thirty-second delay up the outside stairway.

Trayco's Mercedes was a 500 SL, specially fitted with a

souped-up engine, bulletproof tinted glass, and armor-plated doors and fenders. His clientele were not always popular with all their constituents.

We were soon headed west, with two red lights behind us in less than fifty-five seconds. The unusually light traffic was in our favor as Trayco downshifted his way through it. Rounding a natural curve that changed our direction from west to north, we could see the Mirage through the block to our left. Another hotel, much smaller and opposite the Mirage on the Strip, blocked a complete view. Without wings we would have to travel a more circuitous route past the whirlpool of traffic at Desert Inn and the Strip. Luckily there weren't a lot of cars, but half a dozen blocked our way. My heart sank, forcing me to form a prayer in my mind. Any delay might prevent us from getting to the Mirage before Ben. I should have prayed for us.

Trayco yanked on the wheel and spun over the curb and onto the sidewalk, his palm pressed firmly against the horn, scattering a few early-morning tourists into traffic and over a low retaining wall behind a cheap souvenir store. I ducked my head, waiting for the sound of breaking bones, while praying speed into the legs of strangers.

The Mercedes bounded off the sidewalk and into the traffic of the Strip. Cars slammed on brakes, sliding toward one another, missing us by inches on both sides. Pedestrians cleared the crosswalk like sheep who smelled a hungry wolf. Trayco turned, fishtailing at a forty-five-degree angle and heading south between spreading traffic. Releasing the gas pedal, Trayco turned right, easing the unscathed Mercedes into the main entrance of the Mirage, the hotel's man-made volcano in full eruption.

I thanked the good Lord while collecting my stomach out of the backseat. "Trayco! You ever drive like that again with me in the car, and I'll—" He held his hand up as he pulled the car over against the yellow No Parking area, concentrating on his rearview mirror.

"They're coming. Get out and follow my cue!" He opened the door and was out before I could protest.

I jumped from the car, half mad at his treatment and poor judgment, my heart still in my throat, when I saw the black Lincoln less than fifty feet away. Feigning some normalcy, I moved to his side in the entranceway.

I felt Trayco's blow to my chest before I saw it, and I hit the pavement, stunned, gasping for air. The Lincoln came screeching to a halt inches from my head.

Trayco was yelling, shaking his fist, and cursing, dancing toward me as if he were going to finish the job. Then he backed away and began to yell at the Lincoln's driver, who had questioned his parentage for making him stop.

I tried to catch my breath, rolling on my side. His fist had crunched my lungs into the front of my spine, and my chest burned with the pain.

When I heard the car door open near my head, the second bruiser getting out to help do a number on Trayco, I rolled under the front edge of the fender and watched the size twelve Reeboks come toward me. Out of the corner of my eye I saw a crowd gathering on the sidewalk. Then the Reeboks were within reach, and I grabbed a leg and yanked it toward me, hitting his shin against the wheel fender. He yelped and went down as I rolled out, sat astride his massive chest, pulled out the .38, and put it in his face.

Trayco had his gun pointing up the nose of the driver, daring him to move. I got to my feet and told the stranger to turn over and face away from me. Yanking his .45 from his belt, I ordered him to get into the backseat of the car. I slid in beside him and held the gun to his ear, shaking and asking myself what a good Mormon boy was doing pointing guns at people in the middle of a hundred or so witnesses!

Trayco opened the driver's door and pulled him roughly from the vehicle, shoving him toward the rear of the car. Trayco opened the trunk and told Duquesne's messenger boy to get in. The man stiffened with resolve until Trayco hammered him gently on top of his balding pate. He got in, further polluting the air with his verbal garbage.

Trayco slammed the trunk just as the hotel security bolted down the entranceway toward us. He stepped past the car, slipping his gun in its shoulder holster, out of sight under his light jacket, and gave his ID and a soft-soap explanation to security.

Satisfying them, he asked one whom he knew if he would take care of the Mercedes, handing him a fifty for his troubles. Then he got into the Lincoln and sped around the entranceway and back onto the Strip, heading south. Turning at Caesars Palace, he drove us to the freeway and back toward my house. Ben's mouth was shining his Florsheims while my heart thumped against the back of the seat. I made an oath, gently, under my breath. "Never again! Never again!"

After seeing the two thugs secured and under guard, we went into the den and collapsed into various pieces of furniture.

"What'd they want, Ben?" I asked.

"They didn't say, but it wasn't going to be pleasant."

"They're two guns for hire," Trayco said. "Good boys at what they do. We're lucky we caught them by surprise."

"You know them?" I asked.

He smiled wryly. "It's my job to know these kind of people, remember? Those two would kill for their sister's piggy bank and make it look like she deserved it." He paused. "Look, Jerry, I appreciate your position in things like this, but I had to act quickly. Ben was headed for a desert grave; I can almost guarantee it."

I sat down, trying to catch up with the rush of events. Any plan I had remotely decided on was suddenly blown into small confetti. Putting something back together wouldn't be easy. I wanted to dump the whole thing and run for cover.

"Okay, we need to buy some time," I said. "Which one of those muscle-bound trucks was in charge?" The question wasn't directed to anyone in particular.

"The Italian-looking one whose shin you split open," Ben said, smiling.

"Trayco, bring him in here. He's about to call his boss."

At first the man whom Trayco called Angello was reluctant to cooperate. Kentucky Trayco—ex-sergeant, still impossible tough guy—softened him up with a few words and a gun shoved in the man's mouth, the barrel touching the back of his throat. I cringed at the tactics, but couldn't fault the results. We had no time to play games.

The man regained his composure as I wrote out what we wanted said. I had him rehearse the words, then we dialed the Mirage. I listened on the bedroom extension while Trayco positioned his gun on the back of Angello's neck just below the hairline. "This is Angello. We can't find him. We just missed him at the office."

"Missed him!" Duquesne said. "Explain, Angello, and it better be good!"

"He must a gone out through the private elevator. He was

up there—he signed in—but he was gone when we went up."

There was a pause. "Okay," Duquesne said. "He has a place in California. A condo in Newport. Put some people on it and put the word out around here. When he shows up he's to be brought here immediately. Understood?"

"Yessir, but—"

"But what! Can't you hear me? I want him found!"

"Yessir, but what I wanted to tell you was we had to mess up the guard a little bit, and he knows who I am. I've been there before, and we chatted a little. I don't think we should come back to the Mirage. We should keep out of sight for a few days until things cool off." Angello was very convincing.

"Angello! Can't you do anything right! What did you mess him up for?"

"He wasn't going to let us in. He said Stevenson didn't want to be disturbed. When I pressed him he said he'd call Stevenson, so I hit him."

"Okay, okay. You're right; lie low. Did anyone else sign in with Stevenson?"

"No, sir. Just him."

"Angello, you listen. Stevenson must be found. Take care of it, Angello. Do you hear me? He must be here in the morning."

"Yessir. We'll find him."

Trayco was putting the phone back on the hook as I entered the room. Angello wanted to kill us. It was written all over his face.

"Very good, Angello. Remind me to tell your boss how co-operative you were. I suggest that when we let you out of here in a few days you take a long vacation. Fillmore Duquesne would not be pleased with what you have just done."

He shrugged his shoulders. "I work for Owens on loan from my family. That guy, I hardly know, and he don't scare me. He touches me, and they'll never find his body." He wasn't kidding.

"Trayco, what do you think about Mr. Angello's dramatics? Convincing?"

He nodded. "Yeah. His boss shouldn't be suspicious about what you're up to, Jerry, but he wants Ben pretty bad. He won't wait long on that count." He began to pull Angello to his feet.

"Wait a minute. Before you put our guest to bed I have one

more question. Angello, why did Duquesne send you after Ben?"

He looked away, belligerent.

Trayco pushed his gun into his rib cage. "Answer the question. Now!"

Angello was standing on his tiptoes. "All . . . all right. Back off! He was going to kiss him good-bye. Said he didn't need him anymore, and he was a liability."

"Why didn't you just take him out in the desert and kill him?"

Ben's body straightened, and his head jerked in my direction. "He needed to make sure Stevenson didn't leave behind any . . . uh . . . messages to important people. And, he wanted to find out if his information was right."

"What information?" I asked.

"Somebody called and told Duquesne the feds were looking for this guy and they'd better get rid of him. Duquesne told us to bring him in so he could check it out."

"Who told him Ben was wanted by the federal government?"

"I don't know."

"When did the call come in?" I asked.

"An hour ago. Look, I'm only muscle. Duquesne told us to find him. We did. Until you two came along."

"Yeah, sorry to mess up your plans," I said. "How did you know to come directly to the office?"

"The caller said that's where he was."

"That's enough, Kenny. Put the garbage out, will you?"

When Trayco returned I was deep in thought. "Jerry," he said, "we have a lil' ol' fox in the henhouse! Any ideas?"

"Umm . . . Did you check this place for bugs?"

"Yeah. Nothing."

"Is there any chance one of your people . . ." I immediately regretted asking the question. If looks could kill I would have expired on the spot. "Sorry. I'm grasping for straws."

I turned to Ben. "Anyone know you're involved? Anyone, Ben?"

"No one," he said.

"No partners you haven't told us about?"

He shook his head emphatically. "No way! Duquesne brought in the people and threatened our lives if we tried to do so, or if we so much as breathed this to anyone. No way."

Trayco spoke. "It's someone outside Duquesne's direct influence."

"Yeah. Someone who seems to be just one step ahead of us.

"An hour ago. About the time we got what we needed out of Duquesne's mainframe. Someone knew we were there, but didn't know what we were up to." I shook my head, trying to get rid of the cobwebs. Then I changed the subject.

"Duquesne is after you, Ben. You know it, and he knows you know it. He'll lock you out of the computer. I need to get back in there later."

"Probably already has."

I slammed my fist onto the desk. "I should have created a back door."

They looked at me confusedly as I went to the computer.

"If we can still get in by using Ben's password I can have the system log a new password into its memory, allowing me back in when I like. It's called a back door. I should've done it earlier, now . . ."

I used the autodial and called Duquesne's mainframe. "Here goes."

I punched in BEN and waited.

ACCESS DENIED.

"That's it! We're locked out!"

"No way around the password, I suppose?" asked Trayco.

"Not that I know of," I said. "How about you, Ben?"

"None. We're out of it."

"What about some of the other brokers? Does everyone use their first name as their initial password?"

"Some might, but they don't have to. Besides, their initial password is attached to a certain set of access codes, remember. Theirs are not the same as mine. Without their initial password *and* their codes we can't get in."

I flipped off the computer and sat back in my chair. So close, and yet so far away. Without the ability to get back in, my plan to sell him out through his own system was ashes.

30

After a short nap I sat down at the familiar keyboard, the pieces of the puzzle banging around in my mind. Duquesne considered Ben a liability because someone cold and calculating knew we were after him. How? Who? We had slipped the noose for now, but for how long? That someone had to be found.

I shook my head with a deep sigh and then loaded TER-ROR1. I had to admit that the use of that password had been a predictable guess. Sellars had left it attached to Duquesne's file under R and D, research and development. I knew it had to be a password or a code name. What I couldn't figure out was how Sellars got it and why he hadn't used it. But then, maybe he had, and the information I wanted was sitting in another file Sellars had hidden deep within TITAN. I would probably never know.

My good eye stared at the screen, the first page coming up. I always hated puzzles. Why couldn't things be organized and fall into place neatly the way I was used to? As a broker, you organize things, keep them in order, with no room for bedlam or missing pieces. And names you don't know! That's how people lose money. How you fail.

I banged the keys. I ought to have been thanking my lucky charms. Now that we were shut out of Duquesne's mainframe our only hope was what we had already snatched out of his system.

I flipped to the next page and then to the next, scanning. My eyes got bigger with each word. Maybe we weren't so bad off after all.

I found the financial report—$32,300,000,000 invested. It was followed by a list of brokers and their accounts, phone numbers, and code names, but no passwords. Duquesne also kept a file on each broker, giving reasons why they were used. Blackmail in every case, and some of the brokers were pretty nasty people who wouldn't want the SEC to find out about their real past, not to mention federal and state law enforcement. After reading part of Ben's, I understood why he wanted it kept secret.

In addition there was a list of banks, account numbers, wire numbers, and contacts. Everything I needed in one neat little package.

Then came the timetable.

"Trayco! Come and take a look at this. Ben, you'd better come over here. This is crazy." Trayco put down Clancy's latest novel, and Ben got up from the couch, where he was trying to recover from the evening's close encounter.

With one of them over each shoulder, I pointed at the screen.

TIMETABLE

Every single aspect of TERROR1 is reliant upon the success or failure of meeting our deadlines. Timing is critical, and each area of operation must be completed by its projected deadline, or it will lead to serious breakdown in the other segments or, possibly, the entire plan.

Phase One: Investments to control the American petroleum industry, and substantially control the weapons and technological industries, will begin February 1987. It has been projected that 32 billion dollars will be needed, 10 billion each of the first two years, and 12 billion the last year and a half. All investments must be in place by 1 August 1990. Each company we desire is listed later in this report, along with Mr. Duquesne's detailed projections of percent of stock needed, possible expenditures, and projected influential people to be purchased and the method to be used in doing so. It is expected that while the rest of the American economy is falling apart these two industries will turn huge profits because of events we will bring about in the Middle East.

Phase Two: The drilling over the fault line is under the direction of Mr. Winters and Mr. Owens. Dr. Ariel Benson has been hired as scientist. Her proposal is also included, in detail, later in this report. Timing is essential, and the pressure on the fault must be critical and ready to push into a full-scale earthquake on 1 August 1990.

The diversion is planned to be of such consequence to the American people that they will have no desire to get involved in Middle Eastern affairs in any significant way, and will pressure the president to stay at home. It is estimated that nearly 100 thousand will die in the initial quake, that property damage will be in the hundreds of millions, and that the Wyoming oil fields and government storage facilities will be severely damaged. A peripheral disaster may occur at the Idaho Nuclear Engineering Laboratory, causing thousands of other deaths. See detailed report on page 63.

Phase Three: Military invasion of Kuwait on 2 August 1990. Saudi Arabia by 15 August 1990. The Emirates by 10 September 1990. Jordan by 6 December 1990. After these nations come under The New Republic others will follow, either by force or by terms. The New Republic will control the Middle East by the end of 1991. Israel will fall in June 1992.

"What's this?" asked Trayco.

"Can't you read? Look at the date on military action and diversionary activity. That's only two days from now.

"Are the finances in place, Ben?" I asked.

"Mine are. Yes." He answered with a voice barely audible.

"Then in two days they'll rock the West with an earthquake and invade Kuwait, then Saudia Arabia. Diversion and military action.

"The arrogance of Duquesne. None of this is even coded, and some of it's written like a journal." I pushed the down arrow. "Details, dates, places of meetings, who attended, what was discussed. Look at it all! Give this to the press and the world will crucify Duquesne and the others. Why would he leave himself so wide open? Why would the others allow such incriminating evidence to—"

"Without Ben and Sellars, it wouldn't have been so wide open, now, would it?" Trayco responded. "Those pictures Mike showed you tell how they handle people who get too close. You and Bob, the geologist, Sellars—you're all examples. Man! From the looks of this, he's a fanatic for detail and organization. Could you keep track of all of this in your head? Never mind, you can't even keep track of your car keys.

"Another thing. If they succeed—and obviously they think they will—they're figuring on being big heroes to some political factions around the world, particularly to the terrorist world. Their actions would be the subject of ballads and stories for generations to come. If this works, that stuff you're reading is what a lot of kids will read in their history books. Mr. Duquesne and the others wouldn't want to miss their moment of glory because they didn't keep good records, now, would they?" His voice was edged with sarcasm.

I stood and began to pace. Ben took my place and began to read the file more carefully. Trayco planted his great hulk in the Lazy Boy.

I started to talk to myself out loud. "The senator was right; they're planning an act of war against the American people, preliminary to launching their force into Kuwait.

"Only two days to stop them. Not much time, but enough—at least at the oil rig. With this stuff we're back in the ball game and have a great chance of freezing most of their assets."

"Jerry, you'd better take a look at this." Ben's voice sounded strained and frightened. I walked to the computer and stared down at the green words on dark background, Trayco by my side.

"What the . . ."

"No! They wouldn't!" added Trayco.

Under the section entitled "Stage Two: Diversion Detail," it read:

Contingency: In case of emergency or failure to meet timetable by "natural" means, an explosive device is to be used to detonate the well. It should be lowered to 3462 meter depth for maximum effect upon the fault plain. The device should be a plastic explosive and equal to 2000 pounds of surface charge. With the pressure of the forced water this amount will be sufficient to cause an earthquake of ten or better on the Richter scale, with serious damage percussion for a minimum of 200 miles away from the fault line, mild damage beyond. Along the fault line, north and south, the damage will extend 400 to 600 miles.

I had read enough. I picked up the phone and dailed Wyoming.

31

The senator placed a three-way conference call to the White House. The president had been briefed and had taken personal charge of what must come next.

"Mr. Daniels, how bad will it be?" the president asked. "I don't know much about such things, I'm afraid."

I explained what Perrigrine had told us. "He's doing a hypothetical and will have it ready by four o'clock. Then we'll know more."

"But the damage will be extensive?"

"If their methods work, catastrophic, sir. Duquesne's plan calls for more than a hundred thousand lives lost."

There was a pause. "Jim, what do you need to stop them?"

"Jerry and I have talked, Mr. President, and we can get an injunction by this afternoon and move them off the property—"

"Off federal land? For what reason?"

"It's a long story, sir," I said, "but the property belonged to my ancestors long before it belonged to the government. I have a document to prove it."

"The attorney general's office has verified that we can get the injunction, Mr. President," the senator said. "But we're afraid they'll explode the device if we serve the papers to Winters. We can't take that chance."

"I see what you mean," the president said. "You're sure about their timetable, Mr. Daniels?"

"Yes. It's in Duquesne's computer files. We have the information firsthand."

"Then I must move to prepare our armed services both here and abroad; the national guard in the states surrounding the fault line should be notified; and we have to prepare to move into Kuwait if they'll cooperate—and all this despite any catastrophe Duquesne's group creates. I'll put that order out—"

"Mr. President, we must be careful," the senator said. "Notifying the states too soon could be dangerous. Would you be willing to leave that to me?"

"Yes." He paused. "What do you need to stop them at the wells?"

"How close is your nearest Special Forces antiterrorist team, Mr. President?" the senator asked.

"San Diego. We can have them in Jackson late this afternoon."

"Tell them to bring equipment for rugged terrain, sir, and night—"

"They're the best, Mr. Daniels. Don't worry. Can you stop Duquesne and his men's attack on our economy? I can put a freeze on their accounts if you can find out their names and numbers."

"We have them, but—"

"Here's a new number for WASHINGTON," the president said, interrupting. "Call him when you're ready. Any idea—does it say in that file of Duquesne's who Royalty is?"

"No, sir," I said. "and as you know, we have several unidentified players. I understand WASHINGTON is working on that, sir."

"Yes, but chances aren't good and . . . well, gentlemen, I can't keep all of this a secret. There's too much involved! I've got to know who to trust."

"I can't tell you that, sir, not yet. Sellars may have known, and I'm following his path, but I'm not all the way there. Be careful who you talk to, sir. If they find out before we stop them—"

"I know; I know. Darned irritating not to be able to use the people you really need right now. I look at everyone with skewed vision. Even my wife, for pete's sake."

I chuckled. "Rest assured, sir, it isn't your wife.

"May I suggest that Senator Freeman fly to Washington to be of assistance?"

"Not on your life, Jerry—"

"Senator, you need to be there. That's where you'll do the most good, whether we succeed or fail. Others must be told and prepared for this, and the country needs some strong bipartisan leadership as these feathers start to fly. Don't you agree, Mr. President?"

"He's right, Jim. I can't order you, but I do need you here more—much more—than you're needed in Wyoming."

It was decided.

"Mr. President, Duquesne's report gives every indication that they'll proceed in taking Kuwait no matter what happens in Jackson. It also indicates that they'll take Saudi Arabia next. The senator told me about what may happen if they do that. Can they be stopped?"

"I wish I knew, Mr. Daniels. We're not dealing with people who agree with international law. They've set their minds and hearts on Middle Eastern and world domination through both military and economic means. Our intelligence sources tell us they will not be deterred from those goals. If that's the case, force will have to be used."

"No Vietnam?"

"No Vietnam. We'll give our people the weapons and the authority to do what has to be done."

"Can we beat them?"

"Yes, but not without a tremendous cost to everyone involved."

"I don't envy your position, sir."

"I was hoping the senator would offer to fill in for me for a year or so."

"No thanks, Mr. President."

"Mr. Daniels, we can't prevent them from taking Kuwait, but you can stop them here, on our own territory. There'll be enough misery and bloodletting if we have to go to war, without thousands of innocent citizens dying in an earthquake. Stop them."

32

The senator's Cessna Citation V lifted off from the North Las Vegas Airport shortly after noon on 31 July, my mind floating between reality and much-needed sleep. I had printed out a copy of TERROR1 to bring along, and my tired eyes worked at the words.

The first twenty-five pages were the introduction and development of the plan over the last ten years. Iraq's war with Iran was intended to solidify in American minds, and the minds of the rest of the world, that Iraq was a friend to be trusted, an ally against the real enemy, Iran, while also giving Iraq invaluable access to armament support from the United States, France, the USSR, and Germany, among others. The pages gave some outline of recent developments to lengthen the range of the SCUD missiles purchased from the USSR, and the production of a warhead that could house chemicals such as mustard and nerve gas, although this was not quite complete.

It also detailed the development of nuclear weapons for use; a part of the plan that had been thwarted by Israel when they had discovered and bombed the plant. The report stated firm regrouping in that area with the particular help of German industry. There was to be continued research and development with a deadline of late 1991.

The next fifty pages contained the details on the military takeover of the Middle East and the eventual destruction of the state of Israel. It called for the deaths of all opposing leaders and people, and total control of their assets. Kuwait was to fall first, then Saudi Arabia, the Emirates, Jordan, and

Lebanon. The leaders of Yemen and Libya had already secretly joined the alliance, and would receive their fair share of the spoils. Egypt would then be forced to join, leaving Israel surrounded by a formidable and undeniable force that could annihilate them. Syria and Iran were the only question marks, but they could be circumvented. Deadline 1992.

I knew the situation in the Middle East; Liz and I had traveled there in 1984 and had fallen in love with all of it. Jerusalem, the Holy City, was desecrated by war and bloodshed in the name of different gods to different peoples. Mecca, the site of Mohammed's new religion, which had done so much to help a godless people many years ago, was now being used by corrupt leaders for their own ends. There is nothing so formidable as a war in the name of religion, in the name of God.

The descendants of Isaac and Ishmael, two sons of the great prophet Abraham, were killing each other. The hate was embedded deep in the souls and minds of too many. It would not be changed easily.

I shook my head, knowing who was about to be the real losers. Thousands of innocent people would be killed—Americans, Arabs, Israelis, French, British. Every nation would be thrown into this war, like so much fodder, controlled by the greed and the insanity of a few, the fear and indecisiveness of others.

I laid my head back against the seat, tired clear to the marrow, sorrowed by what I knew was a no-win situation. People would die in the next seventy-two hours. Some of it couldn't be stopped; it had already been planned by an out-of-control leader in Iraq, but the rest I must try to stop. If I failed . . .

I adjusted in the seat, my tired and aching bones crying for rest that wouldn't come, couldn't come, not yet. Somehow we must stop them at the well.

The thought made the hair stand up on the back of my neck. Winters and Owens had sufficient forces prepared to defend the rigs if anyone tried to stop their operation. They were also prepared to lower explosives into holes deep inside the earth's surface and, if their calculations were right, create one of the most horrifying catastrophes of modern times. Were they typical terrorists, willing to die for what they believed? Would it take firepower to stop them? No. Not all of them, anyway. Those guarding the wells were hired guns, no more, no less. That, at least, would work to our advantage.

Why the document? It was of no real value now, was it?

The senator was right, wasn't he? If we tried to serve the injunction, they'd blow the wells while keeping us at bay with their weapons until it was too late. Why? Why the dreams? Why had I been led to that document when now it seemed of no earthly use?

Protection of the property after the marines took the wells? Hardly a use at all.

I returned to thinking about the report, shaking my head, bewildered. A reason for that document. There had to be a reason!

The last hundred pages detailed the diversion. The report maintained that America was the only force large enough and strong enough, and with enough unfettered ability, to stop their plan. Russia was too busy with domestic unrest and their economy, and they would be reluctant to fight a long-standing ally. All others were not considered a threat simply because, in the opinion of Duquesne's group, they had neither the backbone nor the armament to do anything. Most of them were highly reliant on Middle East oil and would deal at higher prices before they would try to move in militarily. With the one remaining world power, the United States, out of the leadership role, the rest of the world would hesitate long enough for TERROR1 to complete its military aspect. After that, little could be done to restore the region to even its unstable "stability," leaving the leaders of the "New Republic" free to do as they wished in the Middle East, *and* free to control the world economy through the assets they would have under their greedy little thumbs.

The report was particularly specific about the need for secrecy and keeping the diversion looking natural, with no connection to the Middle East. This must not be a standard terrorist movement, but must appear to be an act of God. No fanatic organizations were to be involved, and the diversion must be under the control and direction of the committee, with Fillmore Duquesne as chairman. He alone was responsible for the instigation of the plan's objectives. He alone would answer to the ruling body, the committee, for its growth and development. He had selected the diversion after careful study of a number of possibilities and had put Winters and Owens in charge of bringing the plan to fruition.

I looked out of the small window. The clouds below were thick and low, with the steel grey of the mountains poking through like spikes. We would be landing in heavy weather.

I looked at the papers again. An almost foolproof plan. How do you prosecute men living outside the United States who have constantly ignored international law, except when it is to their advantage? Extradition? Not these men. No country would want the publicity. If anything was done at all it would be—must be—behind closed doors.

A plan began forming in my mind. There was a way, if everyone would cooperate.

My eyes went to the pages once more, trying to concentrate, working to prevent their success, quickly, quietly.

The last hundred pages dealt with the financial aspect of the plan.

Beginning in 1987 Duquesne initiated the process of buying American oil and military technology companies. Through the use of his computer-system network capability he tapped into national and international sources and compiled files on key people in brokerage houses, banks, savings and loans, and corporations. After a year-long process he had selected a "handful" to blackmail into submission. He engineered it in such a manner as to keep each person separate from the others and without knowledge of the extent of what they were involved in. With the exception of a few meetings with the brokers, and the meetings of the main committee, everything was done through the computer system that Duquesne alone controlled.

The committee held securities in more than seven hundred accounts in twenty brokerage houses. Twenty-eight billion dollars in assets. A dozen cash accounts in banks and savings and loans held another four billion, gathering interest, waiting to be used, and making the total 32,300,000,000. They controlled the stock or management of too many companies to count and were in a position to control oil through control of pipeline companies, processing plants, and transportation corporations, along with many large oil-producing firms themselves, and at least thirty-five percent of technology dealing with weapons and armament production and development. They didn't have to own the firms, only control their stock and voting rights by electing to the board of directors people they could control, then changing presidents, policies, sales—every aspect. All legal and above suspicion. With such power they could withhold oil, causing the price to skyrocket in a failing economy, further precipitating financial failure from the consumer upward.

With control of military technology and armament companies, they could slow down production at a critical time and even sabotage plants and equipment, putting our military months behind, keeping our allies from receiving necessary weapons, stealing our secrets and using them against us. Undermining then dismantling our military capability.

Maybe. The oil companies had treated us in similar fashion before, and we had survived. Of course, one group did not have total control and call all the shots, carefully correlated with production and prices in the Middle East. With those conditions and a financial boondoggle created by this catastrophe . . . they would at least make a lot of money.

Control of companies producing for the military? Even more precarious. They could never control them, but they could do serious damage. And wasn't that all they wanted? Serious damage? Set us back a few years? Show the world what could really be done to the high-and-mighty Americans?

One thing for sure. You couldn't fault them for lack of a big idea! A plan much like Pick up Sticks. Throw them all in the air and see how they land. You're bound to come away with a few points. Not the least of which could be a lot of death and destruction.

Trayco handed me the on-board phone. "It's the senator."

"Hello, Senator. Any action at the wells?"

"Yes, that's why I called. They seem to be shutting down and moving out of areas two and three."

I sat up. "Are you sure?"

"Yes, the sheriff has Burt Sims at two and Dolph Baker at three as spotters. They indicate definite movement to shut those two down. Why so surprised?"

"It just scares me, that's all. Either they know we're coming, or they're ready to start the quake. How did you get those guys close enough to see what's going on?" I was impressed, remembering the encounter Bob and I had had.

"They're both first-class archery enthusiasts and hunters, as well as former military," the senator said. "They went in on foot, full camouflage. Both are sitting within a quarter mile of wells two and three, and they won't be seen unless someone trips over them.

"Jerry, you have to move tonight." He paused. "I have the chopper here, ready to leave in about five minutes. I'll meet you at the airport. Blaznack said you should be landing in about twenty minutes. We've turned this place into a command center, and Bob, Mike, and Charla are running things. The chopper will bring you back, along with a marine colonel, who's head of the special help being flown in. Seems he was caught on furlough in Denver and came directly here. The rest of the team and equipment are coming from San Diego via Hill Air Force Base in Ogden, Utah."

"How's Bob feeling? Are you sure—"

"He won't be doing any push-ups, but he won't be denied."

"Jerry, I feel like I'm deserting the bridge while men are still aboard, even though I know you're right about this."

"Senator, we have a direct line to where you'll be. Heaven above only knows how this thing will end up, and we could have a national crisis—no an international crisis—on our hands. A lot of people aren't going to understand why we have to send troops into the Middle East, and you must help the president convince them. You've got the job; now start earning the money."

"If my daughter didn't like you so much I'd have you shot," he said lightly. "See you at the airport." We hung up.

I was deep in thought when I felt the wheels touch down on the pavement of the Jackson Hole Airport. I looked out of the window at a bleak, rainy day, the Tetons completely engulfed in a gray blanket of moisture-laden clouds.

The chopper carrying the senator landed as we taxied to the hangar. It was a McDonnell Douglas MD350. A six-passenger elite copter with all the latest technology and comfort. With the weather rough I was grateful for state-of-the-art radar and powerful dual turbos, a machine able to handle strong winds and heavy weather.

The senator and I exchanged brief words in the rain, then a firm handshake. In all honesty I was glad I had the easier of the two jobs and the one that would be over the quickest. He introduced us to Colonel Thomas Macklin, and saw us all on board the chopper before he followed Blaznack back to the refueling Cessna for the trip to Washington.

The colonel spoke first. "Great weather! I thought this time of the year things were bright and shiny around here.

"Trayco, good to see you again!" he said with a smile.

"Colonel." Trayco was sitting at attention.

The colonel was a short but stocky five feet ten with a strong neck and shoulders, short brown hair, a long aquiline nose, and round wire-rim glasses. His carriage inspired confidence, but it was Trayco's respect for him that spoke volumes and eased the tension in my stomach.

The trip to the ranch was a short but choppy one, with visibility at less than four hundred feet by the time we flew across Slide Lake. The chopper lived up to my expectations, the radar working like a charm, and the computer adjusting the rotor's speed and balance perfectly as we were hit with constantly changing winds.

When we landed, Mike embarrassed me in front of everyone with a kiss I thoroughly enjoyed, then all of us went into the house and deposited our equipment in the den. The fireplace was lit and added a needed warmth to an overcast, depressing day. I shook the water from my light jacket and wiped it out of my hair. Each of the others did the same, some gathering around the fire to hang rain-dampened clothes on pegs protruding from the functional heavy oak mantel.

I made the introductions while Charla poured hot drinks and passed around sandwiches.

"Anything new, Mike?" I asked.

"Yes. Rigs two and three have been shut down, tight, and all drilling personnel are on their way back to Jackson. They're blaming the storm, but the sheriff says a charter is waiting for them at the airport. They've checked out of their motels, and their destination is Waco, Texas."

"Who's left at rig one?"

"Approximately thirty paramilitaries and some technical personnel, along with Walter Babcock. As Thunderbolt's chief of operations, Babcock's in charge of the deployment of his troops. Winters and Owens were there, but they're presently at the house over by Teton Village.

"For this kind of wet weather it seems like a lot of activity. The spotter says they've added a few more gun emplacements, and he's given us the coordinates. I've located them on the map. He's afraid they have some heavy-duty weaponry sitting on three trucks in the middle of the compound. All the soldier-types are well armed and are patrolling heavily around the perimeter. Our man has had to keep on the move."

"The weather hasn't sent them indoors, then?" I asked.

"To the contrary," she said. "They seem to have loosened up a bit, moving about without fear of someone else showing up."

I moved to the map along with Trayco, Mike, and the colonel.

"This is the site, Colonel Macklin," she said. "The terrain is rough and steep on three sides. A chainlink fence completely encircles the area, and it's topped with razor wire."

Mike pointed to a new drawing on the wall. "These are the locations of the emplacements. In all, eight fifty-caliber machine guns, thirty heavily armed men, and whatever they have hidden under those tarps on the trucks located here, here, and here in the compound."

"Is the fence electric?" the colonel asked. "Any booby traps?"

"The fence is not electrified. Bob and Jerry discovered that the last time they were at the well. The spotter says no activity to plant any mines since he got up there, so I can only assume there are none.

"By the way, there's a building inside the complex that serves as an office and dormitory, but it's small and sleeps maybe fifteen."

"How good is your spotter?"

"Korea. Medal of Honor. Lost an arm to a booby trap. Married and has a fine family. He's the sheriff's top deputy."

"Hmm. Well done, Ms. Freeman. Under the circumstances I couldn't ask for better information. Do you need a job? Join up and see the world, maybe? We've just recently been told we'll be visiting the exotic deserts of the Middle East. Plenty of time for sight-seeing and . . ." He looked at Mike's half grin. "I thought not. The food wouldn't appeal to you, anyway."

I knew the reputation of soldiers like Macklin. Since the embarrassment of Iran and then Lebanon, the directive from the president's office had been to create, train, and hold ready elite groups prepared to combat terrorist actions against American citizens around the globe. The government's method of combating some forms of modern-day Gadiantonism. With things happening in the Middle East, they would be extremely busy in the near future.

He continued. "You should know, people, that this operation is under the direct authority of the president. He's briefed me on the whys and the wherefores, and has been kind enough to allow me to enlist all of you for the next twenty-four hours. With standard hazard pay, of course."

"I wondered how I would pay for my next meal at McDonald's," Bob said. Everyone who had military experience understood and chuckled a little. People didn't join the military for the pay.

Macklin grinned along with the rest, then added, "Actually, you lucky people, for this job only we guarantee forty cents above minimum wage. Now, I know Trayco's talents and experience. How about the rest of you, excluding the ladies. Trayco, let's start with your men."

Trayco nodded at the man beside him. "Tran Quo, sir. A Vietnamese who saved my life. He followed me to the United States when things got bad for our allies over there. Tran is cleared in all field weapons, but he's particularly proficient with handguns and martial arts. He has high government clearance as a part of our work protecting politicals.

"Jack has the same training and clearances. He's retired army, with experience at the end of the Vietnam conflict. Since then he's served in Special Forces and, among other things, has helped train friendlies south of the border, until coming to work for me last year."

"I've heard of his work in South America. Welcome aboard." He nodded at Jack, then looked at me. "You're next, Mr. Daniels."

"Forced retirement from the Marines due to an injury." I touched the glass eye. "I was a chopper pilot in Vietnam. Standard training for the job, but it was a long time ago."

"Very good," he said. "We'll try to put your talents to good use. Lieutenant Freeman, Bob, and I worked together in Vietnam. I wish we could use Bob's greater talents, but this trip he'll be our communications officer. Charla and Mike will aid him and try to keep us from missing some important details."

He removed the glasses and rubbed his eyes, then ran his hand through his short, wiry head of hair. I noticed a sweat mark in his camouflage field uniform. He looked at the map. "Bob, ask the spotter what's going on at well one right now, will you? Ask him if they're still working it.

"Our first concern is a bomb," the colonel said. "Has one been placed in the well or hasn't it? If the spotter says they're still drilling or forcing water down the hole, obviously they haven't armed a device and lowered it into the shaft."

Bob finished talking to the spotter. "Colonel," he said, "the spotter says visibility is worse, but he's pretty sure they're not drillin'. The pump is still runnin', and the trucks are still haulin' water."

"Very good," the colonel said. "What does that tell us, Mr. Daniels?"

"They're still holding to their first priority. A quake as an act of God."

"Bob, notify the sheriff that we want at least five men at each of wells two and three. Have them check for any sign of explosives in or near the wellheads. It's imperative that no one know of their presence. Understood?"

"Yessir."

"Good. Have them maintain constant contact with us."

He put his hands on the desk and leaned forward toward me for emphasis. "Mr. Daniels, my approach to a problem like this is usually a very direct one. Neutralizing before they can hurt you. But I think you are about to propose an alternative plan. One I probably won't like.

"However, the president has given me orders to listen, so you have the floor." He sat back in his chair. "Keep in mind that my first priority is to take those wells and prevent an explosion. I would like to do it without bloodshed, but my duty is to keep innocent people from being hurt while keeping our losses to a minimum, even if I have to use every weapon I have."

"I agree, Colonel."

"Let's hear it," he said.

I nodded, stood, and began. "I want the sheriff to deputize me and give me a uniform and one of his four-wheel-drive outfits, flashing lights and all. Then I will approach the gate and serve the papers."

It was silent in the room. Bob finally spoke. "But that could spur them into puttin' the bomb down the well, Jerry. You've said all along we can't give them forewarnin'."

"I'm relying on Babcock. In the past he was never known to be one for risking his own life when he knew he was involved in a lost cause. He'd shoot you in the back and take any advantage, but if he smelled any chance of defeat he walked, no, he ran away. Using his desire for self-preservation will save a lot of time and blood. If he decides to go for broke, you, Colonel, will be able to move in immediately and neutralize them. Nothing lost."

I let it sink in as I watched the colonel's reaction. His brow was wrinkled, and his eyes had a faraway look. "We could lose *you*, Mr. Daniels, if you're wrong about Babcock or if Winters and Owens are there. You're willing to live with that, evidently.

A possible martyr complex?" His smile was a little accusing.

I leaned forward, placing my hands on the desk, giving him a cold stare. "Colonel, unfortunately I killed enough men in Vietnam to know what it's like and how it's done. If I can't get him to walk away peacefully, I'll be well armed enough to protect myself and to help your cause by coldcocking the one man who could give the order to blow the place up. But the one thing I hated about Nam was the fact that everyone in positions to do otherwise always wanted to shoot first and negotiate later. I wonder to this day how many lives could have been saved if that had been different. As for Winters and Owens, we won't move if they're in the compound."

The words were cold, and the room was very quiet. I waited for him to speak.

He turned in the chair and looked out of the big window. Visibility was cut in half, and the rain continued to pour down. "How rough will the weather be up there?" he asked.

"The wind will be the worst, sir," Bob said. "The choppers all have the necessary equipment, but it is a danger. However, it'll definitely allow the ground troops to get closer without detection."

"Yes, I remember getting caught in a storm like this while I was hunting in Colorado one time," the colonel said. "Between lightning and wind I prayed for a good mortar barrage. It's less scary."

He faced us again. "Listen up." He stood at the desk, and everyone in the room shifted, relaxing. "We'll do it Daniels' way.

"I'm bringing in thirty-two well-trained Special Forces personnel, two transport helicopters, and three McDonnell Douglas Nightfox helicopters. Half those men will be deployed at the rig—four to a side—with orders to neutralize the enemy—"

"Uh, begging your pardon, Colonel," I said, "but that may give us away. That many soldiers in the forest. All the opposition forces probably carry radios; they could notify the main buildings, and it's over."

He smiled indulgently. "The weakness of your plan is not my men, Mr. Daniels. They come from the same cut of cloth that Stinger there did." He pointed at Trayco. "They might even put him to shame, and he was about the best there ever was."

Trayco only smiled back.

"May I continue, Mr. Daniels?"

"Yessir. Sorry."

"They'll move into position and will neutralize the enemy forces *only* if anything goes wrong with Mr. Daniels' plan." He went to his carryall bag and pulled out what looked like a small stereo headset. "One of these will be a part of everyone's gear tonight. You, Mr. Daniels, will have to take it apart so you can wear the earpiece without it being seen. You can attach the speaker anywhere within about two feet of your mouth, and we'll hear your every word. This should eliminate problems of timing or a mix-up on orders."

"Colonel," Trayco said, "I'd a given my left arm for something like this in Nam!"

"Yeah. Wouldn't we all.

"One of the transport choppers will deliver sixteen men early, giving them time to get through the hills. They'll have a special radio that sends a signal to a main unit that Bob will have here, so he can keep them from getting lost in unfamiliar terrain. The other half of my men will be dropped off here, five miles from the gate, and move into positions to take it if necessary.

"Trayco, you and your two men will be with me in the second transport. If needed we'll be dropped in the center of the compound to take the rig.

"The three Nightfox choppers will wait in the wings in case they're needed to eliminate obstacles we cannot take in less than three minutes. Mr. Daniels, they'll enter the fray at my command, understood?"

I hesitated. I knew about the Nightfox, even had a chance to fly one several times early in their development. The elite attack fighter that carries up to twenty-four rockets, two TOW missiles, a 7.52 cannon, and the computer system to make them all as deadly from a mile away as a high-powered rifle at five feet. Night-vision capability, radar-warning equipment, and the ability to fly anywhere, anytime, in any kind of weather. For them an operation like this was a piece of cake, and that's what worried me. Three Nightfox choppers could kill a lot of people in a very short period of time.

"Yessir, understood. If this plan goes bust anywhere along the line, our first responsibility is to the men involved and to those who might be affected by that quake. I don't want anyone hurt unnecessarily, Colonel. All I ask is a fair chance to convince them to throw in the towel."

He looked out of the window again. "Jerry, in Nam your call sign was Deacon, wasn't it?"

"Yessir."

"Good. Mine will be Ghost Leader, and my two groups of sixteen men will be Ghost One and Two. One will be the perimeter troops I have already mentioned. Two will be those in backup, who'll take the gate. Sergeant Delavane will lead One, and Sergeant Kaminsky will be leading Two.

"The choppers will be designated Nightfox Leader and Nightfox One and Two. The transport choppers will be Redline One and Two.

"Remember those names, ladies and gentlemen. If you need help in a hurry you'll want to call in the right people. Also, there'll be constant chatter on the headphones, and if you know who it is it'll help you keep it all straight. Bob, your old call sign was Trapper, wasn't it?"

"Yessir," he smiled.

"You'll be Trapper Base, then." He picked up the phone. "I'll make arrangements for the rest of the equipment to be delivered, along with a substance known as C6-45. Ever hear of it?"

Trayco spoke. "Yessir. We've been trying to get some of it in my protection organization, at the request of a number of our political clients." He paused. "It's new, sir, but very effective. I was impressed with a recent uh . . . demonstration."

"You should be. Nothing like it has ever been developed. Each of you will have a canister. A spray of it in the face of any of the enemy will neutralize them instantly, without lasting complications or illness. Its effects last for about forty-five minutes. Mr. Daniels, keep it handy. If Babcock goes for his weapon we'll want you to use it. Shooting him may cause others to shoot at you. Having him pass out will buy you enough time to jump for cover."

"Thank you, sir," I said truthfully. "I appreciate the thought."

He nodded. "The troops you'll be working with are from the Counter Terrorist Joint Task Force, or the CTJTF. We are trained in counter-terrorist operations and are presently considered the elite of the Special Forces military. All of these men can get within a few feet of the enemy without being seen or heard." He smiled again, and I was glad to see it. "They're the best of the best. I trained them myself."

The smile disappeared as suddenly as it had come. "They have the skills to resolve this problem, Mr. Daniels. That's why

I'm willing to give you a chance to find out for yourself how nasty terrorists really are."

CTJTF. A group rumored to have come out of the failed attempt to rescue the hostages of Iran. They usually operated on foreign ground, and could kill in any of twenty different ways, when necessary. Very disciplined, very elite. Very scary.

"Any field experience, Colonel?" Trayco asked.

He smiled. "These have been in and out of a few places, including Panama and a couple of countries in South America. They've responded very well under extremely difficult circumstances, and none of them will throw up because of spilling blood for the first time."

"There's one other target, Colonel," Bob said. "The communications tower at TriStar's main office in Afton."

"Nightfox Leader will leave early enough to make sure TriStar experiences communications failure due to a lightning strike in a heavy storm.

"Well," he went on, "that about does it. All of you will be supplied with the newer Stoner M63A1 rifles if you want them. Those of us who might be involved in close-quarters fighting will have the Model 22 Type 0 9mm with silencers, the one called the hush puppy. That includes you, Jerry. Grenades, if wanted, and other equipment, including camouflaged fatigues, are available. Bob, will you talk to the sheriff about what Jerry needs?"

"Yessir. Shouldn't be a problem."

The toys of death. I had heard about the Stoner and the Model 22. They were as accurate and deadly a weapon as produced anywhere in the world. The Model 22's silencer made the small millimeter bullet sound like a puff of air and when properly placed could kill instantly. I rubbed the goose bumps on my arms.

Macklin looked at his watch. "It's 3:00 P.M. The rest of my group will arrive at nine o'clock this evening. Redline One will leave at ten o'clock and will be in position by midnight. Redline Two will leave at eleven o'clock with the five of us. We'll drop Mr. Daniels off at a spot predetermined with the sheriff. Jerry, you need to be at the gate by midnight. From there, we play it by ear. If Babcock responds favorably it should be over by twelve-thirty. Any questions?"

There were none.

"Then one last word. Mr. Daniels, Walter Babcock is as

bad as they come. He massacred civilians in Nam and enjoyed it. I don't know what makes you think you can change the tiger's stripes, but the president was clear that I should give you the chance. If I had time I'd have your head examined; as it is I can only wish you luck."

He stood. "Now I suggest those who can, get some shut-eye. It'll be a long night." He still held the phone in his hand. Lifting his finger from the lever, he punched in the numbers and walked to a corner of the room.

"More coffee, anyone?" Charla asked. Several held out empty cups and picked up more sandwiches.

Mike sat down beside me. "Are you sure about this, Jerry?" she asked through a forced smile.

I put my arm around her shoulder and pulled her over. I questioned my own sanity. My stomach was in big knots again. On the plane I had felt good about it, as if it were the way it should work. Now—

"Jerry, you're wanted on the phone," Bob said. "Hank Butcher."

"Huh? Oh. Thanks." He handed me the cordless phone.

It had been several days since I had spoken to Hank. I just plain forgot.

Macklin looked at me from his corner, then held his phone against his chest and spoke to me. "Jerry, at this point remember these are not secured phones. Another hour and Trayco and I'll have a scrambler hooked up, but—"

I held my hand over the mouthpiece. "Yessir, I understand."

The conversation skirted the present plan. "Hank, if I can't get back, the senator and Mike will need your help to bring the other party's financial world to a satisfactory end. Up to it?"

He hesitated. "That serious?"

"Nothing, really. Just have to meet with some reluctant people."

"What are—"

I cut him off. "How's your trial in LA?" I asked.

"Oh . . . that. Fine. He'll only get ten years. Be out in a couple. He deserves more, but I'm too good at what I do, remember.

"Listen, Jerry . . . how do I—"

"Mike will have all the papers."

"She has everything you need? In Jackson?"

"Yes."

He changed the subject. "Anything on the president's nasty friend?"

"We're close. No name yet, but it won't be long." I hadn't told him about all of Sellars' files. There was too much I didn't know. No sense in worrying him.

"Well, then," he said, "anything else I can do?"

"Nope. Just be there if Mike needs you." We said good-bye and hung up.

The rain was still beating down, a solid sheet of water glistening in the dim gray light of late afternoon.

"Okay, Lord," I prayed, "that's plenty of water. Don't overdo it today. Just a nice light fog would be nice, along with a changed Walter Babcock, if you please!"

I took a deep breath, wishing I were somewhere else doing something that had a future.

33

A half hour after the call from Hank, Trayco and Bob had hooked up a scrambling device the colonel had brought, and, with the line secure, I called Phil Perrigrine in Salt Lake City.

The news wasn't good, and it echoed what Duquesne had written in the TERROR1 files. After twenty minutes I put in a call to the president and Senator Freeman.

Estimated loss of life was thirty to fifty thousand along the Wasatch front and north to the Canadian border. Nearly a quarter of a million potential injuries, half a million homeless. Several billion dollars in damage, and untold millions in losses in business revenue. If what they had planned worked, the San Francisco quake of 1906 would be nothing by comparison.

"Jerry, I've talked to the colonel," the president said. "I appreciate your plan and what you're trying to do here, and I respect the moral ethics behind it, but I have to be honest. It makes me nervous. We can't take any chances on this. Unless we stop these men they'll go on to reap their destruction. The slightest miscalculation here—"

"Mr. President," I interrupted, "I understand, but I honestly think a surprise approach is our best bet. If we go in there guns blazing the odds are only fifty-fifty of our successfully dislodging them before they can set the explosives."

He paused. "You're putting yourself in a rather tentative position, Jerry. I would prefer you didn't, and Colonel Macklin says there are other methods involving only military personnel and I—"

"Excuse me for interrupting again, Mr. President. Walter Babcock has a history of running away when he knows he will lose. Someone has to explain to him what we have, and how very much the odds are in our favor. Also, sir, once I get Babcock close enough, I can neutralize him if necessary, leaving his people without a leader."

I took a deep breath. "Finally, sir, I'm the most likely candidate because the others are all needed in critical positions should Babcock decide he wants to grandstand.

"I think they'll give up without a fight. I don't think my life is in that much danger, and the other options guarantee fatalities. You have the power to override me on this, sir, but I hope you won't." I exhaled what little air I had left.

"This will work, sir. I know it! I hope you'll give it a chance."

There was a long pause. "All right. But if they start to shoot, Macklin is to go full bore. Understood, Jerry? We must protect our men, and we must take that well."

"We all understand that, sir. I wouldn't have it any other way. How are things at your end, Mr. President?"

"In place, Jerry, in place. Thanks to your warning we have made tremendous diplomatic progress. The military is on full alert and will be ready to move within two hours of any action by Iraq. Under the circumstances things couldn't be better."

"Jerry," the senator spoke, "the president is right. Things have really moved well. It has been most gratifying to see, but I'm afraid we can't keep it under wraps much longer. All the phone calls, meetings with even a few trusted people, the movement and preparation by the military. The word is going to get back to the wrong people if it hasn't already. If Royalty doesn't know something is going on he's either blind or nonexistent."

"He's there, all right, Senator. And he may have some suspicions. We can't help that. I think he'll want to be sure of his ground before he contacts Duquesne."

The president spoke. "I haven't had time to fill the senator in on this, but WASHINGTON has narrowed down the possibilities on all of the unknown players. Royalty is White House staff, and I have my suspicions as to which one. For now, we're circumventing him. We think we've found Commandant among our military people and have put him under house arrest. We found some rather incriminating evidence in his computer."

"Nothing on Defender?" I asked.

"As you suspected, he's in the private sector, and that

makes things a hundred times harder, but we're working on it." His voice indicated he didn't give it much hope.

"Jerry, I have one other question for you," the senator said. "Did you think to ask Dr. Perrigrine about others who were present at Rangely during those tests using water pressure?"

"Yessir. There were two others with Dooley, both graduate assistants. Ariel Benson—a woman, and the one mentioned in Duquesne's operations timetable—was one of them. It may be helpful to have more information about her."

"I have a pen; give me that name again," the president said.

"Ariel Benson, probably living somewhere in the area of Jackson Hole or Afton. According to Phil she left Montana State University in April of 1987."

"She's been in it from the beginning, then," the senator said. "We'll run a check and have it for you when you get back in the morning." There was a pause.

"Jerry, is everyone present there with you?" the president said.

"Yessir."

"Good. Could you get Colonel Macklin for me? I need to talk with the both of you a moment. The others can listen in if they'd like."

I pulled the colonel away from a conversation he was having with Bob about old times. From the little bit I heard, it was about mutual friends who had come home from Nam and still hadn't adjusted.

"Go ahead, Mr. President," I said. "We're ready."

"Mr. Daniels, Colonel, all of you. The senator and I have met with the appropriate members of Congress. We just wanted you to know this is no longer an intelligence operation, but a military one, against an enemy that seeks to war against the citizens of the United States of America. I give you the full authority of this office to prevent this threat to the safety and peace of the people of this country. We . . . wish you God-speed."

There was silence. "God go with you all," the senator said.

I hung up the phone. The quiet was overwhelming. The words sinking in. Military operation, authority of this office. The first battle of a long war?

Mike came and stood by my side. The rain had slowed to a light drizzle, although the wind was still gusting and blowing the water dripping from the roof in all directions.

"Two weeks ago," she said, "I was a law-abiding enforcement agent for the SEC putting white-collar crooks out of business."

"Yeah. Somehow this whole thing has gotten out of hand. The only way to stop people from killing people is to kill?" I shook my head. "There's something out of whack with that, but I don't know at which end. If you don't stop them they kill more. If you do . . ." I shook my head. "A no-win situation."

"You really believe the document is the answer to the immediate problem, don't you?" she said softly.

"Yes. Is it foolish?" I said with sincere wonder.

"I know some of the others probably think so, and I would have if I hadn't known of your dreams and how it all came about. There is a higher reasoning behind that document. You're right to try and give it a chance to work, to save lives. I'm . . . scared for you, that's all."

"Me too. It's one thing to believe, quite another to act on that belief." I pulled her closer. "It'll be over tomorrow. Then we can go back to living normal dangerous lives on the freeways of Las Vegas." I tried to smile.

"What about Ben?" she asked, changing the subject.

"Right now Trayco's men are protecting him. After this is over he'll lose his license and be out of a job. I wanted to put him in prison because of what he did to me, and what he was involved in. But when I found out he was being blackmailed along with a bunch of others, I decided to save my anger for bigger fish. It should go well with him in the courts because of his cooperation."

"Do you want to get some sleep?" she asked after another moment's pause.

"Can't. I'm strung up like a violin. I wouldn't mind a fresh raspberry shake, though."

"Come on," she said, taking my hand and heading for the kitchen. "By the way, how's your eye?"

"Funny, I haven't even noticed lately, but now that you ask . . ." I plopped out the glass one. "Yup it's okay."

She slugged me in the back as I went through the dining room door. "You know what I mean!"

I worked the eye back in the socket. "The other one is still a little blurry around the very edges, but I hardly notice. I can actually tell your hair is dyed."

She hit me again.

"Hey, careful. You don't want this operation to lose its only madman, do you?"

At that moment the colonel came out of the kitchen with a cup of coffee in his hand, and I just missed knocking it from his hand.

"Woops. Sorry, Colonel."

"No problem, fly boy." He smiled, balancing his coffee cup. "I needed to see you, anyway. Can you spare a minute?" He looked at Mike.

"Go ahead," she said. "I'll join you in a few minutes."

We sat down at the big oak dining table. "My people are due shortly. There's another storm coming in, and they didn't want to take the chance of not getting in."

He sipped his coffee. "When this is over we'll leave immediately to join our group in Saudi Arabia."

"Can I ask you a couple of questions?" I asked. "I'm curious."

"Go ahead. If I can't answer I'll tell you so."

"How deep are the marines into Special Ops? I thought they disbanded Red Five after Nam? You and Trayco and the others were supposed to be the last."

"Umm . . . Political expediency. In times of peace we're still at war. After the incident in Lebanon most branches of the service were told to train elite forces for antiterrorist operations. Red Five was reintroduced then. I was the only remaining member in the service. I got the job.

"We went to SEAL school and learned a lot, but we branched out from there. Survival, escape, and evasion training were intensified with a lot of real-life training against other elite groups. SEALS against Red Five, Red Five against Delta squads." He smiled. "We did very well."

"Necessary evil?" I asked tightly.

"Yes. Covert terrorist groups won't stop harassing United States citizens and interests no matter where they are. What's going on here is a good example." He shrugged his shoulders. "The warfare of the twenty-first century."

"When did the marines start using Nightfox?"

"Part of Red Five's capability is to use needed weaponry from all branches of the service. We get what will serve the situation the best. Nightfox works well in this terrain. Quick, agile, and deadly when need be. Three choppers from Fort Campbell, Kentucky—160th Special Operations, Night Stalkers—were flown into Hill Air Force Base by large cargo plane. They met the rest of my group there.

"Before the night's over I think we'll be glad we have them along."

He paused. "Now answer a question for me, Jerry? How did you get involved in this mess?"

It was apparent that the president hadn't filled him in from the beginning. I did.

"Dick Sellars was a good man," he said, fooling with his empty cup.

"I know, but I don't think these guys killed him."

"From what you've told me, I think you're right. Who then?"

I hesitated.

"You know, don't you, Jerry."

"I have a pretty good idea, but I'm not sure yet. I'll know when we move in on the financial world they have created."

"Umm . . . Do you carry a gun?"

"I do now."

"Good. Be careful. Murderers come in all sizes and shapes, but they have one thing in common, the desire for self-preservation. He may kill you if you let him."

"In this case I hope you're wrong."

Mike came through the door, two shakes in hand.

"Colonel, would you like one?"

"No thanks," he said, stretching. "I need to go prepare a briefing for my men. They're coming in."

I focused my hearing, wondering how he . . . Sure enough, the sound of choppers approaching through the dark, soggy night.

The raspberry shake lost its pull on my taste buds.

34

Thick clouds loomed overhead, blotting out what must have been the last night for a full moon. Pools of water turned packed soil to mud, the grass pungent with moisture that soaked through pant legs in less than half a dozen steps while putting off a fresh, flowery scent. The choppers stood in the pasture south of the house, silent black monsters fully loaded with technological marvels of life and death, depending on perspective.

Each transport chopper carried a maximum load of forty-five with six crew—pilot, copilot, navigator, and three gunners. They loaded from a ramp in the back, and each chopper had six rotor blades driven by two turboshaft engines. The old Sikorsky S-65 used in Vietnam would have been dwarfed sitting next to the behemoth posing like a giant sentinel twenty steps away.

Like the much smaller Nightfox, the transport chopper had all the latest radar toys and flew at better than two hundred knots at treetop level in any kind of weather. As I climbed in the pilot's seat I found myself wishing. Wishing I had been blessed with such an animal under me in Nam. I wondered how many more lives I could have saved with two-inch-thick armor protecting the chopper's vitals and Kevlar-reinforced plating stopping bullets that often killed a third of the men I managed to pick up.

The colonel slid into the other seat. "Dreaming, I see."

I half smiled while continuing to look over the pilot's communication system.

"Weapons of war," he said. "We can't build a car that gives us more than average miles to the gallon and has a hundred things go wrong as soon as the warranty runs out, but we can make monsters like this to kill and maim."

He had surprised me. "A modern-day warrior disenchanted?"

He shrugged. "I've seen this baby in action south of the border, way south. It saved some boys down there, and I was one of them, but if politicians . . . Ah, never mind. Soldiers aren't supposed to bite the hand that feeds them."

"Why do you stay in?"

"Believe it or not I think of myself and others like me as a necessary evil. There'll always be a military establishment, but if we leave it to the ones who want to play soldier, we'll be up that certain creek without a paddle."

"Where do you think this thing in the Middle East is headed, Colonel?" I asked.

He looked out of the chopper's side window, toward the house. "I remember when I was a scrawny kid. Our minister used to rant and rave about something at least three times a year. The way he said it was never boring. He'd say, 'Them what's got it, hoards it, and them what hasn't, wants it. When them what wants it, wants it bad enough, them what has it better look out!' "

I laughed at the way he said it. "I take it you're from the South."

"Yeah. One of five white families in an all-black neighborhood. The white boys, on what some considered the better side of town, called them niggers and us white trash."

"I gather money was the subject of the sermon," I said.

"Nope. Power. My preacher was a rights activist. But he hit the nail on the head, except that today them what has it wants more and is willing to kill anyone and everyone to get it. The hunger for power is insatiable in people like Hussein and this Fillmore Duquesne and his little committee. They'll do anything to get it and all its financial trappings. Doesn't matter who might get hurt or how many people die. What they're doing here is just a matter of numbers on paper to them, a balance sheet with debits and credits. Pay this amount in human life, get this much power and financial return."

"Can the military stop Iraq?" I asked, rubbing away the goose bumps?"

"Yes. But it'll be expensive in money and lives."

"Is it worth what it'll cost?"

"Blood is precious, but you have to weigh the evil against the cost. What if we don't stop him now? What might the cost be later, when he has a bigger arsenal of chemical weapons, more tanks, and even nuclear weapons? Cut him down to size now, or pay a greater price in blood later."

"Even world leaders aren't united on that. They think we'll have to negotiate, give Iraq something."

"Yeah, a lot of them are pretty intelligent people in high places. Negotiate, they say. Hussein won't overstep his bounds. Or, maybe Kuwait would be administered better by Iraq.

"In 1985 I was in Iraq as a special advisor for the Pentagon. We were assigned to give some instructional classes on military Special Forces for Hussein's elite Republican Guards. I disagreed with the assignment, but went under duress. What I saw was a country preparing for war while fighting one. Bunkers, communications systems, weaponry. All the very best. All defensive as well as offensive. It wasn't evident to the untrained eye, but I could see Saddam Hussein planning ahead to a time when Iran was a bad dream, and he would need to pay his bills, and find work for his soldiers."

"Then he was already planning to take Kuwait," I said.

"For years, and from there the rest of the region. But what I saw that frightened me was a military who believed in his cause and whose leaders were willing to sacrifice the lives of their men to accomplish it. They'll force those men into battle until none are left. Terrorism, civilian cities made into battlefields, killing of their own people. They'll do anything!

"These are the worst kind of fanatics—well-armed believers. Before it's over, thousands of their people will die for what they consider a great cause. There'll be no negotiation and no prisoners. When they walk into Kuwait they'll kill anyone who opposes them, and when we stand up to them they'll load their weapons, dig their bunkers, prepare their chemical weapons, and egg us into battle. Then we'll have to kill more of them, and they'll kill some of us."

"Are you telling me his people believe in him?"

"Not all of them, but anyone who voices opposition or refuses to fight is killed, along with his family. Most have made up their minds that it's better to do as you're told than to cause the death of everyone you love."

"A cancer."

"Yes, one we should have removed surgically years ago. Now, because we let evil run rampant, good men will die trying to keep it from trampling everybody." He took a deep breath.

"But you can never stop it all," I said.

"Not anymore. Now it's a battle just to control it."

He turned in his seat and faced me. "You know who sold Iraq most of their weapons? An American arms dealer. He made millions. You know who helped him? Members of our government, past and present! They made a few bucks, too, I'll tell you! And you and I are the ones who elected the bone-heads who think more of the dollar than they do of human life. It's okay to sell the weapons to Hussein to kill Iranians; we can just look the other way. Germans built Hussein his chemical warfare plants and sold him the technology for further research to develop nuclear weapons. German technology has allowed them to build missiles that will now reach Israel. It's all the greedy little politicians, businessmen, and other knot-heads sneaking around for a buck in the fast lane that have created this monster."

"Gadianton robbers," I said, staring out of the window into the chilly night.

"What?"

"People who sell themselves, their beliefs, their country, for money or power."

"Never heard of it, but it fits. All of these birds are part of your robbers. Hussein wouldn't be a problem without them around."

"And this fine piece of technical wizardry we're sitting in would be cars and stereos," I said, smiling.

"Yeah." He smiled back as he got out of the chopper. "And I'd be out of a job. But that won't ever happen, will it?"

I shook my head. "Not in our lifetime."

He held onto the handle of the door, thinking. "As a soldier I do my best to keep an optimistic perspective. It isn't easy when you see what a soldier in my position has to see. But as a Christian I haven't given up hope of finding peaceful solutions. I pray that Iraq will back off, while knowing, deep down, they won't." His eyes bored into mine. "Tonight we'll find out if negotiations can still work with people who have similar traits to Saddam Hussein's. Good luck."

I watched him disappear into the darkness, then took out

of my pocket the small set of military-issue scriptures I had carried ever since Vietnam and flipped the pages, the overhead light shining on the clear, dark print. Liz had shown me section ninety-eight when I was working out the guilt over Nam.

> And again, this is the law that I gave unto my ancients, that they should not go out unto battle against any nation, kindred, tongue, or people, save I, the Lord, commanded them.
>
> And if any nation, tongue, or people should proclaim war against them, they should first lift a standard of peace unto that people, nation, or tongue;
>
> And if that people did not accept the offering of peace, neither the second nor the third time, they should bring these testimonies before the Lord;
>
> Then I, the Lord, would give unto them a commandment, and justify them in going out to battle against that nation, tongue, or people.
>
> And I, the Lord, would fight their battles.

I bowed my head. I wouldn't get a second or third chance to lift a standard of peace, and keep people from dying. Once had to be enough.

35

Ghost One, under Sergeant Delavane, lifted off at exactly 10:00 P.M. Nightfox Leader was next, and at 150 miles an hour he would be in Afton in fifteen minutes.

"Ghost Leader, this is Ghost One. We're on the ground, two miles from target. The rain is intermittent. Should be in position on schedule."

"Roger, Ghost One. We copy." The colonel sat in a flight seat next to the side gunner. The rest of us were strapped into seats along the big bird's innards. I was the only one in civilian clothes; the others were dressed in complete combat uniforms and were heavily armed. All of us had duplicates of Macklin's headsets, which allowed us to listen to each other and to keep track of what was going on.

"Redline Two, this is Ghost Leader. Let's get this bird in the air. Nightfox Leader, are you in position?"

"ETA five minutes, Ghost Leader."

It had begun. I tried to concentrate, thinking things over carefully. The spotter had said Babcock was there and that Winters and Owens had come and gone. They were probably issuing new instructions. The sheriff had put a tail on them with orders to notify us if they headed back toward the rig. We couldn't have them showing up at the wrong time; their answer to what I had to say would be the sound of death in my own ears. Dealing with Babcock, I had a chance.

"Ghost Leader, this is Nightfox Leader. Lightning has struck. I repeat. Lightning has struck. I'm on my way to field green to hook up with One and Two."

"Roger, Nightfox Leader."

The big chopper was brushing against the tops of trees as we skipped over the ridges at nearly two hundred miles an hour. All on board had experienced such maneuvers before, but four of us were a little rusty and began turning a light shade of green.

Mike was still in my mind, walking away as we loaded into the gaping hole at the back of the big transport. I had looked over my shoulder, wanting to go back, wanting to hold her just one more time, feeling emptiness and the gut-churning fear I wouldn't see her again. I had shaken it off at that moment. Now I found myself having to do it again.

Concentrate! Remember the training. Get ready to play the game carefully. Too much at stake to lose my composure. Too many lives.

The big chopper dropped into Hoback Canyon, following the main road at less than a hundred feet above ground. We swung over River Bend Ranch and up the canyon toward Hoback Peak, just barely skimming the tops of trees, my stomach tightening. Redline Two would disembark next, then a rendezvous with the sheriff, who was waiting with the gear I needed.

"All right, Redline Two," the colonel said. "Two minutes to drop. Let's get ready. Everybody up."

They were on their feet, facing the back of the chopper. My heart pounded, and I adjusted the night goggles. In pictures I had seen, the infrared night glasses looked monstrous, almost ridiculous. But these weren't much different than a pair of ski goggles except for the battery packs attached to each side, and I was amazed at how well I could make out even the slightest detail. Macklin had said they weren't available to the average GI—yet.

I grabbed for a handhold as the chopper suddenly stopped and dropped to within a couple of feet of the earth, the back door falling quickly open. The soldiers ran down the ramp and threw themselves to the ground, the big bird barely hesitating before jumping on into the night and leaving them disappearing into the trees at the edge of the clearing. They faced an exhausting five-mile run to the area of the gate where they would wait to see how I fared. I looked at the remaining faces—Macklin, Jack, Tran, and Trayco—intense, ready for battle, ready to go into the compound if they were needed. If I wasn't successful, they and the others could die. I gulped, my mouth and throat dry, my muscles tense.

The big transport reversed its direction, flying low over the valley and then back into the Hoback, turning left, then right up Dell Creek, landing in a clearing where the sheriff waited. I quickly disembarked as the chopper pilot shut the big monster down to wait for its next call.

It only took a minute to slip on the heavy coat—badge and patches attached—pull on the regulation side arm, and drop in place the flat-brimmed hat with the protective rain cover. I stuck the Walther .38 in the coat pocket where I could reach it unseen. In the other pocket I placed the can of C6-45.

"There's an umbrella in the front seat of the Bronco," the sheriff said. "If it starts to rain you'll need it to keep the paperwork readable." I stuffed the fat envelope inside the coat next to my chest. "There's also a shotgun on the rack, and a two-way radio. The doors are armor plated if you need a quick shield, and the four-wheel-drive is standard operation." He looked at me, trying to smile as he extended his hand. "Good luck, Mr. Daniels."

I attached the microphone behind the coat collar. "Thanks, Sheriff. Your men all set to move up when Babcock buckles?"

"We're ready. By the way, we've checked out the other wells. No sign of any explosives. Not even a guard watching them."

"Keep some men up there just in case, will you?" I asked. "If we have to take this place by force and some of them get away they may attempt to go to those wells."

"You got it."

Pushing the earpiece in tight, I checked it out. "Ghost Leader, this is Deacon. Do you read me?"

The return sound was clear and even. "At this distance I'd better!" he said from the chopper door only ten feet away. "Let's just hope when we get a mountain or two between us, and that storm flashing over in yonder hills sends out electricity, it'll do some good. Try it on Redline One. They're the farthest away."

"Ghost Leader, this is Ghost One. We read you. A little broken, but we can understand."

"Roger, Ghost One. How close are you to being in position?"

"Twenty minutes, Leader. Better send Deacon on his way. Out."

The colonel walked over to me, covering his microphone. I

253

did the same. "Good luck, Jerry. One Christian to another, God go with you." He extended his hand, and we shook firmly.

I took a deep breath. "Uh, sir, maybe your plan . . ."

He smiled. "Get in the seat of that Bronco and get moving, soldier. Let's get this over with. Move it!"

He grabbed my shoulder in mock anger, and we walked to the Bronco. "Jerry, we'll be right behind you."

I closed the door, put the already idling vehicle in gear, and started down the valley toward the main highway. Twenty minutes. A speck in time—but enough to have a serious talk with my Maker.

I had to shift into four-wheel-drive about halfway up the canyon. The road was slick and full of ruts. It slowed me down some, but I calculated I'd reach the gate on schedule.

The rain had stopped, leaving a low, misty fog settling on the trees and hills, giving an eerie, other earthly feeling, and I began whistling "The Twilight Zone" to ease the churning in my stomach.

The gate suddenly appeared out of nowhere, two guards standing in front of it. I took three deep breaths in succession as I turned on the blue and red lights atop the Bronco, identifying who I was. The M-16 that each carried pointed directly through the windshield.

I pulled up and placed it in park, opened the door, and got out. "Evenin', gentlemen," I said nonchalantly. "I'm Bill Wilson from the sheriff's department. I have some papers to give to your"—I took the papers out of my coat and pretended to look at the name on the outside of the envelope—"your Mr. Babcock. Is he here?"

"What kind of papers?" said a man with a slight accent that made me freeze. I had heard that voice before. One of the two guys on the hill who had confronted Bob and me when we were looking TriStar over. The short, stocky, dark-complexioned one. I was most thankful for the darkness and shadow created by my wide-brimmed hat.

I cleared my throat. "Well now, young man, that ain't none of your business, is it?" I said coldly, searching for a little deeper voice. "Now, is Mr. Babcock here or not?"

"No, sir, he isn't."

I made a deep sigh. "What's your name, soldier?" I asked with an intimidating voice.

"Uh, Mendez, but—"

"Mr. Mendez, we can do this the hard way or the easy way. I can leave here and bring back another dozen deputies, and we can go through that gate over your bruised and bleeding body, or you can get on that mike you carry and tell Babcock to get his frame down here and talk to me. Now! Your choice." I lifted the strap off the revolver at my side.

He hesitated. "Colonel Babcock has given orders—"

"I'm not going to say this twice, but I think you'd better let him make this decision, don't you?"

Sweat trickled down the back of my neck. "Now, I'm going to sit inside my nice, warm cruiser there until you get him down here. But don't be long. It's late, and I'm off duty in an hour, and I don't want to have to work no overtime!" I climbed in and shut the door, leaving them arguing. Finally Mendez took the small radio transmitter out of his pocket and started to talk. I could tell he was getting a tongue-lashing.

"Ghost Leader, this is Deacon. Do you read me?"

There was no answer.

"Ghost Leader, this is Deacon. Come in please." The earpiece crackled, and there was voice, but it was broken and too far away. I suddenly felt panic. If I couldn't hear them . . . "Ghost One, are you there?" Same garbled reply. More panic.

Mendez was standing at the gate, looking toward the main building in the compound. In the distance through the light fog and mist I could make out a form moving through the dim light of the rig beyond. Panic!

"Ghost Leader, you darn well better be able to hear what's going on here. I can only trust that. Babcock is on his way down to the gate. I . . . ."

The heavens suddenly let loose, the rain pouring down again. As if on cue, the landscape jumped with the brightness of lightning, and my ears filled with the roar of thunder. Visibility was suddenly cut to zero, and I could hardly see the soldier hunkering at the gate. The other one had disappeared, probably to shelter.

"Macklin—if you can hear me—it's raining cats and dogs here. If I need your help the word will be *scramble.* I say it again. If I get into trouble the word is *scramble.*"

Babcock reached the gate. It was unbearably warm, the sweat trickling down my side from underneath my arms. I wiped my hands on the slick cloth of my cotton Levi's. "All right, Lord, here goes."

Clutching the papers in one hand and the umbrella in the

other, I opened the door and stepped into the mud and rain as Babcock strutted through the now-open gate. I had never met him in Nam, but he matched Trayco's description. A solid frame of 210 pounds, large head, mustache, and arrogant nature. His rough face was hard, and he wore the short hair and camouflage fatigues of the professional soldier.

The look on his face said it all, along with a few short but very direct words to Mendez before turning his attention on me.

The smile was as phony as sugar substitutes. "Deputy"—the rain dripped off the beak of his cap—"what can I do for you?"

I had the umbrella in place and took out the papers, protecting them from the moisture. Lightning struck nearby and lit up the mountainside, making us both jump. As the storm seemed to lash out at us, I hoped Macklin's soldiers were under cover and their tiny little headsets fully functional.

"Walter Babcock? Thunderbolt Securities?" He nodded. "Are you the agent for TriStar Oil?" I questioned loud enough to be heard above the pounding rain. He nodded again. "I'm Bill Wilson from the sheriff's department. Would you prefer to talk inside my vehicle, sir?"

He looked irritated. "Get on with it, Deputy. What the devil did you pull me out of my nice, warm office for! And it had better be good!"

I decided to let him have it. "To evict you, *sir!*" I handed him the papers. "That's an injunction and a search warrant. All drilling and work at this and the other two sites owned by TriStar are to be stopped and the premises cleared within the hour. It seems, sir, you are drilling on private property."

"That's garbage. This property has been leased by TriStar from the forest service."

"Not according to a lawsuit filed, sir." I put the umbrella out, sheltering the papers as he opened them. "As you will see, Mr. Babcock, it seems that evidence has been presented to the court that says you have to move out of here. We want your immediate cooperation."

He scanned the papers, then put them quickly inside the envelope. "Sorry, son. No can do. I have my orders from the people who own this rig to keep it under wraps." I put my hand inside my coat pocket as naturally as I could. "Our communications system has been put out by the storm. There's no way for me to clear this with them before tomorrow morning. You have to give us that long."

"Sorry, sir. Within the hour. There'll be another twelve officers here as soon as they finish up a couple of accidents down in the valley. I'm supposed to get things moving now and to begin a search of the premises."

His voice went hard. "A search for what, Deputy?"

"To make sure that nothing released from that well leaves here, sir. It's a part of the lawsuit. Seems they think you might have struck some oil. Leastways that's what I'm to be lookin' for."

He smiled. "No oil. Just water. Lots of water. Sorry again. I can't let you come in here. Not without clearance from the owners."

I took a deep breath. "Then we'll have to evict you forcefully, sir," I said.

His smile from ear to ear evidenced his supposed advantage. The lightning struck again, closer, lighting up every flaw in his granite and in his light gray eyes. I jumped again. He didn't.

"Deputy, around this compound I have enough firepower to blow you and your deputies to kingdom come. Do you understand me? You try and take this place and we'll send you to an early grave."

"No offense, sir, but all I see are two soldiers—both cowering out of the weather over there—with M-16s. Of course I realize you have those eight fifty-caliber gun emplacements, and whatever you're harboring under those tarps is probably at least that big." I hardened my voice. "Along with the thirty some men armed to the teeth. I don't see any of it as formidable, Mr. Babcock. In fact it shouldn't take long to put you out of business." I said the last with emphasis on each word.

The smile was gone, but the defiance was alive and well. "I didn't know the sheriff's department had that kind of firepower," he said mockingly.

"Trust me, sir. We'll have this place wrapped up one way or the other within the hour. You and your men can cooperate and live, or you can fight and die for a piece of land intended only to kill, not make a profit." The hint was understood.

"Who the devil are you?" he asked, shocked.

"Doesn't matter, Sergeant Babcock," I said, stomping on the last two words with my teeth. "Just believe we can do it. We know what's going on here. We also know that at this point you haven't set the explosives, and we aren't about to give you enough time to do it." He started to take a step backward. "Another step in that direction, Sergeant, and I'll have to ruin this coat to stop you." He looked down at where my hand disappeared inside the coat pocket. I made the bulge obvious.

"How—"

"That doesn't matter, either. Now, what'll it be?"

He looked at the envelope and then seemed to collect his composure. "Mendez!" he yelled. "If this man shoots me, kill him!" He said it so fast I couldn't stop him. Mendez trained the rifle on my eyebrows before I could blink.

"Now, Deputy, I don't believe you."

The lightning struck again closer, then another, and the whole sky transformed into bright white and deafening thunder.

"Sergeant, a lot of people might die if you don't. And *you* will be the first."

"He'll kill you before I hit the ground!" he said defiantly.

"So be it. But after that what will your men do? Fight to the death for you? I think not. We'll have this place within the hour regardless of what you do here. Why die for nothing! Fillmore Duquesne isn't worth it!"

The impact of the name and what it meant hit him about the same time as lightning struck again. This time he jumped. "I . . . I need some kind of a sign. I need to know . . ." He shook it off. "No. Names mean nothing. Mendez—"

A thunderous explosion rocked the valley, causing the three of us to shrink before an unbelievable display of light and explosion, the well rig blowing apart like a toothpick tower slapped with a heavy hand. A fireball formed at the center and exploded outward and down onto the floor of the rig, slamming it against the ground, then catapulting it upward into a thousand pieces of cascading electricity and burning wood.

Within seconds it had disappeared, scraps of it thrown into the forest, some landing with a smoldering thud only fifty feet the other side of the gate.

Mendez lowered his gun and stood there with his mouth open.

"What the . . ." Babcock said.

"You asked for a sign, sir," I said gathering my composure. "You shouldn't have. Would you like another?" I was a little unsettled at the colonel's decision to use a Nightfox missile.

"No, Deputy. I think we get the point. How soon can we have transportation here for our people?"

"Half an hour. Two buses are waiting in a canyon twenty minutes from here. Sergeant, I must ask you to wait in my vehicle until they arrive." He nodded. "Mendez. Put out the word. We're leaving. Have the men secure all weapons and get here on the double."

"But—"

"Mendez, what you just saw were the effects of a Stinger or TOW missile. They'd wipe us out in a matter of minutes, and we'd never see them! You want to die tonight?"

"No, sir."

"Then get moving!" Mendez ran toward the emplacements on the right side. "May I get in your vehicle now, Deputy?"

"Yessir, you may," I said, keeping my gun ready. "I'll join you."

The rain stopped as suddenly as it had begun.

"Are these papers legal?" he asked.

"Yessir. My attorney filed them for me."

"You . . . you own this property?"

"Yes. By a strange set of circumstances, I think I do. But the courts will decide for sure." I listened carefully for the choppers, but still heard nothing. I took the radio off its hook on the dash. "Sheriff, this is Deacon. Do you read?"

"Deacon. What's going on up there? We thought we'd lost you? What was that explosion?"

"Apparently my mike is out, and they can't hear me. Get the colonel up here right away. Babcock is with me and has accepted our presence. I need those buses, now, and tell Nightfox Leader 'nice shot.' "

"What—"

"Never mind. Just get up here, all right?"

"On our way."

"Nightfox," Babcock said. "Then it was a TOW 2?"

"Seems so."

The first set of soldiers loitered at the gate as I heard the transport chopper come up the valley, my earpiece coming alive.

"Daniels, do you read me?" It was Macklin's voice.

"Get into the main building, Colonel. And get Ghost One and Two to clean up around here. Babcock and I will meet you."

"You got it! Good work, Deacon."

Babcock was staring at my finger in my ear. "Special Forces equipment. You came with the best."

I smiled. "Some of your old friends. Get one of those boys to open that gate, will you? We'd better prepare your other people for loading. Any of them going to be a problem?"

"Turn on your outside speaker." I flipped the switch. His voice filled the air. "This is Colonel Babcock. We're through here. I want all my people at the gate on the double. Move it, gentlemen, or your pay will be docked by half."

He hung up the mike and flipped the switch back. "Used to be able to threaten them with ten extra miles of running. Now it's with their monthly paycheck. The benefits of being a mercenary." He said it half seriously.

He yelled at one of them to open the gate, and I started inside the compound. "Sergeant Walter Babcock. Good soldier gone bad. I don't think much of what you do, and your reputation tells me not to think much of you, either, but I appreciate your keeping this from getting messy."

We watched as the Redline Two landed in the clearing next to the main building, and the colonel led the others inside.

"I learned a long time ago that being a hired gun has one advantage over being in the armed services," Babcock said. "You don't have to put your life on the line unless you decide to." He said it sarcastically.

"You're going to have to answer some questions, and your men are going to be detained for a few days, incognito. We have a few loose ends to tie up. What do you know about the death of Robert Doolittle?"

"Who?"

"Hmm. Want an attorney?"

He smiled. "Perceptive. But I'll tell you this. I didn't kill him."

We pulled up in front of the main building. "Your cooperation would save a lot of trouble, and probably a lot of lives."

He shrugged. "I quit caring years ago about saving anyone's life but my own. Besides, I have a reputation to worry about. I'll be out and free in a few days, and I can't have it said that I turned on a client, can I? Letting you take me at all will do too much damage." He opened the door and climbed out. I pulled the 9mm from my pocket.

"No offense, Babcock, but empty your pockets of everything but the papers. Throw them on the seat here, will you?"

He smiled. Then he emptied his pockets, turning them inside out as he did so. His .45 bounced on the cloth seat. I picked it up and put it in my pocket as Trayco came from the building. The recognition was immediate and mutually hateful.

"Kenny, finish searching him, then bring him in. Any problems?"

"Look inside," he said coldly, beginning his heavy-handed search. Babcock would have a few minor bruises to show his attorney.

36

Macklin sat on a long leather couch beside a woman in a white dress and a lab jacket. She was rubbing her wrists as ropes were removed. Her eyes held fear mixed with a healthy portion of anger.

Trayco's men were busy. Tran searched the rest of the building one room at a time while Jack untied a slightly built, frail-looking man, who was very sound asleep in a chair in the corner of the room.

The colonel stood, took my arm, and pulled me aside. "Good work, my friend, but I wish you would learn how to operate the equipment I give you. We couldn't hear a thing you said! I almost came busting in with guns booming when that storm grounded us down the valley a mile. What happened?"

"What? What do you mean you couldn't hear? One of the Nightfox choppers or somebody must have heard. They blew up that rig like it was made of toothpicks."

He pulled me further away. "We, my friend, did *not*—I repeat we did *not*—blow up that rig!"

"But"—I shook my head—"I saw it hit. The fireball, and things went up like somebody had kicked a stack of tinker toys!"

He smiled. "Wasn't us. I promise."

"Lightning?" I had to sit down. "Babcock was going back toward the gate, calling what he considered a bluff. I thought you heard what was going on and had one of the choppers fire a missile."

"Uh-uh. Pure luck."

"You're not serious," I said. He kept smiling.

"Let me introduce you to Dr. Ariel Benson."

My head came up. I stood, walked over to the couch, and sat beside her, shaking off the confusion. "Uh, Dr. Benson. You were with Robert Doolittle at Rangely when they—"

"Let me save you some trouble, whoever you are. Yes I was at Rangely, and yes I was hired to start an earthquake here."

"But why would you—"

She interrupted again. "Want to start an earthquake on one of the most dangerous fault lines in the world?" She picked up her purse and took out a small savings-account book and opened it to pages of entries. There were four entries, each for a million dollars, with one withdrawal for half a million.

"I don't come cheap; I just didn't know I wouldn't have a chance to spend it!" she said angrily.

"What do you mean?" I asked.

"When I told them we couldn't start the quake this afternoon they pulled guns on us and tied us up. They said they had another way."

"A bomb."

She nodded. Her face cold and hard as granite. At that moment Trayco shoved Babcock through the door. She spat the words at him. "*He* was supposed to get rid of us after he rigged the bomb." She pointed to some rolls of wire. "He was going to start rolling that out and put plastic explosives down the shaft as soon as the weather dried up a bit. Then a call came saying he was wanted at the gate."

"That true, Babcock?" I asked.

He only smiled.

"That guy over there"—she pointed at the person Jack had untied—"he knows what happened. Wake him up. He'll tell you."

"What did you give him, Babcock?" I asked. "You wouldn't want an overdose of sleeping pills to kill him, would you?"

"Six. He'll wake up in the morning fresh as a daisy. I had no intention of killing them."

"Trayco, take him down to the sheriff at the gate and have him taken to town—separate from the others—and booked for attempted murder, possession of illegal firearms, and anything else they can come up with. Also have the sheriff keep a couple of guys by the name of Mendez and Polansky separate from the others. They know firsthand about the attempt on the lives of Bob and me a few nights ago."

Trayco pushed Babcock back out of the door. Babcock didn't resist. He knew Kenny had a strong desire to slap him around, maybe even kill him. He didn't want to give him an excuse. Trayco's hate for Babcock festered like a big boil, eating at him.

"All right, Ms. Benson. How close were you? And what are the dangers now?"

"No danger of anything major, but there will be a few minor quakes for the next week or so. Another twenty-four hours and we could have given them what they wanted."

Nice lady, I thought. "What happened to Dooley?"

"I liked Dooley, but I couldn't stop what they were going to do." She sat back in the couch and folded her arms tightly. "I have nothing more to say. I want an attorney."

"Jack, pack that guy and put him in the transport. We're taking him back to the ranch. Tran, escort Ms. Benson down to the sheriff. She should be booked as well. Accessory to murder for starters." I looked at her hard.

"Accessory . . . what . . . but I—"

"Get her down to the sheriff, Tran."

I heard the chopper outside and went to the window to watch it land. It was the MD350 sight-seeing chopper, and I wondered what it was doing here. Mike climbed out and ran toward the building. I met her at the door, where she paused to look at the bent and twisted metal of the rig.

"What happened? Your microphone wasn't working. We couldn't hear a thing. Bob figured it was some sort of storm interference. Darn good thing we didn't need flawless communications for a full-scale operation."

"The colonel says lightning hit the rig," I said.

"Hmm. Can't believe everything the marines tell you. Saved your goose, though, didn't it?" She smiled.

"Yeah. You wouldn't believe how close a call it was." I pulled her out of the chilly air and into the office. "Anything new on Winters and Owens?"

"That's what I came to tell you. They disappeared."

"What?"

"Just after the action started, the deputy lost them. The highway patrol is checking traffic while airport security is watching their hangar and plane."

"They couldn't know what happened out here."

"Unlikely. I think they gave the orders here, expecting them to be followed, and figured it was time to find a hiding place."

She changed the subject. "Come on. Let's get back to the ranch. The sheriff notified us that you had taken this place, and we called the president. He'll sleep better when you make a report to him and Dad. Colonel, are your men loaded and ready?"

"Yes, ma'am. A few instructions to the sheriff about the care and keeping of this place, and we'll be right behind you. Jerry, go get some sleep. You've done your part, and you've got more first thing in the morning. You'll need some rest."

I started for the door. I didn't need to be coaxed.

"By the way, Deacon, I don't know what happened up here, but I can't fault the results. I'm glad we did it your way."

I turned and faced him. "Thanks. I'll see you back at the house before you leave for Hill Air Force Base." I took off the coat, hat, and side arm and handed them to him. "Give those to the sheriff, will you? Tell him I quit. The pay isn't worth the stress."

37

2:00 A.M.

"Still no sign of them?" I asked, sipping from a glass of hot cider and watching Bob at the communications console.

"Nothin'. The airport is small enough that two men can keep an eye on it. Winter and Owens' jet is still sittin' in the hangar.

"Nothin' at the company ranch out toward Teton Village, either. They seem to have disappeared."

"Maybe they left by car. Anything turn up in Afton?"

"The sheriff over there is completely cooperative. Nothin'. He set up a roadblock just this side of the junction at Alpine. The highway patrol is coverin' Teton Pass, Warren Bridge to the south, and Moose on the north. If they got out, it was over some pretty tough back roads."

"Mmm. The Lear gassed and ready to go to Vegas?"

"Yeah. It's in Dad's hangar. When you leavin'?"

"As soon as I get a shower and a change of clothes. Mike's going with me. Do you mind?"

He looked up at me and smiled. "No Las Vegas chapel weddings, I hope."

I laughed. "No. She deserves better."

"The temple, huh?" he said, fumbling with some papers.

"Yeah. Want to come along?" I smiled.

"Depends on how long you want to wait."

The colonel walked up, and I couldn't pursue it.

"We have to be back at Hill by 4:00 A.M. to make connections to Iraq. Any of you want to come along? Rejoin and see the world!"

"The deserts of Iraq? Hardly the world I want to see, Colonel." I shook his outstretched hand. "Thanks."

"All in the line of duty, soldier. I'm glad it was you in charge of this event, even if you didn't exactly volunteer."

"Thank your men for me," I said. "Uh, I'm going to be having a wedding soon. Where do I send the invitation?"

"Bob, you're lowering your family standards, aren't you? Blind in one eye; can't see out of the other. Broke. No future. Even the marines kicked him out." He laughed lightly. "I'm glad for you, Jerry. She's a great lady. You'll have cute kids. Just send it to that address." He handed me a slip of paper. "I'll get it."

"Colonel, when will you be back this way?" I asked as we walked onto the front porch.

"Next fall's elk hunt. An invitation from the senator. If you can finagle your way into this family by then you can probably come along." He smiled.

Then he was gone. I watched from the porch as the running lights of the big transports disappeared over the ridge to the south, the three Nightfox choppers in formation to the right, left, and rear. I said a silent prayer for their safety in an explosive Middle East. He was right; there would always be a military machine. It was better to have men like him in it, wasn't it?

I went up to my room, where I found Trayco sound asleep on the bed next to Jack. Tran was on the floor near the window. All of them were still fully dressed in dirty clothes, their wet shoes discarded near the heat duct. I grabbed a towel, shaving gear, and clean clothes and headed for the bathroom. Mike was just coming out in her robe, her hair curly and wet.

I warned her about the dirt and bad breath, but she grabbed me around the waist and kissed me anyway. "If I waited for you to be perfect before I kissed you, our lips would never meet." Then she was closing the door to her bedroom and was out of sight and sound for a rejoinder.

The hot water felt like heaven, but it pricked at the bruises, cuts, and scrapes. The sweat and the grime flowed down the drain. My mind was dull and thought only of getting the soap in all the right places, the whiskers shaved without slitting my own throat, and covering myself in undergarments and a fresh cotton shirt and Levi's.

After my shower as I looked at the battered man in the mirror I noticed a few more gray hairs. Earned. I found myself wondering if Mike minded it. Maybe a little Grecian Formula. I laughed. Not on your life. I'd earned 'em, I'd wear 'em with pride!

I got dressed and went and collapsed on the couch in the den to catch a few hours of sleep before taking the 350 to the airport.

Mike was sitting by my side, staring at me, when my eyes opened four hours after closing.

"Better get moving, Jerry," she said as she ran her fingers through my hair. "The president called. Dad's on his way home and should be here in an hour or so."

I looked at my watch. Nine A.M.

"Ben and Hank called as well. They're nervous. Ben wants you to call. Hank said he'd try later."

We headed for the kitchen. The others were sitting around the big dining room table scarfing up pancakes, sausage, and eggs and gulping down orange juice and gallons of milk. "Morning, gentlemen," I said. "I see you found Mrs. O.'s kitchen. Any complaints?"

"Are you kidding?" said Trayco. "She married?"

The others nodded agreement, but didn't speak with their mouths full.

We joined them. A few minutes into my first stack, Bob came in and filled a plate.

"Still nothin' on Winters and Owens," he said. "My guess is they're hidin' somewhere until things cool down. Any sign Duquesne got word of what's happened?"

Mike answered. "Ben called and said he had talked to one of the other brokers involved. Nothing has changed. No panic sell. If Duquesne does know what's happened here he's staying with the financial game plan."

"Right now," I said, "Fillmore Duquesne is a very frustrated man. Owens and Winters must have told him that something's wrong at the well. He can't get to anyone who really knows for sure what's going on; they're all locked up and out of circulation. Winters and Owens don't dare go anywhere near the rig to find out themselves. They sit and stew."

I took a drink of orange juice. "Duquesne's staying with the financial game plan because he has no choice. His partners will kill him if he fails. He knows that. I would say right now the three of them are trying to figure out what to do next.

"Where's the communications man?" I asked. "We need to have a talk with him before we leave."

"He's at the bunkhouse," Bob said. "The boys are keepin' him happy but under guard. I'll have him brought to the house. Ten minutes okay?"

"Yep. Jack, Tran, you get the gear loaded into the chopper while Trayco and I visit with . . . what's this guy's name, anyway?"

"Wickson. Hyrum Wickson. He was one scared José when he first woke up, but he understands where he is and what's happened at the well. He said we'd come just in time. They were clearing out, and he was pretty sure he was next after Ms. Benson. Other than that he hasn't done anythin' but eat and sleep."

Charla appeared at the dining room door, her face pale. We all stopped eating. Mike got up and went to support her.

"Charla! What's the matter? What happened?"

"They're all dead," she said mournfully. "The . . . the plane blew up . . . over the Grand Canyon . . . last night. Left Vegas for Waco. It just . . . blew up."

"What?" I stood and went to help her sit down. Bob was at my side.

"What plane?" Bob said. "What are you talkin' about?" He was rubbing her hand.

"The rig workers. The ones that left yesterday when they closed down the wells. The federal people think a bomb was placed aboard their plane in Las Vegas, or maybe before. Some terrorist group from the Middle East is claiming responsibility. They're all . . . dead."

Trayco was already out of the door and headed for the bunkhouse.

Hyrum Wickson was a small five feet six with a weasel face and freckled skin. The kind that couldn't take any sun. He was sweating.

I stood at the front of the desk. "Mr. Wickson, your job was running the communications computer, wasn't it?"

"Yes."

"What was the last communication you received?"

"Uh . . . a message to Mr. Babcock from someone in the main office."

"What did it say?" I said a little impatiently.

He gulped. "They were to close down the operation and go to something called 'T1 Contingency.' "

"Was a response sent?"

"Yes, sir. Babcock sent a message saying he would take care of it."

"Did you know the rig workers were to be eliminated?"

He looked quickly down at his hands. I had caught him off guard.

"Wickson, I'm tired. I don't have a lot of patience. You're not guilty of anything here and probably won't see the inside of any jails, but we want the people who are responsible. Do you understand?"

"Yes, I understand." He took a deep breath. "Mr. Winters was at the well yesterday, along with Mr. Owens. They sent a message to Las Vegas. It said that a package should be delivered and put aboard the workers' plane at four o'clock yesterday, when it did a stopover. The message said the package was to be set for delivery over the Grand Canyon."

I inhaled. Winters again. Wickson went on.

"I didn't know what it meant until last night when I overheard Babcock and Ms. Benson arguing. Ms. Benson was very frightened, so I opened the door a little. He slapped her around a little and had her tied up. I closed the door too noisily, and next thing I knew they were tying me up and making me take some pills. I . . . thought it was poison."

"How did you get caught in this mess?" I asked.

He looked sheepish. "I was . . . blackmailed."

I looked at him, unbelieving. *What could he possibly be blackmailed for?* I thought.

Mike spoke. "Did they kill Robert Doolittle?"

"The geologist? Ms. Benson knew him pretty well. I . . . don't know for sure. He came to the well one day and started asking Ms. Benson all sorts of questions about what they were doing putting water into the well. She told him that she knew what she was doing, and that they were only putting enough hot water into the well to liquify the oil and not enough to do any other damage. She said it was all very regulated. When he kept arguing with her, one of Babcock's men threatened him and ordered him off TriStar property. Babcock said they had permission from the forest service to drill for the oil, and they'd drill any way they wanted."

"Did you see Doolittle leave?" she asked.

"Yes. He looked very concerned, and he told them he was going to the authorities."

"Did anyone leave right after that?" I asked.

He looked down again. "I didn't know they were going to kill him, or I would have tried to warn somebody. I didn't know they were going to kill anyone, don't you see, until it was too late."

"Someone did follow him," Mike said, turning away.

"Yes . . . Owens, Sergeant Mendez, and Corporal Polansky. Two days later I heard he had been found dead. Some sort of accident. But I didn't believe it."

"Why not?" asked Bob.

"Because Ms. Benson was screaming at Babcock and telling him he was a fool and she'd get him for what he let them do. Then she went in her office at the back of the building, and I . . . I heard her crying."

The anger was eating at the lining of my stomach.

"Do you know where Winters and Owens might be?" I asked.

"They always stay at the ranch when they come to town, with Babcock and those two henchmen of his, Mendez and Polansky. If they aren't there—Wait. A guy flew a helicopter in a couple of times and dropped them off or picked them up. Some friend of Babcock's, flew for a local tourist and rental place."

I stood bolt straight. "Blaznack!"

"Yeah, that's the guy."

I looked at Mike as Bob jumped to the communications console, Charla right behind him. I looked at my watch. Eight forty-five.

"You don't think . . ." Mike started to say.

"I'm going to the 350 and get it ready. Jack, Tran, is the gear loaded?" They nodded. "Trayco, you three come with me and Mike. Bob, let us know what's going on. If we leave now we can meet the senator's plane when it lands." My insides were in knots again, and I wished I hadn't eaten a full breakfast.

I strapped in, pushed all the buttons, flipped on all the switches, and placed the headset over my ears. While it warmed up I reached over and grabbed Mike's hand. She was pale, worried. This time I knew it wasn't because of flying.

The headset came to life. I turned on the cockpit speaker so everyone could hear.

"Jeremiah, this is Bob. Dad is a little ahead of schedule and is already in a landin' pattern. The tower said Blaznack asked for priority landin'. He told them Dad's not well and said he had already ordered a chopper to meet him at the hangar. I don't like this."

"Yeah, me neither. We're off. Let the airport security know what our fears are. Have them meet the senator."

I pulled back on the chopper's stick and put us in the air, turning immediately to the north and heading down the valley, opening the throttle as far as it would go. We darted across Slide Lake, followed the Gros Ventre River to the mouth of the canyon, and quickly flew over Kelly at better than 150 miles per hour.

"Jackson Tower, this is Jerry Daniels in Teton Tour Chopper Three. I'm on direct line to the airport from Kelly and requesting an emergency landing at Senator Freeman's hangar."

"Tour Three, you are cleared. Bob called, Mr. Daniels. The senator's plane has landed and is moving to the hangar. Another one of Teton's choppers is waiting."

"Thank you, Jackson. Has security arrived at the hangar?"

"Yes, sir. Two of them along with two of the sheriff's deputies, they are awaiting the senator's arrival."

I saw the airport and turned a little left toward the hangar. The plane was coming to a halt north of a plane parking area used by tourists and locals. It seemed cluttered and confusing. Then I saw the other chopper. They saw us at the same time.

The door to the Cessna went down, and the senator emerged, Blaznack close behind. One man got out of the chopper as security emerged from the hangar. He was carrying an automatic rifle and had it trained on the senator. I hovered, my mind darting between solutions. The security police stood back as the gunman pointed the M-16 in their direction and yelled something. Now I could see him clearly. It was Owens.

"Trayco! Scare him off!"

He slid open the side window and stuck the M-16 through the opening. "No problem, but Blaznack has a gun in the senator's back!"

I headed in low towards the senator and Blaznack, trying to force them to get down, and throw Blaznack into confusion. I was banking he wouldn't kill.

"Owens is going to shoot, Jerry." I heard Trayco fire and saw Owens jump back toward the other chopper for cover.

"Keep him pinned down!" I yelled. I was only fifty yards from the senator when he went down. I could only hope it was from fear of getting hit. Blaznack, momentarily confused, held his gun on the senator and then went down beside him as the runner of the chopper passed within inches of his head. I pulled back on the throttle and swung left, trying to avoid the parked planes but disrupting Trayco's line of fire, giving Owens a chance to get up. He hesitated, then went after the senator.

The two security guards had ducked for cover, but one of the deputies perceived what was happening and pulled his gun and fired at Owens. I could see it coming as Owens raised the automatic and chopped the guards legs from underneath him.

One chance left. "Trayco! Disable that chopper!" I had the 350 hovering sideways to the one on the ground. Trayco opened fire, riddling the motor housing. Smoke erupted from it. The blades hesitated, then came to a standstill.

Even at a hundred feet Winters' face was livid with anger. "Keep him pinned down in there, Kenny." I brought the 350 slowly down and shut the motors off, hoping they would consider it a standoff.

Owens had Senator Freeman standing between us, Blaznack at his side backpedaling toward the big Cessna.

I bounded from the chopper, not noticing Mike had slipped from the other side. The other deputy and one of the guards had hauled their wounded friend into the hangar, leaving a trail of blood. Winters had opened the far door of his chopper and had gotten out, Trayco's gun trained on his head.

Owens spoke. "Daniels! You so much as move a little finger in this direction and I'll kill Freeman!" I thought about it. He had nothing to lose, but I ignored him and turned to Winters.

"Same goes for you, Winters," I said. "You even attempt to move and Trayco will stop you!"

He grinned. "Owens! I'm coming over there. If they kill me, you kill the senator! Understood?"

"My pleasure, Jace!" Owens said.

Trayco could see the writing on the wall. He lowered his rifle and stepped from the chopper.

Winters strutted into the open and across the pavement. Half-protected by the senator's body, he stood next to Owens, arguing. Then Winters spoke. "We want the chopper, Daniels.

We don't relish the idea of leaving this valley without finishing our job. If we're followed, or if we see any sign of police or military anywhere near well one, we'll kill Senator Freeman.

"Now"—he was completely composed and in control—"move away from the chopper and take your friends with you."

I waved everyone away. "Take your gear, Trayco, including the C6," I said softly. He looked quickly my way, making sure he had the message. I knew he had a canister. I had seen him save it in his overnighter when we got back from the oil rig.

Trayco reached carefully to get his bag. I saw Mike circling toward the downed chopper, plenty of distance between her and them. Tran and Jack climbed down and made sure their hands were visible, drawing attention to them and away from Trayco.

They moved toward us. Fifty feet, then twenty-five, then ten. Winters motioned with his gun for me to move. I moved back, then away, forcing them to keep their eyes on me.

Five feet. Owens had the senator and slid around the nose of the chopper and toward the passenger side.

"*Look out!*" I shouted. Owens froze as he turned his head toward me. I saw the gun in Winters' hand swing my way, his finger squeezing the trigger. I jumped under the tailpiece, bullets ricocheting off the concrete behind me. I rolled to the far side of the chopper in time to see Owens and the senator hit the ground, coldcocked by the C6. Automatic weapon fire jerked my head toward where Tran stood pumping the trigger on his .45, both his hands braced around the grip for accuracy, while slugs pummeled his own body, trying to knock him backward. Two, four, six shots.

Then it was quiet.

Tran fell, blood soaking his shirt, his pistol clattering across the tarmac.

Trayco sprung away from the chopper and to Tran's side, his own pistol trained on two people sprawled on the pavement on the far side of the cockpit. Winters and Blaznack. Jack had his .45 drawn and was quickly over Winters, kicking the empty M-16 aside. I grabbed Owens' pistol angrily, jerking it from his limp hand. He and the senator were both sleeping like babies.

Mike knelt by me. "He's okay, Mike, I . . ."

I noticed the blood dripping from her arm first, then the scarlet red on her blouse as she fell toward me.

"Mike!" I grabbed for her as she went limp. "No!

"Trayco!" He was already at my side, surveying the damage, then quickly lifting her toward the chopper.

The world was spinning, Jack was cradling Tran in his arms, blood everywhere on his shirt and pants. My legs wouldn't work. I couldn't leave Mike's side and tried to climb in beside them as Trayco got to a seat cradling her in his lap.

"Jerry! Jerry! Get hold of yourself! You have to fly this thing! Move it, man! Move it!"

Something in my head clicked, urging me to the pilot's seat, the cobwebs clearing.

As I pushed buttons to start the rotors, the two security men ran from their holes and across the tarmac, pistols drawn. I yelled at one to take care of the senator. "He's only asleep," I said. "And get some cuffs on the guy next to him." I glanced at Winters' motionless, bloodstained body from out of the front of the chopper, the blades picking up speed. Tran hadn't missed.

Blaznack lay beside him, holding his bleeding leg. I didn't care.

The blades, now in full rotation, lifted us from the ground, security guards moving to tasks below and behind us.

"Jackson Tower. This is Tour Three! Notify Jackson Memorial that we are coming in with two wounded! Gun shots! Very serious! ETA, five minutes!"

I switched frequencies as the chopper flew toward the east butte. "Trapper Base this is Deacon!"

"Deacon, go ahead."

"Your dad is okay, but was hit with some C6. They'll get him to the hospital. Tran"—my swollen tongue choked on the words—"and Mike . . . have been hit. We're on our way to the hospital. *Get there! Quick!*"

"On our way!" The radio went dead.

"No, Lord!" I yelled, looking back at Mike lying in Trayco's lap, blood everywhere. "How bad, Kenny? How bad?"

"One in the arm. One in the chest. Winters. When he fired at Tran she must have been behind him. She's got a pulse, Jerry! Keep your eye on the sky! Fly this thing, boy! You can't do her any good looking back here!"

"What about . . . Tran, Jack?" I asked, trying to get a grip on my emotions.

"He's tough, but he took two in the chest, one in the stomach, and two in the arm. Hardly a pulse! Move this thing, Jerry! Move it!"

I jammed the throttle full open, flying at treetop level, praying to buy every second I could.

"Jackson Tower, what is the hospital Flight for Life frequency?" He gave it to me, and I switched.

"Flight for Life, this is Jerry Daniels. I have two people! Multiple wounds to the chest, stomach, and arm of the man; chest and arm wound in a . . . a woman. ETA two minutes!"

"We read you, Mr. Daniels! We're ready. Land in the parking lot between the hospital and the new construction. It's near the Emergency entrance." The voice was almost too businesslike, but it helped to control my fear.

Dear Lord, please! I couldn't take this again! Please!

The hospital came into view, and I swung in, dropped the chopper on the concrete, shut the blades down as the slides gripped the ground, leapt from the cockpit, raced around the other side, and took Mike in my arms as the doctors came up with a gurney. Carefully laying her on it, I followed as they rushed her toward the emergency doors, ripping at her shirt and then pulling a sheet over her as they fled toward the doors.

Seeing the gaping hole, I cried out. I wanted to throw up. To stop existing. To go back to the ranch. To start over. I had allowed her to come. Why!

We were in the operating room, curtains quickly pulled around us. The doctors were deftly hooking up machinery, checking her pulse, yelling commands.

"Give us three minutes," a doctor cried, shoving me through the curtains. I wiped my tears with my sleeve and, taking a deep breath, uttered another silent prayer, the sweat dripping down the back of my neck.

The seconds seemed like hours.

"Now, Mr. Daniels"—he grabbed my arm, pulling me out of my shock—"I'm a Mormon, and I have oil." He was unscrewing the lid to the key-chain vial as we slipped through the curtains.

"Mr. Daniels, listen to me," he said, taking me by the shoulders. "You're in mild shock. Can you use your priesthood? If I anoint, can you bless?"

"Y . . . yes . . . I . . ." I shook my head, trying to think. *Deep breaths. Concentrate.*

He gently touched a drop of oil on the crown of her head. Another doctor watched the monitor. I noticed the green line blipped slightly upward at erratic intervals. My eyes transfixed on the blip-blip of the barely moving line. Then I realized it was the monitor of Mike's heart.

He finished anointing.

I took a deep breath, spiritually reaching for the words. Nothing.

I laid my hands on her head and closed my eyes. I felt the doctor place his hands on mine.

"Michaelene Freeman. In . . . in the name of Jesus Christ I seal the anointing of this oil . . . upon your head to the end that you might . . . that you might be made well . . . and whole . . . again." My head began to clear, the pressure leaving, words beginning to form. The words I should speak.

I paused, letting them come, one by one gently rising from the dust of my tired mind.

"Mike, your body will heal. There'll be no permanent damage. I bless your torn flesh to mend, the tissue to regenerate quickly, and your vital organs I bless with the strength to carry the load they need for your system to rid itself of infection.

"You are a daughter of God. Your mother is watching over you this day to give you added strength and comfort in your pain. She loves you. And Mike . . . I love you. Now, come back to me." I closed the prayer and backed away as they began to work on her again. Through blurred vision I scanned the monitor; the blips were stronger, even. She would be all right. I knew it.

I felt total exhaustion. My mind whirled as I groped for a chair. Trayco grasped my arm and steadied me. I looked into his pale and drawn face. "She . . . she's going to be okay, Kenny. She . . ."

"I know. Sit, Jerry. Tran—"

Tran! I stood straight again. "Where—"

"Next room." He followed me as I dragged my body toward the door.

They were pulling the sheet over his pale, blood-smeared and lifeless body. I worked my way around to the side of the bed, took his hand, and pulled the sheet back from his face. "He saved my life . . . our lives."

Trayco stood opposite me, tears dripping from his cheeks onto the sheet. I had never seen Trayco cry before.

He wiped his face with the back of his hand. "Tran missed his family. Most of them were killed by the Vietcong when he was just a kid. He used to reminisce about them, have dreams about where they were. He said he always saw them standing in the doorway of a house surrounded with light. He dreamed of living with them, learning from them."

I remembered the scripture: *"Nevertheless, we may console ourselves . . . they have died in the cause of their country and of their God, yea, and they are happy."*

38

Jack accompanied the Flight for Life chopper to bring back Blaznack and the senator. Trayco and I paced the floor in front of Mike's room.

The bishop was the first to arrive, walking resolutely down the hall toward me. His words were the right ones as he asked if I had given her a blessing. I told him about the young doctor.

"Christopher Nethercott. A local boy who has come home and done a lot for medicine here. She couldn't be in better hands."

"A friend died in there." I pointed to the other room. "We would appreciate it if you would have his body taken to a local funeral home. Same ones who took care of Dooley."

"Any relatives?" he asked.

"None on this side of the veil," I said.

Bob and Charla looked pale and scared. I quickly brought them up to date. They could have blamed me, but didn't. I appreciated it. Blaming myself and preparing for the senator was enough of a load.

The chopper landed outside, and I steeled myself. Blaznack—in a lot of pain—was wheeled in first. I ignored him, afraid I might do something rash and hateful.

The senator was walking, but tippy, Jack supporting him down the hall. Bob and Charla met him halfway, insisting he take a wheelchair. I could see the fear in his face, the anger.

He slapped his hands on the wheel handles and shoved himself in my direction. I braced for the worst.

The light blue of his eyes had turned to hard gray. "Jeremiah"—his voice was shockingly soft and managed—"Mike will be all right."

Then it changed. "Fillmore Duquesne is responsible, not you, not me, not even Winters."

I felt the weight lift. I needed to know he wasn't my enemy.

"Blaznack! I helped that kid! I hope his legs fall off!"

I forced a smile. "From the looks of him you might get your wish." I leaned forward. "Senator, I took the liberty of giving Mike a blessing. I know she'll be okay, but I can't say that I'm not worried. She . . . she was shot in the chest and . . . in the arm. It was my fault for taking her along. I—"

"No recriminations, Jerry. I know what you're feeling, remember. We all make mistakes."

Dr. Nethercott came out, blood still bright red against the green of his uniform. Mike's blood.

"All of you sit down, would you please. Senator, we've seen each other under more favorable circumstances. I want you in one of these rooms within the half hour. We'll give you a once-over."

He took a deep breath. "I wish I could have saved them both, but your friend Tran's heart—well, it was a wonder he made it to the hospital." He looked me straight in the eye. "She wants to see you first."

"You mean—"

"Yes, she's conscious. In a lot of pain, but she's going to be all right. I want to talk to you when you come out. Senator, you, Bob, and Charla can go in after Mr. Daniels. And don't be hurt; she says she's going to leave you for him anyway!" The grin was from ear to ear.

"Now?" I asked, impatient.

"Now. But make it brief, please." He stopped and talked quietly to the bishop as I pushed through the door.

Her eyes were closed, her brown skin pale, almost opaque. Tubes ran everywhere, but the monitor was sounding a firm and even beep.

I gently took her feeble hand, feeling the soft squeeze as her eyes opened weakly.

"Hi," I said, wiping a tear from my eye, feeling a little like a small boy at Christmas.

"Hi," she said softly. "Come a little closer."

"My pleasure." Her arm was bandaged and in a restraint

that prevented sudden movement. I touched her soft shoulder lightly and leaned down, placing my lips on her cheek, lingering, letting my tears fall on the pillow beside her head.

"Thank you for the blessing, Jerry. Miracles"—she adjusted a little for the pain—"miracles do happen. I . . . saw you from up there, pulling me back, asking for our miracle with your heart and soul. I wanted so much to reach out and touch you, to come back, but I was afraid—"

"Shh, Mike, your spirit may be strong, but your body has a long way to go. Don't overdo it." I kissed her hand, my heart full of gratitude and love for her.

"Uh . . . Ms. Freeman?"

Her eyes opened, and a soft smile creased her lips.

"Will you marry me?" I asked.

"Right now it would be a little difficult, but . . . you do need someone to keep you out of trouble. Have you . . . asked my father?"

"Uh-huh."

"What did he say?"

"About time the spinster got hitched!" I said mockingly.

She tried to laugh, and I immediately regretted my levity. "Oh . . . don't . . . Jeremiah Daniels, if I could hit you I'd knock you out!"

"Sorry. No more jokes. You rest, Mike, I—"

"Just one more thing, Jerry. It has to be in the temple. It has to be right. He sent me back. It has to be right."

"No other way. Save your strength now. Your family wants to see you."

Her hand went to her hair. I laughed a little, helping her place the curls just right. "You've never looked more beautiful."

That brought a dirty look.

"I love you, Mike. Thank you for coming back to me."

She smiled. Then she closed her eyes, too tired to hold them open.

I walked to the door and let them in. Their faces had perked up some, and the color was back. I stood by the foot of the bed as they touched and talked to her, making sure, seeking reassurance she was going to be okay.

Now I couldn't help it. The tears just kept coming. I took a hospital towel and wiped them away, along with the run of my nose.

The bishop and Trayco were in the hall making arrangements for Tran with the hospital staff person responsible for such things. Doctor Nethercott came out of nowhere, took my arm, and pulled me down the hall to his office.

"I didn't tell them everything, Jerry." He motioned to a chair. "Sit down. I want to share this with you, but just between us, okay?"

I nodded. It sounded serious. Paralyzed? No, she was moving. Damage? It didn't matter, whatever it was.

"She died in there, Jerry, while you were blessing her. The machinery shut down. I know you didn't hear it, but it happened. You brought her back with your blessing."

He paused, considering his next words. "I've seen a lot of miracles, Jerry, man-made and beyond man's comprehension. I've used the priesthood many times, but I've never seen the dead raised, and yet you didn't command. You just promised."

I put my hand up. "You've got it wrong, doctor. And to make you understand I'd have to give you a life history. But I learned a hard lesson a couple of years ago." I leaned back on the couch, exhaustion roiling over my body. "Priesthood doesn't command God. It's what's right that must be discovered, then given to the people we bless. When we tap into heaven we ask first, and then if he tells us to command we do it. By asking first, by tapping into the source, we say the right things. I tried to keep another person, whom I loved as much as I do Mike, alive by commanding, cajoling, yelling, and even threatening. It didn't work, and Liz, my former wife, suffered untold pain because of it. When I finally did it right, peace came to everyone. That's the real blessing of the priesthood."

I closed my eyes. "The hardest thing I did for Liz was find out what was best for her, then have the courage to say it. But once done, the Lord did the rest. Liz, Tran. They're happy, busy, doing what they must, preparing the way for the rest of us. Mike—she has more to do. The gratitude I feel for that is beyond explanation, but the peace I feel for Liz; that is just as real. Both miracles in their own right."

It was quiet. "I thought I understood how it worked," he said. "Now . . . now I think I understand times when it didn't work. Times when it did, and I didn't think it would because, like Mike, I thought they were beyond help."

My eyes popped open. "Beyond help?"

"The bullet clipped a major artery to the heart. At least that was the diagnosis. When we opened her chest after the blessing we found damage all around the artery, but the artery itself was intact." He smiled. "With God, nothing is impossible. I would have been sorely tested to accomplish in a lifetime what he did in a matter of seconds."

He stood and moved to the door. "I've got to check on this Blaznack fella's surgery. Want me to save his legs?" he asked with a smile.

"Please. He'll need them to keep away from tough cons in the federal penitentiary." I smiled back, barely awake.

"Lie down, Mr. Daniels. Get some rest. That couch folds out into a rather comfortable bed. The linen is fresh. I'll holler if there're any changes, but, with all these events in mind, I don't expect any. Do you?"

He walked through the door. I forced myself to stand, remove the cushions, and pull the bed out. Fillmore Duquesne would have to wait another six hours.

Then I knelt, my arms folded on the cool linen. The prayer was short but full of sincere thanks. Then I fell soundly asleep on the floor.

39

At 5:00 A.M. I looked in on Mike. Still pale and weak, she slept soundly through my kisses. The machinery beeped a steady, even message. The nurses were all smiles. Only six hours since the airport. One couldn't ask for more than a miracle.

Reluctantly I turned and left the room, heading for the exit, where I joined a revived senator.

"How is—"

"Fine!" I answered, smiling. "She'll probably sleep right through our trip." I tossed the briefcase in the backseat and stretched out, letting him drive.

The sheriff had kept Winters' death under wraps, and Owens, Babcock, and the others were being held the twenty-four hours without an attorney. It would be enough. I smiled to think of the turmoil Duquesne must be in without any contact from his henchmen.

"May I use your car phone?" I asked.

He nodded. "Just leave a quarter in the ashtray."

After I had made a quick call to Ben, verifying Duquesne's apparent decision to hold and wait, the senator called the state attorney, who informed us the document was valid and would be honored by the state and that he was checking with the federals.

For now, the document had put the rigs off limits. They were being capped with a solid twenty-four inches of concrete and were being protected by army National Guard.

The sheriff had a solid case against Babcock. Possession of illegal firearms, attempted murder, and conspiracy to commit murder. Babcock reacted by pointing fingers at Owens and Winters, trying to make a deal and keep his hide off somebody's barn door. His story was that Winters had ordered the murder of Dooley and that Owens, Mendez, and Polansky had carried it out.

Owens was well trained, hadn't said a word, and gave no sign of breaking. I couldn't help but think he would be back on the street because of some high-powered lawyer with no scruples and a penchant for the big bucks.

WASHINGTON had used TITAN to break into Duquesne's mainframe and had left several misleading messages on his bulletin board that would assure that all the remaining players be in the places I wanted them for our final round. Duquesne had used his computer to keep his thumb on everyone. Without his knowledge we were using it to clean house.

I thought it through. After the market closed at one o'clock Duquesne would go through the motions of gathering the accounts from his brokers and filing them in his mainframe. Then he would send a copy via satellite to somewhere in the Middle East. Then finally he would make a paper copy and a disk copy and put them in his briefcase for twenty-four hours until he went through the process again.

I couldn't help but smile. WASHINGTON had put a thing he called a Trojan horse in Duquesne's program. When Duquesne punched in his password, the "horse" WASHINGTON had placed inside Duquesne's system would let its little men free. They would quickly spread, changing and destroying information, then infect every other system Duquesne had touched. Fillmore Duquesne would be the hand of his own destruction.

I didn't know who owned the computer in the Middle East, but I was pleased that they would lose everything. If somehow Duquesne wiggled free from what we had planned, maybe they would take a shot at him!

Kenny Trayco and Jack had already taken Trayco's jet and were well on their way to Washington. I looked at my watch. In less than an hour they would be in the president's office with what was needed to get court orders to shut down TERROR1's brokerage system. They carried affidavits concerning TriStar, copies of Sellars' files, confessions from Babcock, and several copies of the complete operation and finance plan I had taken out of Duquesne's system. The attorney general had assured the senator that it would be enough to get the necessary court orders to move on twenty-two different brokerage houses and confiscate 721 different accounts containing nearly thirty-two billion dollars in assets.

The money could be used to pay off a portion of the national debt. Duquesne and his partners would never try to claim it. If they did we would nail them for the murders of Robert Doolittle, two brokers, and the workers who were killed over the Grand Canyon.

I hit the switches on Hank's Lear as the senator strapped himself in the copilot's seat. The big engines hummed to life, and after a fifteen-minute checkout we were moving toward takeoff.

My watch said 3:50. We should arrive in plenty of time. Good weather, warm and pleasant in Jackson, hot and very dry in Las Vegas, clear skies all the way. By evening it would be over.

I had asked for a flight pattern that would take me over the rigs. The extra few minutes were worth it. After notifying the sheriff who we were, I went in low enough to see what was going on. The cement trucks were backed up at well one, laying a floor over the hole. The place was crawling with people cleaning up the charred rig and hauling hoses, pipe, and other materials away from the site. A more natural state was soon to be realized.

It all seemed so unreal. A bad dream.

"Jeremiah, if we are about to win, why do I feel empty?"

"Because we aren't really going to win. Because Dooley died, others died, and you almost lost another son. We both almost lost Mike. Because we know, deep down, it isn't over. Iraq will invade Kuwait despite what we've accomplished. We won a battle, senator, not the war."

He sat silent, thinking. "The president contacted Iraq through diplomatic channels. It didn't do any good."

"Did he put us in jeopardy?" I asked anxiously. "Did he tell them what we know?"

"No. Just threatened them."

"Diversion or no diversion, the military aspect of TERROR1 will go as planned," I said. "They don't have much choice, politically. Iraq is broke and in debt. They must have Kuwait's wealth to survive. Taking us out of the picture would have allowed Hussein to go farther, but he must do that much to save face with his own people."

"Duquesne is their sacrificial lamb, isn't he."

"Yeah."

"Does he know it?"

"Yes . . . and no. I think Duquesne saw them as stupid but cruel people. Someone to be used." I took a deep breath. "What I have yet to understand is why he was foolish enough to keep such incriminating records. Reports, diary notations of meetings, names and places. WASHINGTON found gobs in Duquesne's computer beyond what even the TERROR1 file contained."

"For self-preservation?"

"Maybe. Sort of a backup if they didn't come through with what he wanted after their so-called New Republic was set up. An insurance policy. Maybe. Then again, maybe someone else was calling the shots and required the detail."

"Hussein!"

"Not smart enough."

"Who?"

"Million-dollar question, Senator. And the one to which we may never have an answer. Whatever the reason, his record keeping has become the means of his destruction.

"North Las Vegas Airport, this is Lear jet 919, requesting instructions to land."

The response came back, and we were put in a sequence for landing.

"Only a matter of hours, Senator. Maybe Duquesne will be kind enough to fill in the blanks." I smiled.

40

It was 4:30 P.M.

Ben was waiting outside the hangar in my Eldorado, a bit sheepish in the senator's presence. He had talked to another broker over drinks after work and found out Duquesne had given the order to be at their desks an hour before the market would open the next morning, and that they could plan on a big day.

I avoided Ben's questions about what was next, and he seemed to understand it was not for him to know, taking it in stride as I pulled the car onto Rancho, heading southeast toward the freeway. We would have just enough time to get into position. My stomach began knotting up tightly again. If I didn't come out of this thing with ulcers the size of silver dollars it would be a miracle, and I had already had my fair share of those. My thoughts went to Mike. Soon. Soon I would be back and done with this!

Previous to leaving Jackson, the senator had called Officer Carone at the Las Vegas Police Department to make arrangements at the Mirage. We wanted surveillance, but from a safe distance, and no bugs in the suite. Everything had to look and feel normal and, unless I missed my guess, Duquesne had employees at the Mirage, watching, prepared to let him know of anything out of the ordinary.

The car phone rang. "This is Carone. Glad you're here. Duquesne is at the suite now. Been there an hour. My people say he brought a computer with him, like you thought."

An hour. Enough time to get ready for Royalty. Duquesne would want Royalty out of the way now. He wouldn't like Royalty's apparent attempt at blackmail stated in the message we had dropped into his bulletin board.

We drove to the Strip then south a few hundred yards to the main entrance of the Mirage, arriving at three forty-five. Eyeing the spot where he had been rescued only a few days before, Ben's face was somber and matched my own feelings about what might have been had Trayco not reacted decisively.

I pulled into the far end of the back parking lot, where we could keep an eye on things. Carone had said he would let me know when Defender arrived at the back entrance.

We sat quiet, each involved in his own thoughts, the motor and air running to keep the hot afternoon heat from cooking us. I had parked between two vehicles and out of sight of the doorway to the suites. Defender would recognize the Eldorado.

The expensive suites at the Mirage sit behind and to the south in a separate, very swank area away from regular public view. Around two thousand dollars a night, the rooms are the most elaborate in the city.

Sellars had made it clear in his report that the committee used only one particular suite because of its second, very private entrance, its opulence, and its size. It was that one all of us watched as we waited.

A black Cadillac limousine with gold trim and a distinctive license plate approached the annex. I only saw it briefly before it disappeared. It was enough. I had ridden in it several times. My head had told me to be prepared, that all the evidence pointed in that direction. It shouldn't have been a crushing surprise, but one never relishes the discovery of a friend as a traitor.

After giving him enough time the senator and I walked to the suite. I used the key Carone had given me and opened the door. We stepped inside and shut the door behind us.

"Gentlemen, nice of you to come," I said.

They turned a sudden shade of white. A burly man at Duquesne's side who wore a trimly fit suit and had shoulders as broad as the fender on a Mack truck eased a hand inside his jacket. Duquesne motioned for him to stop.

"What's the meaning of this?" he asked.

"Just thought you and your guest here"—I motioned toward Defender—"might want to have some firsthand information on the downfall of your operation."

I turned and faced him. "Hank, glad to have you out in the

open for a change. Skulking around in a red Bronco is not your best talent."

"What are you doing? . . . I don't—"

"Please. No denials. Not yet. Save that for courtroom tactics.

"I don't think either of you have met Senator James Freeman. Senator, Fillmore Duquesne is the one at the oversized desk. Fits his ego. Hank Butcher, my former attorney, is the other gentlemen, and that one over there will probably need to know that his friend Mr. Winters won't be returning and that there's a job opening in the Duquesne empire. Wages are good, but you really ought to ask for hazard pay."

Hank spoke, his ashen face turning red. "I thought . . . the message said . . ." He looked desperately at Duquesne, confused, wanting an answer.

"I had been kidnapped, and Jerry was dead?" the senator said. "Sorry for the deception, but Jerry didn't think you would accept our invitation otherwise. He was right, wasn't he?" The senator was enjoying himself.

"By the way," I said, "before your gorilla there gets nervous and uses that gun under his coat you should know that Sergeant Carone of the Las Vegas Police Department is waiting outside. He has no real interest in you, at least not at this point." The gorilla's hand eased to his side.

Duquesne had gathered his composure. I'd get to him in a minute. "Sit down, Hank, before you collapse from shock." His life was catching up with him very quickly, and his face mirrored it.

"I asked you here for a reason, Hank, so I'll get to it. Take notes. They'll probably help at your upcoming trial."

I could only imagine what was in his head. Desperation? Fear? Maybe he was just trying to look back, checking his mistakes, seeing if I really had anything.

"How's the client in Los Angeles? The one you were supposed to be defending the last few days?"

"My assistant has taken the case, but he'll be free in the next few hours. You always said I was the best, Jerry."

"Yes, I guess I did." I forced my lips into a slight grin. "But at defending murderers, not at being one. Your assistant had the case all along. You have been busy elsewhere."

"Let's not beat around the bush, Jerry. If you have something concrete let's hear it. If not, I have business with Mr. Duquesne; I would like to get on with it." His composure was returning.

I took two steps and bent over, placing both my hands on the arms of the overstuffed chair in which he sat, getting my face down next to his. "You're not quite as clever as you think. Always in the back of your mind was the idea I wouldn't suspect you, that I had no reason to suspect you. That made you careless." I walked to the full-length windows. "Very careless.

"Before I left Jackson, the sheriff was kind enough to hand me these. I had asked him to look for them a couple of days ago." I took the empty shell casings from my pocket. "30-06, 175 grain. With your fingerprints on them. Found on the old logging road where someone took some shots at Mike and me."

I took out a picture of Luke Sievers that Charla had taken when he went to work for the ranch, a safety precaution against hiring crooks looking for a quiet place to hide. "This man was hired by you to help with that little operation. He left the money in his bunkhouse. More prints."

I saved the best for last. "We have your signature on the lease agreement for a red Bronco and on the Visa slip for the 30-06 from High Mountain Hunting in Jackson." I walked over and leaned down in his face again. He looked away. I grabbed his chin and yanked it straight, piercing his eyes with my stare. "Tell me, Hank, how much of what you were doing did Mr. Duquesne know about?"

Duquesne sat at the blond oak desk, a confused look on his face. "Did Hank let you in on things, Mr. Chairman? Did he tell you about Sellars? About sending Winters and Owens to my house to fetch some files he had let slip out of his grasp?" I leaned forward, placing my hands on the glass covering the desktop. "And did he inform you of my involvement, of how much we knew, what we were up to?"

Duquesne's mouth was open, the red of his flushed face crimson. "I thought not." I walked back to Hank. "Well, Hank here is responsible for your failure. It was Sellars who started us on your path, and Hank could have shut him up a long time ago. Because he didn't, we have stopped you."

Duquesne was livid, his face red, steam rising through the skin and developing into sweat.

I smiled, jamming my finger into Hank's chest, emphasizing my words. "From the look on his face I'd say you're in trouble."

Duquesne's face was now sheet white, the pink of his fat lips and nose standing out like flowers against white aged and cracked rock. He spoke very carefully and pointedly. "I don't know this fool!"

Hank walked over to the desk, the bodyguard reaching in his coat again. I mentally checked the 9mm lying comfortably in my belt at the small of my back, knowing I could never get it in time. Fortunately Hank stopped at the front of the desk, slamming his fist into it and cracking the glass.

"Everything," he said, "everything my partners and I own is invested in this deal. I handled our financial matters and those of our wealthy clients, through brokers, of course, and our accountant. I moved money into your system without their knowledge. It wasn't easy, but I got one of the accountants to help me. We, all of us, could've made millions."

Duquesne laughed nervously.

I saw Hank's shoulders slump and the breath go out, the tension in his fist relaxing. "I was trapped! And when Duquesne got Stevenson to incriminate you, Jerry, I saw the chance of everything coming apart at the seams. I couldn't allow it! There was too much at stake. My whole life. My partners. The firm. My family. All of it. I was desperate, Jerry. I had to act to save all of them. To give me time to get out!"

"How did you get involved in the first place, Hank?" the senator asked calmly.

"I can answer that, Senator," I said. "Hank's firm represents a number of clients in the Middle East. Because of his background in international law, and because he speaks the language, he was given the most responsibility."

Hank turned and faced us, the personification of a penitent soul anxious to confess. "That was when I met two members of Duquesne's committee and became their silent partner and legal counsel. They needed someone who understood their liability and knew how to protect them if anything went wrong. In return for services rendered they gave me a sizable nontaxable fee and a promise to get me in if I could raise ten million dollars.

"I advised them privately on how to put all the liability in Duquesne's lap, telling them to keep no records of their involvement and warning them about Duquesne's use of that . . . that computer. I didn't know for sure, but I thought he might be keeping records that could be used against them.

"They were concerned enough to go to work on other members of their group, finally forcing a vote that got me inside Duquesne's system. One of them gave me a password. I found nothing incriminating them, only the timetable, the plans for TERROR1, the information on the brokers, and the financial records. All of which I could use in any court of law to show clearly that my clients were not involved. They established Duquesne's guilt completely."

Hank's head jerked toward Duquesne. "I suspected he had other information on them, but I couldn't find it."

"Yes," Duquesne said arrogantly, "I kept files on them. My insurance policy. You were sloppy. I knew every time you met with them, filling them in on what you thought I was doing. Their choice of a spy masquerading as legal counsel was a stupid one."

Hank turned and went for the symbolic throat. "You think I'm the first they have had watching you? You fool! They never trusted you! They have had spies near you for years! Winters not only kept *them* informed, but he kept his old boss with the PLO informed as well. They used you like they used everyone else, because as an American citizen you could get them what they wanted. But they had already determined to get rid of you as soon as it was over. In the meantime we watched you, and if anything went wrong Winters and I both were instructed to destroy your records even if we had to blow up your entire system! Owens had accepted the responsibility to kill you when they said so!"

I wanted to hear that. Duquesne didn't, and sank back in his chair. It's no fun to be betrayed by someone you trust.

"Sellars, Hank. When you got onto him why didn't you just fire him?"

"I could only watch Duquesne through his computer, and it wasn't enough. Sellars was keeping an eye on things with sources I couldn't get to." He turned and faced outside. "Dick was also very informative on what was happening among my partners in the Middle East. He had agents in close proximity to every one of them. When he found out something that might hurt them, I let them know. He was exchanging information with other groups in TITAN, particularly the CIA. We were able to monitor things very well by monitoring Sellars' files."

"Then you and Royalty were working together?" I asked. I hadn't figured that part out.

"Yes. I recruited him. I knew Royalty through politics. They gave him a million up front and two million when it was over. The rest is history."

He paused, taking a breath, making a decision. "The night Sellars was killed, when you, Ms. Freeman, and I were in his office going through his files, I realized he knew what had happened with your case, and that there must be incriminating evidence in his files. Instead of going home like I told you, I went to my office.

"I have a TR1200, a device that records the numbers that call on my private line and gives me the time of the call and the length of time the caller spends in my system. My security blanket, so I know exactly who looks into my computer. I have to leave it on all the time because of messages coming from Royalty, Duquesne, and the others.

"An hour before Sellars was found dead he had accessed my files for nearly half an hour. In those files I had the passwords for Duquesne's system, and for Royalty's personal computer in Washington, along with the names of the members of the committee and the communications passwords for my contacts. I could think only the worst. Half an hour! Plenty of time to search my files and access those codes. He might have them.

"I panicked, went back to the office, accessed his computer, and did a search. Sure enough, he had the information. It was scattered and mixed, but it was there. I went to his modem ledger and found that two calls had been placed that day. One just prior to his death, to Washington, and one afterward, to your home phone. I called Royalty and told him to find out where the Washington call went. He had no luck. Apparently Sellars had figured out what we were doing and wasn't trusting anyone. He had hidden the stuff in a new file."

"That's when you sent those two killers to my house," I said coldly. "You knew I had sent Sellars' files to my computer."

He nodded. "I told them not to harm you."

"They were going to kill me, Hank. If Jan hadn't come to my door and thrown them into confusion they would have."

"I told them not to."

"If they brought you Jerry's printouts, why did you go after Mike and him?" the senator asked.

"I told him I still had the information," I said. "I trusted him. He had messed things up and was forced to make it right or lose everything."

"I contacted the committee members who were paying me to watch things and told them what was going on," Hank went on, wringing his hands, his face a picture of pain. "They urged me to handle it myself and not to involve Duquesne or his people. I told them I . . . I would do it . . . for the ten million dollars I had given them . . . and they agreed. Jerry, I was desperate to get out!"

"Thank heaven you're a lousy shot," I said.

He faced the window again. Better than facing me, I decided.

Evil is like a bed of quicksand; you don't know how much it can hurt until you step in it, and then the more you move, the deeper you get, until there isn't any way out. Hank had been a friend, and a decent man, once. Then he got in quicksand.

"If it's any consolation, Hank, I know you didn't kill Sellars."

He turned on his heel and faced me, mouth agape. The senator looked stunned, and so did Duquesne.

"What? But he had to. Nobody else . . . I didn't—"

I cut Duquesne off. "I know you didn't, either. My guess is, last you knew you were rid of Sellars years ago when you pulled that little ploy with the phony million-dollar payoff to the president." His body sunk in relief.

"Hank, you didn't arrive at the office until just a few minutes after I did. I know. I saw you come up the main drive as I came through the lobby, and you were in Sellars' office two, maybe three minutes after me. Not enough time to find Sellars and kill him.

"But you are involved in this up to your greedy little eyeballs. What you have done is treason, attempted murder, fraud, and half a dozen other crimes. Do you want to come out of it alive?"

He looked at me with a question in his eyes. "Is . . . is there a way? The people behind this, they . . . they don't let people live when they fail."

"They can be stopped."

The relief spread across his face.

"But I will feed you to the wolves if you don't meet the conditions I'm about to state to you."

"What conditions?"

"You sell your practice to your partners. You return to Jackson and confess to the attempt on our lives. You have no comment for the press, and you serve whatever sentence they give you. Sharp a lawyer as you are, that shouldn't be long, and the money from your sale of the partnership should take care of your wife while you're away, with enough for you when you get out. We'll see that you and your family are protected, and that you get a new identity. You can serve the term out of the mainstream criminal system." I paused. "Last condition. If called on to do so, you will testify against the entire group."

"But what about the money I lost? My partners, our clients. They . . ." His shoulders slumped.

"You're right. They don't deserve to be hurt, but Mr. Duquesne is going to help us with that." I caught the chairman in deep and unpleasant thought. I wondered if he had figured out what came next.

"Me? Not on your life, cowboy!" he said.

"I think you will. Before I leave here I expect to have a check for . . . how much was it, Hank, not counting your own money? Consider that a lesson by experience. We don't want to be unfair with Mr. Duquesne."

"Nine million eight hundred and fifty thousand," he said, still in shock. I noticed the senator. The grin was almost too much.

"Make it a straight ten million. We ought to pay them a fair interest on their money."

"Why are you doing this, Jerry?" Hank asked again.

"Other than guaranteeing you will be a witness for the prosecution, it doesn't matter. Are you willing to meet our conditions?"

He nodded. His face showing a drooped look of relief as he collapsed on the overstuffed chair.

He had deserted Sievers on the mountain that day when Mike and I had come so close to meeting our Maker. I figured Sievers had tried to go through with it on his own. Thinking he had killed Hal, he needed to kill us, too. If Hank had stuck around we might not have survived. He deserved a chance to survive.

Breathing deeply, I went to the window and stood looking at the dusty blue sky. One down. Two to go.

41

After a moment I returned to the couch and let my body sink into the luxurious softness, relaxing a little, preparing for the next round. Duquesne sat at the desk, one eye on the computer monitor, one on the senator and me. I noticed that the briefcase was still held by his bodyguard, the chain attached to his wrist. Hank sat in the overstuffed chair, deep in thought.

"Hank, your partners at the law firm need to be told, and so does your family. I expect to see you in Jackson in no more than a week. Do we understand each other?"

He nodded.

"Good. Your car is waiting. Tell Rod to expect a check, by courier, before the end of the day."

He started to say something, but I put up my hand and waved him toward the door. "I'll talk to you in Jackson. Unless, of course, you're having second thoughts about my terms?"

He walked to the door, looked back over his shoulder at each of us, then left.

Duquesne laughed mockingly. "Protect him? You must be crazy!" His fleshy face turned to stone. "I'll get him! I personally will pull the trigger!"

"Sorry," I said. "I don't think so." I paused as he sat back in his chair, measuring me, deciding how dangerous I was, trying to read my mind, know our plans for him.

"You can't touch us."

I wanted to hear more. I waited, knowing he must fill the

silence in order to remind himself of the strength of the position he thought he had.

"If you try to stop us we'll destroy your economy, your free market system will be in a shambles."

"That's what you have intended from the beginning, isn't it?" I said matter-of-factly. "The quake, the destruction of thousands of lives and millions in property, was only to be the catalyst by which you launched a major selloff on Wall Street, destroying confidence in the system, trying to weaken the economy to a point where anarchy might take over. Did you really believe you could precipitate something like we've seen in recent months in Eastern Europe?"

"Believe?" he asked, his smile cold. "The American system is on the verge of collapse. Your debt is greater than all other nations combined, a tower of cards ready to come crumbling down with the slightest ill wind. Believe? Hardly. We're in a position to make it happen! And when it does, men like myself, men with vision and money, will buy up the pieces and force a new direction. And the people—broke, desperate for a savior to pull them back into prosperity—will beg us to take charge. They'll see the need for a new order here as much as some of my partners—the ones who live in the Middle East—see a need for it there!" He laughed. "Out of the rubble we create we'll build a new economy, a new social system, and eventually a new order of government."

I stood and went to the window. I hadn't noticed that the patio was all enclosed by high walls and was filled with lush plants and trees.

He laughed again, taking out a cigar, biting off the end, and spitting it out with arrogant, bitter force. His guard reached for a lighter.

"Such a pity to smell up this beautiful room, don't you think?" I said coldly.

"You would prefer that I do not smoke?" he said, looking confidently over the tops of his metal-rimmed glasses. "Aw, yes, Jeremiah Daniels, the Mormon bishop. Sorry. I don't mean to offend your uh . . . delicate sensibilities."

He chuckled again. "You see, I do know quite a bit about you. When Winters and Owens found you snooping around our property in Bridger-Teton I did a search on you. Impressive background. War hero, married, widowed, broker caught with his fingers in the till. Tsk, tsk. But, then, that wasn't your fault, was it? I mustn't forget that. It wouldn't be right to include such dishonesty in your resume." He laughed some more. "You're a good man, Mr. Daniels. That's what makes you vulnerable. You let Mr. Butcher off the hook because you have this self-inflated feeling of right and wrong. I'll smash Butcher for making mistakes like he did, and that's why I'm where I am and where you'll never be. Your goodness makes you weak! And weakness, Mr. Daniels, is to be loathed!

"Now. Get on with it, Daniels. I have a meeting with my committee in a few hours, and I must get back to LA."

"How will they feel about your failure?"

"I have not failed. TriStar was a calculated risk. They understood that. The plan will go ahead as scheduled. The rest will not be as easy, nor as devastating, but it will give us the foothold we need, both there and here."

"Then we'd better see if we can stop you." Now I could only rely on WASHINGTON's effectiveness. "The market closed today, up five points in modest trading. At exactly one-thirty you began calling in the reports from nineteen brokers. It used to be twenty, but Ben Stevenson can't seem to be found." I smiled at him. He was unshaken. "Each of those brokers turned in their computer worksheets for the day, and you stored them in your mainframe. Then you sent a copy—I suspect via satellite linkup—to at least one other mainframe in the Middle East." He was fondling his cigar more nervously. "Once that was done you made two backups, one on disk and one on paper. Both are inside that briefcase, and you have them with you at all times." He glanced quickly at it, then calmed himself. "This morning another computer system— bigger and better than yours—used Walter Babcock's passwords and entered your mainframe, leaving what's known as a Trojan horse. But what it's called doesn't matter; what it did, does."

He was turning pale, and I was enjoying it. So was the senator. "Senator, could you explain?"

"My pleasure. The Trojan horse was set up to change any and all information in your system and any other system you conduct business with via satellite linkup. It changed all the numbers in your financial report. When you shredded the old copies and disks, you lost the only accurate copy you have of all transactions. In the new one—the one you saved as of one-thirty today—all the account numbers are jumbled and beyond use, all the figures incorrect, all the phone numbers inaccurate. In short, every number is wrong."

Duquesne grabbed the briefcase—almost yanking the guard's arm from its socket—slammed it on the desk, and used a key to unlock it.

"If you'll look carefully you have something that looks in order," the senator said. "Same format and same look as all the ones of the past, but everything is really quite different. The stock amounts—you should have some of those memorized. Check them. You should also know approximately how much you've spent. If you check that you'll find it's quite an inaccurate figure." The senator was grinning.

Duquesne was thumbing through the papers frantically, his finger going down the page, checking the figures. I could see that WASHINGTON had done a good job. When Duquesne finished he collapsed back in the chair, his eyes fixed with the fear of a trapped animal.

"I suppose your system was necessary, Duquesne, but it was also your nemesis," I said. "Once we got inside we were able to do anything we wanted. Senator, would you like to show Mr. Duquesne a copy of his day-to-day notes and the operational plan and timetable for TERROR1?"

The senator opened his briefcase and took out a few papers. He walked to the desk and slid them across.

"You'll notice that's only a sampling, but we appreciate your penchant for organization. You've given us enough to hang you quite high!" I smiled, then sat down on the couch, letting it all set in as his eyes quickly went over the pages.

"Are you ready for the really good part?" I asked.

If looks could have killed, my next of kin would have received notice in the mail. But he said nothing. He was beginning to get the picture, and his funeral was a part of it.

I continued. "At the opening of the market tomorrow, twenty brokerage house offices will be slapped with injunctions, search warrants, and restraining orders. All your precious accounts will be frozen, all your funds impounded. When Iraq attacks Kuwait and futures go up you'll not care because you'll not be able to do anything about it! You've lost it all to government seizure.

"Of course, you and your partners could lay claim to those accounts and the funds in them. If they really do belong to you we would surely want you to have them." My voice hardened. "But you would have to do it personally, with proof in hand, and you would have to accept the guilt attached as well. According to the evidence we have, that includes the murder of at least forty people—a geologist, two brokers, and thirty-seven innocent people aboard a charter headed for Waco, Texas."

His skin had become clammy, sweat oozing from his overweight pores. He slumped further into his chair and looked as if he would fall right under the desk if he wasn't careful.

"My father used to call this kind of situation a rock and a hard place. Mr. Duquesne, simply stated, we have you, and there's no way out!"

"But you . . . you couldn't have—"

I leaned forward, hissing the words. "But we did! Your egotistical record keeping for posterity, or insurance that you wouldn't be shoved aside when your usefulness was over—whatever the reason—has come back to haunt you."

He stood, angry, spewing the hate. "They'll kill you when they find out what you've done. It's you that has destroyed them. They'll see that, and they'll send people to hunt you down for it!"

"Maybe. I'm willing to take that risk. But I don't think they'll see it that way. You're the one who has failed them. You're the one who has incriminated them. If they live long enough it'll be you they come after, not us."

He sat back down. "What . . . what do you mean, if they live long enough?"

"Pertinent information contained in your TERROR1 and personal files is being sent to the leaders of the governments under which your partners live, with the exception of Iraq, of course. Those leaders will then be briefed by our government on the role each of you played. Under the laws of most nations your committee members will be dealt with as traitors and will be punished accordingly. If there're some who escape that, they'll not escape the monetary sanctions that come afterward. They depend on the very countries they tried to destroy for their business. They'll get that business no longer.

"As for the taking of Kuwait, I wish we'd known in time to stop it, but I don't think we ever could've, under any circumstances. Greedy, evil men that do such things can't be easily swayed with words. But the president has prepared well, both militarily and politically, and Iraq will go no further than that and will find it most difficult to find allies for their cause. I think we'll witness the greatest political solidarity against an invading nation that has ever been seen.

"Second, Kuwait was notified two days ago about Iraq's intentions and has begun moving their assets to other countries. What they can't get out won't be enough to buy the armies of Iraq lunch. Steps have also been taken to freeze all Iraqi assets and to keep them from getting their hands on anything they need while aggressors.

"People will suffer, and there may even be a war, but we are more prepared for what comes than we were a few days ago." I decided to rub it in. "*And* because of *you*, Mr. Duquesne, we have saved many lives both here and abroad. Because of *you*, Iraq will be limited in its aggression and the taking of Arab lives in Saudi Arabia, the Emirates—all of the Middle East. We are pleased with your help. I don't think they will be."

"They'll kill me!" he said, his eyes growing wide with the realization.

"Maybe. No, probably. You've cost them billions of dollars, not to mention their real goal—control of the Middle East and destruction of our economy. They've killed for much less.

"There is evil and there is evil. You're up the scale far above Hank and most of mankind, but others who'll come to kill you are at the very top. Surely you don't expect sympathy from them."

"So that it's clearly understood, our government," the senator said, "will confiscate all assets in those brokerage accounts and hold them. If someone claims them we'll prosecute to the full extent of the law. We have the evidence for a rock-solid case of first-degree murder, along with conspiracy to overthrow the government of the United States. We have witnesses, and affidavits signed by some of your co-conspirators. Those who come to make their claim will rot in prison, and where possible we'll confiscate all other property they own and put them in the poorhouse.

"Needless to say, it would be most unwise for anyone in your group to come even close to the borders of this country.

"You, Mr. Duquesne, have four hours to leave the United States, and never—I repeat never—return!

"Last, by the end of this year, you will have sold all businesses registered in America, or we will confiscate them as well. If you make any attempt to register them elsewhere, or operate them from Tunis, we'll prosecute you to the full extent of the law, in absentia if necessary, and we'll put *you* in the poorhouse. You are out. Your citizenship will be revoked, and your passport as well. Understood?"

There was a silent nod.

"I suggest you buy yourself an army with the proceeds from the sale of your companies," I said. "You'll need the protection."

"Now, about that check I told Hank would be delivered today. Make it out to Clemens, McCloud, and Butcher. Ten million." I took a piece of paper out of my pocket. "Write it on the account in Switzerland, number 003-4296-0077. It's the only one of your foreign accounts that has enough to cover the debt. Everything in this country will be inaccessible."

"Thorough." He reached into his briefcase and fumbled through several checkbooks. Then he wrote the check out and shoved it across the desk toward me.

"Don't cancel it. You won't like the results. Duquesne Industries is worth a sight more than ten million, and we'll take it from you if you try anything stupid. Also, if the senator, his family, myself, Hank Butcher, or anyone else who helped stop you should die sudden and violent deaths, the rest of us will nail your hide to the wall."

I stood and walked over to his computer. Everything should be ready on the other end. I looked at my watch. One more minute. "I'm going to use your computer. No sense you going down alone. Do you mind?" He moved aside as I turned the monitor so he couldn't see it clearly.

He was already plugged into his mainframe by way of the modem next to the monitor. I punched up the bulletin board and followed the instructions WASHINGTON had given me for leaving a message. I typed it in.

▶ ROYALTY:

DIAL THE FOLLOWING NUMBER. WE HAVE A DECISION TO MAKE. THE ENTIRE COMMITTEE IS WAITING.
                              —THE CHAIRMAN.

There was nothing to do but wait, but it shouldn't be long. The note we left in Duquesne's bulletin board had told Royalty to be waiting. I watched Duquesne, who had moved to the window, and his guard a few steps away, the briefcase was closed, but still attached to his wrist. I wondered just how much of all this the gorilla understood.

The phone rang. Then again. "Duquesne, pick that up and say hello, would you? It's for you."

He hesitated, then shrugged his shoulders and moved to the desk on the fourth ring. "Duquesne."

I took the phone, listening to the angry words on the other end.

"What in the name of all that's important are you trying to do! Have things gone that sour? Now you listen—" Royalty was being interrupted. I could hear harsh words, then words of denial. Then the phone fell, hard, onto the floor or desk, then the sounds of a struggle that ended very quickly with the heavy thud of a body falling to the floor. Then a few more seconds of muffled noises.

"Jeremiah, you there?" Trayco's voice asked over Royalty's Washington phone.

"Yeah, Kenny, I'm here. Is the message I sent still on the screen?"

"Yeah. Jack's getting a copy of it for posterity, and the president's here." He laughed. "He just decked Willmore Dutton with one blow. He's got my vote in '92! How you doing on your end?"

"Two down. Good work. Everything set to your satisfaction for in the morning?"

"You, my friend, have moved mountains! It's a wonder to behold, I'll tell you! The house of cards comes down at 8:30 A.M., eastern time!"

"Good." I paused. "Trayco . . . thanks. You really are the best. Heaven bless you!"

"You won't think so when you get my bill!" He hung up with a laugh.

I closed the computer down. "You won't be needing this. Winters is dead, and Owens is in jail. Royalty is now under arrest. Your kingdom has crumbled."

The senator closed his briefcase and joined me at the door. "I hope never to see you again, Mr. Duquesne. I hope never to hear of you again, and believe it or not I hope I don't read about you in the obituaries, although I think it's only a matter of time.

"Nobody deserves to die more than you do, the suffering and deaths you have caused and would have caused, but I think it'll be a greater punishment to wait to meet your Maker while waiting to meet your killer. Good day!"

I closed the door on a broken man. The senator put his arm around my shoulders and patted lightly. "How do you do it?" he asked with a grin on his face.

"Do what?" I said, taking the bait.

"Say all that without using one single swearword?" We laughed and walked quickly through the annex lobby and toward the car.

A plain government vehicle pulled into the drive, and four men got out. They surprised me.

"Mr. Daniels, Senator," the first to get to us said. "I'm David Steen with the FBI. The president sent us to see that Mr. Duquesne goes directly to the airport from here and catches a flight to Tunis. Everything set with you?"

I nodded, looking a little confused.

"We're finished with him," the senator said. "Station two of your men in the lobby and two in the suite. Let Duquesne know who you are and what you're there for. I don't think he'll mind the protection." He looked at me. "Get in the car, Jerry, and close your mouth for pete's sake. It's unbecoming for a man of your stature."

Two down. One to go.

42

I started the Eldorado and let it run with the air-conditioning on to cool the interior a little, then turned halfway in the seat to speak to him.

"Okay, Senator, what else don't I know?"

"Nothing. Duquesne was right about you. You are too kind sometimes. That man back at the Mirage is very smart and innovative. Jerry, once he gets over the shock it's anyone's guess what he might do. The president wanted to take no chances. As much as we know, we might not know everything. There may be other contingencies. You don't trust a man like Fillmore Duquesne. We decided we had to put a guard on him, that's all."

"Okay," I said. "I see it. No harm done, I suppose. It just surprised me."

"You had enough on your mind, so I took care of it myself."

"Are they waiting at the next place as well?" I asked, half grinning.

"No. Your Sergeant Carone will be sufficient, I think. This one is strictly a civil matter." He hesitated, then went ahead. "Do you think you're up to this?"

I didn't answer. I wasn't. How could I be? Putting him in prison for the rest of his life . . . How could anyone be ready to put a friend in prison!

Ben got a confused look on his face as I pulled the Eldorado into a slot in the Pincock Center parking garage. "Why . . . why are we back here?" he asked.

"Ben. Clean out your desk and say good-bye to your secretary. Put Charlie in charge as acting manager and phone the main office and tell them you're through pending an SEC investigation. Belmont, from the local office of the SEC, will be here in twenty minutes to close things down. You'd better warn everyone.

"It's seven o'clock. I phoned ahead this morning and told your secretary to have everyone here for a meeting."

He was going pale. "I knew it was coming, but when you finally face it . . . well it's like dying."

"Not quite," I said.

He smiled. "Yeah. I thought that was going to happen the other night. You're right. Dying is worse. Jerry, I'd like to be able to tell Banner you're coming back, and I'd like to suggest to the main office that you be made manager."

"I'm not a broker anymore, Ben, but thanks for the offer. I've got land to take care of in Wyoming, and I'll be living there from now on. Maybe I'll start a consulting firm of my own, who knows. Besides, Grandpa here will want to have all his grandkids close."

As I got out of the car my feet seemed like weights attached to the end of my legs. It had all started here. Now it was only right that it end in the same place.

I noticed Sergeant Carone sitting in the lobby, reading a paper, ready to come upstairs when needed. The lobby didn't seem as opulent as it had before. Somehow worn, even dirty.

The elevator trip seemed long, but the doors opened, and I stepped into Banner's lobby. All heads turned, each showing different faces. Shock on most, questions on many. Their lives had been changed by all that had happened, and they didn't even know it.

Ben turned and went to his office, his secretary anxiously following him. I went in the opposite direction to my old suite, the senator by my side. I heard the words of brokers: their hellos, their questions. I said something trite to each one, something normal about waiting for Ben's meeting. We were at the door, and my breath was gone. Kirk had been a good friend, his kids like my own. My hand was shaking as I reached for the knob and opened the door.

He sat at my old desk, busy with paperwork and a telephone call. The look of me must have been shocking; he hung up instantly, his mouth open a little, wonder on his face.

"Hello, Kirk," I said. "This is Senator Freeman, from Wyoming. You've probably heard the name."

"Senator. Nice to meet you. Won't you have a seat? Both of

you?" He pointed to the two comfortable chairs we had purchased for their rich look, and because we had a great month. How long ago was that? Seemed like ages. I was suddenly very tired.

"What's up, Jerry? You don't look so hot."

"It has been a rough week, Kirk. Rougher than I can ever tell you, but things are winding down now. Almost finished actually. You're the last loose end."

The fear flashed in his eyes, then it was gone. He gripped the sides of the chair, half a smile on his face.

"What . . . are you talking about?"

"The SEC will be in here in less than half an hour to close Banner down for an investigation. At that time all of our . . . your accounts will be audited. All of your transactions carefully scrutinized. The money you've borrowed from our clients to feather your own nest will be discovered." He grew pale.

"So that you know I'm not blowing smoke, you should know I had Danny's people at the main office in New York look everything over. I know what I'm talking about. Shall we begin?" There wasn't any reply, just the angry look of a trapped animal.

I took a deep breath. "When you weren't given the Powers account you started to snoop around in Ben's computer, looking for answers." I turned to the senator. "For your information, Senator, Banner has a computer in which all client accounts are stored, with each transaction listed in detail. The date of the trade, how many shares, how much cash—everything. Each broker has a password. Usually a very simple one to remember. Mine was JERRY. Kirk's was TRADER, wasn't it, Kirk? Our partnership was GUNGHO, sort of a joke. I knew Ben's was STEVE, short for Stevenson. So did Kirk; I told him when I was acting manager and needed his help in a rush."

I turned back to Kirk. "Anyway, you found more than you bargained for. Huge accounts, big trades, a pattern of stocks. That's where you got onto TriStar. Like any good broker, I suppose, you saw something that looked very big, something you could bring a lot of business into, make a lot of money. Almost insider information. But you needed more. So—and this is a guess, but the police will verify it shortly—you bugged his office, or better yet, probably his computer. That's when you saw what was really going on, and knew you had a good thing going. It's also the way you knew we were here the other night and were able to notify Duquesne."

"Hold it right there, Jerry. I don't have to listen to this. You're accusing me of—"

I stood and approached the desk. "You'd better let me finish, Kirk, because it gets much worse before it gets better."

His jaw snapped shut, and he gritted his teeth.

"You started calling clients. Some went with you; most didn't. Oil stocks and futures aren't real appetizing to the type of client we've gleaned over our years together. My fault, I suppose; I didn't like clients who took risks and were flippant with their money. When they lose it they always want it back, and they sue you for it. So your first round wasn't very successful. You pulled a few in, like Jan. People who don't know the first thing about the market and how it works, and who trust you.

"But it wasn't enough. You started moving money out of their accounts by forging signatures on transfer slips, making phony accounts to receive the cash, and then buying the stocks you saw Ben after. I would imagine that you would have also sent in change of address forms for accounts you pirated so the confirms would not go directly to the client and the monthly statements would be sidetracked as well. A dangerous thing to do, but for a couple of months it could be done.

"We control, for clients, something like five hundred million dollars. I figure half is untouchable—corporate accounts that trade too often and watch their money too close for you to get at. Of the remainder I think you probably got your hands on about ten million. If things had panned out the way you thought they would, you would have had the money back to the owners within sixty days and would have made a healthy profit for yourself.

"But the unexpected happened. I told you Sellars had figured out what happened with Powers and that I might be coming back. That would have blown things sky-high, because once I returned and started looking things over I would know exactly what you had been doing. You couldn't have that.

"You had one of two choices. Get me, or get Sellars. I was in the car, and you didn't know where or who with. Sellars was in his office two floors down. You could get him."

His mouth was turning into a thin slit, his eyes hard as steel, darting.

"You borrowed the key to the private elevator from Ben's office, then came back here and called Sellars' secretary. Acting as a bank executive, you told her that there was a problem with their account and Sellars needed to come down immediately. You knew his habits because of our experience in trying to corner him and get his personal account. I don't know how many times he had used that private elevator to escape us, but we used to joke about it, remember?

"You logged out with the receptionist—I think we can verify that—went down the elevator, and the rest is history. When Sellars went to step in you put the pistol to his head, pulled the trigger, shoved the body out, and returned to this floor."

He glanced at the right-hand desk drawer.

"Sergeant Carone said the bullet that killed Sellars lodged in his brain. It was a twenty-two-caliber hollow head." I took a deep breath while pulling my 9mm from inside my belt and laying it on my lap. "I remember when you bought your pistol. There had been a mugging in the parking garage late one night, and a broker from the firm two floors down was nearly killed while losing several thousand dollars from his wallet. When you stayed late you packed it to the car with you. I thought it was a wise move, really, and that's when I bought one." I nodded toward the gun.

He went for the drawer. I grabbed the 9mm and stepped to his side, putting it against his ear. "Uh-uh, Kirk. That gun has killed enough. Senator, go out and tell Kirk's secretary to call the lobby and ask Sergeant Carone to join us. Get on the floor, Kirk, and spread your arms and legs. *Now!*"

"You can't prove any of this!" Kirk bellowed.

"I won't have to. The SEC will verify the motive, the gun in that drawer, the one you should have disposed of, and we'll do the rest. Now, former partner and friend, get on the floor!" There was a window next to the office door, and our secretary stood openmouthed outside it.

"*Please,* Jerry, don't do this. My wife and the kids. I—"

My anger boiled over. I slapped the back of his head with the palm of my hand. "Curse you, Kirk. Curse you for what you've done! To Sellars, to his wife and family! And to Patty and your kids! And to us and our friendship!"

The tears flowed down my cheeks. Days of frustration and anger and overpowering emotions leapt into my brain. I flipped him over and slapped his face hard. "How could you do this, Kirk? How could you kill a man in cold blood? I thought I knew you! I thought I knew you!" I was shaking him. "I loved you like a brother! And you're a murderer for money!" I hit him again. "I want to kill you myself!" The senator pulled me away, grabbing my arm and pushing me toward the wall. I turned and leaned against it, gasping for air, sobbing.

"It'll be okay, Jerry," the senator said. "It'll be okay. Give me the gun so I can watch him, then sit down and get control."

I sat, grabbing the arms of the chair and taking deep breaths. Kirk was crying, scared, beaten. I did love him like a brother. I took two more deep breaths and prayed for control. Then more breaths.

When the shaking was more controlled I knelt beside him. He jerked his arms up and the senator tensed. I put my arms around his shoulders and hugged, his body erupting into spasms of sobbing, wracked with the anguish of what he had done, what lay ahead. He had killed to prevent the destruction of his dream—to be the biggest and the best broker on the Street. A dream we had talked of often as we wound down at the close of the market, traveled to client meetings, or sat around my pool watching his kids swim while our wives fed us. A dream we had both shared, but in different ways.

Money, Power, Importance—the stuff that his dream was made of.

And the stuff that had destroyed it.

I stood over her, tears filling my eyes. I stroked her forehead, my heart hurting. Hurting for her, for Kirk, for Robert Doolittle. For everyone Duquesne's cruelty had stomped on.

She opened her eyes, a pained smile creasing her lips. "Jerry, it . . . it's over, isn't it? You . . . you won't leave me, will you! You're not in danger any longer?"

I bent down and kissed her forehead, then her cheek and lips. "It's over. And I'll never leave you again. I own property in Wyoming now. Ten thousand acres of it, with three oil wells, remember?" I smiled. "It'll be a full-time job taking care of it . . . and you . . . and a family."

She looked into my eyes. "He would be proud!" She tried to smile through the pain.

I looked at her quizzically. "Who?"

"Finan Daniels. Sun Who Never Sets. Your grandfather. All of them. They would be proud of you, and of what their sacrifice accomplished." The pain seemed to worsen.

I stroked her hair with one hand, pushing the nurse's-station button with the other. "Listen, beautiful. When are you going to marry me?"

"Spring. When"—she shifted again, the pain stronger—"when the flowers . . . are fresh. Spring is always best."

The nurse came through the door, quickly assessed the need, and injected a clear fluid into Mike's IV, bringing almost immediate relief to her creased brow, her eyelids becoming heavy.

I bent and kissed her again as she drifted into sleep, tears welling in my eyes, my heart full to bursting. Her hand loosened its grip on mine, but when I tried to slip it free she grasped it tightly again. I pulled the chair over and sat, caressing her arm, letting her cling to me, silently thanking God for her life.

And my new beginning. Leaning back, hands gently touching, my eyes closed, I slept. A dreamless, peaceful sleep.

> Yea, though I walk through the valley of the shadow of death, I will fear no evil: for thou art with me; thy rod and thy staff they comfort me.

Epilogue

21 January 1991.

The body floated in the pool twenty feet from where she stood, her arms folded, a hard smile creasing her lips. He had failed. They both had known it was only a matter of time before one of their assassins was successful.

She felt no remorse, only relief. No one but Fillmore knew TERROR1 was her plan. His singular death proved she was still free to continue to achieve her goals.

He had been careless. She had known it was over when he sent the last report, and when the computer she had kept everything stored in had been cleaned out by a Trojan horse. She had not bothered to call him, to warn him. Her anonymity would be critical to her own survival, and to her revenge.

From the time they had first met she had used Duquesne and his wealth. Once she had convinced him to move to Tunis she introduced him to all the right people—powerful, rich, and determined people. He had become enamored with his own importance—as she knew he would—not realizing she manipulated it all, used him, to solidify her own position, to open doors she wanted open, needed open, to accomplish her long-ago established goals.

She had made him believe TERROR1 could work, had made him think it was his and that he was to be the one to reap the profits and the power. He had not known she had other things in mind. Things only she could bring to pass without him at her side.

After his defeat he had returned to Tunis like a whipped dog. She had forced him to fill her in on what the trap had en-

313

tailed, how a few lucky amateurs had discovered and destroyed TERROR1. She had become furious, but controlled the anger and the disgust, putting on the airs necessary, allowing him to do as the Americans had demanded, to throw them off and to make them feel they had won, while keeping her own position hidden.

But behind closed doors she had begun to form a new plan. The death of her husband, his body now fully submerged a few inches below the surface of their Olympic-sized pool, was only an inevitable first step she had merely waited for. As his widow she would inherit his vast wealth from the sale of Duquesne Industries and all its subsidiaries. With it she would destroy those who had thwarted her, while strengthening her own position among the leaders of the Middle East.

Although Palestinian by blood, she would continue to maintain her United States passport. It would give her the way to return and avenge herself on those who had been instrumental in stopping what she had taken years to work for.

She had received the final list only hours ago, while they were sitting by the pool going over the intricate details of bank accounts and investments in which her husband had placed their wealth. There were six on that list.

But there was one more responsible than the others. Recent reports indicated he would remain in the state of Wyoming with his new bride. A perfect place for her to find and personally destroy him when the time was right. And it would be soon.

But for now she had too many other things to do. With the war only a few weeks away, the outcome already evident, she must move quickly to distance herself from failure. Her future depended on it.

She went to the diving board, stripping her slim form of the robe covering her skimpy bathing suit. Diving had been her only athletic obsession. She was expert in many other sports, but this one she loved, and worked to perfect.

Standing still, she concentrated on the end of the board, then took the steps and drove her lithe body into the air, twisting and turning, once, twice, then entering the water with nothing but a wisp of a splash.

Swimming to the surface, she dragged her husband's body to the far end. Her bodyguard helped pull the lifeless form onto the tile. She would have to watch this one. She wasn't sure how the assassins had gotten entrance to their little domain. One of *her first priorities would be to find out, to find whom she could trust without question. If Jason were alive . . .*

But he wasn't. Another reason to kill Daniels.

She took a towel and dried herself, looking one last time into the blank eyes of Fillmore Duquesne. Drowned. At least they had made it look natural.

She stood, put on her robe, and crisply walked toward the entrance to their home overlooking the hills. The funeral would be on Tuesday, a week from now. Her period of mourning and seclusion would allow her to slip away and move about freely. She must accomplish many things among her Arab friends before departing for the United States. They must understand her position of support for their cause. Substantial amounts from her newly inherited funds would be a first step. Her future could be a bright one, but it needed careful nurturing through the months ahead, when the potential for change in the Arab world would be dramatic.

She watched the bodyguard and two others remove the body. Funny, accepting it was so easy.

She shook her head, clearing her mind. For now she would have Daniels watched. When the time was right . . .

Unlike her former husband, Jerisha Salamhani would not fail.

But, behold, the judgments of God will overtake the wicked; and it is by the wicked that the wicked are punished; for it is the wicked that stir up the hearts of the children of men unto bloodshed.

—Book of Mormon

About the Author

Robert Marcum was born and reared in Teton Valley, Idaho. He served as a full-time LDS missionary in the East Central States Mission from 1965 to 1967. He attended Brigham Young University, receiving a bachelor's degree in history from that institution, and later attended Idaho State University, where he received a master's degree in education.

The author has served in the Church Educational System for eighteen years and is currently a professor of religion at Ricks College. He also worked for two years with an international brokerage firm in Las Vegas, Nevada.

Robert Marcum has written several articles for the *New Era* and for various professional publications. *Dominions of the Gadiantons* is his first published book.

He is married to the former Janene Andreasen of Grace, Idaho. They are the parents of one daughter and seven sons. The family resides in Rexburg, Idaho.